Praise for Marta Perry

"Abundant details turn this Amish romantic thriller series launch into a work of art."

—*Publishers Weekly* on *Where Secrets Sleep* (starred review)

"Crisp writing and distinctive characters make up Perry's latest novel. *Where Secrets Sleep* is a truly entertaining read."

—*RT Book Reviews*

"Perry's story hooks you immediately. Her uncanny ability to seamlessly blend the mystery element with contemporary themes makes this one intriguing read."

—*RT Book Reviews* on *Home by Dark*

"Perry skillfully continues her chilling, deceptively charming romantic suspense series with a dark, puzzling mystery that features a sweet romance and a nice sprinkling of Amish culture."

—*Library Journal* on *Vanish in Plain Sight*

"*Leah's Choice*, by Marta Perry, is a knowing and careful look into Amish culture and faith. A truly enjoyable reading experience."

—Angela Hunt, *New York Times* bestselling author of *Let Darkness Come*

"*Leah's Choice* is a story of grace and servitude as well as a story of difficult choices and heartbreaking realities. It touched my heart. I think the world of Amish fiction has found a new champion."

—Lenora Worth, *New York Times* bestselling author of *Code of Honor*

Also available from
Marta Perry
and HQN Books

Shattered Silence

Sound of Fear

Echo of Danger

How Secrets Die

When Secrets Strike

Where Secrets Sleep

Abandon the Dark

Search the Dark

Home by Dark

Danger in Plain Sight

Vanish in Plain Sight

Murder in Plain Sight

MARTA PERRY

Amish Outsider

ISBN-13: 978-1-335-00678-3

Amish Outsider

This edition published by arrangement with Harlequin Books S.A.

For questions and comments about the quality of this book, please contact us at CustomerService@Harlequin.com.

www.HQNBooks.com

Printed in U.S.A.

This book is dedicated to Brian, as always.

Death isn't the greatest loss in life.
It's what dies inside of us while we still live.
—Amish Proverb

Amish Outsider

CHAPTER ONE

THE SIGN AT the edge of town was new since he'd been here last. Welcome to River Haven. Michael Forster could only hope the welcome was genuine and that River Haven would prove to be a haven for a man who'd lost everything.

No, not everything. A glance in the rearview mirror showed him Allie, sitting very quietly and looking out the window beside her as the small town came into view. Too quietly for an eight-year-old?

Allie had never been a talkative child—at least not with him. How could she have been? He'd left for work before she was up in the morning, and arrived home, dead tired, just when she was going to bed. On weekends Diana wanted to socialize with her new friends, not spend yet more time with their child.

He could blame Diana's insatiable desire to have more of everything for the life they'd led. But he'd let her ambition become his. He'd devoted himself with single-minded determination to being what the world called a success. Now…now none of that was left. He'd come, finally, to know how empty it had been.

What use was it to blame Diana now? Her death had changed everything, making Allie retreat even more into a silent world of her own. His mind winced away from the circumstances of that death and from the weeks and months that followed—the confusion, the questioning, the suspicion, finally the accusations.

It was over now. He'd come back to River Haven, to the only hope of home he had, with only one aim—to start a new life for Allie.

The state highway became Main Street, as it did in many Pennsylvania small towns, and shops and houses mingled on either side of the street. Off to the left he could glimpse the river, a little high with spring rains, and to the right the valley widened into fertile farmland before lifting to the wooded ridge.

"Daddy?" Allie's small voice surprised him after two hours of silence. "Why are there horses along that building?"

He sent a quick look in the direction she pointed. "That's the hardware store. The horses and buggies belong to Amish people who are shopping there. They don't drive cars, just buggies."

Her tightly controlled face didn't change, but her brown eyes filled with something that might have been wonder. "I wish I could ride in a buggy."

The words hit him like a hammer. He was bringing an eight-year-old into a completely new environment and he hadn't explained even the simplest things she should expect. That didn't say much about his parenting skills. But at least this surprise might be a good one.

"You will, I promise," he assured her. "Your

cousins are Amish, and they ride in buggies all the time. They'll take you for lots of rides."

Would they? A momentary doubt assailed him. Great-Aunt Verna had invited them to share her home—they could be sure of a welcome there. But the rest of his family…

Would they be happy to see him after all the years he'd ignored them? Or would they be as unforgiving as his father had been? Once Daad had made it clear that he didn't forgive, it had seemed pointless to try to contact his brothers and sister.

He'd know soon. They were approaching the other end of town already, and he'd been so wrapped up in his thoughts he hadn't noticed what should have been familiar landmarks.

"There's Great-Aunt Verna's place." He pointed. "See that white house with the greenhouses beyond it? That's her house. That's where we're going to live. She's actually your great-great-aunt, but you can call her Aunt Verna."

No response, unless he could count the apprehension that shadowed her eyes. He wanted to say something to chase it away, but he couldn't.

I promise. I promise I'll protect you. Always.

Michael pulled into the lane that ran between the house and the greenhouses and ended at the small barn and cluster of outbuildings. The racks along the outside of the first greenhouse were bright with spring flowers and herbs. He should have remembered that early May was prime time for the greenhouse business.

There was no time to notice more, because Aunt Verna appeared on the side porch, waving and moving faster than any eighty-three-year-old ought to. He saw who came behind her, putting a steadying arm around her waist, and his heart leaped. Sarah, his "twin," eleven months younger than he was and always both closest ally and direst enemy in the perpetual battle of the siblings.

He stopped the car and went around, opening the door and offering his hand to Allie. She didn't usually take it, but this time she did, gripping it tightly as they moved toward the others.

Aunt Verna, eyes sparkling with tears in spite of her broad smile, swept him into a hug. "So. At last you come home to us."

The words were spoken in Pennsylvania Dutch, and to his surprise his mind switched easily back into that mode.

But he couldn't let that happen. "Englisch, please." He planted a kiss on Verna's cheek, rosy and wrinkled like a dried apple. "This is Allie." He drew her forward, but she clung to his side. "She doesn't know the dialect."

He glimpsed the disapproval in his great-aunt's eyes before her warm smile chased it away. She bent to Allie, reaching out to touch the child's shoulder lightly. "So you are Allie, and I am Aunt Verna. Wilkom. We are wonderful glad you're here."

Michael didn't see how Allie reacted, because Sarah grabbed him, a hand on each arm, pulling him around to face her. For a long moment she stared at him—long enough for him to see the changes that ten years had made. It was an Amish matron who faced him now, not the lively teenager he'd left behind. Then suddenly her face crinkled into laughter, and she was his Sarah again, pulling him in for a hug, laughing and hitting his shoulder all at the same time.

He returned the hug, lifting her off her feet the way he'd done when he'd first grown taller than she was. "It's so good to see you, Sally." The childhood nickname came to his lips automatically.

"I've been right here the whole time," she reminded him, giving him another light punch.

It was in his mind to ask about his father, but a glance at the child who stood next to his sister kept him silent. Daad's reaction to his return might not be something Sarah wanted to mention in front of her daughter.

"This is Ruthie, my oldest." She nodded to the little girl next to her. "Ruthie, this is Onkel Michael. And that's Cousin Allie. She's just your age, so you can be her special friend."

Ruthie had her mother's laughing green eyes and silky blond hair. And it looked as if she shared Sarah's engaging disposition, because she gave him a quick grin and went straight to Allie.

"Hi. I'm your cousin Ruthie. I know where your room is. You want me to show you?"

To his utter astonishment, Allie nodded. She took the hand Ruthie held out. The two of them trotted up the porch steps and into the house, letting the screen door slam behind them.

Michael looked from his aunt to his sister. "If I hadn't seen that, I wouldn't believe it. Allie's always so shy."

"It's blood," Aunt Verna said matter-of-factly. "Cousins always know each other."

"And brothers and sisters just pick up where they left off," Sarah said. "Let us help you unload. My husband and the kids will be here for supper before you know it."

"We thought you wouldn't want a houseful on your first night, so it'll just be us," Aunt Verna added.

He looked at Sarah. "Your family?" He was vaguely ashamed that he had to ask.

"I married Lige Esch. Remember him? Besides Ruthie, we have twins, Jacob and James, and the baby, Sally. So she's Sally now, not me."

"I'll remember." Anyway, he'd try. "About Daad..."

Sarah shook her head slightly, her eyes darkening. "I'm sorry. He's as stubborn as he always was."

He shrugged, turning to the car to pull out a couple of suitcases. Some things didn't change, for good or bad.

Somehow that thought kept running through his mind while he was unloading the car and putting things away in the rooms Aunt Verna had given Allie and him. Daad had always been harder on him than on any of the others. That went with being the oldest son, he guessed. Daad had never been forgiving of even the minor troubles any boy got into. How could he think Daad would change over something this big?

It didn't matter. Nothing did, except starting a new life for Allie.

He shoved an empty suitcase into the closet and stood looking around the bedroom assigned to him. The house was a typical Pennsylvania farmhouse, starting with two rooms up and two rooms down and gradually added onto as families grew. The spotlessly clean room was sparsely furnished, with a handmade double wedding ring quilt on the bed, a sturdy oak dresser and an oak desk with a battery-powered lamp. What else did anyone need?

Michael stepped out into the hall and paused for a moment by the door of the room allotted to Allie. Ruthie seemed to be chattering away, with a word or two from Allie now and then. Not much, but at least she was talking.

A wave of gratitude swept over him for Sarah, who'd done exactly the right thing in bringing Ruthie to be a friend for Allie. He could leave them together.

He took two steps down the stairs, glanced at the bottom and stopped, clinging to the railing. The memory roared over him before he could brace himself.

Eight months ago. He'd come back to the house hoping to talk to Diana, thinking if only they'd sit down and discuss things they could find some solution other than the divorce she'd decided she wanted so badly.

All right, so they hadn't been getting along well for months, maybe years. Diana had wanted to spend the evenings entertaining or being entertained, enjoying the company of the fancy new friends she'd made since they'd moved to an upscale suburb. He'd come home from working crazy hours, trying to make a go of the construction company he'd started so that she could have the endless list of things she needed—the things, she'd pointed out, that would have been hers by right if she hadn't been so foolish as to run away and marry a penniless Amish teen.

Their relationship had gone from bad to worse, right up to the night he'd come home and found she'd packed a bag for him. She needed breathing space, she'd said. A little time apart would do them both good.

Both, nothing. She wanted her freedom; that soon became clear. She wanted a divorce.

He'd arrived at the house that last night to find she'd changed the locks. A simple thing, but it infuriated him. This was his house, built by his sweat and muscle. And she had changed the locks.

He pressed the doorbell, hearing it chiming again and again. Diana had to be there—her car was visible in the garage. He pounded, resisting the temptation to shout. No use rousing the neighbors and having someone calling the cops.

Okay, she was there and she wouldn't answer. She'd find it would take more than a locked door to keep him out. It was the work of moments to pop the lock on the side door to the garage and go in that way. He stormed into the kitchen, calling her name.

Nothing. His thoughts fled to Allie, and he took the stairs two at a time. If she'd gone out and left Allie alone in the house—

But Allie's room was empty, her bed made, the stuffed dog that slept with her gone. Overnight at a friend's? It slid through his mind to wonder why Diana would farm her out on a school night.

He went quickly through the rest of the upstairs, then the downstairs, his anger building. Where was she? Heading through the kitchen, he spotted a line of light under the basement door. He grabbed the knob, yanked it open and choked on her name.

Diana was there. He could see her, but his mind didn't accept what he saw. She lay at the bottom of the basement steps, the back of her head covered with blood.

Somehow he'd stumbled down the steps, knelt beside her, crying her name. Touched her hand and found it cold, stone cold. Diana was dead.

Voices from below recalled him to the present. He was gripping the stair rail in Aunt Verna's house, his knuckles white. The past was gone, and no one could force him to relive it. He made himself let go, to focus on the voice calling his name.

"Michael, supper! Ruthie, Allie, supper!"

"Coming." He heard the clatter of children's feet behind him and started down.

By the time he reached the kitchen he'd put his game face back on. He had no idea how much the family knew, but Harrisburg was only two hours away, and the local papers would have picked up the story.

It was like a splash of cold water in his face. What had he been thinking? This was Diana's hometown as well as his. Her relatives still lived here. Everyone would know. This could be the worst possible place he could resettle.

But he didn't have much choice. At least here there were a few people who still believed in him. Aunt Verna had offered him a home. He could make this work. He had to.

By the time supper ended, with a huge slab of cherry pie and a mug of coffee, Michael had almost persuaded himself it was going to be all right. He sat back, silent, and surveyed his family.

Aunt Verna never changed—if anything, her fiercely independent spirit had intensified. She'd taken over the greenhouse business after her husband's early death, run it her way and turned it into a thriving business. She was scrupulously honest, blunt-spoken, and she had a heart as big as all outdoors.

As for Sarah...he still saw his lively, mischievous, pesky little sister behind the facade of the Amish matron able to serve an immense meal, correct the four-year-old twins' table manners, feed the baby and take part in the conversation at the same time. In comparison, her husband, Lige, was soft-spoken, slow and steady in his movements, able to quiet his sons with a glance and share a look of love and harmony with Sarah that sent a sharp stab of regret through Michael's heart. That was what he and Diana should have had.

He and Lige lingered over coffee, talking about some building repair the oldest greenhouse needed, when Sarah interrupted with a question.

"What are you going to do about school for Allie?"

Allie, sitting on the floor in the corner helping Ruthie build a block tower for the baby to knock over, looked up alertly.

Michael rubbed the back of his neck. Something else he should already have thought through, he guessed. "I don't know. Isn't there still an elementary school on Oak Street?"

Sarah and Aunt Verna exchanged glances, and he suspected they'd talked this over already. "You want to send her to school with the Englisch?" Sarah's voice was carefully neutral.

"That's what she's used to." Irritation prickled. He was trying to do what was best for Allie, wasn't he?

"She would be very wilkom at our school, and Catherine Brandt is a wonderful gut teacher," Sarah said. "Besides, then Allie could be with Ruthie."

"But..." Objections formed in his mind.

"I want to go to school with Ruthie." Allie's voice startled him, even though he'd known she was listening. "Okay?"

They all looked at him, and he had the sense of being both outnumbered and outmaneuvered. "Are you sure? The English school would be more like your old school."

Allie shook her head, her face set stubbornly. "I want to be with Ruthie."

He hesitated, wishing for a sense of certainty about Allie's future that didn't come. Finally he shrugged. "Okay, the Amish school it is."

Satisfaction and approval filled the room, and he

sensed he'd passed the first hurdle on the road home. He wasn't sure he liked that. He'd have said he hadn't missed this life at all, but now it seemed to reach out, surround him and pull him in.

Sarah had begun to make noises about getting her brood home to bed when Lige suggested he and Michael check out the section of greenhouse that needed work.

"You're a builder, ain't so?" There might have been a little challenge in Lige's steady gaze. "You'll want to help with the work."

It wasn't a question. Obviously, he was part of the family so he'd help. "Sure thing. Let's have a look."

The sun had slid behind the ridge, and a cool wind blew across the valley as night drew in. It seemed natural, somehow, to walk along with Lige, discussing the materials that might be needed. He could have been talking to any of the men he'd worked with over the years.

They'd just passed the parked car when Lige stopped dead. "What's that on your car?" He pointed the beam of the large flashlight he carried.

Michael looked, and his stomach recoiled. Blood—splashed over the front of the car. Blood on Diana's head, soaking into the basement floor—

Reason asserted itself. It couldn't be. He forced himself to walk forward, to touch it, to smell.

"It's paint. Looks like someone emptied a gallon of the stuff over the car." His relief was forced out by anger.

He'd come home, all right. But the taint of Diana's murder had followed him.

CATHERINE BRANDT ARRIVED at school early, as always, walking along the path through damp morning grass. She could bring the horse and buggy, and she did when the weather was bad. But on this beautiful spring morning she'd rather walk through the woods and listen to the birds, thinking about her teaching plans for the day.

She paused where the path entered the school yard. The white frame schoolhouse waited, ready for the daily influx of lively young scholars. Catherine crossed the play area, went up the three steps and unlocked the door.

This quiet time in the morning was the point of the day when Creekside School felt most surely hers. She had taught at two other Amish schools, but Creekside was her own school—the one she'd attended, the one she hoped would be in her charge for years to come, if only…

No negative thoughts, she told herself firmly. Teaching might be the only thing she was good at, but she was very good at it, though saying so would be prideful.

Thinking of people who might want to replace her didn't fit with the positive start she meant to give her scholars each day. Dismissing the faint worry, she checked the cloakroom to be sure all was in order before walking into the schoolroom and surveying the rows of desks. Neat and orderly, just as she'd left it the previous day. Walking between the desks to the front, she touched each one lightly, giving thought to the child who sat there, mentally planning the day each would experience.

By the time she'd prepared the chalkboard with arithmetic problems for the fourth graders and spelling words for the second graders, she heard the children begin to arrive. Cathy hurried to the entrance so she could greet them as they came in. She had to smile at how predictable they were…the young ones eager and smiling with their greetings, the older ones either sleepy or wrapped up in each other. It was a challenge to teach children of such diverse ages in one classroom, but she loved it.

Sarah Esch came hurrying to her, grasping her hand and leaning close for a whispered word. "I brought my bruder Michael and his little girl. You heard he was back, yah?"

Cathy's thoughts spun quickly over the rumors that had rampaged through River Haven in the past few months. Yes, she'd heard.

"Allie is Ruthie's age," Sarah went on, glancing over her shoulder at the two little girls. "It's all right for her to come, ain't so?"

Cathy looked from Sarah's apprehensive, questioning expression to the child who stood next to Ruthie—a small, pale face, guarded brown eyes, an air of fading into the background. Next to lively, ebullient Ruthie, she presented as strong a contrast as Cathy could imagine.

But she read need in the child's face, and her heart

opened. "She is most wilkom." She held out her hand to the girls. "Komm, Ruthie. Let me meet your cousin."

They moved toward her, and behind them, matching their steps, was an alien presence. Allie was dressed in what Cathy recognized as one of Ruthie's dresses, but her father wore jeans and a plaid flannel shirt. Michael Forster was advertising the fact that he no longer considered himself Amish, it seemed.

She bent over the little girl, touching her shoulder. "Allie, I'm Teacher Cathy. We're so happy you came to our school."

Allie's lips quirked in the slightest of smiles, and Ruthie burst into speech. "She can sit by me, can't she, Teacher Cathy? I can help her. Please?"

"Of course she can."

One of the nearby scholars said something in Pennsylvania Dutch, and Cathy caught Allie's fleeting apprehension.

"We speak Englisch in school," she said. "If anybody says something you don't understand, just ask Ruthie, okay?"

Allie looked relieved. She nodded, again almost, but not quite, smiling.

"I'll show you, Cousin Allie." Ruthie tugged at her hand, and they scurried toward the smaller desks toward the front of the room.

Cathy straightened and found herself face-to-face with Michael Forster...the man who'd run away to the Englisch and broken his mother's heart, the man who'd come home at last with a charge of murder hanging over his head.

Whatever vague memories she might have had of Michael vanished. Michael could have been any Englischer in his worn jeans and scuffed boots. Taller than a lot of Amish, he had a sturdy frame, the heavy muscles of his shoulders moving under the fabric of his shirt as he waved at his daughter.

But Allie was already sliding into the desk next to Ruthie, seeming completely occupied. His hand fell to his side and he turned a frowning gaze on Cathy.

He looked…worn-out, she decided. As if the past months had drained every bit of energy and life from him. His face was lean, all bones and angles, and his brows were dark slashes above brown eyes that held… What? Suspicion? Wariness? Pain—that was it. He was like a hurt, baffled animal, ready to strike out against a helping hand.

If Cathy had ever seen anyone who needed comfort and caring, it was Michael Forster. Her warm heart opened to him before her rational mind could think that it might not be good to get too close to him.

She blinked, realizing she'd been staring. *Focus on the child*, she told herself. *Allie is your responsibility, not her father.*

Collecting herself, she met his eyes. "Allie looks as if she's going to settle in fine. I don't think you need to stay any longer."

His frown deepened, if that were possible. "Aren't you Mary's little sister Cathy?"

Naturally he'd see her that way—he'd have been Mary's contemporary in school. He couldn't know how much it annoyed her to be constantly classified as the little sister…the runt of the litter, as her brother Eli liked to tease.

"I'm Mary's sister, yah. And the teacher at Creekside School." She managed a smile. "I'd best get the school day started. Is there anything I should know about Allie? Any allergies or physical problems?"

"No." He clipped the word off. "She's been going to a public school. I don't know if coming here is the best fit for her."

He clearly had doubts about bringing Allie here, so why had he? Well, Verna, of course. She answered her own question. Verna Forster always had her own notions of what folks ought to do, and more often than not, she got her way.

"We can give it a try. If it doesn't work out, there's no harm done. It looks as if she's satisfied at the moment." She glanced at the girls, their heads together, one blond and one brown. Even as she watched, Allie smoothed her hands down the front of the plain Amish dress she wore, smiling a little as if pleased with it.

Cathy looked up again at Michael, to find him watching his child with a look compounded of love, protectiveness and bafflement. Maybe he wasn't finding it easy to be a single dad. Her heart twisted with pity, and she longed to reassure him.

"If she gets upset—" he began.

"Please don't worry about it. She'll be fine. If there are any problems, I'll send someone to fetch you. You're at Verna's house, ain't so?"

He nodded, giving her a bleak look. "News travels fast."

"It's a small town." If he remembered anything about River Haven, he ought to remember that.

"Yes. And people have long memories."

There didn't seem to be any answer she could make.

"I'll be here to pick up Allie at three o'clock. Don't let her leave with anyone else." It was an order, and he followed it by striding out the door.

Michael had gone, but he'd left a turbulence in the air. Or maybe the turbulence was only in her.

She'd heard all the stories about him, and her instinctive reaction had been to believe him innocent. How could someone who'd been raised here, who'd grown up nourished on simple Amish values of faith and family, honesty and humility, possibly have done such a thing?

Now she'd encountered him for herself, and she didn't know what to believe. She would have expected to have a sense of the familiarity that linked Amish to Amish. But that hadn't happened. He seemed foreign to her, as if there was no point at which their lives could touch.

Collecting herself, she walked between the rows of desks to the front of the room and picked up the Bible that lay open on her desk, ready for the morning reading. Her gaze lit on Allie, who was watching her with a sort of shy hope in her face.

Cathy's heart warmed, and she smiled. If she looked for a point where their lives touched, it was here in the form of a small child who needed her.

CHAPTER TWO

To Cathy's relief, the school day went forward smoothly as far as Allie was concerned. The child didn't speak at all, but she seemed to understand what was going on and followed directions. Cathy tried to picture one of her other young scholars suddenly placed in an Englisch school, and she suspected Allie was handling it as well as any child could.

Recess might have been difficult, and Allie showed a tendency to cling to Cathy's skirt, but Ruthie coaxed her onto the swings. Cathy stayed close, just in case. If she'd known ahead of time that Allie would be in her class, she'd have prepared the rest of her scholars. She kept a wary eye on them, but other than glancing at Allie with open curiosity now and then, they behaved as well as she could wish.

She was able to relax her vigilance a bit then, and the harmony lasted right up until the time the children were dismissed. Little groups of them started off for home, the older ones careful to shepherd the younger ones along, at least while they knew Teacher Cathy's eyes were on them. She couldn't vouch for what happened after that, but she suspected there was just as much teasing and jostling as there had been when she was a scholar.

The school yard emptied out. Ruthie gave Allie a hug before rushing off to catch up with the older neighbors who walked her home. Then there was no one left but Cathy and Allie, who looked more than a little forlorn as the others disappeared.

“Daadi will be here soon to pick you up.” Cathy stacked the materials she needed to carry home and slipped them into the canvas bag she carried back and forth. “Will he drive the car, do you think?”

“I guess. I wish…” She let that trail off.

What did she wish? That her father had been on time, most likely. Anyone would. No child wanted to be left waiting, the only one at the school.

“Would you like to erase the chalkboard for me, Allie? That would be a big help.”

The small face was unresponsive, but Allie picked up the eraser and started on the board. Cathy let her get started on the bottom half before she began on the top part. They worked together without speaking.

Should she push a little more? Or was it best to let Allie set the pace of their relationship? Cathy had dealt with troubled children before, but she’d never even imagined a situation like this. Did Allie have any understanding of what had happened to her parents?

She tamped down an urge to find Michael Forster and shake some answers out of him. Why hadn’t he taken the trouble to talk to her before arriving at school this morning with his child? If she were to help Allie, she'd certainly need her father's cooperation.

An image of Michael's face, as she'd seen it that morning, filled her mind—stubborn, withdrawn and suspicious. Could she really imagine a man like that cooperating with her?

Allie caught her attention with a tug on her skirt. "Teacher, may I look and see if my daddy is coming?" The child's voice hovered on the edge of tears, and Cathy felt a surge of anger at the absent parent.

"We'll both look," she said. "And if he's not coming yet, I'll walk you home. All right?"

Pressing her lips together, Allie nodded, her brown eyes bright with unshed tears.

Cathy grabbed her schoolbag and followed Allie to the front porch. The school lane curved out to the county road, and there was no sign of anyone coming. Cathy automatically checked the path that led off through the trees. It was the route she normally took to school, and it passed right behind Verna's property, but she doubted Michael would take it. He probably didn't even remember it was there.

Allie had her back turned, but Cathy could see the tremor in her shoulders, and her own temper flared.

"Just let me lock the door, and we'll be off." She kept her voice cheerful with an effort. "We'll walk along the road and maybe we'll meet him along the way. All right?"

Allie had to knuckle the tears away before she nodded. Cathy locked up, pasted a smile on her face and took Allie's hand. It was going to take a gigantic effort to keep from telling Michael just what she thought of him when they did meet.

They walked the lane together, with Allie's hand clasped in hers. A glance at the child's face told her that it was taking all Allie's strength to keep from crying—she certainly didn't have any left to chat.

A cheerful monologue seemed to be the best option, so Cathy talked about school, about the other children, about the swelling buds on the trees that would open in another week of warm weather. Anything to distract Allie from the fact that her father hadn't shown up. She struggled to control her anger. Didn't the man realize how vulnerable Allie would feel on her first day in a new school?

"I'd guess your aunt Verna will have a snack waiting for you when you get home." She'd best distract herself as well as Allie. "My mammi still does that, even though I'm a grown-up woman now. And Aunt Verna will want to hear all about your first day at school. It was pretty good, ain't so?"

Allie's gaze flickered to her face, and she nodded, her own expression lightening, making Cathy feel marginally better. Better, but still determined to make sure Michael knew he'd let his child down.

Even as she thought it, a car spun around the bend in the road ahead of them and came speeding toward them. Taking Allie's shoulders, Cathy drew her back to the side of the road, into the long grass.

"I think that's your daadi." She hoped she didn't sound as grim as she felt.

Brakes shrieked, and the car pulled over and came

to a halt a few feet from them. Michael surged out of the vehicle, his angry gaze fixed on Cathy's face and probably equally angry words brimming on his lips.

Cathy spoke quickly to intercept him, but she spoke to the child. "See? I told you Daadi would be here, and here he is. Now you can hop in the car and ride the rest of the way home." She patted Allie's shoulder and steered her to the vehicle, not looking at him. "I'll see you bright and early tomorrow."

She wasn't looking, but she could hear his quick, indrawn breath and sense his struggle for control.

"That's right," Michael said finally. He reached to buckle Allie into her seat. "Just let me speak to Teacher Cathy for a minute, and then we'll go home."

He closed the car door, and Cathy suspected she knew what he wanted the minute for. He swung toward her. "Why are you walking along the road with my daughter? The traffic danger—"

"The only dangerous vehicle we saw was yours," she interrupted. She went on in a furious undertone before she could lose her nerve. "You said you'd be there to pick her up when school was out. How do you think she felt when all the other scholars left and you didn't come? Don't you know how vulnerable she is?"

His face whitened as if she'd struck him, and he darted a look toward his daughter. "I…" He stopped, his lips clamping shut for an instant. She could only hope he saw the justice in her words.

Michael's eyes narrowed. "I don't need your help

in raising my daughter." It had a note of finality. Would she see Allie in her classroom again?

"You may not," she said, ignoring the little voice that told her she'd gone too far. "But Allie does."

Quickly, before he could speak, she spun and marched away, praying he couldn't tell how she was shaking.

MICHAEL TOOK ALLIE HOME, where Aunt Verna waited with milk and homemade oatmeal cookies. Allie slid onto her chair and then sat there, staring at the milk and cookie in front of her but not moving.

Aunt Verna sent Michael a questioning glance. He shook his head slightly, but he knew why Allie had withdrawn. Because of him. Because he'd failed in the first simple task he'd attempted in their new home.

Cathy's words and expression intruded, and he had the sense that wherever she was, she'd still be frowning at him. Maybe he'd owed her an explanation of why he'd been late. Maybe. Certainly he owed it to Allie.

Pulling out the chair next to his daughter, he sat down, scooting a little closer. He put one hand on the back of her chair, wanting to touch her but afraid she'd pull away.

"I'm sorry, Allie. I should have been there to pick you up on time."

Her face tightened a little, and she didn't look at him. Obviously it would take more than that.

"I had a phone call just when I was going to

leave." An unwelcome call. "It was kind of official. Do you know what that means?"

This time he got a shake of the head.

"That means it was the kind of thing you have to take care of right away." Should he mention the police? He'd tried to shelter her from the events around her mother's death, but he didn't know how much she'd heard or how garbled it had been. "It's a rule. Like the rules you have in school. Does Teacher Cathy have any rules?"

His daughter's face seemed to come to life. "Always be kind. That's the first rule. It's on the chalkboard."

"That's a gut rule," Aunt Verna said. "Everyone is happier when we are kind."

Allie nodded. "That's what Teacher Cathy said."

Michael had a feeling he was going to get tired of hearing what Teacher Cathy said before long. "Well, this is a rule about talking to someone. But it was time to pick you up, so I persuaded him to wait until I got you home. All that made me late. I'm really sorry."

Allie considered for a moment. Then she took a large bite of oatmeal cookie and spoke around it. "It's okay."

"Good." He felt relieved as if he'd passed a test. "I'll go outside and wait for the man I need to talk to, and maybe afterward we can help in the greenhouses."

He stood, pausing to drop a light kiss on the top of her head. Allie seemed to have forgiven him. It would take a lot longer for him to forgive himself.

Michael made it outside just as the police car

turned into the lane. He spotted Lige, working in one of the greenhouses, look up, and waved to indicate he'd take care of the visitor. He'd rather Lige go on assuming it was a customer, at least for the moment.

The car pulled up and stopped in the graveled parking area in front of the first greenhouse. When Chief Jamison climbed out, Michael had a flash of memory—the chief breaking up one of the more rowdy teen parties. He hadn't needed to raise his voice. He'd just looked around, as if mentally taking names, and one by one they'd slipped away.

Jamison hadn't changed much in ten years. His stocky figure might have been a few pounds heavier, and there was a bit more gray in the reddish hair, but Jamison's blue eyes rested on him in exactly the same assessing way.

Michael found himself stiffening, as defensive as a fifteen-year-old caught out after curfew. Jamison approached, giving him an unsmiling nod.

"Michael. It's been a long time."

"Ten years." The less he said the better. He'd learned that lesson in his first go-round with the police, with Diana's body still lying at the bottom of the basement stairs.

When he'd looked his fill, Jamison turned toward the display racks of flowers. "Let's have a look around at the plants. No point in advertising why I'm here."

That was consideration Michael hadn't expected. Together they walked over to the flats of geraniums and pansies.

"Checking up on me?" Michael tried for an easiness he didn't feel.

Jamison shrugged. "Had a call from the Harrisburg police about you."

No point in being angry—he should have expected it. "They want you to keep an eye on me, right?"

"Not exactly." Jamison reached out to finger the leaf of a pink geranium. "Just a friendly alert, you might say. And they wanted to know if you were really here."

"I suppose it does no good to tell you I didn't do it." Bitterness threaded his voice. He wouldn't get away from the effects of Diana's death if he traveled to the other side of the world.

Jamison kept silent for several minutes, but Michael could feel the chief's gaze on him. He stared steadily at the plants in front of him, barely seeing them.

"Well, it's this way." The chief's voice was noncommittal, without the open antagonism he'd received from the detectives who'd been assigned to the case. "Harrisburg might have charge of that investigation, but they don't have jurisdiction here."

That might have comforted him, had he not been through the experiences of the past months. "But you'll cooperate."

"Within reason." There was a slight smile in his eyes. "We figure on treating folks fairly here."

If he really meant it, that would be a reassuring change. Michael was tempted to say that, but if he'd learned anything, it was not to volunteer information. Instead he nodded.

Jamison studied his face for a moment, and then he shifted his gaze to something over Michael's shoulder. "Well, now, who's this?"

Michael swung around to find that Allie had come out of the house. She stood a few feet away, and her gaze went from the stranger to him. Michael held out his hand, and she came and took it.

"This is Allie. My daughter." He didn't think it necessary for Allie to know the chief's name. With any luck, she wouldn't be seeing him again.

"Hi there, Allie." Jamison had always had a quick smile and easy manner with the kids. "I need to get some of these geraniums for my wife. Which color do you like the best?"

To Michael's surprise, Allie actually seemed to warm up a little. She touched a pink geranium with a careful hand. "The pink ones. They're the prettiest."

"You know, I think you're right. Can you pick out a couple of these for me?"

Allie nodded. She scrutinized the plants as if she'd been doing it forever. She picked up one, and then another. "They're all nice, but these two are the best."

"I'll take them. I'll tell my wife they're the prettiest ones, and she'll put them out on our porch." He took the money from his pocket and handed it to Allie.

She took it gravely. "Thank you."

"Your aunt Verna's got a good new salesperson, I can see that." With a smile for Allie and a nod for Michael, he headed for his car.

Prey to a succession of mixed feelings, Michael

watched him leave. If Jamison had meant what he said about fairness… But he wasn't taking anything for granted.

He looked down at his daughter. "When did you learn how to sell flowers?"

She shrugged, and for a moment it seemed she wouldn't answer. "Aunt Verna says this is a family business, and I'm part of the family." Then she smiled. "So it's my business, too."

Emotion seemed to have a stranglehold on his throat. All he could do was smile back at his child.

BY THE TIME she was helping her mother prepare supper, Cathy had managed to push that awkward exchange with Michael to the back of her mind. Maybe she couldn't dismiss it entirely, but she didn't have to dwell on it, did she?

"Cathy, are you going to peel those potatoes or just look at them?" Her mother's glance was half laughing, half questioning. She always seemed to know when one of her children was troubled.

But this trouble wasn't one Cathy thought she should share. She'd rather not look too deeply into the reason why.

"Sorry, Mammi. I was thinking about school." She rinsed the potatoes and picked up the peeler. "We had a new child today."

"I heard already. Michael Forster's little girl, yah?"

Cathy stopped midpeel. "How did you learn about that so quickly?"

Her mother's answer was a chuckle that showed the dimple in her right cheek…the same place Cathy had one. "You should know how fast news flies among the Amish. And when it's about Michael… Well, I guess everyone is curious about him. It's natural, ain't so?"

Curious or nosy? She suspected she knew how Michael would classify it. "Yah, maybe, but I hope that curiosity doesn't extend to Allie. She's only eight, and I hate to think of what she's been through losing her mother like that. And now to be trying to settle in a new place among strangers…"

"Poor child." Mammi's sympathy was immediate. "Is she going to fit in with your scholars, do you think?"

A momentary smile teased at her lips. "She will if her cousin Ruthie has anything to say about it." She'd regaled her mamm with precocious Ruthie's comments more than once. "She's so happy to have a new cousin her age. She just grabs Allie by the hand and leads her through everything."

"Ach, she's a sweet little schnickelfritz, that's for sure. It's gut they're the same age. It will make her feel at home, if anything will."

Cathy nodded agreement, but her thoughts went right back to Allie's dismay when her father didn't turn up on time. Cathy had done her best to reassure her, but it hadn't been Teacher Cathy she'd needed in that moment. It had been her father.

Cathy went back to peeling potatoes, wielding the peeler with such energy that the potato skins flew across the counter. Better to vent her feelings on the potatoes than on any person, including Michael.

Her sister Mary, coming in the back door in a rush, was just in time to see one slice of peeling fly so far it hit the window.

"Mamm, if you don't take that peeler away from Cathy, you won't have any potatoes left. Cathy, didn't I ever show you the right way to do it?"

She came straight to Cathy and attempted to take the implement from her hand. Cathy spun away, shrugging her off. That was Mary all over, always thinking she could do things better than anyone else. Or at least, better than her little sister.

"I've got it." Cathy just managed to add a smile. "What brings you here? Shouldn't you be fixing your own family's supper?"

"I will, I will." Mary planted her hands on rounded hips. She'd put on pounds since the arrival of the kinder, and she looked like what she was…a satisfied Amish matron, running her large family with ease and helping with her husband's orchards as well. "I brought Mamm a bunch of rhubarb. Ours is a little further along than yours. Not enough for a pie, but you could make a dish of sauce." She plopped a bag on the counter, the ruby-red ends of the rhubarb sticking out.

Cathy looked at her, raising her eyebrows. "Sure you didn't have another reason for stopping by? Or didn't the Amish grapevine reach you?"

Mary's cheeks reddened, but she met Cathy's gaze squarely. "Yah, all right. I heard some talk about Michael Forster bringing his child to our school, so I came to find out the truth of the story."

"That is the truth." She didn't mind talking about it with Mamm, but she'd rather not have this conversation with her sister.

Mary made the clucking noise that expressed her disapproval. "Is it wise to have her in your school? Why can't she go to the Englisch school? She'd fit in better there, for sure. It's what she'd be used to."

This might be the first time she had to answer that question, but Cathy didn't think it would be the last. She'd best figure out a convincing answer.

"She's there because she wants to be there with her cousin Ruthie. And because they are living with Verna Forster, and naturally Verna expects the child to be in the school she supports."

Mary frowned. "Yah, I guess I can understand about Verna. But what about Michael? He's lived Englisch for ten years now. Why send his daughter to the Amish school? Unless… Does he want to return to the church?" Amazement entered her voice. Mary was looking at Cathy as if she should know the answers, but she didn't.

"How would I know?" Exasperation came through in her voice. "I wouldn't be so nosy as to ask him."

"For sure you wouldn't," Mamm said, entering the fray. "Komm, now, Mary. It's your sister's job to teach the children who show up in the school. That's what she's doing."

Mary didn't look satisfied. "But Michael… If half of what we heard is true, he was arrested for his wife's death." To do her justice, she sounded troubled, not condemning.

"He was released," Cathy pointed out. "And he was allowed to move away. That must mean the police don't think he had anything to do with it, ain't so?"

"I don't know. But I know the police chief was there at the greenhouse talking to him not half an hour ago, because Elsie Shultz saw him with her own eyes."

Cathy's stomach clenched. *Not more trouble, dear Lord. Think of that child.*

Mamm shook her head reprovingly. "You shouldn't repeat gossip, Mary."

"It's not gossip if it's true," Mary retorted. "I don't want to believe any of the things they're saying about Michael. I'm certain sure the boy I knew couldn't do them. But how do any of us know what ten years in the Englisch world might have done to him?"

"It is not our place to judge." Mamm's voice was firm.

"I'm not judging," Mary protested. "I just wish our Cathy didn't have the child in her school."

For a moment all Cathy could do was stare at her sister. "Why? Allie is just an innocent child. Eight years old, with her mother gone and all of the turmoil in her life—if I can make her happy and accepted there, that's my duty as a teacher."

Mary was already shaking her head. "Ach, Cathy, I feel for the child, but just think. We already know that the Stoltzfus family wants to see their Mary Alice teaching at Creekside School. If there's any hint of trouble about having Michael's daughter in your school, they'd certain sure make a fuss. You only have a year's contract, and—"

"I know that." Cathy interrupted her sharply. She couldn't say it hadn't crossed her mind as well. "But I'm paid to teach the children of this church district, and as long as Allie is living with Verna Forster, that includes her." Her glare dared Mary to say anything more.

Her sister's face softened, and she touched Cathy's hand lightly. "Don't be angry. I understand. I just don't want to see you get caught in the middle of Michael's troubles."

When Mary spoke that way, she became again the patient older sister who'd taught Cathy how to tie her shoes, instead of the sometimes sharp-tongued critic.

"I know." The momentary anger she'd felt seeped away. "I understand that you're worried. I am, too. But I must do what's right for me as a teacher. If I fail my duty to one child—well, it's as bad as failing all of them."

She hadn't articulated it to herself before, but now that she'd said it, she knew it was true. She would do her duty to Michael's child, no matter what it cost her.

CHAPTER THREE

"THAT SHOULD BE RIGHT." Lige lowered the end of the heavy wooden table he carried, so Michael put his down as well. "With Memorial Day coming up at the end of the month, lots of folks should be coming by for flowers."

Michael nodded. "Better have lots out, then." The Amish didn't generally put flowers on graves, but plenty of other people did.

Diana was buried in the Englisch cemetery in her family's plot—her brother had insisted. Would her family be putting flowers on it? If so, they wouldn't come here to buy them.

He eyed Lige as they carried out flats of impatiens and marigolds. If Lige resented his presence or the fact that he'd begun working in the nursery, he didn't show it. Still, he might be wondering how Michael's presence affected his own position here. It seemed generally understood that the nursery would eventually go to Sarah and Lige, and he had no intention of interfering.

"I was wondering..." Lige began and then paused, his usually stolid face troubled.

"What?" Maybe Lige was going to save him the trouble of bringing it up by doing so himself.

"I saw that Chief Jamison was here yesterday. Did you tell him about the damage to your car?"

For an instant he was startled. He'd forgotten that in the rush of other events. "No, I didn't bother. It cleaned right off, so what was the use?"

Even as he dismissed the incident, he knew he couldn't leave it at that. Lige had a right to know anything that might affect the family.

He frowned down at a flat of pansies. "He said… Well, he said the police in Harrisburg had been in touch with him. Making sure I'm really here, I guess." He grimaced. "He was nice about it. Even bought some geraniums."

Lige nodded. "He's a gut man. Not one to stir up trouble where it's not needed."

Something in Michael relaxed. "He said I'd be treated fair by him. I can't ask for more." He glanced toward the house. "Anyone else know about it?"

"Not from me." Lige grinned. "I figure no sense in giving women anything extra to fret over. They find plenty on their own."

"I like the way you think." Lige was treating him better than he'd a right to expect, and he was grateful. "I'd better head out to school to pick up Allie."

"Sarah says you're bringing Ruthie here as well. She can run around with Allie until I go home. Don't let those girls talk your ear off on the way."

Michael smiled at the thought, nodding. He'd give a lot to hear Allie chattering the way Ruthie did.

It took just a few minutes to drive to the school—maybe next time he'd walk. The idea seemed more appealing when he realized a police car was following him down the road, staying a few feet from his bumper even when he pulled into the school lane and down to the school.

His stomach cramped as he got out of the car. If this was Chief Jamison's idea of treating him fairly, he didn't think much of it.

But when the driver got out he realized it wasn't Jamison. For a moment Michael stared, memory stirring. What was his name? He'd been one of the Englisch teens in the gang that had hung around Diana. Big for his age—already bulky and filled out when the other guys were still growing into their height. Smethers, that was it. Guy Smethers.

Something vaguely unpleasant came along with the memory. Smethers had used his size against anyone who was smaller, weaker…a bully.

Judging by the swagger in his step as he walked toward Michael, the patrolman's uniform he wore hadn't changed that aspect of his personality. Odds were he was still a bully.

Michael forced tight muscles to release. No point in borrowing trouble. Smethers could be here on some errand to do with the school.

"Harrisburg get too hot for you, did it? Figure you'd come back here and hide?"

Ten years ago he'd have flared up in an instant at the tone. He was smarter now…at least when it came to the cops. The past year had been full of hard lessons, and that had been one of them.

"Smethers, isn't it? So you're a police officer now." Keeping his voice level took effort.

"That's right." He came uncomfortably close. "And you're a felon. Puts us on opposite sides, don't it?"

"I've never been convicted of a crime." *Don't give him a reason to cause trouble. Remember, Allie is right inside the building. She could come out at any minute.* "And we always were on opposite sides, weren't we?"

That was dangerously close to the edge, but it was true. Smethers had made no secret of his resentment toward any Amish kids who hung around with the Englisch, no matter who invited them.

Guy's big hands knotted into fists. He was right in Michael's face, but Michael wasn't going to back away. He wouldn't raise a hand to the man, but he wouldn't cower either.

"You took Diana away from guys who'd have treated her decent, gave her a crummy life and killed her. And you have the nerve to come back here? Maybe those cops in Harrisburg don't know how to handle you, but we do."

Michael spared a brief thought for Chief Jamison, who'd had him convinced things were different here. Stupid to believe it.

"Unless you have a warrant, get lost." He'd started to turn away when Smethers grabbed him. Steeling his muscles, he stood rigid, not lifting a hand, not moving a muscle.

That threw Guy off. He'd have expected Michael to take a swing. It was what he'd have done ten years ago.

Not now. Not with a cop. He wasn't that dumb. He stared at Guy, expressionless.

Guy's face betrayed his longing as well as his questioning. Could he get away with it? It hung in the balance.

And then the schoolhouse door opened and Cathy stepped out onto the porch. She eyed them coolly for a moment.

"Mr. Smethers. Did you want something?"

Smethers glared at Michael for a long moment. Then he released him and stepped back. He swaggered to the car, where he turned for a final word.

"Get out of town, Forster. There's nothing here for you but trouble."

CATHY COULDN'T MOVE for a moment, trying to assimilate the venom in the man's voice. Here, on the Amish school grounds, to have a uniformed officer talking like that—it was unimaginable.

But she didn't have to imagine it. She had heard it. She had seen Michael's reaction, too. He hadn't turned a hair. Had he actually become used to that sort of anger directed against him?

The police car vanished from view. The momentary paralysis left, and Cathy was nearly overwhelmed by the wave of compassion that swept her. She darted down the steps and across the space that separated her from Michael.

"Are you all right? What possessed the man to behave that way? It was outrageous."

Michael focused on her, but his face was still frozen into what seemed an impenetrable mask. Then it seemed to crack, allowing bitterness to seep through.

"It goes along with being suspected of killing your wife. Don't worry. I've heard that sort of thing before."

"But not here." Not, surely, in their peaceful valley. Amish and Englisch had lived in harmony here for a hundred years or more.

He gave a twisted smile. "Yes, here. Are you really that naive, little Cathy?"

There was an edge to the words, but she didn't think he meant to hurt her. He'd been wounded, and he was striking out at the nearest person. She didn't mind if it happened to be her this time.

"Maybe I am, but that's not a bad thing. It makes me expect the best of people."

"And when they fail you?" His eyebrow quirked, but it almost sounded as if he were interested in what she thought, instead of merely antagonizing.

"I'm disappointed, of course. And sometimes I want to call them to account." She descended from the general to the specific. "I can't believe Chief Jamison would allow one of his officers to behave that way. And here at the school—that just makes it worse." She hesitated, not sure why that should matter, but nevertheless feeling it did.

"You're a kind person, Cathy. But you don't need to worry about me. I've heard worse."

She winced, hating the resignation in his voice. “I should have challenged him. I am responsible for anything that happens on school grounds.”

“No.” The sharpness of his tone startled her. “Sorry,” he went on. “I didn’t mean to bark. But it’s no use trying to fight back against that sort of thing, especially when it comes from the cops. They have all the power. If I had responded to Smethers the way I wanted to…” He let that trail off, as if he wanted to forget it.

But she couldn’t. “What? What could have happened? I know we’re taught to respect authority, but when it is abused that way, it’s not right.”

“Maybe not, but I don’t need you to fight my battles for me. Now, forget it, or I’ll report you to the bishop. Or your big sister.”

She grimaced, relieved that he’d relaxed enough to be able to tease about it. “I’d almost rather deal with the bishop than with Mary.”

“A little bossy, is she?” He managed a smile, but behind it she could still feel the anger and pain fighting for control. “She always was.”

“She hasn’t changed. Come to worship on Sunday and see for yourself. Her family is hosting this week, and I’m sure she’s been driving everyone crazy with her cleaning.”

He nodded, but she could see that his mind was still wrapped up in what had happened.

“What are you going to do about Smethers? Will you talk to Chief Jamison?”

He shook his head. “It wouldn’t do any good.” He

glanced toward the door to the school, which stood open now. "Did Allie hear any of that?"

The sudden anguish on his face at the thought told its own story of his vulnerable place.

"No, I'm sure she'd didn't, not enough to realize anyway. As soon as I heard his voice, I closed the door. I put her and Ruthie to work on cutting things out for a bulletin board, and Ruthie's talking enough to cover up almost anything."

His answering smile was mechanical, and he took a step toward the door. "I'd best take those two off your hands."

"Wait." Her outstretched hand stopped him. "I… I'm not trying to tell you what to do." He'd made it only too clear that he didn't need or want her advice where his daughter was concerned. "But you're still upset. Why don't you give it a few minutes? They're perfectly happy and occupied."

"Maybe you've got a point there." He let out a long breath and seemed to force himself to lean back against the porch railing. "I might be used to this kind of stuff, but I don't want it to spill over onto Allie. That's not acceptable."

"It's also not acceptable for you to be badgered and talked about here." She had a vivid memory of Mary's tale about the police. Some talk would be inevitable, but not the mean-spirited threats Smethers had uttered. "Besides, the police let you go, so…" She stopped, embarrassed. She hadn't intended to mention a thing about it.

Michael shrugged, seeming to accept the idea

that everyone here would know about what had happened. "They didn't have evidence to hold me. That doesn't mean they think I'm innocent. Until they find out who killed Diana, I'll be the main suspect."

"I'm sorry." Cathy responded to the bitterness in his voice. "About all of it. Anyone who knows you must surely know you couldn't have hurt her."

"That's a nice vote of confidence, Teacher Cathy. But I'd guess not a lot of people, even here, feel that way."

"Verna," she said, "Sarah, Lige…there will be others. Just give them a chance."

He didn't seem to hear her. It was as if he'd retreated into his own thoughts and memories. Not very pleasant ones, from the look on his face.

"Michael, don't…" It hurt her to see him that way.

"People will think what they want," he said, not looking at her, pursuing whatever unpleasant thoughts haunted him. "After all, we were separated. Diana wanted a divorce."

That startled her. The grapevine seemed to have missed that tidbit. "Did you?"

He shook his head. "No. And I didn't understand it. I know she missed…well, the things she'd have had if she'd stayed here. But we were doing okay. I just kept thinking if we sat down and talked things through, it would be okay."

She groped for understanding. She knew about divorce, knew Englisch people who had divorced and remarried, but for an Amish person it was not a choice. Marriage was forever. Where were the words that might help him?

"But we couldn't." His voice had flattened out. "I went to the house, hoping to talk, but it was too late. She was dead. And everyone seemed to think I'd done it." His face twisted. "Apparently including my own father. He won't see me."

Everyone knew how stubborn Josiah Forster was. But surely, when it came to his eldest son… "If you could talk to him…"

"You're a kind person, Cathy." At least he seemed to be looking at her now and not into the past. "My father couldn't forgive me for running around with Englisch kids when I was a teenager. Do you honestly think he would forgive me now? Do you?"

She'd like to say yes, but it wouldn't be true. She couldn't see Josiah bending, not for anything.

"I'm sorry." Pity moved her, and she reached out instinctively to clasp his hand. "I'm so sorry."

Their fingers touched, and his hand enveloped hers. Her skin tingled where it pressed his, generating a heat that flowed from her palm right up her arm and straight to her heart. She gasped, unable to stop herself, hit by a feeling she'd never experienced before—a feeling that seemed to wipe every other mild attraction out of existence.

She knew her eyes widened, knew she was staring at him, imagining that his eyes darkened with emotion…

And then he dropped her hand as if it were a hot

coal and turned away. "I'd better get those girls back to the house."

He sounded perfectly normal, but she could only nod because her voice was caught in her throat. Why? Why had this happened to her with Michael Forster, of all people?

And more important, how was she going to hide it?

MICHAEL HADN'T MISSED the fleeting expression on Cathy's face, and it kept recurring all the while he was admiring the children's work and loading them into the car.

He'd been an idiot to spill all that to Cathy. She didn't deserve to be burdened with the ugly details of his life. She was still such an innocent—he'd probably shocked her. And then, because she had a warm, loving heart, Cathy had reached out to him and imagined…

No, he couldn't excuse it by saying she'd imagined what had happened. He'd felt it, too, that sudden rush of attraction. It had felt, for an instant, so very right.

But it wasn't. He was light-years away from Cathy in age and experience. She couldn't imagine who he was inside, and he didn't want her to. The best thing he could do for Cathy was to show that he valued her as his child's teacher, and that was all.

Ruthie chattered in the backseat all the way home, struck by the novelty of being picked up from school in a car. Allie wasn't saying much—she never did. But when Michael caught a glimpse of her face in the rearview mirror, he saw an expression that wasn't her usual quiet interest in what Ruthie had to say. She looked… What? Frightened? Disappointed? He couldn't tell.

His stomach clenched. Cathy had seemed sure that the children hadn't heard Guy Smethers's harsh attack, but what if she'd been wrong? Should he say something about it in explanation?

He couldn't begin to imagine what that explanation might be. How did anyone explain a situation like this to an eight-year-old?

Ruthie broke off her apparently endless stream for a moment as he turned into the lane. Allie spoke.

"I'd rather ride home in a buggy," she said.

"But this is different," Ruthie protested. "Nobody else does this." She sounded as if doing something none of the other kids did was a treat. Somehow he doubted that Lige and Sarah would feel that way about it.

Or maybe they wouldn't care one way or the other. They both seemed pretty well grounded in the Amish way, accepting those bits of modern life that seemed necessary and unobjectionable and discarding the rest.

But Allie… Suddenly he realized he hadn't lived up to one of the first things he'd promised her about living here. He'd said she'd have lots of chances to ride in a buggy, but so far she hadn't done it even once.

A weight seemed to settle on him. Was he ever going to get the hang of being a parent? He certainly didn't live up to the standards of someone like Lige, who was deeply involved in his children's lives on a daily basis.

"We'll take a ride in the buggy tomorrow, okay?" He met his daughter's gaze in the mirror.

She looked at him gravely. "Promise?"

"Yes. I promise."

In return he got that small sweet smile. He could only wish he thought he deserved it.

Since the next day would be Saturday, there would be plenty of time to keep his promise. He wasn't likely to forget, not with Allie's brown eyes studying him, waiting. She didn't nag or pester, the way he'd heard other children do, she just waited.

He'd be happy to believe it was just that she was remarkably well behaved, but he couldn't quite convince himself.

The next morning he and Lige were busy in the greenhouse carrying plants out to display for the anticipated shoppers. At about the time they finished, a buggy turned in the driveway. But it wasn't an early customer—it was Sarah and her family.

The kids scrambled out of the buggy while Sarah, carrying the baby, descended more sedately and grinned at him. "Didn't expect to see the whole crew, did you?"

He gave her a quick hug. "No, but I'm glad. What brings you over?"

His sister linked her arm through his. "Let's get this little one inside first. We figured this would be a busy sales day—such a nice warm day this time in May. Folks will be wanting to get their plants in, ain't so?"

"I guess." He shot a glance at Allie, who had her head together with Ruthie. "I promised Allie I'd take her for a buggy ride today, but if we're going to be busy, I'd best put it off."

"Don't do that." She shook his arm lightly. "A promise is a promise. The girls can help for a bit. Then we'll give the kinder an early lunch, and you can take them all for a trip to town."

He blinked. "All?" He was barely managing one child.

Sarah's face crinkled with laughter. "Ach, Michael, if you could see your expression. Not the baby, for sure. I'll put her down for a nap. But you can manage the two girls and the twins. Take them for ice cream and you'll be the favorite onkel."

Without waiting for a response, she called the children. "Listen, now. You're to help set up until lunchtime. After lunch, Onkel Michael will take all of you to town in the buggy. If you behave yourselves, maybe he'll stop for ice cream."

The twins had looked a little skeptical at first, but the mention of ice cream seemed to win them over. More concerned about Allie, he glanced at her. But Allie, swinging clasped hands with Ruthie, wore a delighted smile.

So a few hours later, Michael found himself driving Lige's family buggy down the road. How long had it been since he'd driven a horse and buggy? Since he'd left home, probably. Apparently it was one of those things a person didn't forget. The movements of harnessing up had come automatically, and the buggy mare was placid and seemed to know her job.

Allie, at least, was quite impressed. She and Ruthie had wedged themselves into the front with him. Her eyes grew a bit wider as traffic increased.

"What if the horse is scared of the cars?" She pressed a little closer to Michael's side.

"Daisy isn't afraid," Ruthie answered before Michael could say a word. "She's been around cars lots and lots. My daadi trained her himself. Sometimes I give her a bite of apple or carrot when we take the harness off. You can, too, if you want."

"You put it right in her mouth?" Allie sounded awed. And scared.

"You put it flat on your hand like this." Ruthie held out her hand stiffly, palm up. "She nibbles it right off."

"I'll bet her lips tickle," he put in. "It'll make you giggle."

Allie didn't look as if she looked forward to that, so he backed off.

"Only if you want to. You don't have to."

She shot him a look of gratitude and turned her attention to Ruthie, who divided her time between pointing out the sights and admonishing her little brothers, who'd started being restive in the back.

By the time they reached the park, Michael decided it was time for a break. He drew the horse up under the trees, where a hitching rail had been provided. Clearly this was familiar to his sister's kids. The boys immediately ran toward the sliding board while Ruthie clutched Allie's hand and led her toward the swings.

So Sarah thought he could manage four kids, did she? She was overrating him. A quick comparison of the height of the sliding board and the size of the twins told him he was needed more there than with the girls. With a few quick cautions to Ruthie and Allie, he trotted across to where Jacob and James were already scrambling up the ladder.

"Take it slow." He remembered to speak to the boys in Pennsylvania Dutch. They had a smattering of Englisch already, but he wouldn't risk it.

"Yah, Onkel Michael." The one in front, Jacob, he thought, responded for his twin.

"You're Jacob, right?"

He nodded, grinning. "How did you know?"

"Just a guess." Actually, Aunt Verna had given him the secret—Jacob, a few minutes the elder, usually spoke for both of them.

A few minutes of watching convinced him that the boys could handle themselves. He'd stay here, just in case they got rambunctious, but he was free to look around.

The park was busy on this sunny Saturday. Ruthie and Allie seemed to be talking to a pair of Englisch girls about their age. He had no doubt that Ruthie started it—she didn't seem to consider anyone a stranger. But as he watched, he saw Allie speaking, too. Tension eased in him at the sight. Allie was warming up. Despite the problems that dogged him, maybe coming here had been the right decision.

He checked the boys again, and then moved his shoulders uneasily. An odd feeling crept over him. A sense of something out of place…something he'd seen that hadn't registered.

Turning casually, he scanned the park again. His gaze stopped at the jogging path where it ran close to the playground.

That was it. One man was visible, dressed for a run, but he wasn't running. He was staring right at Michael.

As if he realized he'd been seen, the man stiffened. For an instant he turned away, maybe to resume his run. Then he turned back and walked quickly toward Michael.

For a moment Michael's mind was blank. Then something about the man…the slight build, the sandy hair, the oddly awkward way of moving, brought remembrance. Randy…Randy Hunter. He had been part of the circle of teens around Diana…hopelessly infatuated with her even when she laughed at him.

There was no time to consider how to handle the encounter…the man had reached him. And a quick look at Randy's face told him that this would be no cautious welcome back. Anger blazed in the faded blue eyes, giving them more passion than he ever remembered seeing.

"I heard you'd come back. I couldn't believe it." His voice was raised, and Michael took a hasty look around.

The boys were preoccupied with each other, laughing as they came down the slide in tandem. Allie, thank goodness, was safely out of reach.

"This is my home." He wasn't going to apologize for existing. But he wouldn't start a fight—not with Randy, not with anyone.

Randy's face twisted. "This was Diana's home before you took her away. You took her away, but that wasn't enough for you. You made her miserable. You killed her." His hands doubled into fists.

"Take it easy, Randy." He kept his voice low. Calm. "You don't want to start a fight here."

He could see the effort the man made to control himself. If he swung at Michael the children would see…

Randy's face tightened, and beads of sweat formed at his hairline. But he stepped back. "I wouldn't dirty my hands." He spun and strode blindly toward the road.

Michael discovered he was shaking. Not for himself. It might have given him pleasure to flatten somebody at this point. But it had been such a close thing. Allie might easily have been standing nearby. She could have heard what Hunter said.

Revulsion swept through him. He could have gone elsewhere—anywhere that he might be able to get a job. But then who would take care of Allie? This was where he had support.

Suddenly Allie and Ruthie were on either side of him, tugging at his hands. "Ice cream," Ruthie said.

"The ice cream truck is coming. Don't you hear it? Mammi said you'd get us ice cream."

Right. The world might be crumbling around him, but the tinkling bell of the ice cream truck had to be answered.

"You didn't forget, did you?" Ruthie prodded.

He managed to grin. "No, I didn't forget. Call your little brothers, and we'll have ice cream."

And then he'd take them home and give some serious thought to where he and Allie went from here.

CHAPTER FOUR

By the time the ice cream had been eaten, Michael found it was necessary to wipe off sticky faces and hands in the water fountain. Fortunately nobody objected to this unorthodox way of washing up.

"It's just water, ain't so?" Ruthie said when James held back for a moment. Michael was beginning to see that Ruthie had her mother's strong streak of common sense. "Put your hands in and don't be a silly."

James obediently followed orders and finished up by wiping his hands on his pants. Whether Sarah would object or not, Michael had no way of knowing, but she was the one who'd landed him with all of the kids, so she could take the consequences.

By the time they were in the buggy and headed homeward, the sour remnants of his encounter with Randy had faded. Maybe it was the company of small children that helped—at least they were distracting.

Ruthie and Jacob were the chatterboxes, while James and Allie listened and put in a word now and then. It amused him to see that Jacob was like his mother while James was as calm and slow-spoken as Lige. They seemed to balance each other.

Why had he so seldom had a simple outing like this with Allie in the past? He'd worked long hours during the week, true, but he could have done more on the weekends.

The truth was that it hadn't occurred to him that he could. From the time Allie was born, his tentative attempts to be involved with her care had been brushed aside by Diana.

That's not the way to do it. It had been a constant refrain, usually followed by a comment that if he wanted to help he could wash the dishes or take out the trash. He'd gradually gotten to the point that he stopped trying.

That had been wrong. He saw that now that he was all Allie had. But surely the distance between them wasn't unbridgeable.

He glanced down at her, sitting so close to him on the seat. "Allie, do you want to drive the horse?"

She gave him a look that mixed awe with eagerness. "Could I?"

"I don't see why not." They were coming down the stretch toward the farm now, with no traffic in sight to scare her. He put one arm around her, holding the lines steady. "Now take hold of the straps, right by my hands."

To his surprise she didn't hesitate. She grasped the reins firmly. "Now, just keep your hands steady. Daisy knows the way home, even to Aunt Verna's."

"She does?"

"For sure," Ruthie said. "Horses always know when they're going back to the barn. That's what Grossdaadi always says when we finish something. 'Time to go back to the barn.' That means we're done."

How strange to hear his father's familiar words echoed in Ruthie's lively treble. It pinched at his heart. Ruthie obviously had a relationship with Daad. No matter how implacable Daad's anger against Michael, anyone would think he'd want to see his granddaughter.

But apparently not. Oddly enough it was regret he felt, not resentment.

There was no time to consider it, since they were reaching home, and in a few moments the children were climbing down, vying with each other in the attempt to tell the adults all about everything.

When he'd unharnessed and Allie had fed the buggy horse the promised apple, Michael headed back to the greenhouse to see if he could be of help. He found Lige carrying flats of impatiens back into the greenhouses.

"Need some help?"

Lige nodded toward the flowers still on display. "We'd best take a few more under cover. Sounds like we might get a quick thunderstorm sometime tonight. You know how those spring storms can bring winds."

"Right." He picked up a couple of flats and started to follow Lige. He stopped, frowning when he saw how full the racks still were. Either they'd been refilling them all afternoon or...

Verna and Sarah were still listening to an account of the ice cream cleanup when he interrupted. "What's happened here this afternoon? It looks as if you've hardly sold a thing. I thought this was supposed to be a big day."

Sarah glanced at his face and then chased the children off to play before answering. "There's plenty of time for sales. Folks will be buying for the next few weeks."

"Come on, Sarah. I still know when you're trying to soften the news. Sales are off, aren't they? Because of me."

There was an echo of instant denials, but he could see the truth when it hit him in the face. People were staying away from the business because they didn't want to be around a man who was, in their minds, guilty of murder.

He should have seen it. If he had thought...but he'd been selfish and ignored the possibility. Well, he couldn't ignore it now.

"We'll have to leave," he said flatly. "That's all."

"Ach, don't talk nonsense." Aunt Verna's tone was crisp.

"It's the truth, it's not nonsense." The words were bitter on his lips. "I should have known better than to come here."

"Where else would you go but to family?" Sarah demanded. "Do you think we're so intent on making money that we'd put it before family?"

"You belong here." Aunt Verna grasped his arm in a wiry grip. "Nothing changes that."

"Folks will komm back." Lige's calm voice took the conversation down a level as he paused in what he was doing. “No sense deciding something serious based on a few hours’ business. Give it time.”

“Yah, that’s right.” Aunt Verna still grasped his arm, and he realized her hand was trembling. “You’ve only been here a few days. Let things settle.” Her fingers tightened. “Yah?”

He couldn’t argue, not when he saw a suspicion of tears in her eyes. So he nodded.

There was a general sense of relief. “Look, here comes a customer now.” Sarah nodded to the car turning in the lane. “Leave those impatiens for now. That’s Mrs. Grandage, and she always gets them for along her porch.”

Michael nodded. Murmuring an excuse, he headed back to the greenhouse, figuring his absence was better than his presence right now.

But this wasn’t over. No matter how much they wanted him to stay, how could he if it was going to ruin the business Aunt Verna had spent years building? He needed time to think.

That was just what the women seemed determined not to give him. Between them, Aunt Verna and his sister kept him busy with a score of unimportant small jobs until he was ready to shout at them that he was fine, just fine.

He wasn’t fine. Wouldn’t be, not unless someone did figure out who’d pushed Diana down those steps. And the more time that passed, the less likely it seemed that the truth would ever come out.

Some people probably wouldn’t believe it even if the cops arrested someone else. Randy, for instance.

He'd been carrying a grudge since they were teenagers, and now it had a focal point.

Finally the afternoon came to an end. The last few flats were carried under cover, and Sarah, with baby Sally on her hip, began collecting the rest of her children. That was when Michael realized that Allie was missing.

"Allie!" A quick check of the house and barn didn't turn her up, and Michael's momentary annoyance turned to fear.

"I'll check the outbuildings," Lige said. "She might be in the henhouse."

It was a matter of minutes before Lige returned, shaking his head.

Panic ripped through him. Where could she be?

Sarah put a hand on his arm. "Don't panic. We'll find her." She eyed Ruthie and gestured the child to her. Ruthie came reluctantly, looking anywhere but at her mother.

Sarah bent to her child, tipping Ruthie's chin up so that she had to look at her. "Ruthie, do you know where Allie is?"

Ruthie's lips pressed together in a straight line. Michael pushed down the need to demand answers. Let Sarah deal with it—she'd get results if anyone could.

"Ruth Ann Esch, I am waiting. What do you know about where Allie is?"

Ruthie held against the power of the maternal tone for another moment. Then she crumbled. Her lips trembled, and tears filled her eyes.

"I'm s-sorry, Mammi. I…"

"Tell me this instant." Sarah's voice allowed no excuse.

"We—we heard Onkel Michael say they would go away. And she cried, and then she said she must hide someplace, but I said that wouldn't help. So she said she must go to Teacher Cathy because she would help." She seemed to run dry.

"And then what?" Sarah wasn't satisfied.

"I showed her the path to Teacher Cathy's house," a small voice admitted.

Michael swung around on the words. The path… through the woods and along the pasture to the Brandt farm. She'd never go that far, would she? Maybe, if she was desperate enough. Michael started to run.

CATHY MOVED THROUGH her mother's strawberry patch, pulling the few weeds that had dared to pop up next to the plants. The tiny berries had begun to get a bit larger every day, and it wouldn't be long until they'd begin to change color. There would be strawberry shortcake to look forward to by the end of May.

Saturdays were a welcome change to the busyness of the school week. She'd do her planning for the upcoming week, of course, but that left time for helping Mamm and working in the garden. After the constant verbal exchanges of a school day, she enjoyed just being quiet for a bit.

"Cathy!" Daad's call startled her, coming so suddenly. She straightened, spotting him by the barn, gesturing for her. "Komm, schnell!"

Jumping lightly over the intervening plants, she hurried toward him, alarmed by the urgency in his voice. He clearly wasn't hurt. One of the animals?

When she reached him, Daad put his finger to his lips to enjoin silence. "Hush, don't frighten her. Just komm." He grasped her hand and led her into the barn, where he nodded toward the corner.

Cathy blinked, her eyes trying to adjust to the dim interior after the bright sunshine. Then she saw. Huddled into the space between the grain barrels in the corner was a small figure. Allie Forster.

Her breath caught. She sent a questioning look at her father.

"I just spotted her when I came in," he said softly. "I tried to talk to her, but she seemed scared. So I thought it best to call you."

She nodded and moved slowly toward the child. Allie did look frightened, and she couldn't begin to guess why. Or why she was here.

"Allie." She kept her voice soft and calm. "I didn't know you were coming to see me."

For an instant Allie seemed to shrink back, her brown eyes wide and blank. And then she burst into sobs and threw herself at Cathy.

"Hush, now, hush." Cathy sat down on the wide planks of the barn floor and wrapped her arms around Allie. "It's all right. You're safe. You're fine."

Allie's body was racked by the sobs she couldn't seem to control. There was nothing for it but to hold her snugly, stroke her shaking back and croon to her softly. The words didn't matter. The comforting sound—that was what counted just now. She might not have a child of her own, but she'd been a child, and she knew what Mamm would do. Hold and comfort until the bad dream, whatever it was, seeped away.

"There, now, that's better." The sobs were lessening, and she could feel Allie trying to control them. "It's all right. Take your time."

She glanced at Daad. He leaned against a stall, waiting with the patience bred in a man who worked with the land and the animals. He answered her look with a nod, agreeing that the child was doing better.

"Take her to the house," he said softly. "Your mamm will help."

Yes, that was the thing to do. Get Allie calm and comfortable in the familiar surroundings of a kitchen, and she'd be able to tell them what was wrong.

"Komm, now," she whispered to Allie. "I'll take you in the house, where we'll be comfortable. No use sitting on the barn floor when my mamm will be sure to have some cookies and milk, yah?"

Allie didn't let go, but her head moved in assent. Cathy smiled despite her concern. The worst of the storm was over. She'd be all right.

Daad gave her a hand getting up, and they headed toward the house, with her carrying Allie. Daad gestured, offering to carry her, but feeling how tightly Allie still clung, Cathy shook her head. She was a light enough burden.

When they reached the kitchen, Mamm seemed

to take in the situation at a glance. She pulled out a chair, and Cathy sank into it, setting Allie on her lap.

"Allie, this is my mamm and my daad. Mammi, I think Allie could do with a glass of milk."

"For sure." Her mother hustled to bring it. "And I have some chocolate chip cookies, just baked this morning. You and Allie can have a little snack together."

The sobs had stopped altogether on the way to the house. Now Allie stirred at the mention of cookies. She sat up, wiping her eyes with the backs of her hands. Cathy and Mamm exchanged glances. It was going to be all right.

Cathy waited until Allie had had a gulp of milk and nibbled a few bites of cookie before she ventured to ask a question.

"Were you trying to find me when you went in the barn, Allie?"

Allie nodded, glancing at her warily.

"That's fine. You are wilkom here anytime. I was in the strawberry patch, so if you'd come a little farther, you'd have seen me."

She paused, longing to have answers but not sure exactly how to ask. Maybe it was best to circle nearer the central question of why she was here.

"Did something happen to scare you that made you hide?"

Allie gave a convulsive jerk, the whites of her eyes showing. Cathy hugged her a bit closer.

"Can you tell me what it was? Maybe we can help."

"I—I was coming on the path, but—but it was dark in the trees. And I was afraid I missed the way."

Cathy patted her back, feeling convinced there was more. "That would be scary."

"It wasn't that." The words came out in a sudden burst. "I heard something. And then a big bird flew down right over my head, and it scared me, so I started to run. And then I saw the barn and I ran inside, 'cause I thought it wouldn't come there. But it swooped right inside, so I hid." The tears threatened to spill over again.

"Swallows," Daad muttered.

"I think you must have seen a barn swallow." Was it safe to smile a little? "It didn't mean any harm. That's how they fly. They swoop down and fly up." She illustrated with her hand. "They have a nest in the barn. Maybe it was a mama bird, trying to bring some food for her babies."

Allie held back her tears. "Do you think so?"

"Well, it could be." She had to be honest. "I know they have a nest up in the rafters, but I haven't been able to see any baby birds in it."

"Ach, they are there," Daad said quietly. "I heard them cheeping this morning."

"There now, you see? It was scary, but you're not scared now, are you?"

"N-no. But…"

"But there was some reason why you came looking for me, yah?"

Allie nodded. She sniffed and rubbed her eyes. "I heard what Daadi said. The grown-ups were talking, but I heard Daadi. He said we'd have to go away." The tears spilled over in a rush. "But I don't want to go. And I tore the bottom of my dress and it really belongs to Ruthie!" She gave herself up to the sobs.

So that was it. What was Michael thinking, to let his child hear him saying something so upsetting? Well, to be honest, it sounded as if they hadn't realized Allie was listening, but he still should have been more careful. The idea of leaving now that she'd found a safe haven was obviously terrifying to Allie, and no wonder.

The comforting had to be done all over again. Then Mamm, always sensible, got out a needle and a spool of thread.

"Now, then, Allie. One thing at a time. Let's fix your dress, all right? Then maybe Teacher Cathy can talk to your daadi and make it better."

Cathy would like to argue her ability to make this better, but Mamm had the right idea. One problem at a time.

Fortunately, Allie was more easily distracted from her crying this time. Once Mamm started threading her needle and talking about how they'd fix the dress, the tears vanished. She even slid off Cathy's lap to hold the dress up by the hem so Mamm could begin stitching it.

Seeing her occupied, Cathy got up, glancing at her father. He jerked his head toward the door, and she followed him out to the porch.

"They'll be fearful, not knowing where the child is," he said. "You'd best stay here in case she gets upset again. I'll walk over to Verna's and tell them she's safe."

"Denke, Daadi. Maybe that will give me time to think what I can say to Michael Forster."

Daad patted her shoulder. "You'll find the words when you need them," he said. Then he strode off toward the path that led to Verna's property.

She stood, staring after him, trying to think. Michael would be upset...probably both because Allie had heard but also because she'd turned to Cathy. Surely there wasn't anything so urgent that he had to wrest Allie away when she was just starting to feel secure.

She was staring absently at the point where the path vanished into the trees when she saw Daad reappear. He wasn't alone—Michael rushed past him. They must have met up almost immediately. And that meant she had no time to think of the right words to say. She could only trust that they'd come to her.

MICHAEL LOOKED UP and saw Cathy on the back porch. The first thing that entered his head was that of course Allie would have gone to her with her trouble. Love and concern seemed to radiate from her, and Allie had responded on instinct.

He'd run along the path through the woods like a crazy person, afraid of what he might find. He'd nearly run right into Eli Brandt. Allie was all right. She was. But he had to see for himself.

Cathy came a little way to meet him. As soon as he was in range, he blurted the important questions. "Where is she? You're sure she's all right?"

"In the kitchen. Yes, I'm certain sure." But she put up a hand to stop him when he'd have rushed on. "Wait a minute. Just wait."

"I have to see her." He brushed her words aside impatiently. "Later—"

"Not later. Now." Cathy's voice was soft and even, but there was a note in it that seemed to compel obedience. "I want… No, I need to say something. And you need to be calm before you see Allie. If you rush in, you'll upset her, and we just got her quieted down."

"I can control myself. You don't need to tell me that." An edge of annoyance sounded in his tone.

"Don't I?" Cathy smiled, and something in him relaxed.

"All right, maybe I do." He took a breath. "You're sure she's okay?" But he knew the answer. Cathy wouldn't keep him talking if Allie were hurt.

Still, she was hurt—just not physically. When he thought of Ruthie's words, he felt a little sick.

"Daad found her in the barn. The barn swallows scared her. You know how they swoop toward their nest. We took her to the house, and she's had a snack. Right now, she's helping Mamm sew a little tear in her dress."

Michael knew what she was doing. She was soothing him with her soft voice and gentle words, just as she'd probably comforted his daughter.

"Did she tell you why she ran off like that?" He supposed she had, but Cathy was safe. She wouldn't be gossiping about it to anyone.

"Yah, she did. It seems she heard something that

upset her very much. You said the two of you would have to move again."

She just waited, not venturing to point out how wrong it had been to let his child hear it.

"I was upset. Something happened… Well, it doesn't matter now. But I shouldn't have spoken—not where she could hear me." He shook his head. "I'd like to think she'd come to me, but she didn't. She confided in Ruthie, and Sarah got it out of her in pretty short order."

"Sarah's a fine mother. She knows her kinder inside out."

The way he ought to know Allie. He managed a wry smile. "Well, Teacher Cathy, can I go in now?"

"Just…just let me say one more thing." Cathy lost her certainty all at once. "Michael, Allie is finding security here already. Please don't let that be taken away by foolish people who believe nonsense."

She didn't seem to expect him to answer. She just led the way to the house.

When he reached the porch, Michael paused to be sure he was composed. *Security*, Cathy had said. Surely that was one of the most important things for a child. It ought to be the least he provided for his daughter. He went into the kitchen.

Allie looked up, her face a little apprehensive when she saw him. "Daddy, I…"

"It's okay, sweetheart." He moved to the table, exchanging glances with Lydia Brandt. She gave an approving nod and gestured for him to sit.

He took the chair next to Allie, trying to find the

words to explain. "I was scared when I didn't know where you were. But I'm not mad at you."

She seemed to be measuring his words, and they must have reassured her. "Not at Ruthie either, okay? She was just trying to help."

He tried not to smile. "That's between Ruthie and her mammi, but I'm not mad at her either."

"And I tore my dress," she said with an air of wanting to clear the slate entirely. She held out the bottom of the dress for his inspection.

"I can't even see where the tear was."

He touched her hand, wishing the space between them could be mended so easily. But that was years in the making, and it would take more than a few stitches to do that.

Now he knew where it had to begin. Security, that was what Cathy had said, and she was right. For reasons he couldn't begin to understand, his daughter had found that here.

He held out his arms to Allie, and she came to him, letting him put his arms around her. "I know what you heard me say, but that was a mistake. Something had made me upset, and I said something silly. People do that sometimes."

He smoothed her hair back where it had come loose from her braid, letting his hand cup her head. She was so young, so fragile, this daughter of his. He had to do right by her.

"I know you love being here. I do, too." Somewhat to his surprise, he realized that was true. "So we're going to stay, even if things sometimes happen that are difficult. Okay?"

He studied the small, serious face. Allie looked up at him, hope in her eyes. "Is it a promise?"

"Yes." He brushed a kiss on her forehead. "It's a promise."

CHAPTER FIVE

CATHY CHECKED THE schoolroom clock. Almost time for recess. Her scholars were already giving her expectant looks—they knew without checking when they were ready for a break. She began the process of sending the younger children to the restroom a grade at a time, knowing they couldn't be counted on to interrupt their play for that necessity.

Her thoughts returned, as they so often did these days, to Michael and the difficult process of adjustment to his new life. Certainly Allie seemed to be happier, more confident, in the days since her father's promise. But how difficult was he going to find it to keep that promise?

He hadn't attended worship on Sunday at Mary's house, although Verna had brought Allie. To questions, Verna had said he wasn't ready yet. The answer seemed to satisfy most, at least for the moment. But people would have opinions about it, no matter what he did or didn't do.

She brushed the thought away. Her concern was only with Allie, and how all of the surrounding factors affected her. Nothing else. It shouldn't be this difficult to stop thinking about Michael.

A shuffling of feet drew her attention back to the schedule. “All right,” she said, smiling at the waiting class. “You may be dismissed for recess.”

No mad rush to the door, of course. The scholars might be eager, but they knew better than that. She inserted herself into the file of children so that she could keep an eye on Allie. So far there had been no untoward incidents, but the freedom of recess might lead someone to misbehave.

Cathy lingered for a moment in the warm sunshine of the porch steps. Spring, after teasing them with what seemed an unfair share of cold, dreary days, had finally come. There was less than a month of the school year left. Would the school board offer her a new contract or not? They’d have to decide soon, she knew.

Her momentary distraction had been a mistake. She spotted Ruthie and Allie with another of the third graders, Mary Louise Yost. Ruthie, hands planted on her hips, seemed to be confronting Mary Louise.

Cathy hurried her steps. She was in time to hear Mary Louise. “I just asked if Allie was really Amish, that’s all.” She glared back at Ruthie. “I want to know.”

Allie’s expression told Cathy something very clearly. She wanted to know that as well. Cathy’s heart seemed to wince. She opened her mouth to intervene, but Ruthie got in first.

“For sure she’s Amish. She’s my own cousin, and I’m Amish. So she’s Amish. See?”

“Oh.” Mary Louise pondered that for a moment before nodding. “Okay. Let’s go on the swings, yah?”

In a moment the three of them, hands linked, were running toward the swings.

Cathy's laugh was a bit shaky. She had barely begun to try and figure out the proper response when Ruthie had taken the wind out of her sails. Her reasoning might not make it past a group of ministers and bishops, but it was enough to go on with.

Allie was not yet of an age to make a decision about baptism into the church. She was being raised in an Amish family now, so she was Amish. Michael might not agree, but it would certainly solve problems on the school yard.

Cathy gave an assessing glance around the school yard, looking for any place where her presence was needed. She often joined in the games, but first she liked to be sure all was as it should be.

Her gaze snagged on the glint of sunshine off metal. Eyes narrowing, she tried to make out what she was seeing. It looked as if someone had pulled a car off to the side of the road just beyond the schoolhouse lane, where the trees masked its presence.

Frowning, she strolled toward the perimeter of the school yard. There were probably a hundred innocent reasons for a vehicle to be pulled over at that spot, but it was unusual. She was the sole adult responsible for the forty-some children in her care—and the only one here today. Many days a parent or older sibling would be present, providing help in one way or another, but not today.

Her stomach tightened. She didn't consider herself a nervous person, but bad things happened everywhere, as the Amish knew to their sorrow. She fingered the cell phone tucked into the pocket sewn onto the underside of her apron. It would connect her in an instant to the police or to the closest Amish business with a phone—the quilt shop run by her close friend, Joanna Kohler. Since someone was always in the shop during school hours, Joanna had agreed to serve as a message center for the school, contacting parents as needed.

Surely the mere presence of a vehicle parked along a public road didn't call for an emergency reaction. If she saw someone—and then she did. A person—a man, she thought, though it could be a woman in pants—was just visible in the shelter of the trees. Her fingers tightened on the phone as the pulse in her neck began to throb.

Slowly, carefully, don't alarm him... She moved toward the older children who were kicking a soccer ball. Forcing a smile, she beckoned the two oldest to her, thankful they happened to also be two of the most sensible.

"John, Caleb, I want you to start the kinder moving into the school. Don't run or act alarmed—I know I can trust you to be calm." Her own heart pounded against her ribs. "There is someone on the school grounds—no, don't look around. Just do as I say and don't alarm anyone."

John grasped Caleb firmly by the arm, as if to prevent him from running. "Yah. We'll do just like you say." Caleb managed to nod, but he looked scared.

She watched them move toward the others, seeming to overcome argument with a few words. Once they were on their way, she dared look toward the intruder again. Was he carrying something or not? She couldn't be sure, but the horrific stories of school shootings forced themselves into her mind.

Another step or two, and she could be sure. There was something—something that gave a small metallic glint as he or she moved it. Cathy yanked the phone out, her heart pounding in her ears as she punched 911. She only got out a word or two before the dispatcher was shouting for the chief.

"Stay on the phone."

Even as the order came through, Cathy turned, mind racing. The last of the children were through the door now. She started to run.

Get to the school, lock and barricade the door, get the children into the supply closet. That was the safest course. Did every teacher think this way when the moment came?

Her racing feet reached the door, where she paused for a quick look back. Nothing. The place where she'd seen the figure held only natural growth, but the branches moved lightly. In the next instant she heard the car's engine and then the squeal of tires as it sped off.

Behind her, in the schoolroom, someone started to cry. But it was over now, wasn't it?

A HECTIC HOUR LATER, the children had all been escorted home—Chief Jamison had insisted on that. Now Cathy sat in her desk chair, feeling oddly boneless. Grouped around her were several parents, a patrolman and Chief Jamison himself.

"It might have been chust a tourist." Lige Esch spoke in his usual deliberate way. "Sometimes they hear we don't like our pictures taken so they try to sneak one anyway."

Lige's calmness steadied her, and she considered it. "It might have been a camera the person held. I couldn't see well enough to tell."

"If you'd taken time to be sure—" That was Zeb Stoltzfus, cut off abruptly by Chief Jamison.

"Teacher Cathy did exactly the right thing. Get the children inside—call us. We'd rather come out a hundred times for a straying tourist than risk something bad happening." He looked around the circle of faces. "I don't need to spell it out to you. We all know that bad things can happen anywhere. That's why we talk to everyone involved with the schools. That's why Teacher Cathy was prepared and did exactly the right thing."

Several people nodded in agreement, and there was a murmur of assent.

Chief Jamison stood, apparently satisfied that he'd gotten his point across. "We'll be keeping an eye out for anyone showing too much interest in your school and the other schools in the area as well. Thank you."

His tone made it clear he expected them to leave. After a moment's hesitation, they filed out, leaving Cathy with the police.

When they'd gone, Cathy looked up at Jamison, expecting more questions.

His face crinkled in the beginning of a smile. "No, I don't intend to badger you with more questions. You've already told us everything you saw and heard. I just thought you might want me to clear them out so you could get off home without answering silly questions."

Cathy hesitated, not sure how she felt about it. "If the parents want to talk to me more, I should be available."

"Maybe so, but not now. I'll drive you home." He took her elbow as she stood, then paused, frowning a little. "You did the right thing. Really. Don't let anyone second-guess you, okay?"

She nodded, but it would be difficult. If the parents of her scholars doubted her, it wouldn't matter what the chief thought.

When they reached the porch, she discovered that everyone hadn't left, after all. Michael Forster stood, leaning against the side of his car.

Chief Jamison glared at him. "Teacher Cathy has answered enough questions. I'm taking her home."

Michael straightened. "I don't have any questions. And I came to take her home."

For a moment the two stared at each other, as if each daring the other to blink. Cathy stepped between them. "Denke, Chief Jamison. If you need anything else…"

His face softened. "I know where you are."

Cathy walked to Michael's car and slid inside before he could open the passenger door. Without a word, he got in and started the engine. It was only when they'd followed the police car out to the road and turned that he glanced at her.

"Was I preferable to the police?"

She smoothed her skirt. "I thought you said no questions."

"Just wondered."

His mild tone seemed to encourage an answer. "I thought my mother might be slightly less upset if I came home in your car rather than a police car. Though she'll have heard by now and…well, I'm her baby, I guess."

"Are you all right?"

Cathy looked at him, startled. "Yah, I am. Allie and Ruthie?"

"Not as upset as I'd have thought. Ruthie strikes me as a kid who'd bounce back, and I guess she must be good for Allie."

"When you came to take them home, I thought…" She let that trail off. She'd thought he looked furious, to be honest. And she'd assumed that the anger was directed at her as the person who should be keeping his child safe.

"I was frantic—we all were." He wasn't looking at her, so she felt free to watch his face. He stared at the road ahead, his hands gripping the steering wheel. "It's a parent's worst nightmare."

"A teacher's, too." Her throat tightened, remembering. "I thought maybe you were regretting putting Allie in our school. Feeling we should have done more to keep the kinder safe."

For a moment he didn't respond, and her heart sank.

If he took Allie away now, what would the result be? She couldn't help feeling responsible, whatever his decision.

"When I came back to the school, I intended to tell you I was taking Allie out. Putting her someplace that had locks and security guards and alarms. They were still inside talking, so I waited, but I could hear the whole thing." Another long pause.

"The chief was right," he said finally. "All the locks and alarms in the world aren't the answer. Human beings are the ones who protect the children." He glanced at her. "No one could have done any better than you did."

Her heart warmed, and some of the tension eased out of her.

"All I could do was remember what Chief Jamison said when we had a meeting back before school started. He told us then to memorize every step we should take—either inside the school or outside—because if it happened we wouldn't have time to think, just act. And he was right."

"Yeah." His face was grim again, his knuckles white on the steering wheel. He made the turn into Daad's lane before he spoke. "We should be able to give our children safety. That was in my mind when I brought Allie here—to the most peaceful place I know. But there isn't any peace."

"Don't think that." She spoke impulsively, reaching out to touch his arm. It was like an iron bar under her fingers. "I know, evil can be anywhere. But peace—peace is inside us." She wanted so much to let him see it as she did. "There's nothing magic about living Plain. We're in the same world as everyone else, good and bad. But this place—it's better than most, I think."

The car drew up to the house then. There wasn't time for anything more. If she hadn't said the right things, it was too late.

But as she opened the car door, he spoke again. "Maybe." His face twisted as if in pain. "I'd like to believe that. Anyway, Allie will be at school in the morning."

BY THE END of the day the community seemed to have come to grips with what happened, at least from what Michael heard. Lige stopped by in the evening to give them the latest.

"So we've set up for Teacher Cathy to have a helper there every day, instead of just a few days a week. And we're scheduling fathers to check the school grounds several times a day."

He shook his head to a piece of apple crumb pie that Aunt Verna held out to him. "Denke, but we just finished supper."

"I'll send some home with you, then." She began transferring several slices of pie to a plate.

Ignoring the byplay, Michael went to the heart of the issue. "I want to be in on that. Just tell me when to go."

He half expected an argument, but Lige nodded. "I said we'd do it tomorrow. I'll take Ruthie to school and walk the grounds then, and you can do a mid-morning check, okay?"

Michael nodded. At least it was something positive to do about the situation.

"Seems like mostly folks are saying it was probably a tourist." Lige shrugged his shoulders in an irritated gesture. "I guess we've got to hope that's all it was and not some crazy person with a grudge against schools. Or against us." They all knew that prejudice against the Amish existed.

"Yah." Aunt Verna handed him the wrapped plate. "And pray."

"For sure." He turned, and Michael walked out with him, holding the door.

Once they were down the steps, Lige raised his eyebrows. "Sure I'm not taking pie you had your eye on?"

"Certain sure." He hesitated. "Do you think it's enough? Not the pie. I mean, checking the school grounds and having a helper there most of the time?"

Lige sobered. "Who can say? It's doing something anyway. Cathy has a phone always with her and a good head on her shoulders. She did fine with just the two boys to help her. Besides, what else could we do?"

"I don't know." He didn't—that was the trouble. It was another area where he felt helpless. He hated that feeling. A man should be able to keep his family safe. Hadn't he been telling himself that since Diana's death?

Lige gripped his shoulder for an instant before climbing into the buggy. "Yah. Me either."

The moment of shared concern heartened him, and he watched while Lige drove out the lane and turned onto the blacktop. Then he started back inside, but before he'd gone a few steps, he'd spotted a car turning into the driveway.

He stood where he was for a moment before walking toward the plant stands. In theory they closed at five, but it wasn't unusual for someone to stop by afterward. Aunt Verna never liked to disappoint a customer, no matter how inconvenient.

Then the car drew up beside him. He stared in surprise as he recognized the driver. Alan Channing, their neighbor back in Harrisburg. Alan and his wife had been the only ones to offer sympathy and help in the days after Diana's body was discovered, taking care of Allie, helping him find an attorney. He'd quickly found how rare that was—most people he'd considered friends greeted him with a muttered word and then hurried away.

"Alan, what on earth brings you here?" He extended his hand as Alan got out of the car and felt it grasped in a firm grip. Alan's open, friendly face was a welcome sight. Here, at least, was a reminder of his previous life that wasn't horrible.

"Came to see you, of course." Alan brushed tousled blond hair back with a familiar gesture. In his pressed khaki pants and striped dress shirt, Alan always looked as if he could pose for a magazine ad.

Too handsome, that had been Michael's first impression of him, but he'd soon found a friendly, self-effacing human behind the glossy exterior.

“All this way for us?” He raised an eyebrow, and Alan grinned.

“I realized my sales route went not far from here, so I headed this way after my last call of the day.”

Alan was a sales rep for his father-in-law’s pool and spa business—the top salesman, he always insisted.

“Whatever brought you, I’m glad to see you. Allie is tucked up in bed already, but come inside and meet my aunt.”

“Sure, but…” He hesitated, glancing toward the house. “First, tell me how you’re doing while we’re by ourselves. Beth and I have been concerned about you—both of you.”

He couldn’t hold back a grimace when he thought of the past few days. “Ups and downs,” he said. “Allie has settled in well. My sister’s girl is just her age, so they’ve become fast friends.”

“Good, good.” His voice was just a shade too hearty. Apparently he’d picked up on Michael’s ambivalence. He glanced around, taking in the greenhouses and the rolling farmland beyond. “This is far from what she’s used to.”

“True. But here we both have family to rely on.” At least, some family. His thoughts flickered to his father. “And she loves her new teacher.”

“That’s fine.” Alan hesitated, looking a little uncomfortable. “We were afraid…well, that it might be worse here, because Diana was from here, too.”

His initial reaction was to keep his problems to himself. But Alan had proved to be a good friend, despite the fact that their backgrounds were as different as they could possibly be.

"There's some feeling against me," he said finally. "I guess that's bound to happen. But weighing it all, this was about the best choice I could make. The legal bills about wiped me out." He forced a light note. "My aunt doesn't charge us rent. And she's about the best cook I ever met."

"So you feel like you're settled here? I only ask because I heard of something that might suit you. A job with a guy I knew in college. He owns a construction business, along with a few other things, and he's looking for someone to manage it for him. He'd treat you right, and it would pay enough to help you get on your feet again." He glanced around, as if looking for evidence of prosperity. "I don't know what you're making here..."

"Room and board." Michael grimaced. He knew his help was needed and welcomed, but it still felt wrong not to be earning his living.

Alan's expression said it all. He couldn't imagine that, no matter how natural it might feel here. Michael found himself looking at it through the world's eyes, instead of Amish ones...looking and judging.

"This job," he said abruptly. "Where is it?"

"Out in Arizona. Jason has a lot of business interests in the Phoenix area."

"Arizona," he repeated. Not just a long way in distance, but a completely new way of life. He could do it, but what about Allie? What about his promise to her?

It felt like burning a bridge, but he knew what his answer had to be. “I couldn’t do it, Alan. It sounds terrific, but Allie—well, Allie’s really started feeling secure and happy for the first time since Diana’s death. I can’t uproot her again.”

“You sure?” He raised an eyebrow.

Michael nodded, more than a little regretful. “I’m sure. But, man, I appreciate it. Other than family, you’re the only one who’s held out a hand to me. I won’t forget it.”

“It’s nothing.” Alan turned away, looking embarrassed to be thanked. “You’d do the same for me.”

If he were in a position to, he would. But he didn’t have the advantages that Alan did, with his Ivy League education and his wealthy father-in-law’s business. Still, he knew he’d do what he could if their positions were reversed.

“Anyway, thanks.” He clapped Alan on the shoulder. “Now, come on inside. If I know Aunt Verna, she’s already making coffee and slicing the pie.”

“Sounds great.” Alan followed him to the door. “But don’t forget. I think the job will be open for a time, so you can let me know if you change your mind.”

“I won’t.” He couldn’t. Allie needed to know she could trust him…that if he promised a thing, he’d deliver. He might not have been the greatest of parents in the past, but from now on, Allie came first.

CHAPTER SIX

BY MIDMORNING THE next day, Cathy sensed that her scholars had settled back into the school routine. She could only trust their parents had handled the situation sensibly, rather than resorting to a lot of what-ifs in front of them.

Allie sat in her usual place next to Ruthie. If she'd had any qualms about coming, they didn't show in her face. Cathy studied that small, serious face. Allie was still keeping her thoughts to herself. Surely she must have questions—she must be wondering why her life had been torn up so abruptly. But she wasn't letting anyone in who might help her find answers.

If only Cathy could breach that barrier she'd erected against the world. Yesterday's events might well have driven the child deeper into her shell. She couldn't be allowed to go so deeply that she couldn't find her way out.

Cathy had considered what she ought to say to her scholars about the previous day and decided to speak to them about it near the end of the day. That way, anyone who had additional questions or seemed unduly worried could stay afterward for a private talk.

And since her helper this morning was Lizzie

Stolzfus, she was doubly glad of that decision. She'd been feeling Lizzie's critical eyes on her for the past two hours and had begun to find it made her second-guess herself.

At least she'd be leaving soon. Joanna Kohler, who happened to be one of Cathy's dearest friends, would be arriving to take her place, and Cathy suspected her own anxiety level would drop appreciably with her friend at hand.

With a glance at the clock, she brought the fourth-grade arithmetic lesson to a close. "You may put your papers in your desks now, and we'll get ready for recess." She nodded to the youngest scholars to use the restrooms first.

Almost before the words were out of her mouth, Lizzie hurried to her desk, her face set in lines of disapproval. "Surely you're not going to send the kinder outside after what happened yesterday."

Cathy made an effort to ignore the scolding tone. It wasn't easy, but she tried.

"It's much better for the students to keep to their usual routine. We wouldn't want them to fear going out to recess, would we?"

The conciliatory question didn't have any noticeable effect. "They're safer inside," Lizzie declared. "Anyone would say so."

Anyone probably being the daughter that she thought would fill Cathy's position admirably. She shouldn't think that way, she knew. Lizzie was worried, just like all the other parents were.

She was as well. But she'd made a decision, and

she'd stay with it unless there was a good reason not to.

"The school board has trusted me to use my own judgment in dealing with this matter." She tried to sound assured. "We will stick to our regular routine."

Lizzie glared at her for a moment before jerking a nod. "You're the teacher."

But not for long? Was that the unspoken message behind her words? Doubt swept over Cathy. Who was she to think she had all the answers? What if she were wrong? What if she was exposing the children to danger?

With an effort, she shoved the doubts aside. She had made the decision she thought was best for the children. She'd have to trust it was the right one.

By the time the children had been ushered outside for morning recess, Cathy had succeeded in beating down the doubts. She kept a careful eye on the small faces as they passed her, looking for any sign of fear or anxiety, but didn't notice anything. Other than a tendency to clump together in small groups for play, her scholars seemed to be taking the situation normally.

Cathy circled the group of children slowly, nodding to Lizzie to do the same. She couldn't seem to keep her gaze from straying to the spot where she'd seen the figure yesterday. No one there, of course. She'd been aware of Lige circling the school when he'd dropped Ruthie off, and most likely someone else would check by soon.

The clip-clop of hooves and the creak of buggy

wheels announced Joanna Kohler's arrival. Cathy walked to meet her, her face relaxing into a smile.

"Joanna, I saw you'd offered to help today. Who is watching the shop?"

"My aunt, of course. She loves it when I go out, so she can be the boss." Joanna slid down from the buggy seat, brown eyes smiling, looking as capable and in control as she always had, even when they were young. They were the best of friends, along with Rachel Hurst—the Threes, people had called them.

Funny, in a way, that they were the only three from their rumspringa group to remain unmarried. The three maidals, she supposed they were now.

"I'm wonderful glad you could be here." There wasn't time to say more, because Lizzie was approaching.

"I'll be going," she said abruptly. "Now that you have your friend to help."

"Denke, Lizzie. I appreciate your assistance."

Lizzie acknowledged the words with a slight nod and marched off toward the road, the shortest way home for her.

Joanna gave her a speaking glance. "Why does she always look as if she's sucking on a pickle when she talks to you?"

Cathy's lips twitched. "Hush, she might hear you."

"Nonsense. She's too busy thinking up a complaint because you have another unmarried woman to help you instead of a mother."

"Ach, Joanna, I don't think she'd say that." She shook her head. "Anyway, she was concerned that

I let the scholars out at recess, but what else could I do? We can't let them live in fear."

If Joanna had any doubts about that, she didn't voice them. Instead she nodded toward the path that opened onto the far side of the school yard. "Are you expecting someone else to show up?"

A quick glance reassured Cathy. "Some of the fathers have arranged to stop by a few times during the day. Lige Esch..."

Then the man stepped into the open. He wore typically Amish garb—black pants, blue shirt, straw hat—but it wasn't Lige. It was Michael Forster. Michael, dressed Amish. Did that mean...

She cut off the thought, knowing she shouldn't speculate about what Michael intended to do. He had enough of that from everyone else. Good intentions or not, she couldn't deny that the sight threw her off balance. Somehow it was easier to keep him at a distance when he looked and seemed so Englisch.

Joanna didn't share her scruples—she was staring at Michael with an open question in her face. Cathy nudged her.

"It's Allie's father. He must be doing the rounds this morning."

Michael was headed straight toward them. Apparently he didn't intend to look around unobtrusively and leave, the way Lige had.

When he reached them, he was looking at the playing children, frowning a little. "I see you're having recess—"

"If you think they should stay inside, that would

do more harm than good." Joanna spoke before Cathy could, automatically moving into the leadership position she'd always taken.

Michael's eyebrows lifted slightly. "I wasn't going to say that." He shifted his gaze to Cathy. "I wanted to ask if Allie seems okay."

Relieved, Cathy nodded. "I've kept an eye on her—on all of them, of course. She's quiet, but she doesn't seem fearful, and they're playing normally." She glanced toward Allie, in a threesome now with Ruthie and Mary Louise.

"Good." Only then did he turn back to Joanna. "Should I remember you?"

Apparently deciding in his favor, Joanna smiled. "Probably not. I was one of the small fry, like Cathy. I'm Joanna Kohler."

"Sorry. I guess you're the teacher's helper for today."

"Part of it anyway." She turned. "I'd best earn my keep, so I'll check on the scholars and leave you two alone." She moved off before Cathy could protest that they didn't need to be alone.

A quick glance told her that Michael looked amused.

"A good friend of yours, I see."

"She is, but what makes you say that?" She took a firm grip on herself, determined that the unexpected sight of Michael in Amish clothing wasn't going to unsettle her.

"She's quick in your defense."

"That's Joanna, all right." Her brief tension dissolved. "So what is this?" She gestured toward the pants and shirt.

"Funny thing—these clothes just appeared on the peg in my room a few days ago."

She had to smile. "Your aunt Verna being tactful?"

"Probably. Although my sister probably had a hand in it. I think these belonged to Lige."

A few days ago—so he hadn't decided immediately to put them on. "What made you..." She closed her lips on the question, remembering her determination not to get too close.

"What made me decide to wear them today?" He frowned a little, his gaze moving over the children again. "After yesterday, it just seemed right. Anyway, it'll make Aunt Verna and Sarah happy."

"Yah, it will. And Allie, I think."

He didn't want to delve any deeper into his reasons, she realized. She couldn't pretend, even to herself, that she knew the answers where Michael was concerned, but she could almost see him change over the short time he'd been back among them. This wasn't the same bitter, withdrawn man she'd met that first day.

"I'm forgetting what I need to ask you," he said. "Would it be possible for you to walk Allie home today? Aunt Verna says you usually take the path that goes right by her place."

"Yah, for sure. I'll be happy to walk with Allie." Happier than he knew. This might be the chance she'd been seeking to get to know the little girl behind the mask. "We can make it a regular routine, if you want.

I walk when the weather is nice, but even if I bring the buggy, I can drop her off."

"Good." He wasn't looking at her. Instead, he was scanning the perimeter of the school yard, obviously alert for any problems.

"It will be a few minutes later than usual," she reminded him. "After the rest of the scholars leave, I'll need to collect the work I'm taking home."

"Right." He brought his attention back to her. "I'm grateful." He smiled, brown eyes warming in a way that was disturbing to her composure. "Lige and I are starting work on rebuilding a section of one of the greenhouses, and afternoons are the best time for him."

"Verna will appreciate that. She always thinks she needs more space for growing her flowers."

It was probably good for him, too, although she wouldn't say that out loud. A man needed to feel he had useful work to do, surely. From what Verna had said, he'd had his own construction company back before all the trouble. Rebuilding his aunt's greenhouse might be a comedown from owning a business, but at least it was a start.

"Yeah, she does." Michael seemed to lose some of the lighthearted feeling of his last words. "Sarah and Lige will take over the nursery business one day, of course, but I want to help. I have to do something."

It was an echo of her own thoughts, making her wonder how much he missed the life and business he'd had back in Harrisburg. And how quickly he'd go back to it if he had a choice.

"There's always work around here for a good builder. Maybe rebuilding the greenhouse will lead to other jobs. There's nothing like word of mouth to let folks know you're available."

He studied her face for a long moment—so long that she began to wonder if she'd said something wrong. Then he shook his head.

"You're an optimist, Teacher Cathy. It's hard to imagine that many people will want to hire me. Not when the Amish see me as an outsider and the Englisch think I'm a murderer."

His expression tore at her heart. "Don't say that—don't even think it. Everyone doesn't feel that way. Give people a chance and they might surprise you."

"Like I said, an optimist. I wish I could believe you were right."

MICHAEL DECIDED IT felt right to have a hammer in his hand again. He'd been away from work too long. "I'll be getting soft if I don't get back to work again. Let's get at it."

Lige had his usual amiable grin. He buckled on his tool belt. "Once we make sure these uprights are in good shape, it'll move along fast."

"If they are." He squatted beside the corner post to check it. "Looks like the drainage worked fine. Did Aunt Verna always use the gravel floor? I don't remember."

"Yah, that was Onkel Samuel's idea. This is the one he built first, Aunt Verna says, and it's still in pretty good shape except for that one corner."

Michael nodded, moving on to the next upright. "A lot of glass has to be replaced. That could get expensive."

"I got a deal." Lige grinned. "There's a guy over toward Bellefonte taking down some old greenhouses, and he sold it to me cheap. We'll just have to get someone with a truck to go along and pick it up."

"A truck with decent suspension," Michael amended. "Some of the rattletraps you see around here couldn't carry a jug of water without breaking it."

"Yah, that's for sure." Lige hefted the first crosspiece they'd need to put in. "Phil Maggio's the guy for the job. We'll have to do the loading and unloading, but he'll drive."

"Sounds like you have it all figured out. Are you sure you need me?"

"This is a two-man job, ain't so? Anyway, you're the construction guy, not me."

Satisfied, he lifted one end of the piece into place, holding it steady for Michael.

By the time a half hour had passed, Michael realized they'd picked up each other's rhythm, working along steadily without any needless hitches. He wouldn't have minded having Lige working on his crew, back when he'd had a crew.

When they stopped for a drink of water, Michael brought up the subject of the clothes he was wearing. "Guess I should be careful not to mess up these pants. They are yours, yah?"

"Were," Lige corrected. "Like Sarah pointed out, I put on a few pounds around the middle the last couple of years. I figure it's her fault for being such a gut cook, ain't so?"

Michael nodded, smiling. It looked to him as if his sister had done fine in picking a husband without his advice. "If you lose the weight, I'll give the pants back for sure."

"No chance." Lige hesitated. "You know, I stopped by the hardware store this morning. Seems like everyone in town heard about what happened at school yesterday."

"They would." His hand tightened momentarily. "You can't keep something like that quiet."

"No. I guess you wouldn't want to. If the guy did mean harm, then everyone should be warned." He worked quietly for a few minutes, but he seemed to have something more on his mind. "Sarah's satisfied herself it was a tourist with a camera, so that's best. Otherwise she wouldn't have gotten any sleep at all."

"You don't think so?" He straightened, knowing Lige's opinion would be of value.

"If it had been a woman, or even a man and woman together, it'd seem more natural. You don't usually see a man doing that kind of stuff alone."

"No, you don't." Lige might be slow to speak, but when he did, he usually had something sensible to say. "I thought about that, too. It still could be—a guy who's crazy about photography maybe, wanting to get something different. But it's odd all the same."

"Yah." Lige looked relieved—not at the conclusion, but at the fact that someone else saw it the way he did. "The patrols are fine, but we'd best be careful not to get onto a schedule."

Michael nodded. "The more pairs of eyes the better. You know, though, I don't think a stranger could spy on the schoolchildren very easily without being noticed. With the trees and the way the site is, I don't think there's any spot that overlooks it."

"Yah, and someone trying to leave a car by the road would be noticed, like Cathy did the car yesterday. It wouldn't be a bad idea to talk to the Campbells and the Warfields. They have those two houses down the road on the other side. Chief Jamison probably talked to them about yesterday, but we could ask them to keep an eye out in future."

"Right. I don't remember them, but..."

"I'll do it," Lige said. "They know me."

"They don't know me." His mouth twisted on the words. "But I'd bet they've heard of me. They wouldn't want me ringing their doorbell."

Lige considered that for a moment, pondering the way he did every new idea. "Could be, I guess. I don't know what the Englisch are thinking."

"Whatever Diana's family thinks," he said wryly.

"Not many left here now. There's her brother, Bernard. He runs the family business. Has a wife, but no kids."

Michael nodded. He remembered Bernard. Much older than Diana, he'd been furious at her for stepping so far out of line when she'd married Michael. Diana had contemptuously called his wife, Janet, a "yes, dear" type of wife.

"What about Diana's grandmother?" He'd been reluctant to ask, thinking of his only encounter with the formidable old woman who'd run the firm and the family with an iron hand. She'd made him feel about as valuable as an ant she'd step on. Once Diana had married him, she had cut her off entirely.

"She's in that rest home place—Maple Crest, it's called. It's out the Sunbury Road. Big, expensive, costs a fortune to stay there, so I've heard. Randy Hunter runs it."

"Does he really?" Somehow he wasn't surprised. Randy had always struck him as one to hang out where there was wealth. Diana would have been the ultimate prize for him—the princess her grandmother adored and everyone admired. But the princess had picked Michael. And then stepped on him.

He shook away the ugly thoughts and checked the time. "Seems like Allie should be getting home about now. Cathy said it might take her a few minutes after the kids left, but it's been more than that."

Lige straightened, stretching his back. "Go on, walk up the path and meet her. I could stand a break."

Michael didn't need urging. The fear generated by the previous day's episode lurked under the surface of his thoughts, but not far. It was ready to erupt at the slightest hint of trouble.

Not that it meant trouble just because Cathy was a few minutes later than he'd anticipated. Still, he strode swiftly along the path, eyes straining ahead for a glimpse of movement or color.

There—not far ahead of him he could see a bit of

blue the color of the dress Cathy had on at school. But it wasn't moving. Heart accelerating, he broke into a run. If something had happened—

He came around the bend where the trees thinned out to brush and berry brambles, and his heart took a leap and then settled into its regular pace. His step slowed, too, then even more when Cathy spotted him and gestured for him to move slowly.

She was kneeling at the edge of some leafy brush, Allie standing pressed against her while they both watched something intently. Michael wanted nothing so much as to run to them and grab Allie in a huge hug, but he hoped he had better sense. Nothing would make Allie fearful more than seeing that her father was.

So he strolled to them at an easy pace, hoping he wasn't scaring away whatever had them so entranced. "What is it?" he murmured, but then he realized that the yellow spots he'd taken for blossoms were actually butterflies—hundreds of them, it seemed, clustering on the low shrubs that grew along a damp bank.

"Look, Daadi," Allie whispered. "Teacher Cathy says they are tiger…" She hesitated and looked at Cathy.

"Tiger swallowtails." Cathy supplied the words. "Because their wings are shaped like a swallow's tail."

"And they're colored like a tiger," Allie explained. "See?"

"You're right." He squatted next to her. "I've never seen so many at one time."

"I haven't either. I think Allie must be very fortunate, because she spotted them."

"I did." Allie's smile was bigger than he'd seen in a long time, and his heart lurched.

He couldn't find any words, so he didn't try. He just squatted next to them. They watched the butterflies, and he watched their faces. Cathy had her arm around Allie's waist, and Allie leaned against her, probably unconscious of how much trust she was showing.

The butterflies began lifting a little higher from the bushes, darting and swooping. They were above Allie's head, and she looked up at them as they formed a yellow cloud of constant movement. Her face was filled with delight. If he could capture this moment, keep it to look at in coming years, maybe he could hold on to just a little of it.

Cathy, her voice still low, was pointing out to Allie how the butterflies were moving farther, as if they were exploring. Did butterflies hear? He had no idea, but her soft words fit the magic of the moment. If anything could wipe away the traces of anger and fear since yesterday, this must be it.

There was so much tenderness in Cathy's face as she talked to Allie, and he realized that Allie was soaking it up the way a plant soaked up sunshine. His heart twisted again. How much tenderness had she received from her mother?

Diana had loved her, of course she had. But had that automatically meant she was a good mother to Allie?

He certainly hadn't done anything to make up for whatever lack there had been. He'd been blind, it seemed to him now, and he was still paying for that. But it seemed unfair that Allie should pay as well.

Cathy moved slightly, probably stiff from kneeling so long. He held out a hand to her. "Need a little help getting up?"

"I guess I'd better—get up, I mean." She looked as regretful as Allie did. "I should be getting home. And Aunt Verna will be wondering where you are." She put her hand lightly on Allie's head.

"I get to tell her about the butterflies. And tomorrow I can tell Ruthie." She grabbed Michael's hand. "You'll let me tell, won't you, Daadi?"

He smiled, as much at the mix of English and Pennsylvania Dutch she'd begun using as at the request. "I won't say a word. After all, you're the one who spotted them. The butterflies are your story."

"They are." She skipped a little, in a hurry to spread the news.

It seemed natural for him to fall into step with Cathy, to feel their hands brush against each other as they walked. "That was a special moment for her."

"And for me." Cathy's eyes seemed to reflect the clear, deep blue of the sky. "Now I really believe that spring is here and summer's on its way."

"Looking forward to summer vacation?"

"No, not that. I'll miss the children." Her face clouded slightly.

"What is it? What's wrong?" He discovered a strong desire to fix the problem, whatever it was.

Cathy shrugged. "I still don't have a contract for next year. I try not to dwell on it, but I can't help wondering. And worrying."

"From what I've seen of the parents, I'd say they appreciate what you do for the kids. I know I do."

She looked up at him, her smile lighting her eyes. "Denke," she said softly, as softly as she'd spoken to Allie.

He ought to look away, but he couldn't seem to do it. She was drawing him in with her warmth, her tenderness, her generous heart. His hand brushed hers, and then clasped it, wrapping his fingers around hers.

This wasn't just attraction. There was plenty of that, but it was mixed up with all the other feelings he'd begun to have for Cathy—admiration, affection…

"Daadi, come on," Allie called to him, impatient.

"Coming." He let go of her hand with reluctance. All those feelings didn't do the least bit of good. A relationship with Cathy was impossible—completely impossible.

CHAPTER SEVEN

CATHY CLUCKED TO BELLE, the buggy horse, as they turned onto the main road. Belle wasn't enthusiastic about going somewhere after supper. Well trained as she was, she still had ways of making her disappointment known.

"Step along now, Belle. The sooner we get there, the sooner we'll be home." Belle might not understand the words, but she got the sentiment and picked up the pace.

To be honest with herself, Cathy was about as reluctant to go out this evening. After those moments with Michael this afternoon, she'd wanted to hole up in her room in private.

But of course it had been impossible. Mammi had been in the midst of making and canning rhubarb sauce, and she'd been plunged into helping. Working together meant talking, and she'd been hard put to find something to chat about that wouldn't skirt dangerously near the person who occupied too large a place in her thoughts right now.

She was alone now, for all the good it did her. Those moments with Michael today had forced her to face facts. She cared too much for Michael Forster.

For the first time in her life she'd found someone for whom she'd be willing to give up her small portion of independence, her satisfying life, and it had to be a man she couldn't hope to marry.

Not that Michael would be imagining any such thing anyway, she told herself quickly. He was attracted to her—she'd seen that in the way his brown eyes darkened when they studied her face and felt it in the way his hand closed possessively over hers. But attraction was a long way from anything serious. If he knew what she was thinking, he'd probably be horrified.

No, not that. But embarrassed and regretting it. He'd responded to her interest and kindness with a kind of surprised gratitude that ripped at her heart. Why should he be so astonished that someone cared about him?

And that was an answer she could see too clearly. His runaway marriage to Diana, his struggle to fit into the outside world and give her what she wanted, the humiliation of admitting he'd failed—all of that was bad enough. Add to that the horror of her death and the suspicions and condemnation he'd faced—no wonder he responded to a little sympathy. That didn't mean he cared, only that he'd reacted like a starving man to food.

The only sensible course for her was to hide her feelings and stay away from Michael. So why was she on her way to his sister's house right now?

Well, he wouldn't be there. She ought to be safe from seeing him, at least. Sarah had asked her to come over to plan a picnic lunch for the schoolchildren since the weather was warmer. Her scholars would love it. Any break in the routine was welcome, especially now that the warmth and sunshine called them outdoors.

The only surprise was that Sarah wanted any help at all. If she knew Sarah Esch, she probably already had the whole thing planned down to the last napkin.

Smiling a little, she turned into Sarah's driveway. She and Lige lived in a house on his parents' farm, although one day she supposed they'd be moving into Verna's place when they took over the nursery. She stopped at the hitching rail, recognizing Verna's buggy horse already there. Sarah must have roped her into helping.

Verna and Sarah were as happy to see her as if it had been months instead of a few days. Cathy eyed them cautiously as they exchanged glances. Were they up to something? If so, it was bound to come out. Verna was well-known for her blunt speech—if she had something to say, she'd have trouble hiding it.

Her stomach seemed to lurch. If Verna knew about what had happened between her and Michael—no, that was foolishness. No one could have seen them on the path. And Michael would surely never mention it.

"Komm, sit." Sarah, all smiles, pulled out a chair at the round kitchen table. "Coffee is ready, or tea, if you want. And I hid a shoofly pie from Lige and the kinder."

"Tea, please. I don't usually drink coffee in the evening. What date were you thinking about?"

"Date?" Sarah's blank look spoke volumes.

Verna hastened into speech. "For the picnic lunch, Cathy means."

Cathy set down the mug Sarah had just handed her. "All right, you two. You're plotting something, and it isn't the picnic lunch. Why am I here?"

Another exchange of looks, and then Sarah began to laugh. "Ach, we should have known we couldn't fool you for a minute. We do want to have a lunch for the kinder, but we can plan that without help."

"I'm sure you can. Now, what is going on? The both of you look guilty—I don't think you're very gut at this."

"All right, all right." Sarah set the shoofly pie and plates on the table and sat down herself. "The thing is that Verna and I were talking, and we got around to thinking about..."

"Let me tell it, or we'll be here all night," Verna said, her voice tart. "It's high time Michael and his father made up their quarrel. We're going to see that they do, and we want your help."

Cathy's first instinct was to flee. She even pushed herself back from the table before Sarah caught her arm. "Just listen, Cathy. Then you can say no if you want to."

Verna's look said she didn't quite agree with the "saying no" part, but she nodded. "Yah, listen. Anybody could see how much you want to help Allie.

You're the best thing that's happened to that child in a long time, it seems to me."

Cathy shook her head. "Not just me. She's living in your house, feeling part of a family. That's so important to a child. She's…"

She hesitated. She'd almost spoken of her longing to break through Allie's barriers and get her talking, but maybe that was best kept to herself.

"She's what?" Sarah leaned toward her. "If there's anything you see that we can do to help her, tell us."

"Just go on loving her." She smiled. "That's the best thing for her."

"Yah, that we can do," Verna said. "Now, Michael… he's harder, ain't so?"

Cathy kept her mouth shut on that one, even though she agreed. Allie's shields were difficult enough to breach. Michael's, she thought, were very nearly impossible.

"Komm, Cathy." Sarah was at her most persuasive. "You must agree that Michael and Daad need each other. It's not natural to hold on to a feud, especially where a child is concerned."

"Oh, I agree. I just don't see what I can do. Josiah is your father. Surely he'll listen to you."

"That's the last thing he'll do." Sarah threw out her hands in exasperation. "When Daadi looks at me, he still sees his little girl. And stubborn… Is anyone more stubborn?"

"Yah," Verna said. "Or at least equal, and that's Michael. They're made from the same mold, those two. Both as proud and as stubborn as can be. The longer this goes on, the worse it gets for both of them."

"I'm sure that's true." Cathy seemed to see that grim line of Michael's mouth, the stern set of his jaw. "But I still don't see what you think I can do."

"I know. But we have a plan, and you're part of it." Sarah's eyes sparkled. "What we have to do is get the two of them together."

"On neutral ground," Verna added. "So neither one of them has to feel like he's making the first move. Men." She grimaced. "They don't use the common sense the gut Lord gave them."

"Where is this neutral ground?" She asked the question tentatively, afraid she already knew the answer.

"The school, for sure. That way, neither one of them should suspect anything."

Verna would think of that. "When? How? At this picnic you're planning?"

"No, no," Sarah said. "We have a better idea. You know the work frolic that's coming up at the school?"

Cathy nodded, foreseeing problems. "On Saturday. There's not all that much to be done—just some tidying up outside the building. But you're not thinking they'd both komm, surely."

Sarah grimaced. "Michael isn't going anywhere that there might be a group of Amish—we've all seen that."

"He's afraid he won't be accepted. I've told him that's foolishness—how can he know unless he tries?" Verna sounded as decided as she usually did.

"If he won't..." she began, knowing as she did that Verna wouldn't accept a lack of trying.

"Sarah will make sure her father is there. She'll tell him they need his help. And then you can get Michael there."

"I can't." Why couldn't they see that it was impossible? Even if she asked him...and how could she? He'd think she was interfering at the least.

"You can," Verna said firmly. "We have it all figured out. I'll send you back to the nursery to get some flowers to plant around the school. You won't be able to carry them yourself, so he'll have to drop them off."

"Once he's there, we'll take care of the rest." Sarah seemed convinced this would work. "When Daad sees him, I don't see how he can hold on to his grudge. I know he's longing to make it up—he just can't take the first step."

"So we'll take it for him. For both of them, with your help."

Verna made it sound so simple. Cathy wished she could believe it was that easy.

They were right—father and son shouldn't live that way, refusing to talk, refusing to bend. Like the prodigal son and his father, each one needed to take a step forward.

What could go wrong? Plenty, and if she let herself become involved, she'd be right in the middle of it.

But they were both looking at her with such hope, convinced they'd found a way to bridge the gap between Michael and his people.

"All right," she said reluctantly. "I'll do it."

And if Michael blamed her for her part in it—well, that would guarantee that she wouldn't get too close, wouldn't it?

MICHAEL PAUSED FOR a moment, glancing from his perch on a ladder over the greenhouse to where Lige was waiting on a customer. The work had been going well—faster than either of them had expected, probably. They worked well together, thankfully not running into any problems.

They'd soon be ready for the glass. Lige had suggested they both go along to pick it up, and he realized that would be the first time he'd ventured any farther than the school or that one trip to get ice cream since he'd arrived. Hiding? He didn't like the sound of that. Sooner or later he'd have to show himself around town, no matter what unpleasantness might ensue.

Lige came back just as he descended the ladder. "That Mrs. Carpenter—she really likes to talk. And she's sharp as a tack. Asked me right away who you were."

He stiffened. "I'm not very popular around here. Having me here might be a problem."

"For her? Didn't seem to be." Lige gave him a look he couldn't interpret. "Seems like you're expecting the worst from people."

"I've had good reason." He'd lived with the reactions of people who'd assumed him guilty.

"Well, not everyone. For sure not Mrs. Carpenter.

She said she's got a couple small projects around her house and wondered if you'd be interested."

"Projects?" For an instant his mind was blank. "What kind of projects?"

"Carpentry work. Not what you were used to, for sure, but..."

He didn't finish the obvious. If Michael wanted to get back on his feet, he'd have to start from scratch. If that meant putting up shelves or mending a broken hinge, he'd do it.

"That doesn't matter, so long as it's work I can do. What did you tell her?"

"I said you'd stop by sometime next week to talk to her about it." Lige grinned. "She has that big, old Victorian house on the corner of Fifth Street. You know the one I mean, with all the fancy trim on it. I'd guess it'd be a full-time job just taking care of a place like that."

He nodded, placing the woman. The Carpenter place was one of the showplaces of town—or at least it had been. "Great. I'll go over Monday." He hesitated for a moment, but Lige deserved to hear it. "Thanks. I guess maybe I have been jumping to conclusions about people. I'll try to do better. As for the job, I'm starting from scratch but I've done it before—I'm not afraid of it."

"Gut." Lige looked satisfied. "We'd better set a time to pick up the glass..." He stopped at the buzz of Michael's cell phone.

Michael took a quick look. Alan. "I'd better take this." At Lige's nod, he moved off as he answered.

"Alan. I didn't expect to hear from you again so soon. Everything okay?"

"Not exactly. I didn't know if I should call you or not, but I figured you'd want to hear." Alan sounded uncertain. But then, he'd probably never had a friend suspected of murder. This was new territory for both of them.

"Whatever it is, I'd rather know. Something's happened with the investigation?" That was the only thing he could think of that would have Alan sounding this way.

"The problem is that the police have been around again. Talking to neighbors, asking questions."

His heart sank. "What else do they think they're going to find out? They must have asked everything there is to ask by this time."

Alan made a sound of assent. "Nothing new about their questions that I could see. We told them exactly what we had before—the truth."

"Something must have started them up again." He forced away the numbing sensation that had set in at the words and tried to think. "Would they come back if they didn't have some fresh information?"

"I don't know. But they weren't the only ones. There was another guy—he tried to pump me. As soon as I found out he was a private investigator and not the police, I told him to get lost."

Private investigator. Why—and why now? "Somebody must have hired him."

"Yes. I wondered...well, about Diana's family.

I don't know anything about them, but is that possible?"

Was it? Diana's brother and his wife had attended the funeral, but their only words to him had been muttered condolences. They'd left immediately afterward, not even showing any interest in Allie. Not that he'd have welcomed that, but it had infuriated him anyway.

He came back to the realization that Alan was still waiting. "I don't know. I haven't seen them or heard anything from them since the funeral."

"I thought maybe since you were living there now, it'd be different."

"No." He wanted, suddenly, to end the call. He needed to think this over—to get his mind working again instead of relapsing into the numb state of shock he'd been in after Diana's death. "Thanks, Alan. I appreciate the call. If you hear anything else..."

"I'll let you know," he said. His voice had warmed a bit. "You still have friends here, you know."

Friends. He considered the word as he clicked off. Not many, but then he never had. The neighbors had been Diana's friends, not his. He could trust Alan and his wife, but what were the others saying to the cops? To the private investigator?

Michael rubbed the back of his neck, trying to smooth the tension away. It was bad enough that the police were poking around again, but add in a private investigator, and the situation was suddenly much worse.

He couldn't think of anyone who would have reason and means to hire a private investigator except Diana's brother. But why now? What had changed?

He considered what little he knew about Bernard Wilcox. Bernard, never Bernie. He must have been more than fifteen years older than Diana, maybe even twenty. Married, no children.

That had caused Michael more than a few anxious moments when it became clear that the police suspected him. What would happen to Allie if he were arrested? Diana's grandmother was clearly unable to get involved, and she'd wiped Diana out of her life anyway. But Bernard and Janet might well have wanted his sister's child.

He'd been relieved when they'd shown no interest. He'd rather send Allie back to his own family than see her raised in what Diana had claimed was a cold and loveless house. He'd never known how much truth was in that claim, but he hadn't been willing to take a chance with his daughter. Not even at the worst of times when arrest had seemed imminent.

Now...now, when he'd hoped he was getting clear of the tragedy, it had broken back into their lives. The reality settled on him like a heavy blanket weighing him down. It would never be over. Never.

ALLIE REACHED OUT to take Cathy's hand as they headed home from school, giving Cathy a quick lift of the heart. She was used to her younger scholars hanging on to her, but this was the first time Allie had initiated holding hands. The gesture coming from such a shy child meant something special to her.

Then she noticed the paper Allie clutched in her other hand—her spelling test, with the bright smiley sticker on top. "Don't forget to tell Daadi and Aunt Verna about your spelling test, will you?"

Allie waved the lined yellow sheet in answer. "I think they'll be happy. Aunt Verna helped me practice my words. She said it helped her remember. Do you think she really meant it?"

"For sure. Your aunt Verna doesn't say things she doesn't mean."

Allie considered that for a moment. Then she gave a satisfied nod. Cathy decided she would give a lot to understand what was going on in that little head.

"Maybe we'll see the butterflies again. The tiger swallowtails." Allie repeated the name carefully.

"We might." Cathy was wary of promising something she might not be able to deliver. "They seemed to like those bushes, but they could have found others, too."

Allie's face seemed to droop. "I wanted to see them again."

"Me, too. But even if we don't, we'll have that memory of what it was like to come upon them. A memory is like having a picture in our minds that we can look at again whenever we want."

Silence for a long moment. Allie seemed to be studying the ground ahead of her. "What if we don't want to see a picture again?"

Cathy had the feeling she'd missed a step in the

dark—surprised and shaken. She shouldn't be, she told herself. Allie had gone through a terrible time when she'd lost her mother. The child was bound to have some memories she'd rather forget.

"Sometimes, if remembering something makes me sad or scared, I can stop thinking about it by concentrating hard on a happy picture." Was that the answer the child was seeking? "Or I might talk to someone about it—a friend, or my mamm or daad."

Allie didn't respond, and Cathy was torn between trying to draw her out and the fear of turning her away by probing. Finally she decided to venture a gentle question.

"Is there a memory you don't want to think about?" She held her breath, half afraid of the answer she might get.

Allie nodded, her fingers tightening on Cathy's hand even though she didn't look up.

"If you want to tell me about it, you can."

Allie sucked in an audible breath. "Sometimes… sometimes I'd hear people talking about Mommy when they thought I couldn't hear."

"I see."

Cathy's mind raced. Based on the way Allie phrased the words, she seemed to be talking about an incident in the past. In the weeks after Diana's death, perhaps? People in the neighborhood would certainly have been talking. She had a spurt of fury at anyone who would do so where a child might hear.

"Did you ever ask anyone about what they said?"

"When I did, they lied to me. Everybody does that."

That calm acceptance of a wrong twisted her heart as nothing else had. This, at least, she could try to put right, but not by making excuses.

"You knew some people who told lies, but that doesn't mean everyone does." She knelt so that she could be at eye level with Allie. "I promise you that I will never lie to you, Allie. I might not always be able to answer a question, but I won't lie."

Allie studied her face, giving nothing away. Then she nodded. It was a tentative acceptance, but at least it was something.

As Cathy stood, the weight of what she'd promised was almost a palpable burden. Allie had been let down in the past. Whatever happened from here on out, Cathy was committed. She wouldn't disappoint this child.

They walked on, but it seemed to her that the silence between them was an easier one now. Allie actually started to skip when they neared the spot where they'd seen the butterflies.

"There are some," she declared. "Look, Teacher Cathy."

"That's right. Not as many as yesterday, but aren't they pretty?"

They stopped, watching, just as they had the previous day. And just as he had then, Michael appeared, coming along the path to meet them.

But today there was no relief at seeing them, and no wonder at the sight that held them there. His face was strained, the skin taut against the bones.

It hurt to see him look that way, and the cut ran

deeper because she knew she couldn't help. Michael's happiness was out of her control, but when she saw the spontaneous way Allie ran to him, waving her paper, she saw that this, at least, she could do. Help Allie. Her responsibility, always, was to the children in her care.

The love in Michael's face when he responded to Allie eased the tension, at least for a moment. He glanced up and held his smile an instant longer for Cathy.

"It looks as if we have a gut speller on our hands."

"Every word was just right. She tells me her aunt Verna helped her."

"She used to help me, but I didn't usually get a smiley sticker. I think I might not have studied enough."

"Aunt Verna says practice makes perfect," Allie observed, taking the paper back and smiling at it.

"That's it, then." Michael touched her cheek gently. "I should have practiced more. Aunt Verna will be wonderful glad to see your paper."

"She will." Allie's confident assertion almost sounded like her cousin Ruthie, and it brought a smile to Cathy's face. "I'm going to go show her, okay?"

"Okay. Just watch where you're going so you don't trip."

Michael watched her run ahead and then fell into step with Cathy. "She's doing all right?" It was a question, not a statement.

"Isn't it obvious? Every day she's a little more outgoing. And her schoolwork is excellent."

"I'm glad to know we have one scholar in the family. I seem to remember spending too much time looking out the window."

"Boys tend to do that."

She wondered if she should tell him a little of what Allie had said. At some point she'd have to, she supposed, but she was reluctant to do it now. Allie had just begun to confide in her. She didn't want to betray that fledgling trust.

And she couldn't ignore the concern she felt about Michael himself. Already his expression was slipping back into that stiff, bitter set, as if he braced himself against a fresh onslaught.

When the silence had stretched too long, Cathy knew she had to speak. "Something has happened to upset you. If it helps to talk about it..." The rest of that sentence slipped away. It was nearly the same thing she'd said to his daughter.

He shrugged. "There's nothing anyone can do. Although..." He frowned, seeming to consider. "Maybe you should hear this. I just realized it might concern you."

"What is it?" She tried not to let herself think what his serious tone might mean.

"I had a call from a friend of mine—a neighbor of ours back in Harrisburg." His expression grew even grimmer, if possible. "He said that the police have been around the neighborhood again, asking questions."

She could see what he was thinking, but... "That might not mean they're focused on you, ain't so?

They could be looking for any clue to who else might have been to the house that night."

"You do like to look at the bright side, don't you?" His gaze softened just a little. "Even if you're right, there's worse. He also said that a private investigator is looking into Diana's death."

It was Cathy's turn to frown, trying to comprehend the significance of that news. "Private. That means someone hired him, ain't so?"

"Right. The question is, who? Who has the interest and the money to pay someone to investigate?"

"You're thinking of Diana's family."

It made sense, she guessed. It seemed odd, now that she thought of it, that as far as she knew the Wilcox family hadn't made any effort to see Allie, at least.

"I haven't seen or heard from them." He echoed her thought. "But I can't think who else would do it."

Her thoughts were already spinning in a different direction. "The man who came to the school—could he be part of that?"

If it were possible for his face to grow any more rigid, it did. "If he is, it has to stop. No matter what I have to do."

He clamped his mouth shut, leaving her afraid to wonder what he meant by that.

CHAPTER EIGHT

BEFORE MICHAEL COULD regret telling Cathy anything about the private investigator, Allie came running back to them. She grabbed her father with one hand and Cathy with the other, so that she could skip along between them.

"Aunt Verna says that was an excellent paper. She put it up on the refrigerator so everyone can see it."

"That's a wonderful gut idea." Cathy swung their clasped hands.

"Right—wonderful." What was wonderful was the way Allie beamed at Cathy's praise—cheerful, smiling, her face lit with pleasure. Even her brown eyes sparkled.

If this was the result of bringing her home to River Haven, then he'd done right for once. Now he had to figure out how to stay here. Here…and out of jail.

Allie let them go suddenly. "I have to go help Aunt Verna. She says you and Teacher Cathy should come and have lemonade and cookies. I get to help pour the lemonade. Come quick." She smiled and corrected herself. "Komm schnell. You will, won't you?"

She was looking at Cathy, and he saw that she could no more turn Allie down than he could.

"We'll both be there in a minute," she said. "I'd love some lemonade."

Allie raced off again.

Michael watched her go, but his mind was on Cathy. He'd had no right to burden Cathy with his problems. Divorce…murder…investigators…those things were as far from Amish life as missiles and moon landings.

He felt her gaze on him. "Would you rather I didn't come?"

"No… I mean, yes, I want you to have lemonade and cookies. Why would you think that?"

She seemed to find her smile. "You were looking pretty grim there for a minute."

"Not about you. Never about you." The words were out before he could stop them. Not that he wanted to when she was looking at him with a smile in those beautiful blue eyes. "Just wondering what I can do about…" He let that trail off. *You weren't going to bring her into your sordid problems, remember?*

But Cathy seemed to take it for granted that he'd discuss it with her. "I just think maybe you should talk to Chief Jamison about it."

He was shaking his head already before she'd finished. "If there's anything I've learned it's not to volunteer anything to the cops."

"Why? Surely Chief Jamison should know if this private investigator is snooping around his town."

"That's not how it works." Michael's jaw tightened painfully. "After I found Diana, I wanted to help so much that I poured out everything—what we'd said, what I'd thought and even the trouble our marriage was in. But I learned. They twisted everything I said around to turn it against me." He seemed to feel again the constant barrage of questions. "I won't make that mistake again."

"Chief Jamison isn't like that." She leaned toward him, intent on changing his mind. "He's always been fair and honest with the Leit."

"This is different. You don't understand." He shook his head. "Look, forget about it. It's not your concern."

Cathy drew back, attempting to hide the hurt she felt. But he could see it in her eyes and the slight tremble of her lips.

"You aren't my business, but my scholars are. Anything that affects you will affect Allie."

He couldn't deny it, but still he shook his head. "Drop it, Cathy. Please."

She gave a curt nod. They were still walking side by side as they approached the house, but they might as well have been a hundred miles apart.

By the time they reached the kitchen, he was berating himself. Why would he alienate one of the few people who believed in him? Sheer perversity, apparently. He stole a look at her face as he held the door for her. She was hiding the hurt now, but he'd seen it.

"Lemonade," Allie declared as they came in. "Aunt Verna made oatmeal nut cookies."

"Yum." Cathy had found her smile. "That sounds delicious."

Fortunately for him, between Aunt Verna and

Allie they carried the conversation, while he sat there and tried to figure out what was wrong with him.

Aunt Verna switched from cookies to the work frolic at the school the next day. "We're all prepared to go. I made a gelatin salad, so I'll bring a cooler. And we can take lemonade as well."

"I'm sure there will be plenty of food," Cathy said. "There always is." She glanced from Verna to him, and Michael thought she looked uneasy.

Was she afraid he'd show up, creating problems with those who hadn't accepted him yet?

"You don't need to worry. I won't be there."

"I didn't..." Cathy began, but Allie interrupted her.

"Daadi, why aren't you coming? Everyone is helping."

"I...I can't, not tomorrow." He couldn't very well tell her the real reason. "Aunt Verna will go with you, and Aunt Sarah and Onkel Lige, too."

"But you should help. Why won't you?"

"I'm busy tomorrow. But I'll go another time and help Teacher Cathy with anything she wants me to do. Okay?"

Cathy stood before Allie could argue. "That's fine," she said, as if the question had been directed to her. "I'll tell Allie to give you a message when I need some work done. Now, I'd better get home so I can help fix supper."

"I'll walk out with you." He rose quickly and followed her out the door.

Once they were out of earshot, Cathy spoke over

her shoulder, not turning to look at him. "If you don't want to help that's fine with me. But Allie was disappointed. She wants—"

"I know. She wants me to be like all the other dads, but I'm not. If I show up tomorrow, it might chase other people away."

"Ach, that's foolishness. No one would leave because you're there."

"Always looking on the sunny side, aren't you? What if you're wrong? What if Allie saw that I wasn't wanted there? That would hurt her a lot worse."

"You're borrowing trouble, I think." She turned now, meeting his gaze. "Are you sure it's not yourself you're fearing would be hurt?"

He stiffened. "I deserve anything that comes to me. Allie doesn't."

Cathy stared at him for a long moment, as if trying to understand what he really feared. Then she shook her head and walked on.

The question lingered in his mind as he watched her disappear into the belt of trees.

CATHY HEADED TOWARD HOME, the hurt like a weight in her chest. She couldn't watch people in pain without wanting to help them. If Michael were a stranger, she'd feel that way, but this was much worse, because Michael was one of their own.

He didn't believe he belonged—that was at the heart of the problem, she felt sure. He was caught between two worlds, unable to move.

When she was small, she'd found a dog stuck in a

tangle of barbed wire once—struggling to free himself and just making it worse, snapping at her when she tried to help. She'd run for Daad, sure that he could make it better. She could still see his strong, gentle hands soothing the creature, talking softly as he pulled each strand loose.

That was Michael, but whose were the hands that would free him when he was determined to reject help? Her heart sank even further at the thought of the plan Sarah and Verna had hatched to bring him and his father together. And of the role she was supposed to play.

As Cathy rounded the barn she spotted a car coming up the lane that led to the main road and frowned a little. It wasn't one she recognized. Instead of going on to the house, the driver stopped as he grew abreast of her. She thought he was going to roll down the window and speak to her, but instead he got out and came over to her.

"Hi there." The middle-aged man was dressed casually in khakis and a plaid shirt—he might have been any Englischer she'd see on Main Street.

"Are you looking for the Brandt farm?" She glanced toward the house, but no one seemed to be around just now. If Daad had been expecting someone, he'd have been on the lookout.

"Is that where I am?" His face crinkled in smiles. "Well, that'll teach me to ask directions from somebody I saw at a gas station. He said, 'Go along the Jonestown Road about two miles. You'll see a big red barn after about a mile, but don't turn there. Go on past where the fruit stand used to be, and take the second or third road…' I ask you, who could follow that?"

She had to smile at his comic imitation. "Yah, I've heard directions like that a time or two. Tell me where you want to go, and I'll do my best."

"Thank you, ma'am. I'd be grateful. I don't want to spend the afternoon driving around one back road after another. I'm looking for a place that sells plants. Forster Greenhouses, I think it's called."

A sliver of uneasiness crept in. "Are you looking to buy some annuals to plant? I know they have a big selection."

"Always like to have some around." His eyes were oddly opaque, making it difficult to imagine what he was thinking. "Is that far from here?"

She suppressed her wariness. She was imagining problems where they didn't exist. "Not far, but you'll have to turn around and go back to the main road to get there."

"Back that way?" He glanced back down the lane. "Okay, will do. Then what?"

"Turn left and drive about a half mile. It'll be on your left. You'll be able to see the greenhouses."

Yes, of course he would. So if he'd come through town, he'd have passed it. He could hardly miss it. And if he'd come the other direction…the uneasiness surged back. He'd said something about getting directions at a gas station, but there wasn't one in that direction for at least fifteen miles.

"So you're neighbors, I guess." He still wore that

genial smile that didn't quite reach his eyes. "You know the Forster family, do you?"

"We're neighbors," she said noncommittally, while her mind raced. Who was he? He wasn't local… She felt more sure of that with every word he spoke. And she didn't think he'd turned down their lane by mistake.

"I guess you know that Michael Forster has moved back, then. Has a little girl, I guess." His gaze wandered to the canvas bag she carried, filled with schoolwork. "You wouldn't be the teacher at the Amish school, would you?"

She sent a quick glance toward the house again. No one. She'd have to handle this herself. She could, she told herself firmly.

"Since you don't seem to need more directions, you'll have to excuse me. My parents are expecting me."

Cathy turned away, but he moved quickly alongside her. "Some reason why you don't want to answer my questions?"

"I don't see any reason why I should." She managed a tight smile. "Excuse me."

"Hey, I'm just looking for information for a client of mine. No harm in that, is there?"

Feeling anything she said might be the wrong thing, Cathy kept walking, her lips pressed together as if any unwary word might escape. She knew who he was now. A private investigator, Michael had said. Poking around where he'd lived in Harrisburg. Only, now he was here.

"What's Michael Forster up to? Does his daughter go to your school?"

Ignoring him as best she could, she marched on toward the house. If he followed her, started pestering Mamm and Daad with questions…

She risked a quick glance, but apparently he'd decided he'd done all he could. He stood still now, staring at her. Cathy pressed down the instinct to run to the door. Somehow it seemed important to behave normally.

But when she reached the kitchen, it took only one look for her mother to know something was wrong.

"Cathy, why are you so pale? Is it that hot out this afternoon? Maybe you should take the buggy to school from now on."

Mamm fussed around, not giving her a chance to respond as she pushed Cathy into a chair and produced cold water and then urged a plate of chocolate chip cookies on her.

"I'm fine, Mamm. It's all right. I'm just a little late, that's all."

"I saw a car out there. Who was it?" Mamm planted her hands on her hips.

She shrugged, trying to decide how to tell the truth without upsetting her. "A stranger. He wanted directions to Verna's greenhouses, so I told him."

Mamm eyed her. "That wouldn't take so long. What else did he want?"

Nothing for it but the truth, then. "He tried to ask questions about Michael and Allie. Looking for gossip, it seemed like. I'd never talk to an outsider about one of my scholars, you know that."

"Yah, of course." Mamm patted her shoulder. "You did right. But it's upsetting. Ever since Michael came back, it seems like things aren't the same."

The urge she felt to defend him startled Cathy with its strength, but she had to push it away. Doing so would just alarm Mamm to no good purpose.

"I'm sure folks will settle down. After all, we've had people return from living Englisch before. It just takes time and patience."

Apparently she hadn't been cautious enough, because Mamm's blue eyes were still dark with concern.

"If he's going to come back to the church, yah. But is he? Verna and I were talking, and all she'd say was that we had to wait for him to decide. But is he going to stay? If not, why would he come at all?"

Cathy rubbed her forehead. Good questions, but not ones she could answer. "I don't know." Maybe because he was fleeing pain and uncertainty and searching for peace?

Peace, it seemed, was in short supply with that private investigator around. And Michael didn't know he was here. He had to be told, and it seemed she was the one to tell him.

MICHAEL STOOD AT the kitchen sink after supper. He and Aunt Verna had worked out a routine in the evening. He cleaned up the kitchen while she supervised Allie's bath and getting ready for bed. She said, and he felt sure it was true, that it was a pleasure for her. He'd heard the lift in her voice at the prospect.

Once Allie was ready, he'd take his turn tucking her in, telling a story and just talking. Upstairs sound had moved from the bathroom to the bedroom, so he finished drying the last pan and headed up.

He stopped in the hallway, listening to their voices. Allie's dialect was improving every day, and she always spoke Pennsylvania Dutch to Aunt Verna now, sometimes pausing to search for a word or substituting an English one. That was a good Amish custom—popping in an English word for one that had no Amish equivalent.

His mother's face appeared in his mind, and he seemed to hear her voice, talking to his child. But that could never be. Would his life have been different if Mamm had lived? She'd always been able to soften Daad's rough edges. And to soothe him down, now that he thought about it. Without her, they'd pulled apart, and there didn't seem to be any way to bridge the gap. "Michael?" Aunt Verna appeared in the doorway. "Allie is all ready for bed."

"Denke." A simple thank-you wasn't enough for all she was doing, but she patted his cheek with a work-roughened hand as she passed him.

Allie sat on top of the log cabin quilt on her bed—with its pattern of pink, rose and white rectangles, it looked designed especially for a little girl. He sat down next to her, and she snuggled up to him.

"Tell me a story, Daadi. Tell me a story about when you were my age."

"When I was eight—hmm, I'll have to think about that. Let me see." Actually, the story popped into his mind without effort. He smiled. "How about one about your aunt Sarah and me, and the time we got lost in the dark?"

"Yah, that sounds good. Did you really get lost?" She looked up, her small face expressing concern.

"Not very lost." He gave her a reassuring smile. "I was eight, so that means Aunt Sarah was seven, and I called her Sally."

"Like the boppli," she said, nodding.

"That's right. Well, Sally and I had decided to build a hideout up in the woods. We wanted to cut some sticks to build it, so we borrowed Daad's saw. It turned out to be a pretty nice hideout, and we played there the rest of the day. But then when we were going to bed, we remembered that we hadn't brought the saw back down."

"Was that bad?" She looked apprehensive.

"We hadn't asked to use it, you see. So we'd be in trouble if he couldn't find it." Funny, that he could still remember that whispered conversation with Sally in her white nightgown, sitting up in her bed. "So we decided we'd better go and get it. It was dark, so we got a flashlight and slipped out of the house." He could almost feel the clutch of Sally's hand. She hadn't let go of him the whole time.

"Everything looked different in the dark, especially when we got up to the woods. Sally started saying we were lost. She was almost crying when I finally spotted the hideout. So I grabbed the saw and we headed back down the hill. We kept hearing things…birds and mice and animals that come out at night. We got more and more scared and finally we started to run. We ran all the way down the hill and never stopped until we got safely home."

"Did your daadi ever find out what you did?"

"We never were very good at keeping a secret, so finally we told him. We had to go to bed early three nights in a row, but I think he figured going up to the woods in the dark was punishment enough."

She nodded, seeming satisfied. "Are you still scared to go in the woods at night?"

He sincerely hoped he hadn't set her up for a bad dream. "No, not a bit. It's kind of fun after dark. Sometimes you might see an owl or even a fox."

"I'd like to make a hideout." She yawned, rubbing her eyes. "I'll tell Ruthie. Maybe we can make one."

"Climb under the covers, and you can have a dream about a hideout of your own."

Allie slid under the quilt, contented, and he bent to kiss her good-night, his heart flooding with love. She was safe and happy, and he would keep her that way.

He went downstairs, finding Aunt Verna settled in her favorite rocking chair with her mending. "Komm, sit," she said.

"I will, but I'll go take a walk around the greenhouses and outbuildings first. Make sure everything is secure."

She nodded, smiling. "Gut."

It was still light outside, though the sun was heading toward the horizon. Days were longer now, and people still dropped by the greenhouse after supper sometimes.

He walked slowly around the greenhouses, checking the doors. It was very quiet, and the peace seemed to seep into him. The strain and despair he'd felt after Alan's call were gone. This place was a sanctuary. If anything could restore him, this would.

Michael rounded the corner of the greenhouse he and Lige had been working on and stopped. Cathy sat on the bench against the wall, very still, very peaceful. She had a dreaming attitude, as if unaware of her surroundings. *Peace*—there was that word again. Cathy's slim figure leaned gracefully against the rough wooden back, and the slant of the setting sun turned her hair to gold.

The face that could quicken with laughter or melt into tenderness showed a serenity he didn't want to disturb, but she must be here waiting for him. For several moments he delayed speaking, but then the smallest unwary movement made enough noise to penetrate her absorption.

Cathy swung around, her face springing into life—into a moment of joy that disappeared almost before it registered. But he'd seen it. He put it away to consider later as she became grave.

"Michael. I thought you'd come out again."

"Why didn't you come to the house?" He sat down next to her, making the bench creak.

"I thought you'd be putting Allie to bed." She smiled. "You wouldn't appreciate my coming in and getting her all excited, would you?"

"We're always glad to see you." His voice was warmer than he'd intended it to be.

She shrugged. "It seemed better to wait. I'd have come to the house in a few minutes, but I'd rather talk to you without anyone else around."

"Something's wrong." He came to the obvious conclusion. "Tell me."

She hesitated, and he realized that whatever it was, was something she thought would hurt him.

"Out with it." He covered her hand with his and felt it warm under his touch.

"You told me earlier about the private investigator your friend said had been asking questions where you used to live." She took a deep breath, as if to arm herself against hurt. "He's here."

"Who?" He felt off balance.

"The private investigator. At least, I think that's who it must have been. He didn't actually say that, but I thought so. Maybe I'm wrong." Hope flared briefly in her face.

He gave her hand a squeeze. "Just tell me what happened. Where did you see this man?"

"Sorry." She managed a brief smile. "That wasn't very coherent, was it? I'll try to do better. When I went home this afternoon, I saw a car coming down our lane. The driver stopped, wanting to talk to me."

He was frowning now, not liking the sound of this. "About what?"

"First he acted as if he'd become lost. He wanted directions." She gestured around them. "To the greenhouse."

"I see. Not a local, then." Anyone local would have known where they were without asking.

"No. I'd never seen him before. He was very friendly, wanting to chat, but he made me feel uncomfortable. As if there was something else going on."

Alarm threaded through him. "Did he threaten you?" He clasped her hand in both of his.

"Nothing like that. But when I started to walk away, he kept asking me questions about you. I didn't answer. I was afraid he'd come to the house and bother Mammi and Daad, but he didn't." She seemed relieved to have it said.

"What made you think he was the private investigator?"

She shook her head ruefully. "Didn't I say? He spoke of a client who wanted to know. If you hadn't already talked to me about the private investigator, I wouldn't have thought of it. But I still wouldn't have talked about you."

"I know that. I think you're right—I don't see who else it could have been." It shouldn't be this much of a blow. He had already known that the man had been investigating in Harrisburg. It only made sense that he'd follow them here.

"I'm sorry." Cathy's voice was soft. "I wish I didn't have to tell you, but I thought you should know."

"It's better that way." He squeezed her hand, even as he thought he shouldn't be touching her.

But she was so warm, so loving. And so not for him.

CHAPTER NINE

CATHY GLANCED AROUND the scene at the school yard on Saturday, marveling as always at the number of people who turned out when there was anything to be done at the school. Even those whose children had long moved past the Creekside School turned out, just as they did for the Christmas program and the end-of-the-year picnic. The school really was theirs in a unique way.

"It's a fine turnout." Michael's father, Josiah, stopped next to her, and Cathy's stomach promptly turned over at the thought of Sarah's plan.

"I was just thinking that myself. It's wonderful gut to see so many people working."

"They want to see the school yard looking nice for the school picnic, so our Sarah says."

"Denke. I'm sehr glad you came to help today." This might be the longest conversation she'd ever had with Josiah Forster, and she suspected he wasn't thinking of her at all. His gaze was fixed on one of the children, and she didn't need to turn around to know it was Allie.

If only he'd say something to the child. She was

his granddaughter just as much as Ruthie was. Surely his grudge against Michael didn't extend to Allie.

Her lips twitched with the desire to say something to him about Allie, but she couldn't. She could only look on and hope he might be hiding love behind that stoic face.

"I'd best help Lige with cutting that ball field if it's going to be done today." With a short nod, he strode off across the school yard.

Cathy watched him for a moment. Josiah must be in his sixties, but he was as lean and wiry as a much younger man. According to Sarah, he worked as hard as a younger man, too, running the dairy farm with his two younger sons to help him.

Unlike Sarah, they hadn't ventured to make contact with their older brother, either because they agreed with Josiah or because they didn't want to go against him. Given the stern quality of his face, she could understand why they might feel that way.

As for her...she felt less and less sure that Sarah's plan was going to work. Or that she could successfully carry out her part in it.

And thinking of Sarah, here she was, hurrying across to Cathy, pulling a child's wagon behind her.

"Verna asks if you'd mind going over to the greenhouse and picking up some more flowers for around the school. You can take the wagon to haul them back."

"There's no one close enough to hear, so I don't think you need to announce it," Cathy muttered. This was going to go wrong—she could feel it.

"Just in case." Sarah's eyes sparkled with mischief. She was obviously enjoying this. Too bad Sarah had picked such poor helpers—Verna just blurted out anything she wanted to say, and Cathy got tongue-tied at the thought of putting on any pretense, especially with Michael.

"This isn't going to work." Cathy shot a look at Josiah. "Your father won't like it, and Michael will be furious."

"It's worth anything if it mends this stupid quarrel. Stubborn as mules, both of them." She grimaced. "Just look at Daad. He keeps looking at Allie. He wants to talk to her, but he won't do it. He'll just keep wanting and not doing, unless someone pushes him into it."

She made one last effort. "I'm not the best person to do this. As soon as Michael sees me, he'll know something is going on."

Sarah grabbed her arm. "You can't back out now. Anyway, I'm not asking you to lie to him. I know you won't do that. Just ask him to help you. Go on."

She gave Cathy a gentle push.

There was no use arguing with Sarah—there never had been. All Sarah could see was reconciliation, but Cathy didn't think she'd get her happy ending, at least not this way.

Trundling the wagon behind her, Cathy set off on the path toward the greenhouse. Apart from all her other hesitations, she hated to leave the work frolic, even for a good reason. Among the workers today were the three members of the Creekside school board…the board that had still not offered her a contract for next year. What might they think if they realized she was gone?

Needless to say, Mary Alice and her mother were prominent among the helpers today. Lizzie didn't miss any opportunity to push her daughter forward.

Mary Alice didn't seem to appreciate it very much. She was only a few years out of school herself, and she'd never shown any burning interest in teaching, as far as Cathy could see. Maybe she should have invited Mary Alice to help as a teacher's aide—come to think of it, it was odd that Lizzie had never volunteered her.

Wondering about Mary Alice and pondering her own future kept her thoughts busy, even if she didn't come to any useful conclusions. It was a jolt to discover that she'd covered the route automatically and was already in sight of the greenhouses.

Trying to steel herself for her task, she walked quickly, only to be halted by the sight of Michael. He was rounding the corner of the greenhouse by the bench—the bench where he'd held her hand and she'd felt her heart melt.

Even now, Cathy could feel heat rising in her cheeks. She longed for a few minutes to compose herself, but it was too late. Michael had seen her and was already coming toward her.

She pressed her hands to her cheeks. He wouldn't notice. And if he did, he'd think it was from the warm day. He'd come from a world where casual touching was commonplace. He couldn't imagine the effect it had had on her.

"Cathy, what are you doing here? Or are you on your way home already?"

She drew in a steadying breath. "Your aunt sent me to pick up some more flowers to plant at the school. She decided she hadn't brought enough." She got the words out all right, but she probably looked as guilty as a kid with her hand in the cookie jar.

"I see." The way he was studying her face flustered her. "Come along, then, and we'll load some up."

Avoiding his eyes, she hurried ahead of him, pulling the wagon behind her. With a sudden step he reached her and took the wagon handle from her, his fingers brushing hers and sending a shimmer of warmth along her skin.

"Anything in particular you want?"

She stared at him blankly, not sure what he meant.

His lips twitched. "I mean, marigolds? Zinnias? Sunflowers?"

"Yah, right." Now she was sure she was blushing. "Marigolds, I think. And some zinnias."

Michael didn't move. He stood in front of her, a frown slowly drawing his dark eyebrows together. "You may as well tell me what's going on, Cathy. That face of yours was never designed for fooling anyone."

She tried frantically to think of something short of the whole story, but it was useless.

Glancing from her to the wagon, he nodded. "I see. That's Ruthie's wagon—the one she and Allie were playing with. I don't have to look very far for the explanation. This is some plan of my sister's, isn't it?"

When she didn't answer, he clasped her wrists in a firm grip, bringing her gaze to his face.

"What's Sarah trying to do, Cathy?"

It was no use. It never had been. "Your daad is there—at the school. She thought, if you helped me bring the flowers, you two would see each other in a—a neutral situation. Don't be angry, Michael. She meant it for the best. This rift with your father is hurting her so much."

She could see that penetrate—see the way he recoiled from the idea that he was causing his sister pain.

Letting go of her wrists, he rubbed the back of his neck with one hand. "I didn't think." His face twisted. "I never even considered how my return was affecting her. All this time I've been accepting her love and her help, and not giving a thought to how it affected her."

He turned away with a single abrupt movement. Grabbing the wagon, he pulled it to the flower racks and started loading.

Cathy's throat was tight with pain for him. For Sarah, too, and even for Josiah. What a tangle it was, and her efforts to help had only made it worse.

Silently she helped him load the flowers. When the wagon was full, she found her voice.

"Denke. I'll take it back. If you want, I could just say that I couldn't get you to come."

Amusement flickered in Michael's face. "You

won't be any more convincing with Sarah than you were with me."

Surprise put a lift in her voice. "You're not angry?"

"Not with you." He grimaced. "Not really with Sarah either. Just mad at the whole situation." He seized the handle. "Let's go by the road. It'll be easier than trying to pull a child's wagon on the path."

She was finally able to smile again. "I did it."

"When it was empty." He pulled it effortlessly to the driveway. "Let's go."

Almost afraid to believe her eyes, Cathy walked beside him. "You're coming, then?"

"I'll help you get the wagon there. That's all I'm promising."

It was something, if not all that Sarah had hoped. She'd have to be content with it. Although, knowing Sarah, she doubted it.

They walked in silence for a few minutes. Then he shot a sideways glance at her. "Now, why do you look so apprehensive? I'm not going to make a scene."

"I know. I was just wondering what Sarah would come up with next."

"She always did have tons of half-baked ideas."

"As I recall, she claims she was the one who followed you into mischief."

"I'd say the blame was about equally divided. Although Daad always figured I could have stopped her." The somber expression came back. "You said Daad was there. How does he look?"

The question took her by surprise. "You have to remember that I've been seeing him every week or so for the years you were away. Any changes would be gradual." She tried to organize her thoughts. Michael deserved a better answer than that. "He's still quite strong—does a full day's work from what I've heard. When I left he was raking grass in the ball field while Lige mowed."

"I haven't asked Sarah much." He stared straight ahead, but she didn't think he saw the gentle curve in the road or the purple spurge along the ditch. "Thought it would be awkward. But that didn't mean I'm not interested."

"I'm sorry." She felt as guilty as if it were her fault. "I suppose everyone hesitates to bring it up. He's well, I'm sure. He runs the dairy farm with your brothers to help."

"I thought maybe Jonah would be married by now and taking over."

"He's just eighteen, although he's courting Becky Fisher. You wouldn't remember her. She's Sam Fisher's youngest girl."

He nodded. "I hope it works out for him." His smile flickered. "In one way, it seems impossible he could be courting age. When I left, he was just the kid brother who wanted to do everything I did." The smile vanished. "Glad he didn't."

There was nothing useful she could say to that, she realized.

"So Daad was there working. Allie went with Verna. Is he… Did he show any interest in her?"

"I think Verna was being careful not to push them together, which was wise." She remembered the way

Josiah had gazed over her shoulder when they were talking together. "He knew who Allie was, of course. He didn't go over to her, but I saw that he kept looking that way…watching her running around with Ruthie."

His face tightened. "He was curious."

Cathy corrected him gently. "He couldn't take his eyes off her."

They'd nearly reached the school, and Michael still wore that closed-off expression, as if he had a big no-trespassing sign in front of him. If he went in like that, who would dare to approach him? Didn't he see that he had to give a little?

The answer to that was clear—no. He didn't.

MICHAEL'S TENSION GREW as they neared the school. People were scattered around the school yard, busy with cleanup projects. Looked like a lot of chatter going on, too, but he noticed the talk ceasing as people turned to look at him. Then they looked away, trying not to stare, trying to pick up their interrupted conversations. Maybe it was his imagination that said they were having trouble with that.

These were people he knew—people who had known him since he was a child. He'd spent more years here than he had away, and still, he wasn't sure how they were going to react.

He tried to focus on the schoolhouse, not the people. He'd been here with Allie, but suddenly he was assaulted by memories. He saw himself going in that doorway for the first time, lagging behind his mother, unwilling to begin what she insisted would be an adventure.

So it had, in a way. Mammi had promised he'd be fine once he got used to it, and he was. Maybe a little too fine, since he'd quickly earned a reputation for mischief.

He'd found a kindred spirit in Jacob King, just his age and just as ready to get into any sort of devilment. That had lasted well into their teens, but when Michael had started hanging out with the Englisch, Jacob hadn't liked it. That had been the first real quarrel they'd ever had. And the last.

Cathy cleared her throat, reminding him of her presence. "We're getting things ready for all the spring events at school." She seemed to be trying to make this easier by talking. "I can't believe how quickly the school year is going."

Poor Cathy. She didn't want to be involved. The least he could do was try to talk naturally to her.

"I know. Picnic lunches and the end-of-the-year program. Is it still hard to get them to learn their parts?"

"Much harder than for the Christmas program. They're too distracted by wanting to get outside." She managed a smile. "Not that we were ever like that."

"Speak for yourself. I couldn't wait for school to be over. You have many eighth graders to graduate this year?"

"Three, all boys. They're a fine group. John is going to be an apprentice at the machine shop, and Caleb will help his older brother in the harness shop.

Joshua's father has a dairy farm, so he has a future mapped out. I just hope he keeps his mind on the cows better than he did on his schoolwork."

He was really just listening to the sound of her voice, letting it soothe his frazzled nerves. But he ought to reply. "You're short of girls this year, ain't so?"

"Yah, but I'll have four next year." She hesitated. "If I'm still here, that is."

That penetrated his absorption. "You mean the school board still hasn't given you a contract?"

"Not yet." She didn't meet his eyes.

"You're a terrific teacher. They'd be ferhoodled not to beg you to stay on."

She just shrugged.

"I'd tell them so, but I guess that would do more harm than good." Then he realized why she wasn't looking at him. Just being involved with him to this extent was probably not doing her any good either.

They reached the school yard, and his sister came hurrying to meet them.

"Denke, Michael. I don't know why we didn't think to bring more plants over."

"Forget it, Sarah. I know just what you're up to, so don't act innocent with me."

He saw her gaze dart toward Cathy, and he shook his head. "Don't think about blaming Cathy. She did her best. You forget I know exactly what kind of sneaky plans you get up to."

"You should." Sarah's eyes crinkled. "I learned from you, ain't so?"

"Not all of it. What were you thinking to involve Cathy in your plans? Being seen with me isn't going to do her reputation with the school board any good."

Shock widened Sarah's eyes, and he regretted speaking so sharply. She honestly hadn't thought of it. That was Sarah, so wrapped up in her plan she didn't see anything else.

"Don't..." Cathy began.

"Cathy, I'm sorry." Sarah swung to her. "I never thought."

"It's all right." Cathy seized the wagon handle. "Let's get these planted. We can't just stand here."

She was right. Carrying on as if everything was normal—that was the only way to handle it. He took the handle back and dragged the heavy wagon to the spot Sarah indicated along the side of the schoolhouse. Once it was in position, he dropped the handle.

"There, flowers delivered. I'll be going."

Sarah grabbed his arm. "Ach, Michael, I'm sorry. But don't rush away. Please. Give people a chance."

It wasn't Sarah's words that changed his mind; it was the expression on Cathy's face. If it mattered that much to her, the least he could do was cooperate.

He nodded.

Sarah had sense enough not to talk about it. She handed him a trowel and together they started setting out the plants. Cathy, with a look of relief, moved off toward a group that was painting the swing uprights.

"Denke, Michael," his sister murmured. "I know you didn't want to stay."

"I guess I ought to do my share. My daughter comes here to school, too."

They worked along the side of the building in silence. When they'd reached the end, Michael leaned back, stretching, and got up. That was when he realized someone stood a few feet away, watching him.

Jacob King. It took a moment to be sure. The years between eighteen and twenty-eight meant changes, but Jacob still had that stubborn cowlick where his hair tried to curl. The laugh lines around his eyes were new. Even with his chin hidden by the short growth of beard, it was undoubtedly Jacob. Michael's lips twitched when he saw that the beard had a tendency to curl as well. How Jacob must hate that.

"Well, Jacob." He waited for the man who'd once been his best friend to act.

Finally a smile tugged at Jacob's mouth, and he moved closer. "You've changed." His tone was wary, but at least he was talking.

"So have you. You're married now?"

"Esther Miller said she'd take me on. We have a boy in school, and another one ready to start in the fall. The little girl is still a baby."

"So now you're a responsible grown-up. Do you ever tell your boy about all the trouble you got into when you were in school?"

"That we got into, don't you mean," Jacob corrected him, and now the smile grew into something more like the one Michael remembered. "Seems to me you were the one with all the ideas, ain't so? Like the time you hid all the chalk so the teacher couldn't find it. How about I tell your little girl about that?"

Michael grinned and shook his head. "It wouldn't matter how many ideas you gave her, Allie wouldn't pull tricks on Teacher Cathy. She loves her."

"Yah, so does my boy. She's a little different from the teachers we had."

"Different, but better," Michael said quickly, relieved when Jacob nodded agreement.

"I better get back to work." Jacob nodded toward the painting project. He hesitated and then clapped Michael on the shoulder. "Komm see us. Soon."

Michael watched him. The same Jacob. And if not the same relationship, there was at least the promise of something good to be established.

He didn't have time to decide what to do next, because Allie raced around the corner of the building, Ruthie in hot pursuit, and hurtled herself at his legs.

"Daadi, guess what?" She clutched him, tilting her head to look up.

"What?" He put a gentle hand on her silky hair.

"Ruthie says that's our grandfather over there." She pointed toward the ball field. "Hers and mine, too. Don't you want to see him?"

He struggled for the right answer, noticing that Cathy was watching them. She'd have seen Allie pointing. She'd guess what Allie was saying.

"Please, Daadi." She caught his hand.

"Let's go." Ruthie, dancing a little with impatience, grabbed his other hand. "Komm. We'll see Grossdaadi. I'll tell him who you are."

He had to stifle a smile at that. His father knew only too well who he was. Knew, had seen him and hadn't approached him. That didn't bode well for any reunion.

He wouldn't be a coward about it, but as he let the girls propel him along, a lead weight formed in his stomach. He could handle it if Daad were harsh, but what about Allie?

Daad saw them coming. He straightened, turning to face them. His face was shadowed by the brim of his straw hat, so Michael couldn't see his expression, but his stance was that of one braced for unpleasantness.

It felt like the longest walk he'd ever taken. People were watching—covertly, trying not to stare, but wanting to know. Was Josiah going to welcome back his prodigal son? If so, it would be a sign for them. If not…

He came to a halt a couple of feet from his father and met his stare. Daad's eyes were like flint, and his face was fixed and forbidding—enough to scare anyone away.

But Ruthie reached out to grab his hand and tugged at it. "Grossdaadi, here are Allie and Onkel Michael. You are Allie's grossdaadi, too, ain't so?"

With what seemed an effort, Daad looked away from him, tilting his head to look down at Ruthie. Her lively face turned up to his, her eyes danced. "Ain't so?" she said again. "Don't you want to say hello to Allie?"

Michael felt his jaw turn to rock. If Daad did or said anything to hurt Allie…

Slowly, very slowly, Daad squatted down so that he was level with the two girls. He looked searchingly at Allie, and she returned the stare, her brown eyes serious and intent.

With the effect of ice breaking up, Daad smiled. His face warmed, and he reached out a tentative hand to Allie.

"So you are Allie. I am wonderful glad to meet you, Allie."

For an instant, Allie's shyness kept her silent. Then, at a nudge from Ruthie, she nodded. "I am wonderful glad to meet you, too."

Daad blinked, as if he had something in his eyes. He touched her cheek, very gently. "You and Ruthie must come soon to see me, yah? We'll have a picnic. Would you like that?"

She nodded but then glanced up at Michael. "And Daadi, too."

Michael winced. His father rose to meet his eyes.

"You've come back at last."

"Yah." No point in trying to put a gloss on the reason. "Allie and I needed a home."

"You can—"

But he was destined never to know what his father might have said. A police car, with a wail of the siren, pulled up in front of the school. The driver got out—Guy Smethers. But it was the man who emerged from the other side that engaged his attention. Davis Moreland, detective with the Harrisburg Police Department and the man who'd worked so hard to gather enough evidence to bring charges against him.

So Alan had been right. They were investigating all over again, and they'd followed him here.

"Michael—" Daad said his name, but Michael couldn't turn to look at him. He could only stare at the two men who were advancing on him.

They came to a stop. "Get in the car, Forster." Smethers didn't bother to be polite.

A glance told him that Guy was itching for a chance to manhandle him. Moreland must have seen it as well, because he stepped between them.

"We need to have a talk, Forster. Let's not create a fuss here. Just get in the car quietly, and there'll be no trouble."

No trouble. Michael had an insane desire to laugh. What did the man call trouble if not coming here, siren and all, to take him in, in front of his family and neighbors?

He could feel his father, standing behind him, could imagine how his face would look. He'd take it as a personal humiliation. Michael couldn't look at him.

Instead he bent to give Allie a gentle hug. "I have to go and talk to these men," he said. "Aunt Verna will take you home, and I'll see you later." He dropped a kiss on her forehead and hoped he was telling the truth.

CHAPTER TEN

Michael staggered as Guy gave him a none-too-gentle shove into the backseat. The doors slammed, and he took a quick look back for Allie. She still stood with Daad, and he had pulled her and Ruthie to his side in a protective gesture. But the face he turned toward Michael was implacable.

So much for any hope he might have had for reconciliation. Now that it had been snatched away, he realized he had been hoping…actually wanting to find his place in the family again. He'd never know what Daad had been going to say.

The police car moved past silent groups of Amish, all looking at it…at him…with solemn expressions. Except for Cathy, who looked stricken. She caught his eye and made a pitiful attempt at a smile. Then they were gone, swinging out onto the main road and heading for town.

Michael forced himself to focus on the men in the front seat. Not Guy—he fancied himself a big deal, but it was the Harrisburg detective who called the shots in this situation.

"What is it you want from me, Detective Moreland?" He kept his voice even. Aggressiveness wouldn't pay.

"We just have a few questions to go over with you, Mr. Forster." Moreland's gaze met his in the rearview mirror and flickered away.

"I can't imagine there's anything you haven't asked me at least a dozen times."

Guy moved slightly, as if he wanted to speak, but a glance at the detective kept him silent.

Michael leaned back, folding his arms. "I'm here. Go ahead and ask me."

"We'll wait until we have a little privacy."

"Privacy?" Anger threatened to overpower him. "Your method of setting up a talk wasn't very private." Bad enough in front of the people who trusted him—worse in front of half the church, to say nothing of his father.

He caught a quick, sidelong look from Moreland that wasn't hard to interpret. He'd make a guess that coming to the school had been Guy's idea.

The anger surged again, but he was prepared for it this time. He wouldn't let it take over. Doing so just gave credence to the idea that he was a man who'd let emotion turn to violence.

As he'd assumed, they were headed to the police station. He got out as soon as the door was unlocked, walking ahead of them up the three steps to the entrance.

Chief Jamison was waiting, his face expressionless. He opened the door to his office and gestured them in, but when Guy attempted to follow, he shook his head.

Balked of his obvious desire to participate, Guy moved away from the door, but not far.

Jamison closed the door firmly and headed for his chair. Now it was the detective's turn to shake his head.

"There's no need for you to sit in, Chief Jamison."

"My jurisdiction," he said. "My office." He sat down behind the desk.

"Certainly, if you have time." Moreland covered his reaction smoothly. "Sit down, Mr. Forster." He indicated a seat to Michael, but then sat on the edge of the desk so that he loomed over him.

Michael sat, planted his feet firmly and crossed his arms again. He vaguely remembered his attorney advising against that position, saying it implied a negative attitude. If so, then it implied just what he was feeling.

He met Moreland's gaze, not blinking. Moreland had wanted this. *Let him do the talking.*

"Let's just go over again what happened on the day your wife died." Moreland's tone was casual. He looked at Michael expectantly.

Michael answered with a frown. "We've already been over every minute of that day. If you have something new to ask me, ask. If not, let's not waste each other's time."

"I'm in no hurry. Humor me. For instance, when did you tell your wife you were coming over that evening?"

Michael stared at him. Moreland knew better

than that. Did he think Michael's answer would have changed?

"She didn't. I didn't tell her."

"Why not?" He shot the question.

Shrugging, Michael forced himself to go back. "It seemed to me she was avoiding setting a time for us to discuss the separation. I figured if I just dropped by, I'd stand a better chance of seeing her."

"Sure you didn't call her? How about a quick text, just to be sure she'd be home?"

"No."

"Didn't run into a neighbor and mention it?"

Michael's frown deepened. Why the emphasis on this? "No. There was no occasion for me to see any of the neighbors. It was a workday. I was on the job all day, then I showered, grabbed something to eat and went over."

"You went over. And then what? How did you get in?"

"She'd changed the locks." That still rankled after all this time. "I got a screwdriver from the car and popped the lock on the garage door."

"Carried the screwdriver in with you, I suppose."

Michael stared at him. "No. Why would I? I put it down on the walk, thinking I'd pick it up when I left."

"Tell me what happened after you stepped inside."

"I've already told you." He didn't want to relive it again. It never got any easier.

"Tell me again. Everything you did."

He sucked in a steadying breath, grasping the edges of the chair with his fingers, and began. He went through every moment, every action and almost every thought. When he'd finished, his palms were wet against the wooden edges of the chair.

"I see." Moreland was unaffected, his face revealing nothing. "Let's go over it again."

"No."

The detective stared at him for a moment. "If you're as innocent as you claim, Mr. Forster, I'd think you'd want to cooperate with us."

"Cooperate? After you burst into a gathering of families and kids at the school and haul me off in a squad car? I've cooperated as much as—"

"Hold on." Chief Jamison stood, his square face reddening, his jaw tight. "A word with you, Detective." He nodded toward the door.

Moreland rose slowly. "What's the problem?" Resentment tinged his voice.

"Outside." Jamison could be intimidating in his own way. The Harrisburg cop met his steely gaze for another moment and then nodded.

Left alone, Michael tried to assess what had just happened. Something had lit a fuse under the chief, that was evident. He could hear the murmur of voices from the other side of the door. Then came something he could hear.

"Smethers!" The chief's bellow could carry to the next building. "Get over here."

Guy's answering footsteps sounded reluctant. He said something Michael couldn't hear.

"You're telling me you took this officer to the workday at the Amish school? I said to drive him to the house to talk to Michael. Not to burst into an Amish gathering. You have any sense in that head of yours? You know how I worked to gain the trust of those people? You think our good relationship comes easy?"

Guy and the Harrisburg cop both seemed to be protesting at the same time.

"Enough." A hand slapped the wall. "Smethers, get out on patrol. I'll figure out what to do with you later. Detective Moreland, I think we're finished here."

"I'm not done questioning..." Moreland had raised his voice, but the chief ran right over him.

"I said I'd cooperate. I have. In my town, I decide when you're done."

A few more murmurs ensued, and footsteps retreated toward the outer office. Michael sat, waiting, wondering.

About the time he thought they'd forgotten about him, Chief Jamison came back in. "Sorry for the wait. Come on—I'll drive you home."

He'd refuse, but he wanted to get back to Allie as quickly as possible. At least he was going home. He followed the chief out to the police car. This time he was ushered into the front seat.

"Sorry about what happened at the school." Jamison started the car and made a U-turn, narrowly avoiding pickups coming from both directions. "It shouldn't have. I'll be calling on the school board to deliver my apologies in person."

"Thanks."

He wasn't going to say it hadn't mattered, because

it had. More than Jamison could know. But there was no undoing it. Still, as long as the man was in a conciliatory mood, maybe he'd be willing to open up.

"Would I be right in thinking something prompted Harrisburg to send someone up here?" He held his breath, half expecting to be slammed down by an official answer.

Jamison stared at the street ahead for a long moment. Then his face cleared. "Let's say in general terms that wouldn't be likely to happen without something new having come up."

"He didn't ask me anything new," Michael observed.

"No. Well, again, in general terms you understand, I'd guess that either someone started pushing for action or they got a tip they thought was worth investigating. Or both."

He suspected he wasn't going to get anything more, but it was certainly enough to make him think. Either way, it meant that someone other than the police was behind this new interest in him.

Did that someone know anything? Or just want to cause trouble? Maybe he should see this as a positive step. If the police would stop focusing on him, they might be able to find the person who'd taken Diana's life. No matter how bad their relationship was, he needed to see justice done, for Diana's sake as well as for his daughter's. Allie ought to be able to think of her mother without wondering and uncertainty.

Either way, it seemed living here quietly and keeping his head down wasn't a viable option. He'd been kidding himself to think the past was over.

CATHY HAD BEEN shaken beyond anything she might have imagined when the police car drove off with Michael in the back. What did this mean? She hadn't been near enough to hear what the men had said to Michael. One had been a familiar figure—Patrolman Smethers, who'd hassled Michael at the school. The other was a stranger.

She had to force herself to swallow, to breathe normally and to compose her face. Allie might need her. She should check on Allie.

The two girls still stood next to Michael's father. Josiah had squatted down and was talking to them in a low voice. She hurried toward them, registering gratitude that Josiah seemed to be handling the situation well, at least where the children were concerned. What this would do to Sarah's hopes of getting her father and brother back together, Cathy couldn't imagine.

Before she could reach them, Verna got there, sweeping Allie up in a hug.

"It's all right," she was saying when Cathy reached them. "Daadi will be home soon."

Josiah made an involuntary movement, as if he had doubts, and Verna impaled him with a glare. "Yah," he said, patting Allie's back with an awkward gesture. "He will. And you and Ruthie can come to the farm soon to see me. The barn cat has some new kittens you can play with."

"That will be fun, won't it, Allie?" Ruthie seemed aware that something was wrong, even if she didn't know what, and she was trying to make it better. "Maybe we can name them. You'd like that, wouldn't you?"

Allie responded with a nod, but her face was closed, as if she'd locked and barred her real self to keep trouble away. From what she'd heard, Allie had been at the home of Michael's friend the night her mother died. What would people have told her? How could anyone explain that in a way that wouldn't leave overwhelming pain behind? Cathy's heart ripped a little, and her throat grew tight.

"Denke, Ruthie." She managed a smile. "It sounds like fun. You and Allie can look forward to that."

Verna exchanged glances with her. "I think it's best if Allie and I go home now. When they... When he gets a ride back, he'll go there, most likely."

Cathy nodded. "Is there anything I can do for you?" It was hard to feel so helpless when people you cared about were in trouble.

"Nothing." Verna glanced at Josiah, then down at Allie, as if thinking that at least one good thing had come out of this day. Holding Allie's hand, Verna headed toward her buggy. Lige was already harnessing up the mare, apparently assuming she'd want to go home.

Of course, she was right. She couldn't imagine Michael walking back into the work party after having been taken away by the police. A wave of anger burned through her. Surely, whatever the police wanted, they could have waited. They hadn't had to come here for him—he'd have been home in another hour.

The fact that they'd burst in on the work party looked like malice on someone's part. Usually Chief Jamison bent over backward to avoid problems with the community's Amish, something they appreciated. As a result, the Leit were more likely to go to the police in case of trouble than they would be in some places.

Josiah was still watching Allie and Verna walk toward the buggy when Sarah reached them. Her face was clouded, and she looked as if she held back tears. She looked at her father over the head of her small daughter.

"Daad, I—"

Josiah cut her off with a shake of his head. "No need to talk. You meant it for the best."

Sarah blinked several times. "Yah. I did."

Anything more she wanted to say could probably be said better without an audience. Cathy slipped away, trusting others would have sense enough not to butt in on them.

Maybe so, but she hadn't gotten more than halfway to the school building before Lizzie Stoltzfus grabbed her arm. "Disgraceful. Having the police interrupting our work frolic. I never heard of the like. You should have done something."

Suppressing the desire to ask what she or anyone else could have done, she just shook her head. "I have to check on something. Excuse me."

But Lizzie had a firm grip on her sleeve. "You must—"

Whatever Lizzie thought she must do, she wasn't destined to hear it. Someone grasped her other arm and turned her around. Joanna, of course. She smiled firmly at Lizzie even as she gently pushed Cathy toward Rachel Hurst, the other member of their little group of singles.

"Lizzie, you're just the person I wanted to see." Joanna was sweeping the woman away from Cathy with her usual brisk determination. "Come, we have to talk. I need your advice."

Rachel put a comforting arm around Cathy as she led her away. "We thought you needed rescuing." Her voice was as comforting as her warm hug. "Komm inside. I think there's some coffee left in the urn."

Fortunately Rachel didn't seem to expect her to say anything sensible, because her throat was tight and her mind a jumble of hopes and dread. Cathy gave a sigh of relief when the schoolroom door closed behind her.

She tried to speak, but discovered that her voice was too unsteady to trust. Rachel didn't bother to speak, she just put her arms around Cathy in a warm hug.

"It will be all right," she murmured eventually. "You're not to worry. Nothing will happen to him."

Cathy drew back, mopping her eyes. "How did you know?"

Rachel shook her head. "Do you really think you could love someone without Joanna and me seeing it?"

Pressing her hands against her cheeks, Cathy longed to sink into the floor. "I'm not… I mean…"

"Yah, you are." Rachel patted her arm with a gentle touch. "It's all right. No one else knows. Your secrets are always safe with us, ain't so?"

Cathy nodded, her tension easing. If Joanna had been the leader and spokesperson of their little group, Rachel had always been the heart. She seemed born for the role of comforter, stepping in to mother her younger siblings when their mother passed away, always patient, always caring, even as her own life passed her by.

Sinking down on a desk, Cathy felt herself begin to think rationally. "There must be something I can do," she murmured.

"What?" Rachel said, her tone practical. "Verna is taking care of the little girl. As for the police… well, that's out of everyone's hands."

"True. I'm being foolish. There isn't anything I can do except get on with the workday."

"They are doing fine without you. Just stay here for a bit. I'll get you a cup of coffee."

"I don't need coffee."

"No. But you need a reason not to go out and get caught by Lizzie Stoltzfus or someone equally talkative." Rachel sugared the coffee and handed it to her. "This is a fine excuse."

She wasn't so sure, but the coffee, still hot from the insulated carafe, warmed her all the way down.

There's nothing you can do, she repeated to herself. Maybe, eventually, Verna would send word that

Michael was safe at home again. She couldn't very well pester the police with questions about their actions.

Did this mean they had something new against Michael? Her fingers closed around the cup, seeking warmth. She didn't know, and she couldn't ask. She didn't have the right to do anything where Michael was concerned. Except love him.

CATHY KEPT HERSELF busy inside the school as much as she could while the volunteers finished their work, afraid if she heard people talking about the police taking Michael away, she'd be unable to control her feelings. When she heard people begin to leave, she went back outside, knowing she needed to be there to show her gratitude.

It had been a shock to learn that Joanna and Rachel had guessed. She'd hardly spoken with them in the past week, but that didn't seem to matter. Would she be as insightful if it were one of them? She hoped so, but she wasn't sure. Still, it had been a relief to have someone know and sympathize. Rachel hadn't even bothered to point out the problems involved in caring for someone who was no longer Amish. She'd just expressed caring, and that had been enough.

Sarah, chasing her daughter toward the family buggy, paused for a word with her. Sarah's face was drawn with anxiety, even as she tried to smile. "I wish we'd hear something," she murmured. "Surely they won't keep him long."

She felt more helpless than usual in the face of Sarah's pain.

"I hope not. I can't understand why they'd do such a thing. I'd think after all this time, the police would have moved on."

She said it having no idea whether it was reasonable or not. Her limited exposure to the justice system was a disadvantage right now.

"Just when I thought…" Sarah didn't finish, but Cathy knew what she'd thought—or maybe *hoped* would be a better word.

"How is your father?" The quick glance she'd dared to take at Josiah's face hadn't been encouraging.

"Not talking." Sarah grimaced. "Ach, I'm nearly forgetting. Aunt Verna asked if you'd stop at the house on your way home."

"Yah, of course. Did she say why?"

"She's worried about Allie, that's for sure. You're so gut with her. Maybe you can help."

"I'll do anything I can." That was an easy promise to make, but she suspected only her father's reappearance would really help Allie now.

"Gut." Sarah squeezed her hand in a quick farewell. "I must go. Call me the minute you know anything. I'll be haunting the phone shanty until I know what's happening."

Cathy nodded, watching until their buggy was out of sight. In a few minutes everyone had gone, and the school yard carried its usual atmosphere of Saturday peace. She checked that the doors were locked, and headed for the path that led home.

The walk was so familiar she could do it with her eyes closed. Still, she'd never done it while carrying such a load of pain and helplessness.

How had she come to let herself love Michael? She knew perfectly well a future with him was impossible. He didn't return her feelings. He might never be able to contemplate marrying anybody after what had happened to him. And if he did, it wouldn't be to someone for whom he'd have to turn back to the Amish life he'd run away from.

Hopeless. But the feeling was like nothing she'd ever experienced before—so powerful it swept everything else ahead of it. All she could do was try to keep anyone else from knowing what she felt, including Michael himself.

She emerged from the patch of woods, and the cutoff to Verna's house was ahead of her. Cathy paused for a moment, murmuring a silent hope for guidance in dealing with Allie. Then she strode toward the collection of greenhouses and the house, telling herself that Michael would be there, the worry ended.

But as soon as Cathy entered the house, she knew that hope was futile. Verna's face fell when she saw who it was. Allie, seated at the kitchen table with paper and crayons, took one look and went back to her drawing, pressing the crayon furiously against the paper.

One look was enough to tell her that Allie had

retreated again—her face blank, her defenses up against intruders. Cathy's heart twisted. She and Verna exchanged a silent message, and Cathy pulled out the chair and sat down next to Allie.

Instinct told her a question wouldn't get any answer. "I like that picture of a barn. It looks very real." Nothing. "Drawing is a good way to fill the time until Daadi gets home. Then you can show him your picture."

Allie didn't speak, but her hand stopped its movement. Then she picked up a yellow crayon and made a few strokes. She hesitated.

"Can you show me how to draw a kitten?" Her voice was tightly controlled, but at least she spoke. The relief that washed over Verna's face was probably reflected on her own.

"Let's see if we can do it together," she suggested, picking up an orange crayon. "If a kitty is sitting, its back makes a curve, like so. And if it's looking at you, its face is sort of like a triangle pointing down, only more rounded, ain't so?"

Allie nodded, painstakingly copying Cathy's movements. Cathy watched her, smiling. "And what about whiskers?"

"Yah, whiskers." Allie drew them in, concentrating, the tip of her tongue peeking through her lips.

That was better—at least Allie was focusing on something she could do, instead of worrying about things she couldn't control. They could all stand to learn that lesson.

Before she had time to put that into practice,

Cathy heard the sound of a car pulling up and moved quickly to the window.

"It's Daadi," she said, and Allie's face lit up. She slid off the chair, grasping her picture.

Cathy watched as Michael stepped out of the police car. He bent over to say something to Chief Jamison. It looked as if they were on good terms, and her tension eased. In another moment he was coming in, to be met by Allie rushing to him.

He picked her up, holding her close. Their faces were next to one another, and he murmured something, so softly no one else could hear. Cathy found she was blinking back tears.

Michael straightened again after setting Allie on her feet. "Everything's okay," he said, glancing from Verna to her. "No problems."

Whether Verna believed that or not, Cathy couldn't tell, but she certainly didn't. Michael might try to hide it, but she could read the tension and anger that rode him.

She could do nothing about it. Forcing a smile, she crossed the room. "I'm glad you're back. I was keeping Allie company, but I'd better be going."

"Wait a second. I'll walk out with you." He bent to touch Allie's cheek lightly. "I'll come right back. Did you save any cookies for me?"

Cathy was already out the door, so she didn't hear the child's reply. He ought to stay with Allie. Cathy was having too much difficulty controlling the complex feelings that threatened to overwhelm her. It would be easier without him.

She hurried her steps, but he caught up with her before she reached the greenhouse. "Hold up, Cathy. You don't need to rush off."

Averting her gaze, she sought for a reasonable answer. "Allie needs your attention right now. And you should call Sarah. She was worried, and she'll be waiting for a call."

"Right." He touched her arm lightly. "Sorry all of you were worried. I didn't have much choice." He sounded puzzled, probably at her reaction.

"I know. But when they put you in the police car..." Her voice ran out, thank goodness. She was betraying herself with every word.

"I'm sorry. Sorry for all of it." Anger threaded his voice, but she knew it wasn't directed at her. "I've done nothing but cause trouble for people since I got here."

"That's not true, and you know it. This is your home."

His face twisted. "I doubt that everyone would agree to that. Especially after today."

Lying to him would do no good, even if she wanted to do so. "I'm sure it's given folks something to talk about. But you're here, aren't you? It can't have been anything too serious, can it?"

"Serious enough." He released her arm and shoved his hand through his hair. "That was the detective from Harrisburg who investigated Diana's death."

"What did he want? He surely doesn't have any authority here, does he?"

Michael shrugged. "I guess if he asked for Chief

Jamison's cooperation, he had to give it. But I'd say it was grudging. And the chief was furious when he found out they'd come to the school."

"It didn't seem like something he would do. But what did the man want? I thought…"

"What? That Diana's death was in the past? It'll never be in the past until they find out who killed her."

"They won't find out by harassing you," she retorted.

That brought a slight easing of the tension on his face. "I'm glad you think so."

She was frowning, trying to reason it out. "That detective—he must have some reason for coming here now."

"He didn't tell me—just went over the same ground again. But the chief did say…"

"What? I won't repeat it."

"No, I know you won't." His quick smile nearly undid her. "Chief Jamison seems to think that either they got an anonymous tip that pointed to me, or that someone was pushing them to act."

"The private investigator," she said instantly.

"Right. Someone hired him. Someone who thinks I'm guilty." He made a quick, angry gesture. "The first time around, I was so numb I couldn't believe it was happening. It was all I could do to answer questions, let alone think through it. Now…now I'm thinking. And I'm angry, not numb."

"In this case, angry is probably better than numb."

"Yah. It has to be Diana's family. Who else would hire an investigator?"

She nodded, seeing no other possibilities. The person who'd killed Diana might want suspicion pointed at Michael, but surely not to the extent of hiring an investigator who could manufacture that truth.

The grim look on Michael's face alarmed her. "What are you going to do?"

"That's what I've been asking myself since I saw that police car. I'm past the point of being numb, and running away won't help any. So I guess it's time I fight back."

CHAPTER ELEVEN

IT WAS ALL very well to make a decision to fight back, Michael realized as he made the rounds of the greenhouses and outbuildings that evening. Finding a way to do it was an entirely different challenge.

He did have one advantage—his experience of the outside world. The average Amish person would be hampered in that respect. He wasn't. On the other hand, the average Amish person wouldn't be in this position to begin with.

Not that the Amish were saints, by any means. They were generally law-abiding, more likely to be victims than perpetrators. But there were cases of physical abuse, alcoholism, drugs—no one was entirely safe from those ills.

If he could trace the person who'd hired the private investigator, that would be a step forward. Unfortunately he didn't have a name—Cathy hadn't asked the man for identification. Well, why would she? It wasn't the sort of thing she could ever have imagined happening to her.

Alan Channing might be of help there. If he hadn't gotten the name or the company, someone else in the neighborhood might have. He could call…

He walked around the corner of the shed and nearly walked right into Lige. "Hey, steady." Lige grasped his arm to keep him from stumbling. "Sorry. Guess I startled you. Aunt Verna said you were out here."

"It's okay." He moved forward, out of the shadow of the building, so that he could see Lige's face more clearly in the spring twilight. "What's wrong?"

If he'd come to break the news that Daad was more set against him than ever, he needn't bother. Michael had already figured that out, but given what a friend Lige had become to Michael, he'd probably want to show his support anyway.

"Nothing. Well, nothing's wrong with us. I came by to see how you're doing after...well, what happened today. It must have been rough."

He shrugged, but at least he didn't feel as if he had to protect Lige from the truth. Lige had a clear way of looking at things that made him a good ally. "It wasn't pleasant, that's for sure. Seems like that detective from Harrisburg is convinced he doesn't have to look any further than me for Diana's killer."

"Can he do that? Keep coming after you, making you answer questions, intruding like that?" Lige grimaced, probably remembering the scene at the schoolhouse.

He might as well bring it out in the open. "That was bad, wasn't it? Cops at the school work frolic."

Lige's expression eased a little. Obviously he'd find it easier to talk about once Michael had brought it up. "Gave folks something to talk about, that's for sure."

"Kind of messed up Sarah's plan, didn't it?"

Lige and Sarah might well be regretting their championing of him by now. The thought of losing their caring and support shook him more than he'd have expected.

"Well, yah." Lige studied the ground for a moment. "I told her it was a mistake to meddle, but you know Sarah. She's got her share of the family stubbornness."

He had to smile. "She always did. It's okay. I'm sorry you got caught in the middle."

"That's where we belong, according to Sarah." They started walking slowly toward the house, and Michael caught the sound of spring peepers from the direction of the creek. "She… We're sorry it didn't turn out better."

"If Sarah's blaming herself, she shouldn't. Tell her so from me, okay?"

Lige nodded. "Won't do any gut, but I'll try."

He should have thought of the effect on his sister. She'd always tried to be a buffer between him and Daad, and she'd just ended up getting pushed by both sides. "Maybe, if the cops hadn't shown up, things between me and Daad might have improved." He wanted to relay something positive to his sister. "As it is…at least he seemed to take to Allie."

"That's certain sure." Lige sounded relieved. "Well, how could he resist his own granddaughter? Ruthie's already got him around her little finger, and Allie will be just the same. That is, if you're okay with him seeing her." Lige's glance was questioning.

The thought of refusing was tempting for about

ten seconds before he knew he couldn't. "I'd be a pretty poor excuse for a father if I tried to deny Allie a grandfather, wouldn't I?"

"If you were looking for a way to get back at your daad, that'd be one. I'm wonderful glad you won't, though. Makes it easier for us."

True enough, but he was thinking of Allie. Her life had been empty of relatives until he'd brought her home to River Haven.

"I know what it means to Allie to have aunts and uncles and cousins around." It was the sort of thing an Amish child took for granted. "I'm fine with her seeing Daad."

"Gut." Lige seemed to relax. "That was what Sarah wanted to know, because your daad asked if she'd bring Ruthie and Allie over sometime this week after school. Okay?"

Michael nodded. He'd said what his conscience insisted on, but that didn't mean he felt any differently toward his father. If he'd ever tried to understand his son…

But that was past. Wasn't he just wishing he could leave the past behind him?

They were getting closer to the back porch, and he slowed his steps deliberately. There were things he needed to know about Diana's family, and Lige might have some of the answers.

"I remember you told me about Diana's grandmother being in the nursing home. Do you know if she's…well, still there mentally?"

"So I've heard." Lige chuckled. "In fact, word

is she didn't want to move out of her house and she practically disowned her grandson for pushing it."

"Why did she leave, then?" From what he remembered of Diana's grandmother, she wasn't one to give in. She could give his daad lessons in stubbornness.

"Don't know, exactly. I suppose if Bernard had her doctor and her lawyer on his side, he'd get his way."

Michael could hear the distaste in Lige's voice. He'd never think of such a thing. Folks took care of their parents and grandparents in his world.

"So Bernard and his wife are living in the Wilcox house now?"

Lige nodded. "They've had some work done on it. I saw the trucks there when I went past one day. Bernard's heading up the family businesses, so I guess it's right that he take over the property."

"He can't be pleased that I've come back to River Haven to live. Reminding him."

"I guess not." Lige eyed him. "What are you thinking?"

"Just wondering if Bernard is behind the police taking so much interest in me right now." They came to a stop at the porch steps, where warm yellow light spilled out from the kitchen.

Lige considered. "Could be, I guess. But I don't see what you can do about it."

"Neither do I. Yet."

But he would.

HOLDING ALLIE'S HAND on Monday after school, Cathy headed for the familiar path home. She had been glad that it worked out so that yesterday was an off-Sunday. The intrusion of the police into the work frolic had focused attention on Michael's return—too much attention for comfort. A worship Sunday would have given the entire community an occasion to talk about it.

She glanced down at the child. "What did you do yesterday, since it wasn't church Sunday?"

"We had a picnic at Aunt Sarah's. Onkel Lige made hamburgers on the grill. And afterward we had s'mores." She had a satisfied smile. "It was easier than when we have church."

Cathy chuckled. "I suppose so. Was it hard to sit still for so long in church last Sunday?"

Allie seemed to consider whether she should be honest. "A little bit," she said at last.

"When I was your age, I thought the benches got harder and harder. When I got the wiggles, my mamm would do something to distract me."

"Like what?"

Allie sounded so interested that she suspected Verna hadn't anticipated the needs of an eight-year-old. "Well, she'd make a little doll for me out of a handkerchief—like a baby in a cradle. I could play with it."

"Do you think Aunt Verna knows how to do that?"

Cathy smiled. "If she doesn't, I'll show her how. All right?"

Allie nodded. "I liked the songs, but I didn't know the words like everybody else."

"You'll remember them soon enough. Some we

sing every time, so they'll be easier. And you're wonderful good at remembering."

"Like spelling words," she said. She grew silent, her face somber, as if remembering something unhappy. "Did those policemen think that Daadi was the one who pushed Mommy down the stairs?"

For a moment Cathy was too stunned to reply. Did Michael realize that Allie knew how Diana had died? She'd certainly had the impression that he'd tried to protect Allie from the details of her mother's death.

Allie was looking at her, expecting an answer. She had to say something. "What makes you think that was what happened to Mommy?"

"I'm not supposed to know. When I stayed with Mr. Alan and Ms. Beth, they pretended everything was okay. But I heard them talking when they thought I was asleep."

Cathy wasted a moment on hopeless anger at someone who'd allow a child to hear something that upsetting. Why hadn't they taken precautions?

Too late for that now, and she had to deal with the question. And while remembering her promise never to lie to Allie.

What would Michael think? Well, no matter how angry it made him, she couldn't fob Allie off with feeble excuses or outright lies. And surely, knowing as much as she apparently did, it was better for Allie to talk about it than hoard it to brood over.

"I think the police are still trying to find out what happened to your mommy. So they wanted to ask your daadi some more questions. Just in case he remembered something else."

Allie frowned. "Didn't he tell them what he remembered before? He went to help the police. That's why I stayed with Mr. Alan and Ms. Beth."

"People can remember something long afterward."

"Mostly I forget things after a long time."

This was proving a lot harder than she'd anticipated, especially since she kept seeing Michael's face, his eyes glaring at her. She scoured her brain for an example.

"Once when I was a little older than you are, my daadi came in the house carrying a piece of torn-off paper with a star on it. I hadn't thought about it in months, but all of a sudden I remembered that I had been carrying my arithmetic test home from school a long time earlier. I was so eager to show Mammi that I took a shortcut across the field where the bull was. He chased me, and I had to run as fast as I could to get away. I was so relieved to be safe that I never even thought about my paper, until Daadi found it stuck on a raspberry bramble."

Allie had listened intently, but Cathy suspected she was more interested in the bull than the point of the story.

"I wouldn't go in a field with a bull. No matter what." Her tone was emphatic.

Maybe it was just as well. At least she was distracted from the subject of the police.

"Do you think Daadi remembered anything?"

Apparently she'd been wrong. Cathy chose her words carefully. "I don't know. You could ask him."

That didn't seem to satisfy her. Allie walked in silence for a few more minutes. When she did speak, she didn't look at Cathy. "I might remember something."

It took her breath away for an instant. Then she tried to respond calmly. "If you do, you should tell Daadi about it."

"Even if he doesn't like to talk about what happened?"

Feeling she was in over her depth, Cathy could only respond in the way that seemed right. "Even then. Talking to Daadi is the best thing you could do."

As if she'd called him, Michael appeared around the bend in the path, coming to meet them. Allie darted on ahead to greet him. Cathy reached them in time to hear the end of what Allie was saying.

"...said that the policeman just wanted to know if you remembered anything else. That's all."

To her surprise, Michael didn't seem to resent what he might see as her interference. Maybe he realized it had been important to explain and reassure Allie. "She did, did she? That's good."

"Allie asked me," Cathy added, wanting him to understand how it had come about.

"I see." He shot her a grateful look before turning back to his daughter. "How about running ahead and seeing if Onkel Lige is waiting for me? I need to speak to Teacher Cathy."

Allie nodded, always glad to have an errand, and ran off.

"I didn't bring it up," Cathy said once Allie was out of hearing. "I'm sure you've already explained it to her, but she seemed to need a little more reassurance." She paused. "She's coping with it, you know. I don't think you need to worry too much about her reactions."

His jaw tightened. "Worrying seems to come with the territory. I never know whether it's better to try and explain or to say as little as possible."

"It is difficult," she admitted. "But I think it's best to assume she needs reassurance." She hesitated, realizing there was something she needed to bring up, even if it was difficult. "Did you realize that Allie knows how Diana died?"

"What?" His dark brows drew together in a fierce frown. "What are you talking about? She doesn't know anything about it. Don't you think I was careful?"

"I'm sure you were." She spoke as cautiously as if she were treading on ice. "But someone wasn't. She says she heard Mr. Alan and Ms. Beth talking about it. That's the friend who came to see you, isn't it?"

He nodded, his face grim. "I thought they had better sense. If she knows..."

"If she knows, you have to talk to her. It isn't good for a child to be holding on to something that scary."

"No." For an instant the muscles of his face quivered. "I was so sure. Stupid of me, I guess."

She hated to see him beat himself up over his parenting. He'd been put in a situation she couldn't even imagine. "You were doing your best."

"It wasn't good enough." The anger in his voice was all for himself.

"All anyone can do is their best." She knew how trite it sounded even as she said it. Why couldn't she find the words that would help him? Worse, she had to go on and tell him the rest of it—the thing that Allie only hinted at.

"Michael, that's not all. She said… She implied, anyway, that she remembered something she hasn't talked about. I told her she should tell you."

He stared at her. "Impossible. She's just a child. She couldn't know anything, because she wasn't there. Diana had taken her to Alan and Beth's for the night. And if she did, she'd have said…" That trailed off, as if he knew it wasn't true even as the words came out.

Cathy hesitated, but she had to tell him why Allie was so compelled to keep silent. Even though she knew it would hurt him.

"She won't say anything because she's sure you don't want to talk about it."

He didn't want to accept it—she could see the struggle in his face. "She can't…" The words trailed off into silence, and her heart hurt for him.

"Allie isn't unusual in reacting that way." She forced herself to sound calm, even detached. He'd take it better that way. "Small children often hide things they don't understand, worrying but not able to say it out loud for fear of making things worse. Anyone who works with children would tell you that. What they imagine is often worse than the truth."

"In this situation, the truth is surely worse."

"Perhaps. But if she knows a little, she probably needs to hear an explanation from you. Not details, of course, but enough to feel there's not something worse lurking in the shadows."

They walked on in silence, and she began to think he'd forgotten she was there, deep as he was in his own thoughts.

But when they reached the fork in the path and she started for home, he caught her arm.

"Wait a second."

He looked so fierce she thought he intended to yell at her.

"I should go..." she began.

"Just wait a second." He seemed to be coming to a conclusion. "Allie talks to you." He grimaced. "Sometimes I think better than she does to me. I think you'd better be the one to ask her what she remembers." He looked at her with a mix of hope and discomfort, as if he wasn't used to asking for help.

The thought was overwhelming. "Are you sure?"

"I'm not sure of anything just now. I had no idea she knew anything about how Diana died. If there's more she's holding back, I have to know, so I can deal with it." His jaw clenched until she thought it would break. "Please, Cathy."

Her heart twisted. She was the one God had put in this place, so she had to do what she could. "Yah, if you think it will help."

"Good. I'll get Allie. Meet us at the bench by the greenhouse." He strode off as if determined to get it over with as quickly as possible.

Cathy stood where she was for a moment, trying to collect her thoughts, but they scattered in all directions. What was she thinking to take this on? And yet how could she have refused? With a silent plea for guidance, she walked toward the greenhouses.

Lige was busy in the first of the greenhouses, so it was simple to slip around to the bench without being noticed. Not that she wanted to hide from Lige, but the upcoming talk with Allie would be difficult enough without the need to make conversation with Lige when she was already so nervous.

She reached inside herself for the calm core. She'd been put into this situation for a reason, she reminded herself. Anytime that she could help a child, she had to do it. She'd been given this gift, and it was meant to be used for others.

Michael was back almost before Cathy had time to take a few deep breaths. Allie skipped alongside, holding his hand. When she saw Cathy, she scurried ahead and jumped onto the bench next to her.

"Daadi said you wanted to ask me something, Teacher Cathy."

At the sight of the trusting little face, her courage almost failed her. Almost, but not quite. "Daadi and I were talking, Allie. He didn't mean for you to think that you couldn't talk to him about when your mommy died."

Allie shot a questioning look from her to Michael. She'd been afraid the child would be angry that she'd told Michael, but she didn't seem to be angry—just uncertain.

Michael responded, sitting down on the other side of Allie and taking her hand. "That's right. You can talk to me or to Teacher Cathy about anything, and we'll try to answer."

He glanced at Cathy, seeming to hand the ball over to her.

Swallowing to ease the tight muscles in her throat, Cathy put her arm around Allie. "Do you remember anything from that day, Allie?"

Again that uncertain glance. But whatever she saw in Michael's face must have reassured her. She nodded. "I remember everything."

"Do you? What did you do in the morning?" It was in her mind to take her through the day first, just to get her talking.

"I got up when the clock rang, and I got ready for school. And Mommy said hurry or I'd miss the bus, so I went out front."

"Did the bus pick you up in front of your house?"

Allie nodded. "It picked up me and Kristin and Jamie from across the street."

"Did you have a good day at school?" At least she seemed to be talking easily. She leaned against Cathy, her head against Cathy's arm.

"It was okay. I like our school better."

Her heart warmed at the sweet thought, but they were approaching what might be a dangerous point. "So after school you rode the bus back home, I guess."

"Yah. When I got in the house, Mommy was sweeping the rug, but she stopped then. She said..." She frowned, as if with an effort to get it right. "She said I was going to go to Mr. Alan and Ms. Beth's house for the night, so I should get ready."

"Did you like to go to Mr. Alan and Ms. Beth's house to stay over?"

She nodded, wiggling a little closer. "They're nice. Ms. Beth likes to play Chutes and Ladders with me. We had supper, and Ms. Beth fixed hot dogs 'cause she knows I like them. And then Mr. Alan had to go out. But Ms. Beth and me played games until bedtime, so that was okay." She was still for a moment and Cathy waited, giving her time to say anything else she wanted.

Nothing. Was it because she didn't want to talk about what happened the next day?

Michael cleared his throat, as if he found it hard to speak. "Did Mommy say why you were going to spend the night?"

Allie shook her head, but intuition told Cathy there was something else. "I'll bet you guessed, though, didn't you?"

"I thought she was going to have company. Sometimes she did. And that day she'd fixed her hair and put on a new sweater, and when Mr. Alan picked me up he laughed and asked if she had a date."

Something seemed to have frozen inside Cathy. Michael had never given any hint that there had been someone else in Diana's life.

She risked a sidelong glance at him and winced. Michael looked as if someone had hit him with a two-by-four.

Allie glanced at them, as if thinking they didn't believe her. "Mommy did have company sometimes."

"Of course she did," Cathy said, finding her voice with an effort. "Did you see any of her company?"

"Sometimes." Allie's face eased, as if reassured that it was all right. "Ms. Beth and Ms. Barbara came for coffee, and they sat in the kitchen and talked, but I didn't stay overnight then." She paused. "One time I was looking out the window at Ms. Beth's and I saw someone, but I didn't know him. So maybe he was selling something."

"You're sure you didn't know him?" Michael's voice had roughened with emotion, and Allie squeezed closer to Cathy.

She hugged the child, sending a warning look at Michael. "It's okay, Allie. Daadi isn't mad."

"No, no, for sure I'm not mad." He put his arm around Allie, too, so that their arms crossed each other, holding her snugly between them. "I just wondered if it were someone I knew. Did you see what he looked like?"

But Allie seemed to have run out of surprises. She shrugged. "Just ordinary." She wiggled again as if to get down this time. "Aunt Verna has lemonade and snickerdoodles today."

"You wouldn't want to miss those." She dropped a light kiss on Allie's forehead. "I'm wonderful glad you talked to me."

"Me, too." Allie slid down, then gave Cathy a throttling hug. "Do you want some snickerdoodles?"

"Not today. My mamm is waiting for me to help her make rhubarb sauce. Another day."

Allie nodded. "Daadi?"

"I'll be there in a minute, pumpkin. Save a cookie for me, okay?"

"Okay." Allie ran toward the house. Maybe it was Cathy's imagination, but it seemed to her that something had lifted from the child's mind.

Unfortunately it had settled on Michael's now, and he understood what it might mean.

"I'm sorry," she said softly, thinking how much he must hate having that come out in front of her. "It might be nothing at all."

His face twisted. "Would you believe I never thought of it? Seems so obvious now. The whole thing—saying we needed time apart, insisting I move out—she'd met someone she liked better, that's all."

"Michael, you don't know that." She put her hand over his to find it clenched into a tight fist.

"What else could it be? I was so blind. Don't you see? If she was expecting company that night, he must have been the person who killed her."

Her first instinct was to wince away from his words, but she couldn't. She couldn't pretend she hadn't heard any of this—she was too involved now to draw back.

And if Diana had been expecting a man—a lover—that night, who else could have killed her? It hadn't been Michael, so that left only her mysterious visitor.

"You should tell the police…" she began.

“I can’t. I can’t let them start questioning Allie. Think what that might do to a child.”

He was right. The detectives would never take Michael’s word for it. They’d insist on talking to Allie, putting her right in the middle, with what could be terrible consequences.

“But if you don’t tell them, he’ll get away with it.”

His face hardened, and he wrapped his hand around hers, holding it so tightly it seemed she could feel the pulse thudding in angry beats. “That’s not all. If the police find out there was someone else, they’ll say it gives me a perfect motive for doing away with her.”

CHAPTER TWELVE

As soon as he'd said the words, Michael realized the full implication. He was trapped. He could see a possible way out of the nightmare and at the same time see it was closed to him.

"Surely it's better to speak the truth about it. If you hide this from the police, they may never know what really happened."

"They're not interested in what really happened." He spoke from the depths of his bitterness. "All that detective wants is enough evidence to take to trial. He doesn't care about truth."

"Ach, Michael, that can't be true. He's the police—he's supposed to find out what really happened."

"You don't know—how could you?" Cathy was way out of her depth. No one here could understand—and certainly not his father. He sent a fleeting regret after the possibility of a reconciliation with the old man. "You've been sheltered from that side of life. You don't know what trouble is."

Cathy's gentle face tightened in a rebuke. "Trouble comes to everyone, Michael. You know that. The Amish aren't immune. We just have to trust."

"Trust?" Anger swept over him. "Who am I going

to trust? Diana, who betrayed me? All the friends who turned their backs on me? My father? Him least of all."

"You might trust God."

He made a short angry gesture. "I don't want to hear about it. I'm not that naive any longer."

Cathy paled, and he knew he'd hurt her. "You say that everyone has let you down. You're forgetting the ones who didn't—the people who tried to help. The ones who welcomed you back."

Shame battled with anger. It wasn't fair to take out his feelings on Cathy. And she was right. "All right. I'm sorry. Not everybody. Not you, or Verna, or Sarah and Lige. But my own father—he's so stubborn he can't let go of anything. You don't know what it's like."

Answering anger sparked in Cathy's eyes. "You blame your father for being stubborn, but you're just as bad. You don't give anyone a chance to help you. You push people away because you're so sure you know what's best."

The words struck at his heart. Had he really been doing that? He hadn't wanted to put his burdens onto other people. He wanted to protest that it was necessary, but he wasn't sure that was true.

"You don't understand." He put his hand over hers, wanting her to see it from his perspective. But something happened when his fingers closed over her wrist. He felt her pulse fluttering against his hands, her warmth against his skin.

That warmth spread from his palm, radiating up

his body until it enveloped his heart. He warned himself to look away, but he couldn't. His eyes met hers, and he sank in the clear blue depths.

Cathy's breath caught. Awareness of him filled her face. The surroundings faded until he couldn't see anything else.

Without thought, he bent toward her. Their lips met, and the longing to be closer overwhelmed him. He slid his arms around her, and she came willingly, clinging to his shoulders. Trusting him.

Trusting. The word acted like a bucket of cold water in his face. He pulled away, leaving her dazed, her eyes wide and her lips parted.

He couldn't. Cathy trusted him. He couldn't give in to the longing to accept all the warmth and caring of her generous heart. Not when he knew there was no possible future for them.

He shot off the bench, grappling for control. "I'm sorry. That was a mistake."

"Michael." Her voice was gentle. Soft. As soft as her lips under his.

"It didn't feel like a mistake." He thought there was a smile in her voice.

"It was." He was at the end of his tether. He might long for a different answer, but there wasn't one. "Go home, will you?" His voice broke on the words. He wanted to hang on to her, to share everything with her, good and bad. But he couldn't put that onto her. Maybe, someday, but not when Diana's murder loomed over him.

He couldn't look at her, but he felt her movement

as she stood. She took a few steps away and then stopped, maybe waiting for him to speak.

Clamping his jaw, he walked away. When he reached the corner of the house, he looked back. She was gone.

CATHY HAD NEARLY covered the distance home before her numbed senses began to register the world around her. She couldn't let her mother see her, not until she'd recovered a little. Her skin, her lips were burning. Her mother would see something was very wrong in an instant.

Emerging from the band of trees, Cathy crossed the open space to the barn, standing still for a moment to let her eyes adjust to the dim interior. Blackie, one of the buggy horses, whickered a soft greeting.

She patted him automatically. She must still look and smell the same to him, even though she felt like an entirely different person than she'd been this morning.

Not that she hadn't been kissed before. But none of those hurried, fumbling kisses had made her yearn to repeat the procedure. Even the boy she'd had a teen-age crush on had left her feeling unmoved when he'd finally kissed her—especially when he'd attempted to put his hands on her breasts. She'd smacked his face and never felt a moment's regret.

Michael's embrace had been so different in its ef-fect on her that it seemed laughable to call it "just a kiss." It had been more, far more. The touch of his lips had brought an overmastering surge of longing and tenderness, a fierce need to be closer to him.

When Cathy thought of the way she'd responded to him, her cheeks began to burn again. She should be ashamed—but she wasn't, not in the least. Not until he'd pushed her away so abruptly.

She leaned her head against the rough wood of a stall upright, and Blackie craned his head around the corner to butt at her gently.

"Ach, you're a greedy one. I don't have anything for you, not now."

Greedy—was that what Michael thought she was? A woman greedy for male attention and willing to sacrifice her self-control to get it?

Instinct denied it. He was trying to protect her from involvement in his ugly situation. Didn't he see that she was already involved? Even if he'd repelled her, she couldn't have stayed aloof, not when a child's health and happiness were at stake.

He'd made his wishes plain by pushing her away. He didn't want anything between them. Nothing but her help with Allie, that is. So all she could do was accept it. She'd have to put these unfamiliar emotions aside and do what she could for the child.

Cathy patted Blackie again and headed toward the house. Mammi undoubtedly had plenty of work waiting for her. Work was surely the best cure for her bruised heart.

She walked into the kitchen to find the room hot and steamy. The water bath canner could be counted on to produce plenty of heat and humidity. Mammi, turning to greet her, was red and perspiring.

Cathy hurried to wash her hands. “Looks like you need a rest. You sit down and I’ll take over.”

“I have a better idea.” Clutching the pot holders, Mammi slid the canner off the burner. “We’ll both work on the last batch, and then we’ll both take a rest. You can start ladling that rhubarb sauce into jars.”

Cathy suffered a pang of guilt. She should have been home earlier to help her mother, but how could she? Allie’s confidences had required immediate action. If she’d felt able to explain, Mammi would have sympathized, she felt sure.

Working together, the chore went quickly. Mamm already had rows of rhubarb sauce finished, the glass jars glowing a deep pink where the afternoon sun touched them. Cathy ladled, capped and put jars into the canner rack before lifting it into the still-hot canner. A pressure canner would do the job more quickly, but Mamm clung to the way her mother had taught her.

She smiled slightly, thinking of her oldest sister. Mary took pride in doing things the way their mother had taught them, but she’d noticed a brand-new pressure canner the last time she’d been in Mary’s kitchen.

“What’s funny?” Mamm asked, glancing at the clock to time the load.

“Nothing. Just thinking of Mary and wondering how she’s doing with her new pressure canner.”

“Ach, she was just raving about it to me this

morning. Insists I should get one, but I'll stick to the way I know. I wouldn't trust that thing not to explode all over the kitchen."

"I don't think it'll do that, as long as Mary is careful."

Her mother sniffed. Apparently Mary had been urging the virtues of her new canner a little too fervently. She never had figured out when it was best to stop giving advice.

"We'll let those jars sit awhile before we move them to the shelves." Mammi put the pot holders she'd been using handily on the counter. "Let's take some lemonade out on the porch and relax."

"You go ahead. I'll bring it. I haven't done my share yet."

Mammi gave in, departing for the shade of the porch swing. Cathy poured glasses of cold lemonade, congratulating herself on giving nothing away. No one needed to know how she'd let herself be carried away.

Taking the glasses, she headed for the porch. She had no more than sat down when her mother spoke.

"Now, then, tell me what is wrong."

She'd congratulated herself too soon. "Nothing. Why do you think that?"

"Komm, now." Mammi put her hand over Cathy's. "Do you think I don't know when one of my kinder has trouble? Something has happened to disturb you today. Tell me."

Cathy's throat tightened, but she managed to

smile. "And you'll fix it? I don't think you can make this better."

"When your kinder are small, they have small troubles. When they get big, the problems get big as well. You'll still feel better when you talk about it."

She pressed her fingers against her forehead, trying again to collect herself. She'd have to tell her mother something, if not all of it.

"Is it Allie?" Mamm asked. "I know you worry about the poor child."

"Partly," she admitted.

"Ah." Mammi studied her face. "Allie and someone else, too. Michael Forster, yah?"

"In a way." What could she say? Not everything Allie had told them, certainly. "Allie has been opening up to me when we walk home from school together. It's gut for her, I think. She holds too much inside."

"Yah. And she doesn't have a mammi to know."

Somehow Cathy didn't think that Diana had been a mother to confide in, but that was only a guess. "She said something that led me to believe that her mother might have been seeing some man."

Mammi nodded, not even seeming surprised.

"I thought…well, that Michael had to be told. It could be important in clearing himself."

"Yah, I see that. You did the right thing, so that would not be troubling you. There's more." She held Cathy's hand tightly. "You care for him, ain't so?"

Cathy couldn't look at her, knowing it would hurt her. Staring down at their clasped hands, she nodded.

Her mother was silent, so Cathy rushed into

speech. "Don't be worried. He doesn't feel anything. And even if he cared, he wouldn't want to involve me in his troubles, and I'll have to accept that fact."

"Are you sure about his feelings?"

That wasn't a question she'd anticipated her mother asking, and for an instant she was speechless. "I… Sometimes I've thought that he cares." She heard the yearning in her voice. "But I must be wrong. He just appreciates my help with his daughter, that's all."

But that kiss—didn't it mean anything?

"Ach, Cathy, is it so strange that a man should care for you?" Mammi's tone was gently scolding, and Cathy met her eyes with a sense of surprise.

"It's not what I would choose for you," her mother went on. "It would come with troubles, that's certain sure. But I don't like to hear you thinking you're not worthy of a man's love."

"I don't. I mean… I don't think I feel that. It's just best not to wish for something I can't have." She'd been sure her mother was the last person on earth to encourage such a course.

"So you are giving up. You didn't give up on your teaching just because of obstacles, ain't so? You should have more trust in your own judgment."

"I do," she protested.

Her mother shook her head. "It is my fault. You were my baby, and I knew there would be no more after you. And your big sisters didn't help—they thought they were taking care of you, but they were quick to do things for you that you should have done for yourself."

It wasn't at all funny, but she couldn't help smiling. "You mean I grew up lazy?"

"Ach, no." Mamm gave her a quick hug. "I mean you don't have enough confidence in your own self. You have grown up to be a fine woman. Just don't let other people tell you what you should feel—not even the ones who love you. Listen to your own heart. Promise me."

"I'll try." It was hard to speak around the lump in her throat. "Denke, Mammi."

Her mother had given her a very different view of who she was. At least part of what she'd said was true, that was certain sure. Except when it came to anything affecting her pupils, she slipped away from disagreements, finding it easier to go along.

Standing up for yourself was not something integral to Amish beliefs—sacrificing yourself was. And even if Mamm was right, she didn't quite see what she could do about it. Michael was out of her reach, and most likely he always would be.

MICHAEL CAME DOWNSTAIRS dressed in his English clothes that afternoon and saw the flash of fear in Aunt Verna's face. He should have realized—she'd taken his acceptance of dressing Plain as a sign he was staying.

"It's okay." He touched her arm lightly. "I want to see Diana's brother." He grimaced. "I figure I'll get further this way."

The fear abated, but he could see she didn't like it. "Isn't it best to leave well enough alone? We don't want him to start bothering us."

"If he hired that private investigator, he's already doing it."

"Ach, Michael, let him be. Nothing good comes of going up against that family."

He'd forgotten the way most people in River Haven regarded the Wilcox family. The people who lived in the big house, the ones who controlled the biggest payroll in town…even their friends had always trodden softly. But he'd been too long in the wider world to fall in line with that attitude.

"If he hired the man who was prowling around the school, I'm not taking that quietly. He has to be told to stay away from Allie."

She nodded, but with a little doubt still in her eyes. "Yah, that was wrong. But what can you gain by antagonizing the man?"

"Don't worry, I'm not intending to start a fight." He gave her a reassuring pat and headed for the door.

"Promise you won't lose your temper." She made a last effort to affect what she seemed to see coming.

"I'll try." He made his escape before she could demand something more definitive than that.

Funny, how strange it seemed to be behind the wheel of a car again. Even after such a short time, it felt strange.

He took the road toward town, careful to stay within the speed limit. Guy would like nothing better than to give him a ticket.

Keeping his mind focused on what he was going to say to Bernard Wilcox was an antidote to thinking about Cathy and what had happened between them. The trouble was that once he let her in, he couldn't keep from reliving those moments.

Not that reliving them helped him make any sense of his actions. As soon as he pictured Cathy in his mind he felt her kiss, saw the dazed look in her eyes.

He swore softly to himself. The best thing he could do for Cathy and for himself was to stay away from her. Since that was impossible, he'd have to make sure nothing of the sort ever happened again. There was no room in his heart for another woman.

He forced himself to itemize the changes in Main Street since he'd left town. There weren't many. River Haven, like a lot of long-established small towns, resisted change. The only grocery store in town was the small, locally owned one. If people wanted a supermarket or a big-box store, they drove several miles to the strip development on the highway.

The river made its way through town, defining the limits of development. The town was here because of the river—the early settlers came by boat, picking the wide, shallow curve of the Susquehanna River as a good place to settle, accessible by river and later by canals before the railroad was even thought of.

He had to turn off Main Street to reach the mill, assuming that Bernard would be in the company offices there. Despite the changes in manufacturing and trade, the mill managed to keep going, switching from one product to another as demand changed.

Bernard could easily afford to retire, but from what Michael had known of the man, it wouldn't suit him to see someone else in his position.

Funny, in a way. Bernard had nearly twenty years or so to get used to his position as the heir apparent when Diana came along—the baby no one had anticipated. Her grandparents had doted on her, and Michael had just begun to realize how much her leaving must have devastated them. It took maturity and having a child of his own to make him empathize.

The mill spread out over several acres at the lower end of town, where the river curved. It looked much as it always had, but the section that housed the offices was new and modern in comparison to the rest.

Cars filled the fenced-in lot devoted to employee parking, but a little farther on was a strip of eight spaces designated for visitors. He pulled in and parked, sitting for a moment to assemble his thoughts.

Hold on to his temper, that was the main thing. Express his concern about an outsider spying on the Amish school. He didn't see how anyone could take offense at that, not that he really cared whether Bernard was offended or not. But for Verna's sake, he'd try to keep it low-key.

He headed toward the entrance, trying to look like any ordinary visitor. Apparently Bernard wasn't worried about security, since there was no obvious precaution at the main door. A reception desk stood in the middle of the hall, ahead of the staircase. A quick glance at the list of offices showed him that the one he wanted was upstairs. The woman at the desk wore a harassed expression as she responded to the phone.

"Yes, yes, right away," she muttered before turning to him. "I'm so sorry. If you wouldn't mind waiting just a minute, I have to take care of this."

She was escaping toward a hallway as she spoke. Apparently taking his silence as assent, she sped off on her errand.

Michael didn't wait for her return. He went quickly up the stairs. Luck must be with him—he hadn't even thought of a reasonable excuse to get himself past the receptionist.

The first door he faced on the second floor bore frosted letters, Bernard Wilcox, President, Wilcox Industries. A few quick strides took him to the door. He opened it to find a very businesslike woman looking at him in a manner that suggested no one just walked into this office. "Yes?"

"I want to see Bernard Wilcox." Short and not so sweet.

"Do you have an appointment?" She didn't bother consulting an appointment calendar, so the answer was obvious.

"No. It's personal business."

"I see." Thinly arched eyebrows lifted. "Your name, please."

Would Bernard have cautioned her about him? Maybe or maybe not, but it wasn't a secret.

"Michael Forster." His brother-in-law, he didn't add.

"Just one moment, please." She'd kept her polite

demeanor, but she obviously knew who he was. "I'll see if Mr. Wilcox is free."

He beat her to the door by a hair, not wanting to take the chance of being escorted out before he'd seen Bernard. "He'll see me," he said and opened the door.

Behind a massive desk, Diana's brother looked up with a frown that turned to alarm. "What do you mean by walking into my office?" He rose to his feet as he asked the question, a paunchy, slightly balding man who carried an air of affronted dignity at the moment.

"We need to talk." Michael moved forward until only the broad expanse of the desk stood between them.

"I have nothing to say to you. Ms. Thatcher, call security."

"I already have, sir." She didn't sound particularly alarmed, but she knew her job. Or maybe just her employer.

"Then I'll talk fast." Michael planted his fists on the desk. "The investigator you hired has been snooping around the Amish school."

"How… What makes you think I did anything of the kind?"

So he'd guessed right. Bernard had nearly asked how he knew.

"The Amish school is out-of-bounds. And so is my daughter. He can poke around my life all he wants—he won't find anything. Just keep him away from the children."

Bernard's face flushed. "You killed my sister.

There's proof somewhere, even if the police are too stupid to find it."

"Did it ever occur to you that there's no evidence against me because I'm innocent?"

No, it clearly hadn't. Nor anyone else, it seemed.

Before he could say another word, he was seized from behind by two beefy security guards. Exercising more control than he'd thought he had, he didn't struggle. He let them propel him to the door, where he stopped short, giving himself a moment for another word.

"Stay away from my child, Wilcox."

They hustled him out. Well, he'd had his say, and a fat lot of good it had done him. Still, there was a certain amount of satisfaction in letting Wilcox know he knew.

By the time they got downstairs, Chief Jamison was coming in the front door. He surveyed Michael and nodded to the guards.

"Okay, boys. I'll see Mr. Forster out."

They walked out together, with Jamison not even going through the motions of taking his arm. Apparently the chief didn't see him as a threat.

They walked in silence to Michael's car, where Jamison leaned casually against the door. "Making yourself unpopular, aren't you?"

He shrugged. "I've never needed to try with the Wilcox family."

"True enough, but what did you hope to gain by charging into Bernard's office, other than to get kicked out?"

Michael's fists clenched. "He hired a private investigator who's been snooping around. He was probably the person spying on the Amish school."

"You have any proof of that?"

"Not that he was the man at the school," he admitted. "But I was told about the private investigator by one of my neighbors in Harrisburg. And the man actually stopped Cathy on her way home from school and tried to question her. But can you think of a better explanation for the guy at the school?"

Jamison shrugged. "I don't see what he'd hope to gain by doing that."

"I don't either, but I don't want anyone like that around my child."

The chief was silent for a moment before he gave Michael a sharp glance. "You think he wanted to question little Allie?"

Michael shrugged, wishing he'd avoided any hint of that. "That's the only reason I can come up with. It wouldn't do them any good anyway. Allie wasn't there when it happened."

"I know."

Of course he'd know. He'd probably made himself familiar with every aspect of the case.

"Did the cops in Harrisburg talk to her?"

"Certainly not. Do you think I'd let them upset her? She's had a hard enough time losing her mother without being asked a lot of questions she can't answer."

"It's probably just as you say." Jamison's tone was mild. "Still, there might be a way of having someone she trusts talk to her without upsetting her."

That was so close to what had actually happened that he could only pray his face didn't betray him. Jamison saw too much. That soft-spoken way he had got under a man's guard.

His mind flickered briefly to the man Allie had glimpsed. Would it do any conceivable good for Jamison to know about it? He couldn't see how. The chances that the man could be identified by a child's tentative impression were slim to none. All it would do was give a motive for him to have a violent argument with Diana.

"Well?"

He'd been unresponsive for too long, and that in itself must have roused the chief's suspicions.

"Allie's finally recovering from what happened. I'm not going to risk that to satisfy somebody's curiosity." He reached past the chief to grab the car door handle.

"Okay, okay." Jamison moved away from the car. "Just one thing." He put a hand on the door as Michael started to open it. "I'll look into this private cop business. If someone like that is in my town, I want to know it. Meantime, you stay away from Bernard Wilcox." He moved back with a fraction of a smile. "I've got better things to do with my time."

Michael got in the car with an unexpected sense of satisfaction. He'd gained nothing from Bernard, and if anything, just put him on his guard. But Chief Jamison showed a surprising willingness to look at matters with an open mind. Maybe that justified a glimmer of hope in a dark world.

CHAPTER THIRTEEN

By late afternoon, it seemed likely that everyone in the community had heard about Michael being kicked out of Wilcox's office. When the third person stopped at the nursery ostensibly to get plants but really to ask about it, even Aunt Verna's temper was growing short.

"Put up the closed sign," she snapped. "I've had enough of nosy folks with nothing to do but mind other people's business."

Michael pulled the sign into position. "I'm sorry. I didn't mean to cause problems."

"I told you..." She clamped her lips shut. "Ach, well, I guess you had to see the man, at least. Folks will get over it. So long as he doesn't mean to cause trouble."

"Most likely he doesn't want talk any more than we do." He expected that would be Bernard's attitude, but he couldn't know for sure.

Allie came running toward them then, putting an end to the conversation.

It was just as well, he guessed. There wasn't anything else he could say to reassure her, not that Verna was one to expect the impossible. If he'd realized how much trouble it would cause when he came back here, he'd have thought longer, though in the end he didn't see what else he could have done.

"Can I help with something, Daadi?" Allie looked at him hopefully. The past few evenings she'd helped him with some simple chores—the sort of thing an Amish child took for granted, and she seemed to love it. There was something to be said for expecting a child to participate in the work of the family.

"I'm thinking we should get the weeds out of the strawberry patch. How about giving me a hand?"

"Yah." She grabbed his hand. "Show me."

"Be sure he shows you which ones are the plants," Aunt Verna said, her good humor restored.

Allie nodded, understanding the message. "I'll be really careful."

Leading the way to the berry patch that spread behind the toolshed, Michael realized he'd begun to look forward to moments like these. Working side by side seemed to encourage sharing confidences, and he'd learned more about his small daughter in recent weeks than he had in all the time Diana was alive.

What had it been in Diana's nature that hadn't allowed her to share him with their own child? Or maybe it was that she hadn't wanted to share Allie with him. Either way, she'd arranged their lives to give him a minimal amount of time with Allie, and he hadn't even realized it until too late.

He should have, and he blamed himself as much as Diana. At least he had a second chance, and he was determined not to mess it up.

"This is easy," he said, kneeling at the first row of berry plants. "You can see which ones are the plants. See what the leaves look like? And there are the tiny berries, ready to get big and sweet."

"They're green." She touched a berry with her finger.

"That's because they're not ripe yet. When they're ready for us to pick, they'll be bright red."

"Like the ones in the stores." She nodded to show understanding.

"But better." He smiled at her. "You've never tasted anything sweeter than a fresh-picked berry. You'll see."

She looked a little doubting, but she nodded. "So I just pull up these little pieces of grass, ain't so?"

He nodded. "Everything except the berry plants." He started pulling the weeds, making a pile on the edge of the row.

"Okay." Allie worked steadily for a few minutes, her fingers nimble as she pulled grass from around the plants. Then…

"You didn't come to meet me and Teacher Cathy today," she said. "Why didn't you? We looked for you."

"Did you?" But it was Cathy he was thinking of. Had she looked for him?

"Yah. We wondered. Where were you?"

"Onkel Lige and I were working on the greenhouse. When we're up on the ladders it needs both of us."

Which was true enough, but not the reason he hadn't shown up. He'd been avoiding Cathy. That was the least he could do for her. He'd done enough damage with that kiss. Now it was up to him to make sure she understood that there wasn't anything between them.

Maybe he was flattering himself. Maybe she didn't think that at all, just that he'd been too forward and embarrassed her.

Either way, staying away from her was the only thing he could do.

"I like it when you meet me after school." Allie moved on to the next row. "And I like walking home with Teacher Cathy, too. We talk."

He could imagine Cathy drawing Allie out of her shyness. "I know. But school won't be in session for too much longer, you know," he pointed out. "Before you know it, you'll be on summer vacation."

Allie drooped—there was no other word for it. She looked like a plant without water. "I don't want it to be summer vacation. I'd rather be in school every day."

He couldn't recall ever feeling that way himself. "You'll like vacation. You'll have more time to play and to help around the greenhouse. I know you like to do that."

"Yah. But Ruthie..."

He should have realized seeing Ruthie every day was part of the appeal of school. "You'll still see a lot of Ruthie. I'll talk to Aunt Sarah and Onkel Lige about it. She can come over here and help, and you can go over to her house."

At least he hoped so. Sarah and Lige would understand why he couldn't just leave things alone, wouldn't they? Diana's death was hanging over his head like a heavy limb about to fall. He had to do what he could to avert disaster, even if it meant treading on toes.

"I want to see Cousin Ruthie. And my other friends. But mostly I'll miss Teacher Cathy." Her lower lip trembled. "I like it when we talk while we're coming home. She makes me feel…safe."

The word hit him in the heart. He'd known she was attached to Cathy. That was obvious. But by the look on her face, it was a lot more than that. She needed Cathy. She trusted her. She loved her.

He tried to swallow the lump in his throat. Allie hadn't had all that many people to love during her short life. Cathy was special. Maybe he'd been blinded by his own needs, but he knew that. Cathy was very lovable.

He needed to stay away from her, for both their sakes. But he couldn't deprive his daughter of someone who meant so much to her.

"Suppose we make sure you can see a lot of Teacher Cathy over the summer. Will that be okay?"

"Could I?" Her smile lit up her face. She didn't need any words to communicate how much it meant. Then she drooped again. "But how? If we don't have school…"

"Maybe we could ask Teacher Cathy to help you with something over the summer." He was fishing, looking for some way Allie could spend time with Cathy, even knowing the more he saw her the harder it would be to resist the strong appeal she had for him.

"Aunt Verna said she'd teach me to make a doll quilt this summer. Maybe Teacher Cathy could do that." Allie's eyes lit with her idea.

"Don't you think Aunt Verna would be disappointed if you didn't do the sewing with her?" he asked gently.

"Oh." He watched her process the thought. "I don't want to hurt Aunt Verna's feelings. Not for anything. But I *need* to see Teacher Cathy." Her lower lip trembled.

"We'll find something," he said, hurrying to avert tears. "Suppose we asked her to help you learn Pennsylvania Dutch? I know you've picked up a lot of words, but she could help you really understand and speak it."

"Yah, that's it." The threat of tears vanished. "Oh, Daadi, can we ask her? Will you explain so she'll want to do it?" Hands clasped together prayerfully, she looked at him.

He was a goner. He couldn't resist Allie, that was for sure. The question was, if life kept throwing them together, could he resist Cathy?

AT THE END of school the next day Cathy lingered a bit longer in the classroom than usual. Allie, bending over a picture she was drawing, was intent and occupied. Cathy slid a notebook into the canvas bag she carried back and forth and then took it out again. That wasn't the notebook she needed—she was getting absentminded.

That might do as an excuse, but the truth, if she

admitted to herself, was that her mind was on Michael. It was fruitless, but she couldn't seem to stop.

He hadn't shown up to meet them when she walked Allie home yesterday. Lying to herself would be foolish—she'd been disappointed. Chances were good he wouldn't be there today either. That kiss had changed everything between them.

Strange, that a kiss could have the power to turn life upside down. She'd known, in that moment, the thing she didn't want to admit. She loved Michael. Not in a comfortably caring kind of way either. This was the kind of loving that made her heart turn over at a touch, that made her willing to sacrifice for his well-being, even if she couldn't have him.

And she couldn't. Even if she'd been willing to give up her faith to marry him, which she wasn't, it wouldn't matter. Diana had apparently destroyed any possibility of his loving again.

She'd begun to think of Diana in that light—as someone who destroyed everything she touched. Being ashamed of her attitude didn't seem to help. She couldn't understand the woman, and she never would.

Cathy brushed a hand across her forehead in an attempt to chase away the idea. Moving slightly, her glance caught the window, startling her. The day, already cloudy, had darkened appreciably. If it was going to rain, she'd best get Allie home right away.

"Better put your crayons away, Allie. It looks as if rain is coming, so we must leave."

Allie looked as surprised as she had been, but she obediently started putting crayons back in the box.

The spelling book…she didn't need that, but she'd better take the upper grades history text home to plan for the next day. She reached for the spot where she normally kept it and realized that, with the perversity of inanimate objects, it had migrated to the edge of her desk. As she picked it up, her fingers touched a folded paper that lay beneath it.

Sliding the book into her bag, she flipped open the paper.

And froze. It wasn't a piece of schoolwork, as she'd supposed. It was a roughly printed message. An unsigned message.

Everyone knows about you and that man. He killed his wife. Stay away, or he'll do the same to you.

The paper slid from her fingers, closing to blank out the words. It didn't help. She could still see them—imprinted on her mind. Ugliness seeped from the words, staining everything it touched.

Who had done this? And how?

A rumble of thunder sparked a quick movement from Allie. "Teacher, the storm—"

"It's far away. We have time to get home." Reassuring Allie, she forced herself to pick up the paper and shove it in the bag. She couldn't leave it here for anyone to see. Little as she wanted to carry it with her, she'd have to consider the possibilities before setting a match to it.

"We'll go now," she said, grasping the big black

umbrella from the stand in the corner. "Do you have a sweater or jacket?"

"Yah." Allie scurried to get the dark sweater from the peg. She pulled it around herself as she followed Cathy out the door. A gust of wind caught it, and she had to struggle to pull it closed.

Cathy grasped Allie's hand and headed for the path. "We'll hurry, right?"

Allie nodded, trotting along next to her, seeming glad to cling to her hand. Not talking, they hurried their steps, and Cathy's thoughts hurried as well.

How had that ugly thing gotten into her schoolroom? It wasn't the work of a child—she was sure of that. The words and thoughts weren't those of a child, not even one of the older ones. Besides, she knew her scholars better than that.

Then who? And how did it get there? And more important at the moment, what should she do with it?

She thought, as always, of her parents, but she couldn't show it to them. It would upset them terribly, and although she'd often thought there was nothing Daadi couldn't handle, she knew this was beyond even his gentle wisdom.

The answer made her stomach twist. She should show it to Michael, even though it made her sick with shame at the thought of his seeing it.

She argued with herself. Maybe it would be best just to burn it and forget it. Except that she couldn't forget, not now that she'd seen it. Besides, it might be important in some way she couldn't know. What if it wasn't just a crank? What if it was somehow connected to everything else that had happened to Michael?

That was ridiculous, wasn't it? But much that had happened to Michael seemed impossible, and yet it happened.

They'd reached the band of trees. The wind, sweeping suddenly down the valley, sent the branches tossing, turning the leaves to show their paler undersides. Rain was coming—she could smell it in the air.

She glanced at Allie and paused for a moment. "Better put your arms into your sweater. The wind is chilly."

Allie hurried to obey, obviously not wanting to be outside a minute longer than necessary. "It's going to storm, isn't it? With lightning and thunder and rain." Fear was obvious in her words and her face.

"Ach, what's a little rain?" Cathy said, keeping her voice cheerful. "We aren't made of sugar. We won't melt even if we do get wet, ain't so?"

The idea of being made of sugar earned a giggle from Allie. She buttoned her sweater more cheerfully and then caught Cathy's hand again.

"Daadi says it will be school vacation soon," she volunteered.

"That's right. We have two and a half weeks of school left." And the school board still had made no move.

Maybe they'd made up their minds not to renew her contract and wanted to wait until school was out and tell her. That was a depressing thought.

"I asked Daadi about the summer vacation."

Something in Allie's voice snagged her attention. Allie was going somewhere with this conversation, so she needed to pay attention.

"Are you going to do something special after school is out?"

"Well, I asked… Daadi said… We thought maybe you'd help me with learning Pennsylvania Dutch this summer." She rushed to get it all out. "Will you, Teacher Cathy? Daadi said we'd see what you said, and I really want you to. Will you?" She stopped, tugging on Cathy's hand. "Please?"

Cathy could see the pleading in Allie's face and hear the need in her voice. It was the need that caught her heart in a bruising grip. Allie needed her. There was nothing for her and Michael, but his child needed her. If any child needed her, how could she refuse?

"If you want, I guess I could teach you that. Yah, Allie, I'd like that fine."

"Really?" Delight filled the child's face, and she threw her arms around Cathy. "Thank you, thank you."

Cathy managed a chuckle. "It won't all be fun, you know. You'll have to try hard to catch up."

"I will. I'll work really hard. I promise."

"All right. It's a deal." She unwound herself from Allie's arms to the sound of thunder—louder now. Much louder.

"No more talking now. We have to hurry."

It was when they started walking again that Cathy felt the strangeness. The electricity in the air, she told herself. *That's all it is.* But the fine hairs on the back of her neck rose, and a chill shivered down her back. It wasn't the storm. It was someone—someone watching her. Hating her.

Impossible. Her imagination was working overtime. She resisted the urge to rub the back of her neck—the longing to turn around and see if someone were behind them.

It didn't help. The feeling didn't leave. If anything, it intensified. She took a firm grasp on the handle of her umbrella. It was a good sturdy one, but could she really strike someone with it?

She believed wholeheartedly in nonviolence—it was bred in her. But if it were a question of keeping a child safe, she would do what she had to do.

A sound behind her—a dry branch breaking under an unwary foot. Her stomach twisted, but at least it told her the follower's location. Behind her and to the right—probably hidden behind that low growth of bushes along the edge of the path.

If he came out into the open—but it didn't seem he intended to. The faint rustling indicated he was moving along behind and to one side, staying in the shrubby growth, maybe not wanting to be identified if she looked back.

She wouldn't. Every instinct told her that if she showed awareness, it could drive him into action.

A spray of raindrops blew into her face. "Let's run," she said, her voice pitched above the noise of the wind and water. "See if you can get to the greenhouse first."

Pushing Allie gently ahead of her, Cathy gave her a head start—every muscle quivering with the effort to stand still even as the sound of footsteps, muffled by the wet grass, grew nearer. She had to stay between the follower and Allie—that was the thought that filled her mind. She had to.

"Here I come," she called to Allie, and put on a spurt of speed.

Her own footsteps made enough noise to cover the sound of pursuit, but he was there—she could sense it. The need to look back pressed on her nerves, but she didn't dare take her eyes from the wet path ahead of her. If she fell… If she fell, she couldn't protect Allie.

She had to. The refrain repeated itself to the sound of her feet. The path curved, and then she could see the greenhouse through the trees…could even see movement inside it.

Almost there…please, please… Allie ran into the open, laughing a little, not realizing anything was wrong. She'd reached the greenhouse. She was safe.

But the footsteps were close behind Cathy. She made a desperate effort. Once she was in the clear, she'd be all right. Something brushed her skirt—a hand? Fear gave wings to her feet, and she darted into the open, heading straight for the greenhouse and Michael's reassuring presence.

WHEN ALLIE CAME running to the greenhouse, Michael was waiting to swing her inside, wishing he'd sent her with a rain jacket. "About time you're getting here. You're wet."

"Not very." She grinned, seeming exhilarated

by the dash to escape the rain. "We ran fast. I beat Teacher Cathy."

"I see that. Hang your wet sweater over the chair, okay? We'll wait here until the rain stops."

Allie nodded, stripping the soggy sweater off as she headed to do as he'd said. He turned, frowning, toward the door. Surely Cathy would have had an umbrella?

She bolted through the door, grasping the umbrella as if it were a weapon. The look on her face chased everything else out of his mind.

"What's happened? You..."

"Hush," she murmured with a meaningful glance at Allie. Even with her face white and her hands shaking, she thought first of his child. He clasped her cold fingers in his.

"Quietly, then. Something's wrong." He kept his voice low, moving close enough to hear the slightest breath.

"Someone was chasing us." The whites of her eyes showed as she darted a look back at the path.

He gripped her hands firmly. "Are you sure it wasn't the noise of the storm?"

Cathy shivered. "I heard someone behind me. I didn't imagine it. He was there."

"Stay here," he ordered. Yanking the door open, he brushed away her attempts to stop him and raced toward the path.

Anger thudded through his body with every swift beat of his heart. Someone watching the school, following his child—it was too much. When he caught up with the man, he'd wish he'd taken up some other line of work.

It must be that private investigator—who else would it be? He'd settle with him. And then he'd settle with Bernard. They weren't getting away with this.

His clothes were soaked and clinging to his body by the time he reached the shelter of the trees. Not as noisy here, now that he couldn't hear the rain drumming on the glass panels. He stopped his headlong rush to listen intently.

Nothing. But the tall grass at the edge of the path had been flattened, as if someone or something had brushed through a moment ago. He surged after it, feet squelching on the wet ground.

The trail he was following ended where the trees were dense enough to discourage growth beneath their canopy. He paused again, scanning the area. Nothing that he could see. The man must have fled as soon as Cathy was in reach of the greenhouse.

He'd probably have gone toward the road. He must have parked a vehicle somewhere. Michael headed in that direction, unwilling to give up despite the creeping conviction that he was too late.

When he reached the road, Michael was forced to admit it was no good. He hadn't a chance of overtaking the man. The only hope was that Cathy had caught a glimpse of him.

His rage settling down to a simmer beneath the surface, Michael trudged back to the greenhouse. By the time he neared it, the rain had stopped. For an instant he veered toward the house, but he spotted Cathy standing at the greenhouse door and headed there instead.

"You didn't catch him." She made it a statement, not a question.

He shook his head. "Too late. I didn't even get a glimpse. Did you?"

"No." She spoke quickly, probably recognizing the hope in his voice. "I'm sorry. By the time he was close enough that I could have known him, I was afraid to look. If I'd tripped and fallen—" A shiver went through her at the thought.

"You did the right thing." He clasped her hand, realizing he was dripping cold water on her but needing to touch, to comfort. "I take it Allie's in the house with Verna?"

"Yah. I thought I'd best stay so we could talk without their hearing."

"Good. We need to hash this out. When did you realize someone was following you?"

She hesitated, obviously thinking back. "It was about the time the storm started to hit. At first I thought it was the storm making me nervous. Making me imagine things. But it wasn't."

"You're sure? Yes, of course you are." Cathy wasn't the type of person who'd panic at nothing. "What happened next?"

"We were getting closer—about where we saw the butterflies that day, remember? Then I could hear him. Eventually he didn't bother being careful about the noise. Allie didn't realize… I suppose she thought it was the rain. I put her in front of me, and as soon as we were in that last stretch, I said we'd race to the greenhouse." A shiver stopped her words.

She didn't really need to say any more. Obviously she'd been protecting Allie, keeping herself between Allie and the follower, putting herself at risk for his daughter.

His grip tightened on her hand. "Did he touch you? Say anything?"

"He didn't speak. Just as I started to run, his hand brushed my skirt." She gave a short, impatient shake of her head. "It panicked me."

"Maybe that was best. I just wish I could prove it was that investigator. He ought to be in jail for that. At least you're both all right. But what was the point of it all? That's what I don't get."

What did the man think he had to gain? Frightening his daughter and her teacher wouldn't help him learn the truth about Diana.

"There's something else." Regret saturated the words. "I'm sorry, but..." She took something out of her book bag—a folded piece of paper—holding it gingerly, as if it were dirty. "I found this when I was getting ready to leave. It was under a book on my desk."

He took it with a sense of foreboding. He flipped it open and read what it said.

It took an effort not to crush the offensive thing in his hand. So they'd sunk as far as leaving anonymous letters for the teacher.

After a moment the facts penetrated. "It was on your desk, you said. When did it show up?"

"There's no way to be sure. It could have been there all day. It was only when I picked up the history book that I found it."

He frowned at it. "One of the older kids—"

"No, I can't believe that." Her tone was decided. "They wouldn't. I'm sure of it."

"How did it get there, then?" He thought she was being awfully quick to eliminate her scholars from suspicion. They were the most likely not to be caught planting it. Or one of her helpers.

"I don't know." She folded her arms, hugging herself in a gesture of defense against his words. "Maybe even during the night. Anybody could get in if they really tried."

"Did you see any sign of someone breaking in?" He was frankly skeptical. It could well be that the anonymous letter was totally unrelated to the man who'd followed Cathy and Allie. He glanced at it again. It felt more as if it had been written by an Amish person, not an Englischer.

"No, but I didn't look. You can't assume that someone from the church would be playing tricks like this. It's unheard-of. They'd be risking discipline if it came out."

Was she right about that? He wasn't sure. Maybe he'd become cynical during his years outside. He'd like to think he'd come home to a way of life he could believe in, but he just wasn't sure.

He had to decide what to do next. Maybe this

was actually a case where telling the police was warranted. Chief Jamison hadn't liked the idea of a private eye on his territory. He'd like it even less if he thought the man were frightening the Amish teacher.

"How would you feel if I talked to Chief Jamison about this?"

Alarm filled her face. "You can't. Please, Michael, you mustn't do that. Everyone would hear." Her cheeks grew scarlet. "My parents, the children and their parents—I couldn't handle it."

"If he promised to keep it quiet…"

But she was already shaking her head. More than that, her whole body was shaking. He'd kept her there talking in her wet clothes, not even noticing how uncomfortable she must be.

"Never mind it now. I won't do anything until we've hashed it out completely. Let's get you home before you catch pneumonia."

He'd have to drop it for now. But he'd also have to do something about it, and soon.

CHAPTER FOURTEEN

To her relief, Cathy found that her mother assumed she was upset because she'd become drenched by the storm. Cathy didn't correct her. Anything was better than letting Mammi know the full story. She'd just worry, and there was nothing that could be done about it.

Michael thought there was. Now he wanted to go to the police, after being so determined to stay away from them. She couldn't blame him. If he thought someone threatened Allie, he had every right to do whatever he thought best. She was selfish to pull back just because it would be embarrassing for her.

But how could she possibly cope with the results? People would learn about it, even if Chief Jamison promised to respect her privacy. Nothing stayed secret forever in a small community.

Her family would be in an uproar, wanting to protect her, yet no doubt feeling a sense of shame at the notoriety she'd brought on the family. And as for her teaching career—she couldn't conceive that anyone would hire her if the contents of that anonymous letter became known. Too many people thought that if something was in writing, it was true. No smoke without fire, they'd say.

She could only be thankful that the evening promised to be busy enough to keep her thoughts and hands occupied. Her friend Joanna had an open house in progress at her quilt shop, and both Cathy and Rachel had been recruited to help.

As soon as she arrived at the quilt shop, she and Rachel were settled at a table with fabric squares, helping customers create a small nine-patch square. It was Joanna's idea, of course. She ran events at her shop several times a year, and she claimed the brief introduction to quilting brought her more customers every time.

"Here they come," Rachel murmured, looking a little apprehensive as a couple of visitors bore down on them.

"Relax." Cathy produced a welcoming smile. "You'll do fine."

And naturally, Rachel did, as soon as she started working with one of the women. She'd always been shy, with a wary look that reminded Cathy of Allie. Rachel had to brace herself each time she was pulled out of the familiar surroundings of her father's farm, where her time was completely filled with raising her younger siblings and catering to her widowed father.

Joanna privately insisted that Rachel's father selfishly took her for granted, but Cathy always pointed out that Rachel was contented…she seemed born to take care of people. It was too bad she wasn't expending all that love on a family of her own, but life hadn't worked out that way. She, along with Joanna and Cathy, continued to be the maidals, the old maids, of their age group.

"That wasn't so bad," Rachel said, as the women moved on to a different activity. Leaning back in her chair, she took a long look at Cathy. "Is something wrong? You've been distracted. Is it Michael?"

The unexpected reference caused Cathy to jab herself with the needle. "Ouch. You and Joanna have been talking again, haven't you?"

"We know you have feelings for the man." A smile tugged at Rachel's mouth. "Wouldn't that ruffle some feathers if it comes out?"

"That's not all it would do."

"I don't see why. After all, Michael was raised Amish, and now he's come back. He'll join the church like he should have done years ago, and a widower with a little girl needs a wife, ain't so?"

Cathy felt sure her cheeks were scarlet. It wasn't often that gentle Rachel was so outspoken. How she and Joanna had seen her feelings—

About to deny it, she stopped short at the sight of an approaching figure. "Hush. That's Janet Wilcox, ain't so?"

She knew it was so without asking the question. Janet was a familiar figure around town—a fixture at every charitable drive and a volunteer for every good cause. Some said she did it to fill up a life that was otherwise empty. They had no children, and Bernard apparently didn't want his wife to have a job.

If that was so, she was sorry for the woman, but

she didn't want to be trapped in conversation with her, not when Michael and his daughter occupied such a large portion of her thoughts.

But Janet was clearly intent on her. She sat down across from Cathy, smiling a bit tentatively. "You're the teacher at the Amish school, aren't you? Catherine Brandt?"

"That's right." Cathy hastily pulled an assortment of fabric scraps in front of her. "Would you like to make a nine patch? Just pick out any nine pieces that you think would go well together."

"Oh, of course." She looked for a moment as if she'd forgotten why she was there, and then she began idly moving scraps around with her fingertip, pushing several together and then sweeping them aside.

Thinking she needed more instructions, Cathy smoothed out a completed patch. "You see how it will look when it's finished. Then if you want, you can turn it into a pot holder." She gestured toward a table where Joanna's aunt was demonstrating the finishing.

"Yes, well..." Janet Wilcox stared down at the bits of fabric she kept moving, but Cathy sensed she wasn't seeing them. "Really, I wanted to talk to you."

Cathy's nerves stood at attention. Her mind scampered from one possibility to another. What did the woman want from her? She'd never expected this sort of attention.

"You're Allie's teacher, then." The nervous fingers paused, and an odd expression crossed her face. "My...my niece."

She seemed to have run out of steam, and Cathy wasn't sure what to do. Michael probably wouldn't want her to talk to the woman, but she couldn't be impolite, especially not at Joanna's event.

"Allie is in my class, yah."

"I wish..." She shook her head in regret. "I would like to have done something...maybe sent a gift... when the baby was born, but Bernard's grandmother wouldn't hear of it."

"It's a pity to hold a grudge." She offered the only thing she could think of.

"Exactly." Janet smiled as if she'd said something profound. "That's what I said to Bernard. His grandmother won't know anything about it now. Why not be friends?" Her face clouded. "But when it came to Diana, Bernard's view was the same as his grandmother's."

"I'm sorry." She really was. The woman's sorrow seemed genuine. Perhaps in Allie she was imagining the child she'd never had.

"Is she well? Happy? I've wanted so much to know, but there was no one I could ask."

Surely it was all right to answer that, at least. "Very well. And she's settled in so nicely at school. A little shy at first, but coming out of it more each day and making friends."

"Diana was never shy. Why would she be?" A trace of envy, perhaps, colored her voice. "She was always the center of attention."

Janet's memories of Diana seemed tinged with

distaste. Did no one have any good memories of the woman?

With a sudden movement, Janet rose. "Thank you. I should go. I wouldn't want Bernard to hear I'd been talking with you." She cast a quick look around, as if half expecting to see him watching her, and then hurried away.

Cathy stared after her, going over that odd conversation in her mind. It had been strange. Not that she wasn't familiar with family disputes and grudges—those happened in any family, Amish or English. But why should Bernard Wilcox be so ready to extend his quarrel to an innocent child? Surely they should all want what was best for Allie.

Was that really all Janet had wanted—to know that Allie was all right? And was she going to tell Michael about the encounter?

By the time the door was closed and locked after the last customer, Cathy was more than ready to forget the whole thing. But Joanna seemed to have other ideas, because she came straight to Cathy with the light of curiosity in her eyes.

"All right, tell us. What did Janet Wilcox want with you? Was it about Michael and his daughter?"

"Nosy, aren't you?" She tried to evade, but she and Rachel both advanced on her.

"You can't keep secrets from us," Joanna said, and Rachel nodded.

"We tell you everything, don't we?"

"There's nothing much to tell," she protested. "Mrs. Wilcox just wanted to ask about how Allie is doing, that's all. Apparently her husband forbids any connection, and she's interested. It's to her credit, I think."

"Any normal woman would certain sure feel that way." Joanna gave a determined nod. "But that's not everything. You've been edgy since the moment you walked in the door. Come on, talk."

Cathy tried to hold off, but realized she actually wanted to hear their reaction to what had happened that day. Joanna and Rachel were safe. They'd kept each other's secrets for years. So in the end she told them everything—the anonymous letter, the follower and even Michael's idea of going to the police.

There was silence for a moment when she'd finished. Joanna frowned, considering. "It sounds like you both assume this is connected to the investigation into Diana's death."

Cathy blinked. "Isn't that logical? I mean, what else could it be?"

"The letter," Rachel said. "It must have been someone Amish, ain't so? Someone who knew how to get into the school."

"I—I don't know. I guess, if it weren't for all the other things, I'd think it was written by someone in the church."

"Rachel has a point," Joanna said, her quick mind jumping several steps ahead. "The letter isn't necessarily connected with the person following you. Just because one thing happened shortly after another, that doesn't mean they're connected."

"No, but surely…that's twice that someone has

been lurking around the school since Allie has been there."

"That is serious enough to involve the police." Joanna's tone was firm. "You're just holding back because of the note, but that could be entirely different."

"And what if the man wasn't spying on Allie?" Rachel put in. She sent a fearful look around the shop, perhaps afraid someone might be watching. "Maybe he was interested in you."

"A stalker." Joanna nodded in agreement. "It could happen."

"Not here," Cathy said, instantly denying the idea. Such things didn't happen here, in their peaceful community.

"Anywhere. Surely we've all learned that there are disturbed people, even evil people anywhere."

Joanna was right, she supposed. Bad things did happen. But she still could scarcely believe that the watcher had been after her. What had she ever done to draw such attention?

"If you want to make me afraid to drive home alone, you're succeeding," she said.

"We just want you to take it seriously, that's all." Joanna gave her a quick hug. "Tell Chief Jamison about the man following you from school. Nobody could blame you for doing so. And you know it's the right thing to do."

She'd argue the point, but she had a sinking feeling she agreed with them. Not about the stalker notion… that still seemed far-fetched. But the man had been lurking around the school. She couldn't pretend it hadn't happened, not if it might put a child in danger.

MICHAEL LEANED AGAINST Cathy's buggy in the alley that ran alongside the quilt shop. He had to talk to her again, so he'd walked into town to catch her away from her family. He didn't want to go to the police without her agreement, but the thought of someone lurking outside the school and creeping after Cathy and Allie turned his stomach. When it came to Allie's safety, he wasn't taking chances.

He'd seen the shoppers leave and heard the door lock behind them. Cathy was probably helping her friend clean up, but she wouldn't want to get too late a start on the drive home. Dusk was already slipping away into darkness.

He risked a cautious look in the window. The three of them had their heads together, talking, their faces intent. Was she talking to them about him? He had an urgent need to know what she was saying, but he wouldn't, not unless she told him.

Finally they moved toward the door. He heard a chorus of good-nights. Someone seemed to be picking up Rachel—that must be one of her brothers. Rachel was offering to take Cathy home, with Cathy insisting she had her buggy and would be fine. In another moment Rachel's buggy rolled off.

Cathy came around the corner. It was dark enough here that she didn't spot him until she had taken a few steps toward him. Then she stopped.

"Who's there?" Her voice trembled slightly.

"It's me. Michael." He moved toward her. "Sorry. I didn't mean to scare you."

"You didn't," she snapped, but the very fact that she snapped at him told the tale.

"You ought to be. What's the idea of coming into a dark alley by yourself? You should have someone picking you up. Did you forget so easily about what happened this afternoon?"

"No, I didn't. But since I didn't want to tell my parents, I couldn't very well ask Daad to pick me up when he knows I'd normally drive myself."

"That's the trouble with keeping secrets. They come back and bite you." He walked alongside her, his hand naturally going to her lower back to guide her to the buggy.

But when he started to climb up to the seat next to her, she put out her hand. "Hold on. What are you doing?"

"We need to talk." He swung up beside her. "In private. So I'll ride along with you. Don't worry, I don't expect you to take me home. I'll walk from the turnoff."

"I'm not worried about that." She sat still, the reins slack in her hands. "But if anyone sees us..."

She was right, he supposed, but the need to convince her to go to the police was strong, and it was compounded by the instinct to protect her. He couldn't let her go alone—that was the bottom line.

"An unmarried Amish woman doesn't usually go somewhere after dark with a man unless he's a relative or they're courting. Since you don't fit into either category..."

He stopped her by taking the lines into his hands and clucking to the horse. "No one is going to see us." He tilted his hat down to hide his face. "This town closes up in the evening, and we're not likely to see anyone from the church on this short trip."

Cathy made a tentative movement toward the lines, then sat back and clasped her hands in her lap. "Maybe I'm being too nervous. Or don't you think that's necessary?"

"I'd rather you'd be wary. That'll do more to keep you safe. I'm saying your safety is more important than what gossips might say if we were seen together." He frowned, trying to figure out how to start what he needed to say. "I know you're upset at the idea of contacting the police about what happened this afternoon, but I'd like you to think about it."

"I have thought. I've done little else." Her fingers twisted together as if they struggled. "I... Well, to be honest, I think you're right." Before he could exclaim, she held up her hand. "But I'm concerned about what will happen if you show Chief Jamison that anonymous note."

"No one needs to know what it says. He'd respect your privacy."

She gave him a pitying look. "You've forgotten what it's like around here if you think that it wouldn't get out. And once it does...people might not want to believe it, but they won't be able to help it. 'No smoke without fire.' That's what they'll say."

He'd been trying to deny it, but with her eyes on him, he knew that what she said was true. She'd be tainted with the slur. As for him—well, they'd probably say that it was just what they'd expect from him.

"Okay. You're probably right. I don't like it either. But are you willing to put that before Allie's safety?"

He saw her flinch at the sharp question. She stared down at her hands, writhing in her lap, and he suspected she was fighting back tears.

"No." Her head came up, and her chin firmed. "No, I can't put Allie at risk, no matter what it costs. You win. I'll talk to Chief Jamison."

Silence for a moment, broken only by the rumble of the buggy wheels and the clop-clop of the horse's hooves on the blacktop. Michael had what he'd come for, but he felt a flood of nausea at the thought of the repercussions. He rubbed the nape of his neck, searching for another answer. Any answer.

And then he realized the thing he was missing. "Wait a minute. Why should we tell the police anything at all about the anonymous letter? It might have nothing to do with the rest of it."

Cathy glanced at him warily, as if not sure she'd heard him properly. "It's possible, I suppose. In fact, that's what Joanna and Rachel think—that it's something totally different."

"You talked to them about it?" He seemed uneasy with that.

"Of course." She seemed surprised. "They're my closest friends. I can tell them things I wouldn't even tell my family." Then, maybe misinterpreting his reaction, she went on. "You don't need to worry about it. They've never spilled any of my secrets yet, and I don't suppose they'll start now."

"You're that sure of them?"

Cathy nodded, the movement barely visible in the glow from the buggy's battery lanterns. "Don't you have friends you trust that way?"

"When I was a kid, I guess." He thought back to his friendship with Jacob King. Maybe, if he'd stayed here, that friendship would have ripened into the sort of bond Cathy was talking about. There hadn't been anything that close after he'd left. Even his friendship with Alan was more the casual companionship of neighbors, not reaching beyond that to their working lives or inward to their secret feelings.

"All right, I accept that they'll keep your secrets. What do they think about the guy who followed you and Allie?"

She hesitated, and he thought she was embarrassed. "Joanna said that maybe…maybe the man was after me, not Allie. I can't believe that, but she was serious."

That explained the embarrassment. A stalker. Such things did happen, and to a twisted mind, there could be an odd temptation in the shape of an innocent Amish woman.

"It's possible," he admitted. "The simple answer is that if there's trouble here, I brought it with me. But it is possible." He reached out to cover her hand with his. "Are you worried?"

"Not really. I know with my head that bad things

can happen anywhere, but I guess my heart doesn't really buy that idea."

His fingers tightened on hers. "You'd better, because it's true. Still, I don't think it's likely in this case." He was silent for a moment, thinking it through, his hand still clasping hers.

"Okay, here's what we'll do. I'll go and see Chief Jamison and tell him about the guy who followed you from the school. Even if there wasn't anything else involved, it's alarming to think he was hanging around, watching the school. It may well have been the man you spotted before."

He paused, watching her for signs of rebellion. She looked solemn, but she didn't seem ready to back out.

"He'll want to talk to you. We'll have to set up a meeting."

"Not at home," she said quickly. "I don't want to alarm my folks."

That troubled him—to think of her on that isolated farm. Her father was a capable man, but if she kept him in the dark, he'd have no reason for suspicion.

"Don't you think your daad—"

"No." She yanked her hand away from his. "You have to promise me you won't tell him if you want me to do this."

He doubted she'd be able to keep it from her parents for long, but at the moment he could do nothing but go along with her.

"Okay, if you feel that way about it." He considered. "Suppose I ask him to meet us at the school. Well after all the kids and parents have left, so no one will know. You can talk to him there."

"What about Allie? She'd be with me, unless you're going to take her home first."

He frowned. "Can't you find something that will keep her busy while we talk? I'd say I'd take her outside, but I think I should be present with Chief Jamison."

"I suppose so. But you're not going to mention the anonymous letter, ain't so?"

"Not if you don't want me to. Have you any idea who would do such a thing?"

She shook her head, but he suspected she was holding something back. "I think it's most likely one of us." She seemed unaware she'd included him among the Leit.

"No jealous boyfriends in your life?"

"No boyfriends at all." Her lips quirked. "Unless you count Isaac Stoltzfus."

"Who is Isaac Stoltzfus, and why should he be counted?"

"He's the uncle of the girl whose parents have been pushing to put her into my job. He's a widower with five preschool-age children, and supposedly he told my brother-in-law that he thought I'd make a fine stepmother."

"I take it you discouraged him, since he doesn't seem to be around."

"Well, I would have, but James, my brother-in-law, did it for me. He says it's well-known that Isaac is a skinflint who can't get along with any woman, and he certain sure didn't want to be related to him."

There was soft laughter in her voice when she told the story. It seemed to have distracted her from the interview she was clearly dreading, so maybe this was a good time to part.

He slowed the horse. "I can get down now, if you want. It's not far."

She put her hand over his to stop him. "No, not yet. There's something I need to tell you. It probably doesn't mean anything," she added quickly.

"What is it?" Not more trouble for her, he hoped. He seemed to carry trouble to everyone he came near.

"You know that I was helping with Joanna's open house this evening. We… Rachel and I had a table where we helped visitors to make a quilt patch, so you see, we were sitting and talking with various customers."

He nodded, wondering where this was going.

"I was taken aback when Janet Wilcox came and sat down with me. Bernard Wilcox's wife, you know."

"What did she want? Did she make a scene?"

"Janet? Ach, she would never do that. She's not that kind of person. But it was obvious that she wanted to talk to me, and not about quilt patches."

"About me, I suppose." He felt sure she'd heard all about his very brief talk with her husband. And how he'd been kicked out.

"Not really. I don't think she mentioned you. She wanted to know about Allie."

"What about Allie?" All of his alarms went off.

He'd half expected some effort on their part to take custody of Allie after Diana's death, and he'd been ready to fight it. But they hadn't, and he'd thought he could stop worrying about it. "They've never shown any interest in her at all."

"I had the impression that was Bernard's doing. Janet said she'd wanted to get back in touch with Diana after his grandmother went into the nursing home, but he wouldn't hear of it. And she apparently doesn't stand up for her opinions."

"Why now, then? And why did she come to you?"

"I suppose she thought coming to the open house would be an unobtrusive way of talking to someone who'd know about Allie. She knows that I'm the teacher at the Amish school, and I suppose word has gotten around that Allie goes there."

"No doubt. But what did she ask?"

"She just wanted to know how Allie was doing. It all seemed innocent enough. I'd rather not have talked to her at all, but there was no way of getting out of it. So I just said that Allie was doing well. That she seemed to enjoy school and she was making new friends. That's all, really. You couldn't be upset by that, could you?"

Cathy had turned toward him on the buggy seat, tilting her face to his, looking for reassurance. It gave him a nearly irresistible urge to kiss her.

Almost irresistible. He managed to control himself. He'd caused enough trouble in that direction.

She seemed to catch the wave of attraction. She

sat back suddenly, turning away from him. "Anyway, it was nothing to worry about."

"I guess not." He pulled the horse up abruptly. If he didn't want to do something he'd end up regretting, it was time to get out of this situation.

He thrust the lines into her hands and jumped down from the buggy. "I'll walk home from here. I'll be in touch after I've seen Jamison."

He started walking. A brisk walk in the cool night air—that should settle him. He hoped.

CHAPTER FIFTEEN

AFTER SCHOOL THE next afternoon, Cathy lingered in the schoolroom, making a show of being busy. Meanwhile Allie bent over the small table in the corner, totally absorbed in the picture she was drawing.

At least, Cathy hoped she was absorbed. Michael would be here with Chief Jamison any minute, and they should be able to chat in the back of the room without Allie hearing and becoming upset. The child hadn't realized they'd been followed on their way home from school, and Cathy wanted to keep it that way.

The sound of footsteps sent her scurrying to the back of the room. Chief Jamison came in, closely followed by Michael, looking strained.

They separated immediately, with Jamison waiting for her while Michael crossed to Allie. She heard their animated voices behind her as she showed Chief Jamison to a seat.

Jamison nodded his approval of the arrangement. "This should work," he said, his voice quiet and calm. "Now, tell me all about what's troubling Teacher Cathy."

His use of the title reassured her in a way nothing else could have. She managed to smile.

"I hope it's not a wild-goose chase." She glanced out the closest window, seeing nothing but the familiar apple tree by the corner of the porch and the lawn beyond. "You're sure no one saw you arriving?"

"I can't be positive, but I don't think so." He seemed to understand her stress at the thought. "I drove my own car, not the cop car."

"Denke. I'm sure it sounds silly, but I'm afraid..."

"Forget it," he said. "I understand."

He understood, but what she feared was the other people who wouldn't.

"Just tell me exactly what happened and let me decide how serious it is. That's what I'm here for."

Cathy nodded, reassured. He reminded her, quite suddenly, of her father. Not in appearance, of course, but in the quiet confidence which said he'd never run into anything he couldn't handle.

"Someone followed us—Allie and me—when we walked home from school yesterday. You'll think I imagined it with the storm coming on and all, but I'm sure. Someone was there, watching and following." She looked at him with a touch of defiance, expecting to be doubted.

Instead he nodded. "You never struck me as someone to imagine things. Now, if you were Ethel Bredbenner, seeing Martians landing in her backyard, I might be skeptical. But you're a levelheaded woman. If you say someone was there, I believe you. Especially when we know that private investigator is hanging around. I haven't run him to ground yet, but I will, and he's going to get an earful when I do."

Cathy breathed easier, but she still had a hurdle to get over. “That’s the first thing I thought of. And if it wasn’t the investigator, I guess I assumed it was connected to Michael’s trouble.”

His sharp eyes questioned her. “And don’t you think so now?”

“Yah, I still think that’s most likely. But Joanna and Rachel said it might be directed at me, and not anything to do with Michael and Allie at all.” She shivered a little. “I don’t see how it could. Do you?”

He considered. “I wouldn’t rule it out, no. But let’s hear all the details first.”

“Didn’t Michael tell you?”

“Just assume I don’t know anything and take me over it.”

He was serious, she could see. Cathy went over what had happened each step of the way—rushing out because of the storm coming, gradually sensing that someone was watching, hearing the rustle of a body moving through the tangle of bushes, coming closer. Telling Allie to run ahead, and feeling the brush of someone’s hand on her skirt as she bolted. When she’d finished, she was shaking inside and her fingers had started to tremble.

“It’s okay.” Michael had come up behind her without her hearing him. His hand rested briefly on her shoulder, sending comfort flooding through her.

“Right,” Jamison said. “That’s nice and clear. I know a sensible woman like you wouldn’t imagine something like that.”

Levelheaded, sensible… They were good things to be called, so why did it sound so flat…so ordinary?

"You want to hear about me chasing him again? I never got within a mile of him, most likely," Michael said, frustration clear in his voice.

"That's pretty clear." Obviously the chief had already heard Michael's account. "Suppose I walk back along the path with all of you, and you can show me where the tracks were that you followed."

He pushed back his chair, focusing on Cathy. "I hope I don't need to tell you that you should take precautions. Have your cell phone on you always, and call if anything happens that seems odd. No matter how trivial, you hear me? And don't go walking anywhere alone or with just a child. Okay?"

She nodded. He'd moved away from any subject that might lead to the anonymous letter, and she was relieved. No one had to know about it.

Chief Jamison got up. "I'll wait outside for you."

"I just have to get my things." And convince Allie that her picture was finished, she added to herself, moving to where the child sat, still engrossed.

"We're going home now," she said, touching Allie's shoulder lightly. "What a nice picture."

In actuality, she wondered what it represented. Usually Allie's pictures were of farmhouses and barns, but this was different.

"Whose house is this?" she asked.

"That's our house, where we used to live." Allie's clear little voice reached Michael and sent him turning around in surprise.

"And that's the man who used to come. Mommy's friend."

Cathy's breath caught, and now it was Jamison who turned. He looked at Michael. "Seems that's something I should know about," he said. "Did you know about this?"

Michael's face hardened. "I just found out a few days ago myself. I was trying to figure it out."

But Jamison didn't wait for an explanation. He came to the table and squatted down next to Allie. "Can I see your picture?"

Allie eyed him for a moment and then pushed it over to him.

"Very nice," he said. "I especially like the tree you put in."

"I didn't put it," she explained with no sign of embarrassment or shyness. Apparently Chief Jamison's ability to put people at ease worked with children as well. "It's really there."

"That makes it a true-to-life picture, then," he responded gravely. "Who is this coming up the walk?"

"That's Mommy's friend," she said as she had before. "I don't know his name."

"I see. Did he often come to see you?"

She actually giggled at that, sounding like Ruthie for a moment. "He didn't ever see me. Mommy always had me go to a friend's house when he came."

"So you just made him up to go in the picture, then."

"No, he's really real. Like the tree. I saw him outside from the bedroom window at Mr. Alan's house."

Cathy's fingers were clenched so tightly that her nails dug into her palms. She glanced at Michael. His face had actually eased a bit, maybe because Allie didn't show any signs of distress. She'd come a long way in a few short weeks.

"I see you used a brown crayon. Does he have brown hair?"

Allie nodded. "I could see that, but I couldn't tell what color his eyes were, so I made them brown, too."

"Good idea. Was he taller than your daddy or shorter?"

Allie wiggled, showing signs of tiring. "I don't know." She started to roll up the picture. "Is it time to go home, Daadi?"

"Yah, it is." Michael's look at Jamison warned him not to interfere.

But the chief seemed satisfied he'd heard all Allie had to say. He rose, nodding to Cathy.

She acted with alacrity, grabbing her bag with one hand and Allie with the other. "We'll go now."

No one objected, and she hustled Allie to the door, leaving Michael to walk with Chief Jamison. He'd be asking questions, trying to identify the man. It would come out eventually. It seemed that everything did.

MICHAEL TRIED TO clear his mind of everything except the task at hand that evening. He was doing yet another job at the home of Mrs. Carpenter, who seemed to have an endless list of repairs needed to her aging Victorian house. Tonight it was shoring up the rough wooden steps going down to the basement.

He frowned. What he should be doing was putting in a railing. He shuddered at the thought of the elderly woman plunging down toward that unforgiving concrete cellar floor.

He'd have to suggest it, even if she thought he was trying to drum up business. It was too dangerous to ignore.

One thing he'd learned about her—if she thought that, she'd say so. Blunt, outspoken, even a bit abrasive, that was Mrs. Carpenter. It probably put some people off, but he couldn't help admiring her. And being amused by some of her blunt comments. She had no illusions about people, it seemed.

He moved down a step, checking carefully for any signs of weakness.

Unasked and unwelcome, his mind returned to the case the police had against him. He hadn't heard anything more from the Harrisburg detective, but that didn't mean the man was idle. Chief Jamison, at least, didn't seem to take his guilt for granted.

When they'd walked back along the path, identifying where Michael had gone in pursuit, Jamison had been intent, obviously eager to find something that would tell him who it had been.

That didn't mean he had any illusions about the chief. If he found indications that Michael was guilty, he'd act. He'd pressed the subject of the friend when they were alone, and it was impossible to tell if he believed Michael hadn't known.

He'd been good with Allie, though. Michael had to admit that his worries there had been unwarranted.

Jamison had struck the right note, managing to elicit the information he needed without alarming her. It was a testimony to how good this life was for Allie that she seemed to have no fears.

He'd reached the bottom, checking the treads and underpinning as he went. Then he went back up, stepping heavily on each tread and detecting no tremors. Satisfied, he emerged into the kitchen… old-fashioned by Englisch standards, but typical of houses of that period.

Mrs. Carpenter was waiting for him. "All done?"

"It's as good as it can be, but—"

"Is it safe? That's all I want to know." She never hesitated to interrupt.

"It won't collapse under you." He could be just as blunt. "But it's not safe. There should be a railing. Don't take my word for it. Ask any contractor, and he'll tell you the same."

Her answer was a short grunt. With her square, bulldog face and strong jaw, she didn't look as though she'd take anyone's advice readily.

When he didn't say anything, she glared at him. "No more arguments?"

"I've had my say. If you want to take chances, it's up to you. But you need a railing."

Silence for a moment. Then she shrugged. "I'll think about it." She thrust his money toward him. "Thanks."

He nodded. That was progress. His work hadn't always rated a thanks. "Okay. Just let me know if you need anything else done."

He picked up his toolbox and headed out. He'd reached the door when her voice stopped him.

"Wait a minute. No need to be in such a hurry." Getting up, she grabbed her cane and stumped over to him. "Got a hot date?" She let out a crack of laughter.

Michael smiled in return. "With my daughter. It's almost her bedtime."

"How's she doing? Fitting in okay?"

He hesitated, but it seemed well-meant. "More than okay. She's happier than she's been in a long time."

She nodded. "Folks are happier when they're where they belong."

He wasn't sure how to respond to that, but she didn't give him time anyway.

"There's been talk going around about you."

He'd expected that was true, especially after his attempted interview with Bernard Wilcox. "What are they saying?"

"They wouldn't say anything to my face." She let out a crack of laughter again. "I judge people by what I know, not what others say."

"So what do you know?" Was she building up to saying she didn't need him any longer?

"Just that you should be careful, that's all. And take care of that little girl."

"I intend to." If he sounded grim, he meant it. Nobody was getting to Allie.

"Right. Go on home now. You can stop by tomorrow and give me an estimate on the railing."

Before he could collect himself and thank her, she stamped away.

He went out and closed the door carefully. Well. She'd been warning him, that was sure. And declaring herself on his side, it seemed.

But what, exactly, was threatened?

WHEN MICHAEL HAD settled Allie for the night, he came downstairs to find that Lige had come back. He was sitting at the kitchen table, with Aunt Verna cutting into a pie.

"What brings you back again?" He sat down across from Lige. Before he could refuse, Aunt Verna had set wedges of cherry pie in front of them.

"He brought a present for Allie." She turned to lift something from one of the pegs by the door. "A new dress Sarah made."

The dress was a clear green color, bright and pretty. When Aunt Verna held it out to him, Michael ran his hand down the fabric, touched at his sister's thoughtfulness.

"It's great. She didn't have to do that. Allie will love it."

"Ach, I should have thought of it." Aunt Verna smiled, hanging the dress up again. "Sarah is wonderful kindhearted. Every little girl wants a new dress all her own."

"She's been happy with the dresses Ruthie lent her, but she'll love having one her aunt Sarah made just for her." He might have thought of that himself, instead of just accepting what had been given.

His feisty little sister had turned into a generous,

thoughtful woman. She had her hands full making clothes for her own kinder, without taking on Allie, too.

Aunt Verna, finishing pouring coffee, sat down with her own cup. "You did some more work for Mrs. Carpenter, ain't so?"

"Mending her cellar steps." He frowned. "She ought to have a railing on them. Somebody her age shouldn't take such chances. I told her so."

Lige choked on his coffee, and Aunt Verna set her cup down hard.

"You didn't say so to her. She doesn't like people interfering in how she lives."

"Is she giving you any more work?" Lige struck a practical note.

He shrugged, amused at their reactions. "She said she'd think about the railing. And told me to come back and give her a quote on the work."

"She did? Ach, I wouldn't have believed it." Shaking her head, Verna stood.

"Where are you going? You didn't finish your coffee."

She lifted down the dress. "I'll hang this in Allie's room so she'll see it when she wakes up." She smiled, touching the dress tenderly. "She'll be wonderful happy."

Lige forked up a large bite of pie. When they could hear her footsteps on the stairs, he nodded. "Verna's the one who's happy. She's starting to feel like Allie's her own granddaughter, ain't so?"

"It's good for Allie, too. She's never had grandparents." Or much other family.

"That reminds me." Lige looked as if he contemplated walking on eggs. "Sarah wanted me to remind you that she's supposed to take Ruthie and Allie to your father's house tomorrow after school." He seemed braced for an explosion.

Michael felt a flare of resentment, but he forced it down. His father was the way he was, and there was no changing him. That didn't mean he couldn't be a good grandfather to Allie.

Finally he nodded. "Okay." He hesitated again. "If Allie has a chance to have a relationship with her grandfather, I don't want to mess that up. Tomorrow after school." He forced a smile. "She'll want to wear her new dress."

Lige seemed relieved. "Gut. Sarah will be happy. Not satisfied, but happy."

"Sarah wants a happy ending," he said. He shrugged and then moved on to another thought. "If Mrs. Carpenter does hire me to build the railing, I could use another pair of hands. Feel like working a few evenings?"

"Sure thing." Lige grinned. "Always glad to earn a couple bucks. I—" He stopped at the sound of a car coming down the drive. "Wonder who that is at this hour? It's dark out."

"He's going too fast." Apprehension sent Michael to his feet. Even as he spoke, brakes shrieked and there was the sound of gravel spattering.

In the next instant, it seemed, they heard the crash of breaking glass. Michael charged to the door, with

Lige right behind him. Together they burst out into the night.

Three men were attacking the nearest greenhouse. Michael saw the swing of a bat and yelled.

As if his shout had been a signal, the men raced toward the waiting car. Michael ran to cut it off. By the time they turned, maybe he could get there and stop them. It was already moving as the last man jumped in.

It swung in a circle, turning, and then headed out the lane. If he could just get in position to see the license number…

The car veered and suddenly it was headed right at him. He froze for an instant, heard Lige shout and then dove to the side, rolling over in the soft grass. The car spurted by, turned onto the road away from town and vanished.

He stood, panting, his fists clenched. If he'd gotten his hands on one of them…

Lige's hand fell on his shoulder. "You okay?"

"Yeah. Could you see the license plate?"

"No chance, not with the lights off. There's no way of telling who it was. Let's see how bad it is before Verna gets out here."

It was too late already. Verna had paused to grab a battery lantern. Face grim, she held it up to focus on the damage.

Michael's stomach twisted. Thank Heaven the men hadn't reached the other greenhouses, but they'd done plenty of damage to the first one, where Verna kept the annual plants that were currently selling best. Shattered glass—that was the first thing that struck you. Glass had scattered far and wide—they'd have to find a way to clean it all up. And then the repairs…

"I'm sorry." He couldn't find any way of comforting her. "This is my fault. It's because I'm here."

To his astonishment, Verna put her arms around him, holding on tight, as if finding comfort that way.

Lige, face working, put his arm across her back awkwardly. "We'll fix it," he said, his voice husky. "We'll make it gut as new, ain't so, Michael?"

Michael nodded, but was it really for the best that he help? If he left now, this persecution would cease. "If I left—"

"No." Verna's voice was sharp, and Lige was already shaking his head. "That's not how we deal with trouble." She straightened, standing on her own. "I will call the police."

He and Lige exchanged looks as she marched toward the phone shanty. "I never thought she'd do that." Lige was the first to speak.

Michael rubbed the nape of his neck, trying to think. "I guess it's best," he said slowly. "This is what Mrs. Carpenter meant, I guess. She said people were talking. Stirring up feelings against us."

Lige shrugged. "It's happened before. It'll happen again. It goes with being Amish."

"It shouldn't, not this time. This time it's because of me."

Lige eyed him seriously. "Best if you quit saying that. It doesn't help. We're all in this, not just you."

Lige's severity shocked him, but at the same time it woke him up. Whether or not it was his fault didn't matter. The fabric of Amish life was woven so tightly that what touched it affected all. Declaring that this trouble was his alone would be seen as pride, in an oddly inverted way.

He nodded. "Okay. You're right."

"I'll get more light," Lige said. "We'll have to see what we can save from inside."

Michael roused himself to concentrate on the immediate problem. "Right. I'll go up and check on Allie first." Without waiting for a response, he headed inside.

Tension tightened his muscles as he hurried up the steps. If only she could have slept all through it. This ugliness couldn't be allowed to shatter the peaceful world she'd found here.

He eased her door open. Allie slept curled up on her side, her face relaxed, her loose braid hanging over her shoulder. Her breathing was even and relaxed, and the stuffed dog was under her arm.

Michael smoothed the quilt over Allie's back with gentle hands before heading back downstairs to face the current crisis.

The police had arrived in the form of Guy Smethers. Michael stifled a groan. Smethers was the last person to be helpful in the current situation.

"Got some trouble," he was saying as Michael approached. "Not much we can do about it when you didn't even get a description of the vehicle."

"You mean you only investigate when other people have done your work for you?" Michael snapped.

Smethers flared up instantly, fists clenching. "If these people want to escape trouble, they'd be better off without you. You were trouble when we were kids, and you're trouble now."

Before Michael could say what he wanted, Lige and Verna had moved next to him. "We are family." Lige's tone wasn't combative, but it was firm.

Smethers seemed to fight for control. It hung in the balance, but then another car turned into the lane, dissolving the tension.

The new vehicle drew to a halt, and Chief Jamison stepped out. For a moment he stood surveying the chaos of the greenhouse, and then he came to Aunt Verna.

"I'm awful sorry about this, Mrs. Forster. We'll do our best to get to the bottom of it." He turned to Smethers. "Guy, get some photos of those tire tracks where the vehicle turned around. Let's have a look for any paint scrapings. They might have hit something in their hurry to get out."

Smethers seemed to hold back a retort. Then he turned to follow orders.

"We need to save what we can from inside," Lige said. "Okay for us to go in?"

"Did any of the men go inside?" He looked from Lige to Michael.

They both shook their heads. "They ran along this side. I saw rocks and one man had a baseball bat."

Jamison nodded. "Right. Lige, how about if you start while Michael answers some questions?"

Lige turned wordlessly toward the greenhouse. When Verna attempted to follow him, Jamison spoke up. “Mrs. Forster, do you think you could make a fresh pot of coffee? That’d be a help.”

Verna hesitated, but then she nodded. Michael breathed a little easier. She was in shock, and it would do her more good to be working in the bright kitchen than out here with the dark and the damage.

He and Lige would have to cope with the destruction. He felt a burst of gratitude to Lige, who’d become as good as a brother to him so quickly. Still, this was on him, and somehow he had to find a way to repay his family for all of this grief.

CHAPTER SIXTEEN

CATHY TOOK THE horse and buggy to school the next morning. Mindful of the chief's warning, she'd decided she wouldn't be walking through the woods for a time. Mamm and Daad were sure to question why she was driving if she did it every day. She could only hope this situation would be resolved before it came to that.

She drove into the Forster lane to pick up Allie and stopped, appalled at the sight that met her eyes. The greenhouse—for a moment it looked as if it had been hit by a tornado. Then reality asserted itself. This hadn't been done by nature. Someone had vandalized the building.

She'd barely formulated the thought when Michael came striding toward her, his movements quick, his shoulders tense. He leaned against the buggy seat to speak.

"Allie will be out in a minute." He jerked his head toward the greenhouse. "You see that we had visitors last night."

"It's…it's terrible." She didn't have the words. No wonder he looked so strained. He was blaming himself, of course, for having brought this trouble on the family. "Who was it?"

Michael's hands tightened into fists. "I wish I knew. Lige and I were in the kitchen when a car came racing in. We ran out at the first sound of breaking glass, but they did a lot of damage in a short space of time."

"You couldn't identify them?" But he'd have started with that if he could have.

"Three men, that's all I could say. Youngish, from the way they moved, but not kids. They piled back into the car and beat it before we could catch up with them."

"Poor Verna. She must be so upset. What can I do?"

His eyes softened. "Just keep Allie occupied. Verna's surprising us. She's already forgiven. I'm afraid I'm not able to meet her standard. At least the damage is nothing that can't be fixed."

Michael turned as the back door opened and closed. Allie came hurrying toward the buggy. Cathy's heart winced when she saw the child's face. Allie was all closed in again.

But then she reached Michael, and her expression blossomed into a smile as she took his hand. Cathy's tension eased. Allie was turning to her father in a way that seemed natural. They were finding their way to each other, and that was the best thing that could happen to them.

"Okay, off you go to school in your pretty new dress." Michael lifted her to the buggy seat next to Cathy. "Don't worry. You'll be surprised at how much Onkel Lige and I will have cleaned up when you get home today."

Allie nodded, accepting his words, but Cathy was still concerned. This vandalism had hit Allie on an emotional level, and she thought it was worse because Allie had begun to see this place as belonging to her, too.

"We'd best get moving," she said with a cheerfulness she didn't feel. She clucked to the mare, turning in a wide circle to head back out the lane. "I'll see you after school, then," she called to Michael while trying to send a message with her expression.

I'll do my best for Allie. She hoped he understood.

They rode in silence for a few minutes, and she waited, hoping Allie might speak. But Allie had retreated firmly behind her barricades.

Cathy hurt for her, and she knew she had to open something that was bound to be painful. Still, it was even worse to keep silent.

"That was a terrible thing that happened last night," she said, watching for cues. "Did you hear it?"

Allie shook her head. "Daadi told me when I woke up. Why—" She stopped, clamping her lips closed.

"Why do bad things happen?" Cathy asked, hoping she guessed right.

Allie's mouth compressed even more, but her eyes were alive with a mixture of feelings—most likely anger among them. It was like watching a pot come to a boil.

Then the lid seemed to pop off. "Why do they happen to us?" It was a cry so many people had made, but Allie wasn't to know that.

"You have had a lot of bad things happen to you

in the last year, haven't you?" Cathy kept her voice calm, feeling her way. "Maybe you started to feel as if you did something wrong to bring all these bad things on."

Allie shot a glance at her, as if weighing whether Cathy thought that. Whatever she saw must have reassured her, because she seemed to lose a little of the tension she carried.

"Do you think that's why?" she asked, her voice very small.

Cathy reached across to take one cold little hand in hers. "No, I'm sure it's not. Very sure. It's not you."

"Then why?" The words had tears behind them. "Why?"

Why do bad things happen? She was asking the biggest of questions and expecting an answer.

"Sometimes people do bad things," she said, praying for the words. "It's not your fault if you're hurt by one of those bad things, any more than it would be my fault if I were hit by lightning. You see?"

Allie nodded, but she was clearly not satisfied. Cathy would have to dig a little deeper.

"You didn't do anything to make those things happen. And it's important to remember that there are more people doing good things in this world than bad."

She mulled that over for a moment. "Are you sure there are more?" This sounded almost like a challenge.

"I'm sure." She smiled at Allie. "Tell you what. We'll have a game. We'll count up all the good things that happen today, and we'll tell each other on the way home. Okay?"

"Okay." There was still doubt in Allie's tone, but she managed to smile. It was a tiny smile, but it gave Cathy hope. Somehow she had to make sure that Allie had good things happen to her today.

When they reached the school, Cathy kept Allie with her while she unharnessed the buggy horse and turned her into the small paddock. By the time they'd done that, some of the other scholars had started to arrive.

Cathy cringed inwardly when she saw who her helper for the day was. Mary Alice Stoltzfus. She'd wondered why Mary Alice seldom volunteered to help, since she supposedly wanted to be a teacher. Now Cathy had a chance to find out. But almost any other day would have been better to have Mary Alice watching her.

The morning went on its usual course, but Cathy, with an ear well tuned to her classroom, could tell that some of them had already heard what happened at the greenhouse the previous night. That settled it in her mind. She'd speak to the children about it. Children relied on the grown-ups in their lives to set the tone of their reactions.

As the time for morning recess approached, she closed out the current lessons and asked that books be put away. As they did, her scholars looked at her expectantly. Mary Alice rose from the corner where she'd been listening to the third and fourth graders reading aloud.

Cathy came around her desk to be closer to the children, looking from one face to another. "Some of you have heard about what happened last night at Verna Forster's greenhouse. If you didn't, you must know that several people attacked one of the greenhouses and made a mess."

She didn't need to explain that the attackers had been Englisch. They'd know that without thinking.

The children exchanged glances, some looking shocked and others a little frightened.

"All of you know Verna, Allie's great-great-aunt, and you understand what a mean thing that was for someone to do. Do you have any questions you want to ask?"

A tentative hand went up, and she nodded.

"Will they… Will they do that to us, too?" Anna Schmidt, whose family ran a large farm stand, looked as if she imagined it the target of an attack.

"I don't think so, Anna. I'm sure your daad will be watchful to keep you safe. But we can all imagine how it would feel if it happened to us, can't we?"

Heads nodded solemnly, and more than one child glanced at Allie.

"What do we do when one of the Leit needs help?"

Ruthie's hand shot up. At Cathy's nod, she said, "We help them."

"That's right. We all know that, don't we?" Heads nodded solemnly. She scanned faces, looking for any dissent, but found none. If any of their parents were inclined to think Verna had brought it on herself by taking in Michael and Allie, they hadn't apparently shared that with the kinder.

"So we will look for ways we can be kind and

helpful, remembering that's what we are called to do. You may go to recess now."

Mary Alice hesitated for a moment as the children began to file out. Then she went to take hands with Ruthie and Allie as they moved toward the door.

Well. That surprised her...she couldn't deny it. She wondered if Mary Alice's mother would approve. Probably not, but perhaps Mary Alice was developing a mind of her own.

As for Allie...she suspected that the friendship the other children showed her would help her heal more than any words Cathy might say.

LIGE PICKED UP one of the ten-inch geranium pots and shook it gently, to be rewarded with a small shower of broken glass. He glanced at Michael and made a face.

Michael shrugged. "We may have to ditch the lot of them."

"Ach, don't give up so easy," Lige said. "We'll set them aside, and maybe we can figure out some way to save them."

It sounded like Lige had a lot more patience than he did. There were bigger problems facing them, like how to get all the broken panes replaced. A few of the frames were damaged as well—he'd guess the baseball bat had done that.

"Even if we save those, we might not find anyone wanting to buy them. People tend to avoid a place once there's trouble."

Lige stared at him for a long moment. "Out there,

maybe." His gesture seemed to indicate the world beyond the ridges. "Not in River Haven."

He'd like to believe that was true, but he couldn't.

They had moved one row of geraniums when Michael saw a buggy turn into the drive—Sarah, with the three younger children in the back. He headed toward the drive, intent on discouraging her from trying to take part.

Aunt Verna emerged from the kitchen, where she'd been washing breakfast dishes, pulling on garden gloves. "Ach, Sarah, what are you doing here?" Obviously she felt the same way as he did. "Now, don't say you've come to help. You have plenty to do with the kinder, and you won't want them around the broken glass."

Sarah was already lifting down a basket and putting it in Michael's hands. The two boys scrambled down on their own and stared wide-eyed at the greenhouse while Sarah lifted little Sally into Aunt Verna's arms.

"That's a couple of shoofly pies and a box of sandwiches." She nodded toward the basket. "Boys, you take that into the kitchen for Aunt Verna."

They cast a wistful glance toward where their daadi was working before obeying her.

"The men will work up an appetite this morning, so we'd best start the coffee and get things ready." Her voice was brisk, and she swept Aunt Verna toward the house as she spoke.

"What men? Lige and I…"

His sister gave him a mischievous look that

transformed her into an eight-year-old. "Wait and see. I predict you'll have more help soon."

Michael started to protest, but she didn't wait around for it. And apparently she was right, because another buggy was turning in already—Lige's two brothers and his daad, he realized quickly.

Lige had come out at the sight of them, and he grinned at Michael's expression. "Save your breath," he said. "They're here to help, and you won't talk them out of it."

Oddly enough, he wasn't even tempted to do so. This place must be having an effect on him. Or maybe it was the people. Lige's family was probably here because of him, but their help would be most welcome.

Throughout the morning, another eight men had shown up, including Cathy's father, along with a handful of women carrying food into the kitchen. When he glanced toward the kitchen window, he could see what looked like a cheerful beehive of women, all talking and working at the same time.

"It's going fast," Lige said as he and Michael pulled out a broken frame. He sounded satisfied, and it was no wonder. They'd completely emptied the greenhouse and were well underway with cleaning up the broken glass.

"Yah, but it'll need another trip to get the replacement glass." *How long would that take? And what would it cost?* That should be on him, as he saw it.

"At least it didn't happen earlier in the spring,"

Lige pointed out. "We're not going to have frost now, so the plants will be safe enough outside."

He could stand to have a little more of Lige's boundless optimism, he decided.

He and Lige were both startled, it seemed, when a car pulled into the lane. Probably Lige was wondering, as he was, if the police had come calling again.

Then he recognized the car—it was Mrs. Carpenter's elderly station wagon. He and Lige exchanged glances.

"I'll talk to her. She must not have heard." Michael walked quickly toward the car, trying to frame an explanation. But there wasn't one, other than the truth.

"Good morning." He hurried to intercept her before she got out of the car. "I'm afraid we're closed for repairs."

"Nonsense." She shoved the door open abruptly and swung herself out, hanging on to it as she straightened. "You can always stop long enough to sell something." She walked past him, headed straight for the rows of geraniums they'd put on the ground.

"I could bring you anything…" he began, but as usual, she cut him off.

"No need for that. Just load up these geraniums in the back of the wagon. I'll take all you can fit in."

Lige had joined them by this time, and he protested. "We haven't had a chance to check them all. There might be broken glass."

"Do I look like I'm afraid of a little glass?" she demanded, scowling at him. "Start loading them."

She definitely had Lige intimidated. He immediately started picking up pots.

"Look, Mrs. Carpenter, we appreciate it, but I can't let you pay for plants that might be damaged."

She shrugged. "Doesn't matter to me who I pay. Lige will take the money, or I'll leave it under a flowerpot. Mind you come by and give me that estimate. It's time we got started on that railing."

He'd have continued to protest, but she'd already stumped off toward the car to supervise the loading. Resigned, he picked up an armload of pots. Despite their obvious differences, Mrs. Carpenter reminded him of Aunt Verna, and he never had been able to win an argument with her either.

CATHY TURNED THE buggy into the lane, smiling at the sight of Allie's face when she saw workers swarming over the greenhouse. Phil Maggio's truck was pulled up close, and he and two other Englischers were unloading glass panes that would replace the ones broken by vandals.

"All those people are helping." Allie's expression was one of awe. "Look at them."

"'Course they are." Ruthie bounced on the seat, as if ready to launch herself into the work party. "Look, there's my daadi."

"Remember what we talked about this morning?"

Allie met her gaze, and her smile transformed her serious face. "We'll both count this one, ain't so?"

Cathy nodded.

Ruthie, predictably, turned to Allie, her eyes

alight with curiosity. "What do you mean? What are you counting?"

"Good things," Allie said softly. Suddenly she put her arm around Ruthie and hugged her, surprising Cathy as much as it did Ruthie. "You're one of my good things."

Michael approached them, his gaze questioning. "I thought Allie and Ruthie were going to my daad's place this afternoon."

"I received a message from Sarah to bring them here instead."

He gave each of the girls a hand as they jumped down. "See all the people who came to help us? That's wonderful good, isn't it?"

"Did you ask them?" Allie said.

Michael shook his head, smiling. "They just came. Now, I'll bet Aunt Verna and the others could use your help in the kitchen."

The two of them consulted wordlessly. Then they ran off toward the kitchen.

Cathy had to smile. "Those two have reached the point that they don't need words to communicate. It's nice to see."

"It is." His brow furrowed. "How was Allie today? She seemed so upset when she left that I wasn't sure sending her was the right thing to do."

"Talk to her," she suggested. "I think you'll find being in school today was good for her. The other scholars rallied around, just as they should." She nodded toward the greenhouse. "Just as the grown-ups did."

Michael leaned against the buggy seat as if prepared to chat. “I’d guess that the example set by Teacher Cathy had something to do with it.”

She shook her head, smiling. “All I did was remind them who they are. That’s all.”

“We all need that, I guess. When I see things like this, I think I know.” He gestured toward the men working on the greenhouse. “But sometimes it’s hard to be sure.”

Cathy’s heart twisted. She knew what she hoped his answer was. But how could she be sure it was right for him? Impulsively she put her hand over his. “Give it time. It will come to you.”

He glanced at her hand, and she took it away hastily. What was she thinking to be touching his hand where others could see and interpret?

“I guess Sarah knew she’d be here helping, so it was best to pick up Allie and Ruthie here to bring to my father’s.” Michael turned, as if going to the kitchen.

“I think there might be another reason.” Cathy had just spotted the man who emerged from behind the greenhouse. “Your daad is here.”

“He’s not...” Michael began, and then fell silent as he, too, saw his father.

Josiah Forster looked intimidating at the best of times, and his expression was stern as he approached his son. It suddenly occurred to Cathy that she was intruding. She picked up the lines.

“I’ll get my buggy out of the way and then check in with Verna,” she said quickly. But Josiah had reached them already, and his sternness melted slightly at the sight of her.

"Teacher Cathy." He nodded in greeting. "You brought my granddaughters, yah? Denke."

"I was happy to do so." Her own smile broke through at the thought of Josiah dealing with the two girls. "They chattered the whole way."

He couldn't seem to hide the doting look in his eyes. "Ach, little girls are different, ain't so?"

She nodded, thinking it was high time she scooted. "I'll just get out of the way."

Josiah stopped her with a hand on the buggy frame. "I'll just keep Michael for a moment." He turned to his son as if there had never been any estrangement between them. "Lige asks will you komm? He wants your opinion on the framing before we start."

For a moment it seemed Michael was too stunned to speak. Then he nodded. "Yah, fine. Let's go, then."

Cathy watched them walk toward the greenhouse together. They were so much alike, allowing for the difference in ages…both tall and wiry, with the same glossy brown hair the color of a horse chestnut, though Josiah's was sprinkled with gray.

A little bubble of happiness teased her. If only this could be a new beginning for the two of them—that would go a long way toward allowing Michael to find his place.

After she'd tied her horse to the hitching rail, Cathy walked back toward the house, pausing to wave at her father. Was it too much to hope that as Daad worked with Michael, they'd develop a liking for one another? It could be, but she suspected her motives for seeing that happen were totally selfish.

Cathy stopped short of the porch when a car came sweeping up the lane…not the police car, but Chief Jamison's own vehicle. He was being tactful, but he could have picked a better time to come.

The car pulled up beside her, and Jamison got out. "Hi there, Cathy." He glanced toward the greenhouse. "Looks like everyone is hard at work. Could you find Michael for me?"

She nodded, heading for the spot where she'd last seen him. Was this good news or bad? Impossible to tell from Chief Jamison's expression. She couldn't stop apprehension from rising in her.

Michael turned, seeing her and beyond her, the chief's car. Their eyes met for a moment, and he nodded. As he started toward her, Cathy saw his father hesitate for a long moment and then follow Michael.

Murmuring a probably incoherent prayer, Cathy returned to Jamison. "He's coming. I—I'll let you speak with him privately."

"No, stay." He put out his hand to detain her. "I'll need to show you something, too."

Feeling like an awkward fifth wheel, she lingered, hoping futilely that no one was noticing.

"Michael. Josiah." Jamison nodded to them. "Just wanted to let you know that we've got them—all three of them."

"That was fast." Michael looked as surprised as she felt. "How?"

Jamison's eyes twinkled. "Not so hard. We found

them bragging about it over beer at the Rusty Gate Tavern. Bartender called us."

"These men…were they people we would know?" Josiah asked, and Cathy thought she could hear apprehension in his voice. That was what she dreaded as well. That the vandals would be people they'd thought were friends.

"I doubt it. Couple of lazy loafers who'd do anything for the price of a drink, and a teenager who'd come along for the ride."

Michael was frowning. "Does that mean you think someone put them up to doing it?"

He'd been quicker than she was, but she saw it now, too. Why would random strangers suddenly decide to pick on Verna's greenhouse?

"Could be." The chief was cautious. "They're not talking, if so. But I haven't given up on it. Thing is, it won't be the first time the two older ones have spent thirty days in jail. As for the kid, well, I don't believe he knows anything. Scared him enough to make him think twice, I hope."

"If someone incited them, then it's not over." Michael said the words evenly, but Cathy could sense the pain behind them, and her heart ached for him.

"I can't kid you. There's no way of knowing unless one of them talks." The chief pulled something from his pocket. "Here's pictures of the three of them. Mean anything to you?"

Michael took them, scanned them and shook his head. Josiah did the same. He started to hand them back to Jamison, but he shook his head.

"Let Teacher Cathy take a look. Any of those faces familiar to you? Like maybe you might have seen them somewhere near the school?"

"You think one of them might be the person who was spying on recess that day," she said quickly, trying to keep him from mentioning the person who'd followed her and Allie from school.

"Have a look anyway."

She took the photos warily, realizing that Josiah was as reluctant to hand them to her as she was to take them. But the faces were strangers.

"No, I've never seen any of them."

Josiah spoke for the first time. "Whoever they are, we forgive them."

"I wouldn't expect anything else," Jamison said. "But they've broken the law, and they'll have to face the consequences."

Cathy's thoughts honed in on Josiah's words. He could forgive the vandals so easily. Couldn't he forgive his own son?

A moment later she had her answer. Josiah put a hand on Michael's shoulder. "Komm. We'd best get back to work."

Another person might think that Michael was unmoved, but Cathy knew him too well for that. She read, so clearly, the sense of relief in his eyes.

Whatever else this trouble might have done, it had closed the chasm between father and son, and her heart overflowed with gratitude.

CHAPTER SEVENTEEN

THE GREENHOUSE HAD been restored to like-new condition by the time folks began heading home. Michael was staring at it, still amazed, when Jacob King clapped him on the shoulder.

"What's wrong? Didn't you think we could do it?" His grin took him back to when they'd both been about ten or so.

"I knew you could. I just didn't think you would."

"You know better than that, ain't so? The Leit would come together no matter what caused the trouble." His bright blue eyes turned thoughtful. "Maybe even quicker when it's an attack on one of us. Comes from all those stories they drummed into us when we were small from the *Martyrs Mirror*."

He found himself smiling. "I seem to remember you having nightmares of being crushed to death as punishment for being Amish."

"That was because my little brother was sitting on my chest when I was sleeping." He shook his head. "Enough old times. Let's get down to business."

"Business?" Michael looked at him blankly. "What business?"

"My business. You're a skilled builder. I have a

construction business. Seems like a good fit. How about coming to work with me?"

He wanted to jump at the chance, but his conscience wouldn't let him.

"Have you really thought that over? I'm not exactly popular these days. If I work for you, you might lose some jobs because of it."

"Ach, I've got more work than I can handle anyway." Jacob's good humor was unimpaired. "Besides, I always wanted an excuse to boss you around."

"You and who else?" he retorted, taken back to elementary school again. "If you're sure, there's nothing I'd like better." Mrs. Carpenter popped into his mind. "Only thing is, I've been doing some jobs for Mrs. Carpenter in the evenings. I wouldn't want to stop..."

Jacob waved that away with his hand. "No problem. Lots of the guys do little jobs here and there. Long as you have the energy to do both, it's fine with me. We have a deal?"

"Yah, I guess we do. Denke, Jacob. I can't tell you what it means—"

"Save it. I've got somebody to pick up my crew, so he'll come by around seven thirty tomorrow."

"I'll be waiting at the end of the lane. And thanks, Jacob. For the job, and for today."

Jacob responded with another clap on the shoulder and marched off. Michael saw Aunt Verna intercept him before he'd gotten far. He'd have to listen to her thanks, too, even if it embarrassed him.

As for him—elation bubbled up in him. He had a

job. He'd be bringing in a paycheck, doing work he loved for someone whose friendship had stood the test of time. What could be better?

Cathy. He had to tell Cathy the good news. He took a step toward the house and then realized that Daad was standing a couple of feet behind him.

"You heard? Jacob offered me a job."

"Yah. That's gut. You and Jacob will work fine together. You always did."

He nodded, letting his mind drift back into the past. Jacob had been like a brother—closer than his own brothers, who were so much younger than he was. If he'd followed Jacob's advice when they were teenagers…

"It'll be good to have a real job again. I'll still help Aunt Verna and Lige, that's certain sure." He glanced toward the house. Cathy had come out with the two girls, and she stood talking to Verna.

"Looks like Cathy is headed home. I should thank her for helping."

"Michael." Something in Daad's voice kept him from moving.

"Yah?"

"You're wanting to tell Teacher Cathy your gut news, ain't so?"

He felt himself stiffening at the hint of disapproval in the question. "She's been wonderful good with Allie. I think she'd like to hear it."

"I hear she's a fine teacher. And everyone knows she has a generous heart, especially for the young ones."

Michael couldn't help but feel Daad expected him to draw some sort of lesson from the words.

"She is that. I don't know how Allie would have settled down here if it hadn't been for Cathy."

"You've seen a lot of her."

Now he knew what Daad meant, and he couldn't say he liked it. "Because of Allie," he said. "And since they're close neighbors, she offered to take Allie back and forth to school. That's all."

"No one would be surprised if a man grew fond of Teacher Cathy, seeing her so much."

"But I shouldn't, that's what you mean, isn't it?" He felt the familiar spark of resistance at having Daad tell him what to do, even if it mirrored his own thoughts on the matter. And then, just as quickly, it was gone, leaving him feeling flat.

He wasn't a teenager any longer. He was a man who carried a load of trouble with him wherever he went. That load of trouble had a way of slipping over onto other people when they got close to him. He only had to look at the greenhouse to know that.

Daad was still standing there. He waited with a lot more patience than Michael had ever known him to show while Michael found the answer for himself. Maybe he wasn't the only one who'd grown and changed in the past ten years.

"I know," he said finally. "Teacher Cathy has risked her job, most likely, just through her kindness to Allie. I can't let her risk anything else because of my actions."

"If you came back to the church…" Daad began.

"I can't. Not now. Maybe sometime, but not now. Don't you see?" If only he could make his father understand, maybe it could close a bit more of the gap between them. "I'm not free of what happened to Diana. I don't see how I can be unless someone finds out the truth of it."

He stared at his father for a long moment, trying to see some glimmer of understanding. Maybe it could never be there. Maybe… "Why don't you ask me if I'm responsible for her death? Is that what you're thinking?"

A spasm of what could only be pain crossed his father's face. "I don't ask because I know that you are innocent of that, at least."

Michael closed his eyes for a moment, grappling with it. Daad trusted he wouldn't kill, but there was still a qualification. As Daad saw it, he'd done plenty of other wrongs.

Well, haven't you? The voice of his conscience sounded remarkably like his father's at the moment.

Yah, he had. Not just things the church would call wrong, like driving a car and working on the Sabbath. Things he knew in his heart were wrong—not spending enough time with his daughter, failing to heal the breach between himself and Diana, letting his family think he was indifferent to them. And most of all, not loving Diana in a way that satisfied what she wanted from her life.

Michael took a deep breath and squared his shoulders to support the weight of the burden he still had to bear.

"The last thing I'd ever want to do is hurt Cathy. I can't let her care for me when I have nothing to offer but a ruined reputation and a child who needs to be my sole focus right now. But I can't stop seeing Cathy because Allie needs her so much. It's not easy to balance." Ruefulness entered his voice on the final words.

No, not easy. It might be the hardest thing he'd ever done, but somehow he had to bring it off.

Slowly, very slowly, Daad reached out and clasped his shoulder in a strong grip. "You will try hard, yah? And trust God to handle the rest of it."

He couldn't imagine that God would have much use for him after the mess he'd made of things. But if Daad could trust, he could try to do the same.

"I'll try."

His father nodded, and for an instant he thought he saw a sheen of tears in his eyes. He didn't speak, just tightened his grip in a wordless gesture of support.

"You'll come to supper soon, you and Allie? It's time you got to know your brothers again, ain't so?"

"We'd like that. Soon."

Several giant steps forward, he decided. But there was still a formidable obstacle between him and any kind of normal life.

"WHICH ONE DO you think?" Joanna held up two baby quilts, one with animal designs and one with flowers.

"Take them both," Cathy suggested. "They're beautiful." And melancholy for someone who had little hope of ever needing a crib quilt for a child of her own.

She gave herself a mental shake. What was she doing? It was only since Michael had returned that she'd found she was mourning the future she didn't have. Well, it was time to stop that nonsense. Michael might be attracted, but he was as well aware as she was of the impossibility of anything between them.

"Cathy?" Joanna and Rachel were both staring at her. "What's going on? I've answered you three times, but you were lost in a world of your own."

"Sorry." She tried to smile, sure that her face was getting red. "I just thought of something."

"Must have been serious." Joanna's face was openly curious.

She managed a laugh. "Just thinking that Rachel's awfully happy about an evening out packing things for the Mud Sale."

It was Rachel's turn to flush. "I am happy. I don't have the exciting lives you two do—seeing people every day. Now that my brothers are mostly grown-up… Well, Daad isn't much for talking."

Guilt pricked her. She shouldn't have used Rachel as a distraction from her own troubles.

Cathy gave her a quick hug. "Never mind. You can talk all you want to us. But if you think a roomful of schoolchildren makes for good conversation, you'd best think again."

"And you haven't lived until you've tried to talk Emma King out of getting pale pink for a new dress.

It'll make her look like she faded in the wash, but there's no convincing her."

Joanna could be counted on to come up with something to cover Cathy's mistake. Though she'd probably demand answers later.

"Anyway, to get back to work," she went on, "I can't carry everything in the store over to the sale. Some of the things I have on consignment are supposed to go, but some people wouldn't think of it, even if it is for charity."

"What's the money going to this year?" Cathy asked, putting quilted pot holders into a box. Joanna would know. She always knew what was going on in town.

"Half to the volunteer fire department," she said promptly. "And the other half is to be divided between the two Amish schools."

"Really?" Visions of new books danced in her mind. "The committee has never done that before. Why now?"

Joanna smiled. "Well, I might have pointed out that without all the donations and work of the Amish, the sale wouldn't be much of a success. And last year, they made a donation to the elementary school playground, which our kinder don't even use. Someone might have mentioned that, too."

Cathy shook her head. "I never knew you were such a manipulator, Joanna. Don't tell me your aunt knew about this, because I won't believe it."

Joanna's aunt Betsy lived with her in the apartment above the shop. That was the only way Joanna's parents could ever be brought around to the idea of their daughter living there. But Aunt Betsy was busy with her own job at the bakery, and she spent more time out than in, as far as Cathy could tell.

"Aunt Betsy is the ideal person to share an apartment with," Joanna said. "We both want our freedom."

"I'm not sure I could live with any of my aunts. Mamm is more understanding than all of them put together."

"You're blessed in that way," Rachel said. "Even if things..." She let the sentence trail off, looking at Cathy and then as quickly turning away.

"Even if what?" Cathy said. There was some meaning behind that quick glance, and she wanted to know what it was.

"Nothing, nothing." Rachel busied herself folding a quilt. "I was just talking."

Cathy and Joanna both advanced on her, and Joanna took the quilt from her hands and put it aside. "Komm, now. You think we don't know when you're hiding something?"

"That's right." Cathy caught the hands Rachel extended as if to fend them off. "Talk. What is it?"

Rachel's soft eyes filled with tears. "Ach, Cathy, I don't want to tell you. I was just so upset I couldn't help myself."

Cathy felt her teasing smile freeze on her face. This was serious. It wasn't one of their usual jokes. Rachel wouldn't weep unless she was hurting.

"Whatever it is, it's best for Cathy to know,"

Joanna said, her tone firm. "Just tell it. No one is blaming you."

Rachel wiped her eyes with the backs of her hands like a child. "I wasn't meant to hear, I think. But I went out to the barn last night after supper, and I realized someone was there with Daad. He was telling him..."

"Who was there?" Joanna clasped Rachel's hand.

The tears threatened again, but she blinked them back.

"Zeb Stoltzfus."

Cathy's heart sank. Mary Alice's father wouldn't have had anything good to say, she guessed.

"It sounded as if he'd been going around trying to get people to talk to the school board members." Her eyes avoided Cathy's. "To make them decide not to renew Cathy's contract."

"And he had exactly the right candidate in mind to replace her, I suppose." Joanna was fuming. "Mary Alice, and she couldn't teach her way out of a paper bag!"

Cathy wasn't sure whether to laugh or cry at her friend's quick defense of her. "Now, Joanna, she's not that bad. She needs training and supervision, but she might be a teacher one day."

"But not now." Joanna's anger wasn't assuaged. "Of all the underhanded things to do. Zeb and Lizzie should be ashamed of themselves."

"They think they're right." Cathy could see that, even through her pain. "Did Zeb tell your daad why I should be let go?"

"He… Well, first he talked about how the police had been at the school, and he didn't like that."

"Cathy did exactly the right thing. Would he rather have the kinder in danger?" Joanna's temper was a simmering kettle ready to boil over.

"I know! I'm certain sure Cathy did the right thing, and I believe Daad thought so, too. But then Zeb started talking about…about Michael. And Allie. He said Allie was an Englischer and shouldn't be in our school."

Cathy winced. Poor Allie. She was just finding a place to belong. Did they really want to take that away from her? Her resolve strengthened. If she wasn't willing to fight back for herself, she ought to defend Allie.

"That's not all, is it?" She controlled herself with an effort. "He talked about me and Michael, didn't he?"

Rachel nodded. "He hinted mostly. But, Cathy, I'm so afraid folks might start to believe what Zeb and Lizzie are saying. We have to do something."

"What? What can anyone do?" She wanted to protest this injustice, but how could she protect herself against rumors? It seemed impossible, and if Allie were hurt by this, she'd never forgive herself.

MICHAEL MOVED ALONG the peak of the roof, ready to start another row of shingles. His first day on the job, and already he felt as if he'd been working with this crew his whole life.

Maybe it was the product of the eighteen years

he'd spent here before he'd run away. He'd grown up working alongside the others, with each year bringing a new job with greater responsibility. Amish boys learned how to work from working alongside someone—moving from carrying water to the workers, to fetching and carrying, to taking those steps toward doing a man's job. There was no juggling for position or slacking off or feeling pride because you could do something a little better than the next man.

Jacob moved up a row behind him, pausing long enough to grin at him. "Going okay?"

"Great."

A sense of well-being washed over him. This is what he was meant to be doing. Jacob worked alongside his crew, something Michael had lost the chance to do in the outside world. There, he'd felt pressure to reach for more—bigger jobs, bigger crews, losing the pleasure of working with his hands in exchange for supervising others and making more money.

Had it been worth it? Not in the long run. No matter how much he made, he hadn't been able to keep Diana happy.

Something flickered through his mind—an image of what his life would have been like now if he'd stayed here. He and Jacob had been the best of friends. They'd both enjoyed the same kind of work. Maybe they'd have been partners in a business like this one by now.

"Finish up," Jacob called. "Once we get it all under roof, we'll knock off for the day."

Naturally they wouldn't stop until that was done.

Jacob had his standards, and Michael had already realized that despite Jacob's soft-spoken way of managing the men, he expected the best. And he seemed to get it.

Eventually they were off the roof and clearing up for the day. Jacob paused next to him. "So, got some sore muscles, ain't so? I'd guess it's been some time since you've put in a day like this."

"The day I can't keep up with you, I'll take to my bed," he retorted and then grinned. "Maybe a little bit achy. I bet Aunt Verna has some liniment that'll cure it." Aunt Verna always had remedies for everything, most of them homemade.

"Yah, I could use some. This has been a big job." Jacob looked with satisfaction at the work. "And another one waiting—over at that fancy nursing home."

"Where Diana's grandmother is?" Michael's eyebrows lifted. He hadn't imagined Jacob pulled in those kinds of jobs.

"Don't worry. You won't run into her. We'll be outside, not in." He'd misinterpreted Michael's remark, but it didn't really matter. He wasn't eager to run into the woman. Once had been enough, the time she'd warned him away from her granddaughter.

"No problem. I..." He broke off, as the sense of something one of the other men was saying broke through to him.

"...don't know if it's true or not, but that's what I heard. A bunch of people are planning to get rid of the teacher at Creekside School."

Michael swung toward the voices. The speaker

was Thomas Baylor…not someone he knew well, since Thomas lived at the far end of the county, in a different church district. But he'd said Creekside.

It must have registered with Jacob a second after it had with him. "What's that you're saying, Thomas?"

Thomas was young, gangly, with an air of still growing into his work clothes. He flushed at the sudden attention from the boss.

"I—I don't know if it's true. I just heard some talk at the lumberyard, that's all."

"What kind of talk?" Michael took a stride toward him and was conscious of Jacob's hand on his arm.

Thomas kicked at the gravel, looking unhappy. "Didn't mean anything much to me. I mean, it's not my school. Or my church district. I didn't think about it being yours, or I wouldn't have said anything."

"Take it easy, Thomas." Jacob took over. "Tell us what you heard."

"Some guy was talking—Stoltzfus, it was. He said that the teacher had caused a lot of trouble and got herself talked about, and they couldn't have that at the Amish school. So they figured to get her replaced. That's all I know, honest."

"Yah, all right. Get loaded up, everyone. Time we were out of here."

When the men had scattered, Jacob gave Michael a wary look. "I heard Cathy's been helping you with Allie. You want to talk about it?"

"No." He clipped off the word and then realized how it sounded. "I mean, not right now."

Not until he'd talked to Cathy. He saw it clearly,

and he had no doubts at all. He'd brought this trouble on her. He had to tell her how sorry he was. And then he had to figure out a way of fixing this mess.

Unfortunately, the opportunity to see Cathy didn't come until well after supper. He was late getting home, and they were waiting supper for him. It was only when Aunt Verna swept Allie away for her bath that he'd been able to slip away.

He approached the Brandt place by the trail through the woods, emerging into the area behind the barn. He and Cathy needed a private conversation, something that wouldn't happen if he went to the house and asked for her.

He was fortunate, it seemed. When he neared the barn he heard Cathy's voice, crooning something softly to one of the horses, he supposed. He slipped in the back door, and she looked up, startled, when she heard it open and close.

"Michael? What are you doing here? Did you want Daad?"

He walked quickly to her. "I needed to see you." He plunged ahead, not waiting to wrap it up pretty for her. "Did you know Stoltzfus is saying the school is going to get rid of you?"

Once he was close enough, he saw the shadows around her eyes and the drawn look of her face. "You already heard."

"Last night. A friend of mine had actually heard him. He was trying to convince her father to bring pressure on the school board."

"Because of me." His tone went flat. Somehow

he caused trouble for anyone he touched. Now it was Cathy.

"No, not because of you." She was quick to deny it. "Zeb and Lizzie Stoltzfus have been trying to get the school job for their daughter for the past year. This is just the latest effort."

"Okay, so they want your job." He couldn't get rid of his guilt that easily. "But I'm the weapon they're using to accomplish it."

Cathy pressed a hand to her forehead. "It's not your fault." Her voice sounded choked. "They're talking about when the police came to the school, making it sound as if I overreacted. And..."

"And you've been trying to help me and Allie." He caught her wrist, turning her to face him more fully. "Stop trying to save my feelings. I can see as far as the next person. You've put your job in jeopardy because of me."

She managed a faint smile. "Mostly because of Allie. And if you think I'd do anything any differently, you don't know me very well."

"I think I do." He looked down at her wrist, encircled by his fingers, and fought the longing to pull her into his arms. "But I can't just let this happen. I'll go to the school board and—"

"Don't. Ach, don't you see that would just make it worse? If they're going to let me go for doing what I know is right...well, then, they'll have to do that. I can't change."

"Nobody with any sense would want you to change." The feelings that swept over him were leading him in a dangerous direction, and he had to back up. He let go of her wrist. "I'm sorry." He took a step away from her for safety's sake, rubbing the back of his neck in frustration. "All the mistakes I made with Diana—it seems like they're going to follow me wherever I go. And cause trouble for anyone I touch."

"Michael, please." She sounded desperate—longing to help him but not knowing how.

There wasn't any way. The closer she got, the more trouble she'd be in.

"It's true. I messed up with Diana." He put his hands on the nearest stall bar, feeling like he wanted to hit something. "I didn't mean to, but I did. I could never make her happy."

"Did she make you happy?" Cathy's voice was soft, but the words seemed to go right to his heart.

He'd like to avoid the question, but he couldn't. "No. Ironic, isn't it? We made this grand gesture, running away, giving up everything for love. But the truth was, we couldn't make each other happy. I knew that long before she told me to leave."

What must she be thinking about this? He shouldn't be saying these things to Cathy, but they seemed to come out without volition.

"I wasn't giving up, you know. Even then, when I was out of the house, I'd have gone back to her, have tried to make a decent life for her and Allie. For Allie's sake, if not for hers. But I didn't get the chance."

"Everyone has things they regret." In her eagerness to help, Cathy had moved dangerously close to him. “You were trying to do the right thing. You still are.”

He nodded. What she’d said was true. He was trying to do right, and that meant getting away from Cathy before he found himself kissing her, trying to drown his pain in her soft sweetness.

She reached out a tentative hand, and he flinched away. “I have to go. I’m sorry, Cathy. Truly sorry.” He left, knowing if he stayed a moment longer he’d go a step too far and never be able to go back.

CHAPTER EIGHTEEN

MICHAEL REALIZED HE was walking back home even faster than he'd gone. An outside observer, he thought wryly, might even say he was fleeing. And he'd be right.

Slowing his pace as he neared the house, he tried to think what had possessed him to go there. He knew it was dangerous for him to be alone with Cathy. She was sweet, innocent and loving—and he was afraid of doing the wrong thing with her, just as he was with Allie. Caught up in the warmth of her sympathy he'd almost forgotten that he was to blame for her problem.

Cathy faced losing the job that was the most important thing in her life because of him. The worst part of it was that he could do nothing. She'd probably been horrified to hear him say he'd go to the school board. If anything, that would tip the scales against her.

No, the best thing he could do for Cathy was to leave her alone. Even if, through some miracle, he was cleared of all suspicion in Diana's death, he still wasn't the man for her. After he'd failed so miserably, how could he risk marriage again?

He emerged into the yard to spot someone sitting on the back porch. Alan Channing, obviously waiting for him.

Michael strode quickly to the porch. "Alan. It's good to see you. If you'd told me you were coming..."

"That's a little hard to do when your cell phone is turned off." Alan smiled, pumping his hand. "You're really getting sucked into this life, aren't you?"

"It's got a lot to recommend it," he said, a little annoyed by the unconscious superiority of Alan's comment. "I use the phone so seldom it's a nuisance to keep it charged up. You're back in the area again already?"

He shrugged. "A minor hiccup with one of our customers. It was resolved in the office, but the old man thought it warranted a personal visit, so I turned on the charm."

The old man being Alan's father-in-law, he knew.

"I'm glad to see you anyway. Didn't Aunt Verna welcome you?"

"Sure thing." Alan gestured with the coffee mug he'd apparently set on the porch railing. "She wanted to feed me pie, but I said I'd wait for you."

"Good, I'm glad." For more reasons than one. His mind had gotten back on track after being derailed by his feelings for Cathy. He'd intended to talk to Alan in any event. He might be able to shed some light on the "friend" of her mother's Allie had mentioned.

"I wanted to see if you'd thought any more about that job I mentioned." Alan glanced around, as if wondering what the appeal of this place was. "I understand it's still open."

The temptation to run away was there, but his decision had already been made. "Thanks. I appreciate it, but I'm staying here. It's a lot better for Allie than going to another strange place."

Alan nodded, seeming to understand. "Allie's most important, I know. I always seem to get here after she's gone to bed. Tell her I said hello, will you?"

"Sure thing." Michael hesitated. "Speaking of Allie, she said something the other day that has me wondering."

"What's that?"

Wariness showed in Alan's face, startling Michael. What did his friend have to be wary of?

"She said that one time when she went to stay overnight at your house, she saw someone heading for our place. A man. She referred to him as Mommy's friend. Who was she talking about?"

"How...how would I know?" Alan made an effort to smile. "You sure she knew what she was talking about? Kids that age can imagine things. Anyway, how could she see anything?"

Doubt settled in. Alan was protesting too much. He might have been convinced if Alan had stopped with a simple denial.

"You know something," he said, his voice flat. "What was Diana up to?"

Alan stared at him and then glanced quickly away. "I don't know, not for sure."

Impatience rode him. "Okay, then, what do you *think* was going on?"

"Suspicion, that's all we had." He grimaced. "You know how it is. Diana kept asking if we could have Allie for the night. Of course, we were glad to help out, but...well, it made us wonder if there was a man in the picture."

Michael fought down anger. Another man. So that was what her talk about having a little time apart meant.

"Who was he?" He shot the question at Alan.

"I don't know. Really, neither of us did." He seemed to attempt to force certainty into his voice. It didn't work.

"You know something." His fists clenched. "What is it? You..." He stopped, aware of something shamefaced about the way Alan evaded his eyes. "You? It was you?"

"No!" Alan held up both hands as if to fend him off. "Not me. Not really."

"What do you mean, *not really*? Either you were having an affair with my wife or not."

"No, no. It never got that serious. It's just... She was..." His voice died out. He cleared his throat and started again. "A flirtation, that's all. She let me kiss her once. Afterward I could hardly look at myself in the mirror. I'm not that kind of guy. I love my wife." There was desperation in his face when he looked at Michael. "Afterward...that last month before she died...that's when I thought she was hiding something."

The urge to punch someone or something ebbed slowly away, to be replaced by a determination to get to the end of it.

"Why? What made you think that?"

"We both did. Diana asked us to have Allie twice before…before that last night. And Diana said something odd. She said she was going to have the life she should have had."

She should have had. Michael put that thought away to consider later. He had to make sure he had everything Alan knew, because he didn't think they'd ever see each other again.

"Allie caught a glimpse of the man once. You must have been curious to see who Diana preferred. Don't tell me you didn't try to see him."

Fine beads of sweat had formed along Alan's hairline. He was trying to decide whether to talk.

"All right, then, I did. But it didn't amount to much. I couldn't very well walk over and introduce myself. You know how far it was from our windows to your front walk, and there's that cedar tree in the way. I just got a glimpse of him."

"So you got a glimpse. Did you know him?"

"No, no." He sounded startled at the thought. "He was a stranger. Maybe about our age—average height, not heavy or anything."

"What about his face? Hair? Coloring?"

"Khakis, a dark shirt, I think. He had a windbreaker on, and a ball cap. Just looked ordinary, that's all."

"Would you know him again?"

Alan was already shaking his head before he got the question out. "I couldn't possibly identify him. Listen, Michael, you've got to keep me out of this. If my wife hears about it..."

He didn't need to say more. He wasn't going to do anything to risk his marriage or his cushy job with his father-in-law.

"Right." His jaw tightened with the effort not to say what he thought of him. "You won't mind if I don't invite you in."

Alan turned away quickly as if afraid he'd change his mind. "Sorry," he muttered and hurried to his car.

Michael watched it peel out of the driveway. So that was it for his friendship with Alan. All that support...easy enough to do, especially when Alan knew about the other man. And didn't want to say, for fear of his own relationship coming out.

It wouldn't have needed to. Alan could have helped clear him, but he'd been too worried about himself. As for that helpful job offer...clearly Alan would have been happier if Michael and Allie were safely on the other side of the country from him.

He knew more now about what had gone on in Diana's life in those last months, but was it going to do him any good? Jamison would listen with an open mind, but if the city police talked to Alan, he couldn't count on any help there.

He headed inside. Maybe a piece of Aunt Verna's pie would take the bad taste out of his mouth. He had a piece of the puzzle now, at the cost of what he'd thought had been a friendship, but he wasn't sure how much good it was going to do.

CATHY HAD HEADED straight to the fire company grounds after dropping Allie off from school. She'd promised to help Joanna set up her stand for the Mud Sale so she was here, though she'd rather be somewhere else. Somewhere quiet, where no one would know about the trouble brewing at the upcoming school board meeting.

"What are you fidgeting about?" Joanna handed her one end of the line she was stringing to hang some of the lighter-weight items. "You look as if your mind is a thousand miles away."

I wish I *were.* "It's nothing. Too long a school day. I'm like the kids—I need a recess." Before Joanna could voice the argument she saw forming, she hurried on. "Where's Rachel? I thought she'd be here."

Exasperation flashed in Joanna's eyes. "Her daad raised a fuss. As if he couldn't dish up his own supper when she had it all ready for him. I think he's the most selfish man I ever met."

"I wouldn't be surprised." If there was anything Rachel's friends agreed on, it was that her father imposed on Rachel's sweet disposition with his tyrannical ways.

"She said she'd stop by later, but I told her not to bother. She can help on Saturday. You'll be here, won't you?"

"Bright and early," Cathy said. She knew the format. Joanna couldn't put out the items she'd be selling until Saturday morning, and it would be a rush to have everything ready before the first customer showed up.

Joanna's only answer was a distracted nod, since she'd noticed that one of the hooks for the line was crooked. The wooden booths were stored from one event to another, and sometimes they came out a little the worse for wear.

Given a moment when her thoughts weren't distracted, Cathy's mind went immediately back to the things that troubled her. If she managed to stop worrying about the school board meeting, she'd switch back to Michael, and that was almost worse.

He'd left so abruptly that she'd remained standing there in the barn for a good twenty minutes, trying to wrap her mind around what had happened between them. They'd hardly touched, but she had never felt closer to anyone else in her life. It was as if their minds and hearts touched, if not their hands or their lips.

Did it frighten Michael to be so close to her? He seemed sometimes to believe that he'd never be free of the stain of Diana's death, never be able to live a normal life.

She'd been relieved not at the pain he'd undergone with his wife, but simply that he'd said it aloud. A thing that was kept secret and hidden from daylight could fester and poison the whole body.

But Michael might not see it that way. Probably the only reason he'd spoken was that he'd been rocked off his balance by the thought that he was responsible for the loss of her job.

As for her…well, looking back over everything that happened, she couldn't see a decision that she'd change if she had it to do over again.

No, not even tumbling into love with Michael. It hurt already, and it would probably hurt worse before it was over, but she could never regret having experienced such love.

"You're worrying about the school board meeting, aren't you?" Joanna's question was so far from what she was thinking that for an instant she couldn't come up with an answer.

"I suppose," she said at last. "There's nothing I can do about it, so it's silly to worry."

"If you tell me it's God's will, I'll shake you," Joanna declared, planting her hands on her hips. "There's nothing remotely good or truthful about the machinations Zeb and Lizzie Stoltzfus are going through to get rid of you."

"Maybe so, but there's nothing I can do about it."

"Now, there's where you're wrong. There's plenty to be done, and Rachel and I are more than eager to help. We can organize any number of people to attend that meeting and raise a fuss over what's going on. It's simple."

Cathy was already shaking her head. How could she convince Joanna that everything in her cringed at the thought of an open fuss about her? Joanna didn't fear anything, and she never had.

"I can't," she protested. "Please, Joanna, try to

understand. If they don't want me teaching the kinder, there's nothing I can do about it. I'll have to leave." Her voice choked on the words.

"If you're thinking about the scholars, you'll stay and fight, not give up. Everyone knows what a wonderful teacher you are. How will those kinder feel if you just give in because of a few people? You can't let them make decisions for you."

"I'm not." But what Joanna said seemed to echo something Mamm had told her. Was it true? She wanted to deny it, but a tiny doubt niggled at her.

"Here's Michael," Joanna announced. "Maybe he can talk sense into you." She swung around and busied herself at the back of the stand.

Michael reached out and took a screwdriver from her hand, making a show of securing the screws that held the stand together. "What is your friend so upset about?"

He didn't look at her, and Cathy suspected he didn't like having been maneuvered into this situation.

"Joanna is a very strong personality. She's upset that I might lose my teaching position, and she wants me to fight back. It's what she would do, but I don't think I can do it."

"You should. Don't you think I'd do it if I could? I'd tell those people what I think about this in a heartbeat, but I know it would make things worse, not better."

She was taken aback at the passion in his voice. For a moment she let herself envision him standing up to the school board for her. But he was right—it would be a mistake.

"Denke, Michael. I…I wish I could be a person who'd do that."

He was silent for a moment, and then he shook his head. "I guess you have to be true to yourself. Just don't forget that you're a strong person, too, and you're important to all those children. There's nothing false about you. You—" He stopped abruptly.

He'd seemed to be talking about her, but she suspected someone else had been in his thoughts, prompting what he'd said.

"What is it, Michael?" she said, keeping her voice soft and her eyes on the piece of twine that she was winding around her fingers. "Something about Diana, ain't so?"

His jaw tightened so much it seemed it would shatter. "Diana." He repeated the name, and she sensed a struggle between the need to speak and the desire to keep silent. "I talked to my old neighbor last night," he said abruptly. "A guy named Alan Channing. A friend—well, I thought he was a friend." A muscle in his jaw twitched. "That was before I knew he'd had a thing for Diana."

He didn't seem to hear her gasp, which was probably just as well.

"Not an affair, he claimed." Michael might have been talking to himself. He seemed totally unaware of her in that moment. "Just a kiss or two. As if that made it better."

"I'm sorry," she whispered. She couldn't find anything else to say.

He focused on her suddenly. "I shouldn't be telling you this, but you're the only one I can say it to."

"Of course you should be telling me. You have to confide in someone."

"That's not the worst of it. He's convinced there was someone else—the man Allie saw. The *friend.*" His voice rasped on the word.

"But, Michael—" Realization hit her. "That could be the one. The person who killed her. Did he tell the police?"

"No. And he won't. He's too busy trying to keep his own infatuation secret."

"But you could tell them what he said. They could look for him."

"They could, but they won't. Without Alan to back me up, I have nothing, except more motive for me."

"But surely—" Wouldn't he tell the truth if questioned by the police? Surely someone who'd been a friend wouldn't let Michael go on suffering.

Cathy had to force herself to face the obvious truth. If the man had a conscience, he wouldn't have stayed silent this long.

She didn't want to give up on the chance. Surely there was some way to make him speak. But Michael clearly didn't think so.

"So that means there's a killer in Harrisburg walking around free when he should be paying for his crime. If Alan won't speak, he never will."

"The chief knows that Diana had a male visitor,"

she pointed out. “That alone should be enough to make the Harrisburg police take it seriously, even if Alan won’t talk.”

“I wish I could be sure it would work out that way. I’m just afraid of doing the wrong thing with Allie. What if the police pursue it and want to question her themselves? I’m trying to keep her out of it, not push her into the middle of it.”

“I know.” Heedless of whoever might be watching, Cathy put her hand over his. “I can’t answer that—I don’t know enough. But think about it. You could see what Chief Jamison says. He’s a good man. He wouldn’t want to do anything that might hurt Allie.”

He didn’t move for a moment, and she thought he wasn’t going to respond. Then his fingers tightened on hers before withdrawing, and his face relaxed a little. “You always look on the bright side, don’t you? I just wish I could do the same.”

THE VAN TAKING the crew to work the next day passed through a pair of modernistic pillars and onto the grounds of the Maple Crest Retirement and Convalescent Community. Michael eyed what seemed like acres of rolling lawns dotted with buildings, and nudged Jacob.

“Pretty fancy, isn’t it? And Randy Hunter owns all this?”

“Owns? Not a chance.” Jacob gestured toward a street of duplexes, each with its own garage and pocket-size yard. “The residents own those, but ownership returns to the corporation when they move on to another level of care. Some big corporation owns the whole thing, and Randy manages it for them."

"Quite a position. I wouldn't have thought he was up to it." The kid he'd known had been a follower, not a leader.

Jacob shrugged. "Maybe he doesn't think he is. He certain sure fusses a lot. You wait—see if he doesn't come out while we're working with a half dozen things he's reconsidered." He shook his head. "As if we couldn't put up a gazebo without him standing over us."

"That's the job, then?" He should have been showing more interest in what they were doing, instead of just seeing it as work to keep him too busy to think.

"Yah. There's a nice little courtyard where they have what they call the memory care unit. We're doing a good big gazebo in the middle, so the patients…residents, they call them…can sit out in the shade."

There wasn't time for more, since their driver was already pulling up at the destination. The men scrambled out, and in a moment were unloading tools and equipment.

"Vans can't pull into the site, so we're carting everything through those doors. Everybody, grab what you can, and we'll use the hand truck for the bigger things."

It took several trips, but eventually everything had been assembled in the middle of a grassy plot. By then they'd attracted an audience—a number of older people lined the wide windows facing the courtyard. Michael spotted an elderly man at one of the doors, obviously wanting to come out. A woman in a pale pink uniform seemed to be discouraging him.

Jacob noticed the direction of his gaze. “They agreed to keep the residents inside while we’re working. Not that I mind folks watching, but I sure wouldn’t want anybody to get hurt.”

“You said this was the memory care unit?” A hazy memory connected with that was trying to surface. “Is that where Diana’s grandmother is?”

“Guess so.” Jacob frowned. “Is that a problem?”

“Not for me. And I don’t suppose she’d know me if she spotted me anyway.” He’d only met her once, and that had been enough for him.

Jacob set the men to work quickly. The foundation had been laid, so they could start framing out the building. It would be good-size as far as gazebos went, but not a big job for a crew like this. He suspected Jacob saw it as a step toward bigger projects. A place like this could be a profitable client for a small construction crew.

The work went smoothly, almost too smoothly for Michael. It gave him too much time to think, and none of his thoughts were very pleasant. Sometime in the night it had occurred to him that he’d accepted Alan’s explanation at face value. How did he know that Alan’s relationship with Diana was as minimal as Alan wanted him to think?

If they had been more deeply involved…if Diana had been pressing him for a commitment…somehow he didn't think Alan would have been ready to throw over his comfortable life and promising position as the boss's son-in-law for a new love. Maybe he had been Diana's path to having the life she'd wanted.

A desperate man could do desperate things. He'd accepted Alan's friendship and support after Diana died. He'd believed him to be a friend. He certainly hadn't been that, on his own admission. How much further might his relationship with Diana have gone?

Michael tried to stand back and look at the situation dispassionately, but it was impossible. Maybe Cathy had been right. Maybe he should talk to the police about Alan's admission.

He probably shouldn't have talked about it to Cathy, but it had become the most natural thing in the world to confide in her. And she must feel the same, or she wouldn't have told him as much as she had about her problem. If only he could get her to see what a good, strong woman she really was, and how much all of those children needed her. He'd grown to care so much for her, almost without realizing it was happening. Now it was too late to go back. Even if they could never be together, he was a better person for loving her.

Think about something else, he commanded himself. *Anything else.*

A distraction presented itself almost immediately. One of the doors had opened, and a figure stepped into the courtyard and started purposefully toward them. Not a patient—it was Randy Hunter.

He wasn't dressed for jogging this time. Instead,

he wore a tailored suit…gray, lightweight…that fit his slight frame so perfectly it was clear he hadn't bought it off the rack. He looked like a man who fit in at a place with extensive, rolling lawns and expensive amenities.

Mindful of Randy's attitude the previous time they'd bumped into each other, Michael moved behind an upright, letting a couple of the other guys screen him. No use in causing trouble for Jacob right off the bat.

From his position he could hear Randy well enough without necessarily being spotted. Dressed just like the other workmen, he blended into the background. After all, Randy's business was obviously with Jacob. He was already saying something about the plans.

"Are you sure you're following the plans we drew up? It doesn't look as large as I'd expected it to." Fussy, like Jacob had said.

"All according to the plans." Jacob handed over a sheaf of papers. "See for yourself. Those are the plans you signed off on."

Randy made an annoyed little clucking sound, like a hen disturbed on its nest. "It seemed larger on the plans. Really, I don't know…"

"The foundation has already been poured," Jacob pointed out. "If you want it larger, it will add considerably to the cost."

"I suppose it'll have to do." He still had that discontented note in his voice, as if his whole life was a series of small disappointments. "Just be sure you finish on time. I don't want to have to keep the residents penned up inside a moment longer than necessary in this nice weather. I'm not sure it wouldn't have been better to delay this project until the fall."

By this time Jacob had turned back to his work, apparently taking the balance of Randy's complaints for granted. Michael had to suppress a grin. Randy hadn't changed that much, not really. He might wear a suit and tie now, but he was still the one who stood back and let other people make the first move.

Funny, even in that memorable fight when Guy had decided he'd overstepped the bounds by dating Diana, Randy had stayed well on the sidelines, looking poised to fade away from the hint of trouble.

Michael turned to look up and check one of the support braces just as Randy moved back, leaving a clear line of sight between them. For an instant their gazes crossed. Randy's face stiffened.

"Jacob!" He snapped the name in a tone that seemed to surprise even himself.

As Jacob turned to him, he gestured toward Michael. "What is that man doing here?"

Jacob assumed the blank expression they used to call his "dumb Dutchman" look when they were kids. "What man?"

"Michael Forster. You never said you were bringing him on this job."

"I never said I was bringing Isaac King or Joseph Kohler either."

"You know what I mean." His anger was giving Randy a more emphatic tone. "I don't want—"

"We don't discriminate on my jobs." Jacob's tone was final. "It's against the law, ain't so?" he added, with a craftiness that surprised Michael.

"That…that's not the point." Randy seemed to be losing some steam. "You ought to know…to know Mrs. Wilcox is a resident here. Seeing him might upset her. He'll have to leave."

Jacob straightened. "Anybody leaves, we all leave." As if it were a signal, the other men put down their tools. The courtyard went suddenly silent.

Michael's momentary amusement was replaced by guilt. He didn't want to be the cause of Jacob losing what was probably a lucrative contract because of him. He opened his mouth to say so, but Joseph, standing next to him, gave him a nudge. He nodded toward Randy.

Sure enough, Randy was backing off. Literally. He took several steps backward, clearly looking for a way out of the situation he'd brought on himself.

"Maybe you could keep Mrs. Wilcox away from the windows on this side," Jacob suggested.

"Yes, yes, I suppose so. The nursing staff ought to be able to do a simple thing like that, given how much we pay them." Randy had found an alternative scapegoat. "I'll have to see to it." He scurried away.

Unaccountably moved, Michael cleared his throat. "Denke," he said.

"Can't let him get the upper hand," Jacob said easily. "Else we'd be here till Christmas doing this project. Forget it. We have."

True enough. The men were turning back to their

work as if the incident had been an entertainment put on to break up the day. He followed suit, not sure what he'd done to deserve the loyalty he was receiving.

Nothing, that was the answer. They behaved that way because he was one of them in their eyes, at least. If not in his.

CHAPTER NINETEEN

CATHY'S HELPER AT school was supposed to be Mary Alice Stoltzfus. She wondered whether she'd actually show up. Somewhat to her surprise, Mary Alice walked into the schoolroom behind the last group of older boys and girls.

Turning from greeting each of the scholars, Cathy received a shock. Mary Alice looked paler than ever, and her eyes were red rimmed, obviously with weeping.

"Mary Alice, what's wrong?" She reached out to the girl without thought.

"Nothing." Mary Alice evaded her eyes, but she clung to Cathy's hand for a moment.

"I can see you're upset." She kept her voice low. "If you'd rather not come in today..."

"My mother wanted me to stay home. Because of the school board meeting tonight. But I wouldn't." A little spurt of defiance sounded in her voice. "I said I'd help today, so I'm here."

If Mary Alice had actually defied her mother, it must surely be for the first time. Cathy wasn't quite sure what to think about that, but she gave the girl an encouraging smile before moving toward her place at the front of the room.

So the school board meeting was tonight, and no one had notified her. Did that mean the board had already made a decision? Surely they wouldn't do that without hearing what others in the church had to say.

Of course, she didn't normally attend school board meetings, nor did any of the parents. The board's work was primarily taken up with repairs to the building and decisions on new purchases. There was seldom anything in that to draw a crowd. But apparently tonight's meeting would be different.

It was harder than she'd expected to cultivate an attitude of reliance on God's will when she thought of losing her job. Maybe she'd better try harder.

Ruthie approached her desk, clutching a handful of violets. "These are for you, Teacher Cathy. Because we love you."

She had to blink back a rush of tears as she accepted the damp flowers, their stems hot from being clutched in Ruthie's plump little hand all the way to school.

"Denke, Ruthie. That was very thoughtful of you. Mary Alice, will you put some water in a small cup for the violets?"

Mary Alice nodded, heading for the cloakroom, and Cathy realized that Ruthie was actually glaring as she watched Mary Alice.

Her heart sank. If the Stoltzfus family got what they wanted and replaced her with Mary Alice, she feared the girl wouldn't have an easy time of it with the scholars. At least certainly not with Ruthie, who had undoubtedly already decided where she stood on the subject.

"You may take your seat, Ruthie," she prompted when Ruthie showed no signs of doing so. "It's time to start, everyone."

That reminder usually got her scholars into their seats and quieted the flow of chatter. This morning they seemed to have a bit of trouble getting settled, and the occasional whisper still reached her ears even as they moved into the morning routine.

Finally, when she'd gotten the lower grades started on their arithmetic practice, she sent a quelling glance toward the seventh and eighth graders, who were supposed to be reading in their history books.

"Komm, now. I know it's a lovely spring day and we're going to have a picnic lunch, but we must get some work accomplished first. Ellie and Margaret, have you finished your reading?"

"No, Teacher Cathy," they said in unison and bent their heads over their books.

She smiled a little, remembering how the longing for summer vacation sometimes became overwhelming on a beautiful day like this. She could be tempted to stare out the window herself, admiring the way the blossoms on the apple tree made delicate shapes against the gnarled bark. That tree had been old when she was a scholar here, and the scent of its blossoms could always take her back to moments spent dreaming, gazing at it.

The morning wore on, and the sound of the third graders reading aloud to Mary Alice was like the soft drone of bees on a summer day. The sound of a buggy coming down the lane caused an instant faltering in the reading.

Cathy and Mary Alice exchanged glances.

"Yah, it's the mothers coming to set up the picnic for you," Cathy said. "But first you will finish the work you're doing. We'll let you know when the picnic is ready."

She swept the classroom with a firm look as she headed back to the door to have a word with the arriving mothers.

Sarah was the first, trailed by her two boys, each carrying a basket as carefully as if they were filled with eggs. "Set them down under the trees," Sarah instructed. "I told you we didn't need them until we had the tables ready."

She turned to Cathy with an apologetic smile. "They're so excited to be allowed to come for the picnic."

"It's fine," Cathy assured her. "Believe me, the kinder inside are even more excited than your two boys."

"I'm sure. I wanted a moment to talk to you, but I guess that won't happen until we get everyone fed." Two more buggies had pulled up by now, and Sarah turned to begin organizing her volunteers.

Cathy retreated back into the schoolroom. Mary Alice would need her help to keep order until it was time. She suspected she knew what Sarah wanted to talk to her about—the school board meeting. Cathy felt herself cringe inwardly. She couldn't take her mind off it, but that didn't mean she wanted to talk about it.

There was the usual flurry of activity when the picnic started, but eventually everyone was fed and the scholars scattered around the school yard, giving their mothers a chance to relax and enjoy a second glass of lemonade or tea. Leaving Mary Alice to keep an eye on the children, Cathy made her way over to Sarah, thanking mothers as she went.

Verna pressed a glass of iced tea on her. "Just the way you like it," she urged. "Komm, sit for a minute with me and Sarah."

Nodding, she sank into a chair. "I need a minute. The kinder were buzzing so much this morning that I had trouble getting them to focus. Spring fever, I guess."

Sarah gave a decided shake of the head to her comment. "More likely they've heard all the talk that you might not be here next year."

Cathy's glass tipped, spilling a few drops of the tea onto her hand. "People wouldn't talk about it in front of the scholars, surely."

"Ach, kinder always know everything, even when the grown-ups try to keep it from them." Verna glanced at one of the women who'd begun to drift over to them—Donna Ascher, mother of Margaret.

"I'm that sorry, Cathy. I'm sure I never spoke of it to Margaret, but she heard it someplace. Asked me if it was true. Well, I had to say there was talk, but I hoped nothing would come of it." She had a sweet smile for Cathy. "I certain sure don't want to lose such a gut teacher. My kinder have never been so happy to come to school."

"Are there others who…" she began, and then she realized she didn't want to ask that question.

But it was too late. Donna's gentle face showed her distress. "Some, I'm afraid."

"Folks who say there's no smoke without fire," Verna snapped. "I've no patience with them."

A small silence greeted those words, making Cathy wonder just how many folks agreed with that sentiment.

"Maybe you should talk to your scholars about it," Donna suggested diffidently. "If they knew—"

"If they knew, maybe they'd put some pressure on their parents," Sarah exclaimed. "That's a wonderful gut idea, Donna."

Cathy was already shaking her head before Sarah had finished talking. "I couldn't do that. I couldn't bring it up even. That would be putting the school children in the middle of a grown-up dispute."

"They're in the middle already," Sarah said. Impassioned, she leaned forward to clasp Cathy's hand for an instant. "They are the ones who stand to lose if they—"

She broke off abruptly. Looking up, Cathy realized why. Mary Alice stood a few feet away, her face stricken.

"Mary Alice…" she began, but the girl shook her head.

"I know what you're thinking. That it's me who's behind this. But I know I'm not ready. I'd like to spend a whole year learning from Cathy how to be as fine a teacher as she is."

"If you feel that way, why don't you tell your mother that?" Sarah asked the obvious question.

Mary Alice paled. "I couldn't," she whispered.

"Leave her alone," Cathy said, pity for the girl swamping every other consideration. "None of this is her fault. I've done what I felt I had to do as a teacher, and if the board doesn't agree, then there's an end to it."

And an end to the life she'd made for herself. She felt as if she'd cut herself loose and was being blown away by the wind. Nothing that she'd thought stable and secure seemed that way any longer.

Sarah looked at her in exasperation. "What are we going to do with you? Neither you nor Mary Alice can stand up for yourself. Well, maybe we'll have to find another way."

Cathy blinked back tears again, determined not to show weakness. "I appreciate what you're trying to do, Sarah. Really, I do. But I can't bring the kinder into a grown-up argument, and I don't want to cause a rift in the church. If anyone is willing to speak for me, I'd be grateful, but others have to decide that for themselves. We can't let it be a…a popularity contest."

By the time the mothers had finished clearing up and her scholars were back in the schoolroom, Cathy felt as if she'd been running an obstacle race. And no sooner had she gotten them settled in their seats than one of the older girls raised her hand.

"Yes, Anna Mae?"

"Teacher Cathy, there...there's something we want to ask you." She looked around at the other upper graders, as if for moral support.

Cathy waited, afraid she knew what was coming.

Anna Mae took a deep breath. "Is it true? Is it true the school board won't let you be our teacher anymore?"

Donna and Sarah had been right—they did know. Only Allie looked confused—confused and more than a little frightened.

Cathy took a deep breath of her own. What to say? But she didn't really have a choice.

She took a step forward, letting her gaze embrace the whole class. "I have never lied to you, and I won't do it now. What I know is that there are some people who think I should be replaced as teacher."

A murmur of voices responded to her words.

"Please don't be upset. I love being your teacher, but if the board decides to replace me, I hope you'll be as good for her as you have for me."

She could see that they weren't satisfied, but what else could she say to them? Sometimes life didn't turn out the way you wanted. Still, she had to put on a brave face for the children, no matter how much she was grieving inside.

MICHAEL CLIMBED OUT of the van at the end of the lane, raising a hand in combined thanks and good-bye to the rest of the crew. Physical fatigue slowed his pace as he headed toward the house, but it was a good tired. Always before he'd end the day with worries about the next job hovering over him. Now he just felt satisfied with the day.

It wasn't a matter of the boss carrying the worries. He didn't suppose Jacob lay awake at night fearing the next job wouldn't be bigger and better, the way he had. There was no place here for being better than the next guy. As long as there was work to do that fed his family, Jacob was satisfied.

Aunt Verna's property opened up before him, as familiar as the farm where he'd grown up. Light clouds scudded across the blue sky, and there was a hint of showers in the breeze. The new windows in the greenhouse sparkled where the sun hit.

A little spurt of anticipation reminded him that he and Allie were going to Daad's for supper tonight. It would be interesting to see who did the cooking now that Sarah was married. Daad or one of his little brothers? He'd soon find out.

Tomorrow he'd stop by and talk to Chief Jamison about Alan. At some point today he'd realized that Cathy's instincts had been right on target. She'd responded with what he'd needed to hear. He wasn't justified in keeping Alan's confession to himself. The police had to hear it. The decision had brought with it a measure of peace.

He realized suddenly that the buggy pulled up in front of the greenhouse was Cathy's. She'd obviously just brought Allie home, and she stood talking to Aunt Verna and smiling down at Allie.

They'd both be better off, probably, if he confined

himself to a simple greeting, but he knew he wouldn't. It wasn't even possible to stay away from her in their small, close-knit community.

That description of community clung to his thoughts for a moment, oddly appealing. But if he committed himself to stay, he'd grow impatient with its restrictions, wouldn't he?

"Daadi!" Allie came skipping to meet him. "We're going to Grossdaadi's for supper tonight, remember? That will be fun."

"It sure will, sweetheart." He put his hand on her shoulder, aware of the fragility of small bones and soft skin, and was momentarily overwhelmed at the thought that she was his to love and to guide. He had to do it right, if he didn't do another thing in his life.

"Komm and wash up and have a snack," Aunt Verna said. "It will take Daadi a little time to get ready before you leave."

Allie obediently changed course to go with her. "Bye, Teacher Cathy. See you tomorrow."

"Bye, Allie." Cathy's smile included him, but she was already turning back to her buggy.

"Wait a second."

He put out a hand to delay her, touching her hand lightly. Even in that gentle touch he could feel the warmth of her skin. His pulse gave a jump, and for an instant he forgot why he'd stopped her.

"Yes?" Cathy seemed to make an effort to control herself.

"About last night. I'm sorry. I said things to you I shouldn't have. Please, forget it. All of that stuff about Diana—that's my unfinished business. I didn't mean to burden you with it."

He'd promise never to do it again, but even now he felt the longing to tell her what he'd decided, as if her approval was the most important thing in the world.

Something that might have been hurt flickered in her eyes, as if she felt he'd shut her out. "It's all right. I understand."

He'd hurt her, but he couldn't let her become involved in a murder case. "I have to handle it myself. I can't rely on anyone."

He'd relied on Diana, and that had been a mistake. On the sanctity of their marriage vows. On Alan's friendship. All mistakes.

"Nonsense." Cathy's voice cut sharply through his morbid thoughts, stunning him with its force. "No one can rely only on himself. We're put here to rely on each other—it's in the nature of life."

"Of Amish life. I know. I've seen that since I've been back here. But Diana's death and everything around it didn't happen in this world. Outside this valley I feel as if you have to rely on yourself or you get trampled."

"I don't believe that. You think it because people you trusted were false, but that's not all people. Haven't you learned yet that you have to count on others? You can't raise Allie all by yourself, no matter how good a parent you are. You need others who love her to help you. It's the same with this."

"No. It's not." The anger was a shield to cover the longing to hold her, to forget everything in the warmth of her embrace. "You don't know a thing about it."

"I know that you're letting it turn you into someone you're not. You're a good man, Michael. You didn't harm Diana, and it's not right that you should go on paying for it. It's not right!"

Her passionate defense of him shook him, reaching into his chest to grab his heart. How was it she could believe in him so strongly, despite everything? That belief seemed to turn everything upside down, shattering barriers he didn't even know he had.

"Cathy—" He should say something—something that would keep her away from him unless and until it was safe for him to love. But he couldn't find anything. He could only feel—longing. Passion.

Without thought, he pulled her against him, his lips claiming hers with a fierce need he didn't entirely understand. This wasn't teenage hormones and rebellion—this was something bigger, something that drowned his reason in longing and desire.

For a long moment it seemed the world was suspended. But then Cathy pulled herself free of him. He longed to hold her, but he couldn't. She would jump into the buggy and flee, and it was no wonder. How could he—

But she didn't. She leaned against the buggy, her breath coming fast, her lips red from his kisses. But when she spoke, there was a calm finality in her voice.

"I love you, Michael. It doesn't make any sense, but that's how it is."

When he made an instinctive movement toward her she warded him off with her hand.

"But there's no future for us. Not as long as you deny what you are—who you are. So now we both know."

"Yes." It was true. He couldn't see a future for them, but knowing she loved him—it pulled his heart together and then broke it again.

CATHY DROVE HOME AUTOMATICALLY, letting the buggy horse have her head. She knew the way to the barn all right, no matter what Cathy did or didn't do.

Numb. She couldn't seem to feel anything at all for a time. Then she woke to the painful realization that it was over. All over. The numbness was better than this tearing pain.

Telling herself she'd known from the beginning it would end this way didn't seem to help. It didn't soothe the pain in the least.

Nothing would. All she wanted now was to crawl into her bed and cry herself out, like a wounded animal seeking a hiding place. She understood that reaction now.

But when she reached the house, the first thing she saw was her sister's buggy. The second thing was Mary, leaning out the kitchen door to gesture to her.

"Hurry and come in. We have to talk, and I don't have much time."

None of that was an incentive to hurry, but Daad was already taking the mare's head.

"Go on." He jerked his head toward the house.

"May as well get it over with." His sympathetic smile bolstered her, though he couldn't guess the pain she bore.

"There you are." Mary swept her into a brisk hug the instant she walked into the kitchen. "Now, I don't want to see you moping around about this thing."

For a crazy moment Cathy thought her sister knew about Michael. But she couldn't.

Mary was surging on without drawing breath. "Just because this teaching plan didn't work out, that doesn't mean there's nothing you can do."

Her sister assumed the school board had already decided against her. Was that based on actual information, or was it just her assumption that, as usual, Cathy couldn't accomplish anything on her own?

"I happen to know that Esther Eshel needs someone to mind her kinder while she's helping in the furniture shop. You could do that easily, and it would keep you busy. I'll find out when she wants you to start and let you know."

"Mary, just stop." Desperation made her voice louder than she'd expected, and Mary stared at her, openmouthed. How was it she could be in such control in front of her class and so unable to speak up to her own sister? It was time to change that now. "I don't need a job with your friend Esther. I won't even know what's happening with the school until the meeting tonight."

Mamm had been standing at the counter, and she leaned against it now, giving Cathy a look that seemed meant to encourage.

"You're not going." Mary was appalled, her

already-rosy face reddening. "You don't want to sit there and listen to them discuss you. No, you listen to me, and everything will be fine. We'll take care of you."

To do her justice, Mary did love her. She wanted to help. She just didn't seem to understand that Cathy wasn't a shy six-year-old any longer.

"I'll take care of myself. I love you, Mary, but I don't need your help."

"But..."

Before Mary could go any further, Mamm was gently but firmly ushering her to the door. "You heard, Mary. Cathy is all grown-up now. You go home and take care of your own family."

Still gaping, Mary allowed herself to be shoved out the door, but she turned for a final word.

Cathy braced herself for an argument, but it didn't come. Instead, her sister looked at her with what might have been respect.

"All right, if that's how you feel about it, I won't interfere. But you know I just want what's best for you."

Before she could draw breath for more, Mamm closed the door, still smiling gently.

"Denke, Mamm." Cathy struggled to produce a smile. "Is it... Is it really decided already?"

"Not that I know of. Surely not without telling your side of the story. I expect better than that of the school board."

"You think I should go to the meeting." The very thought made her shake inside.

Mamm came to put her arm around Cathy. "We will support you whatever you decide."

That put it squarely on her. She wanted to be treated as an adult, didn't she? Beneath the fear there welled up a tide of resolve. This issue wasn't just about her—it affected Allie, too. And all of the children. Michael had seen that—why hadn't she?

Their faces seemed to form in her mind—eager, bright, questioning children, looking for answers. If she let this injustice take place, she was letting them down. And that was one thing she'd never do.

"Denke, Mamm. I will be going to that meeting tonight."

CHAPTER TWENTY

IT DIDN'T TAKE long for Michael to discover that his brother Jonah, who was eighteen already, had become the family cook in a house of single men. They'd eaten their fill of pot roast with potatoes and vegetables, and when Jonah produced a blueberry pie, it was all he could do not to groan.

"How about a break before dessert?" he suggested. "My stomach could do with a rest."

"You don't need to worry," Adam piped up. "Jonah didn't bake that. Sarah sent it over."

At sixteen, Adam had turned from the lively six-year-old Michael remembered to a gangly teen still getting used to his long legs and arms. But he was still the family joker, it seemed.

"The pot roast was great. So good it made me overeat."

Jonah's rare smile lit his usually serious face. "You're just lucky Adam didn't try to cook for you. The last time he almost set the kitchen on fire."

"Showing off," Daad growled, but there was a twinkle in his eyes. Maybe he'd learned to take it a little easier on his sons over the years.

"I just wanted to see how many times I could flip a pancake. I don't know how the curtains got on fire."

"You never do know how things go wrong," Jonah retorted. The bickering between the two was friendly—even Allie seemed to understand that. She just smiled, her eyes going from one to the other of her young onkels.

"Why don't you two show Allie the swing you put up for her?" Daad asked.

"For me?" Allie's voice squeaked in surprise.

"For you and Ruthie." Jonah held out his hand to her. "Komm."

She skipped out the door, holding hands with the boys.

Daad set a mug of coffee in front of him and poured one for himself. "So what do you think of your little bruders?"

"I'm impressed." It was the truth. "How did Jonah learn to cook?"

Daad gave a snort that might have covered a laugh. "When he realized his big sister was moving out, he figured he'd best learn if he didn't want me cooking for them. She taught him a few meals. He's not bad, ain't so?"

"I'll say. He told me he's an apprentice at the machine shop."

Daad nodded. "Amos Burkhart seems to think well of him. Says he'll offer him a partnership when he's a little older."

Michael gave a low whistle. "He must be good, if Amos is talking partner. He's got high standards."

"I'm wonderful glad to have him settled. He never

had the feel for the animals that Adam does. You can't run a dairy farm without that."

Michael could only nod. He'd never had it—that was certain. Seemed as though Daad was pleased with the idea that Adam would take over for him one day. Not that he supposed he'd be ready to retire anytime soon. He was as lean and leathery as he'd always been, and he seemed just as strong.

"They've turned out well. I'm sorry I wasn't here to see it happen." He was surprised to hear himself say the words, even more surprised that they were true. He hadn't realized how much he'd missed until he saw his two little brothers all grown up.

Daad seemed pleased with the response. He didn't say it—he wouldn't, that wasn't his way.

Instead he glanced at the clock. "We'd best not dally too long over the pie. The meeting starts at eight."

The reminder hit him like a blow to the gut. The meeting—the school board meeting that would decide Cathy's fate—was tonight. It had been on his mind every second of the day, and now it was almost here. It wasn't fair—it wasn't right for Cathy to lose the job she loved because of her kindness to his daughter. And to him.

She loved him. He was still trying to get used to that idea. Despite all the reasons for holding him at arm's length, she had actually grown to love him. He ought to be dismayed by that, but instead it created a warm glow inside him that persisted despite all reason.

"You're planning to go to the meeting?" He tried

to sound casual, but he didn't suppose he fooled his father.

"For sure. Anything that affects my granddaughters affects me." Daad's stern expression would warn anyone to watch out. "Zeb Stoltzfus ought to be ashamed of himself. Cathy's a fine teacher—one of the best we've had. And that girl of Stoltzfus's is no more ready to take over than my prize heifer."

Michael couldn't suppress a snort of laughter. Daad was right about Mary Alice, from what he'd seen, but Cathy seemed to detect some talent in her.

His father was directing a challenging look in his direction. "And you? Aren't you going to be there?"

He stared down at his coffee, wishing he could see an answer there. "I'm afraid of making it worse by being there. Reminding people that I'm an outsider now."

"That's just plain ferhoodled. You're the father of one of her scholars. The way I see it, Teacher Cathy needs all the support she can get. Nothing could be worse than staying away and leaving her to face it alone."

He'd told himself he wasn't susceptible to Daad's scolding any longer, but this time it hit close to the heart. This time Daad was right.

"You're right. We'll go together."

That got him one of Daad's all too rare approving looks. "Yah," he said. "Together."

AN HOUR LATER Daad was driving his buggy into the lane at James Miller's home. James, one of the numerous members of the Miller family, was president of the three-member school board, and according to Daad the usual meetings were informal affairs held at his house with nothing more important to consider than the schedule for schoolhouse maintenance.

"They're going to have a lot more than that on their hands tonight," Michael said as they neared the house. "Look at all the buggies."

"Looks like a worship Sunday." Daad pulled into a lineup of buggies, and one of the Miller boys came running to take the horse.

They climbed down and headed for the house, with Michael's apprehension building every moment. Had he done the right thing in coming? With the weight of the investigation pressing harder on him with every revelation, he'd begun to feel as if every step he took might plunge him into a chasm he'd never climb out of.

They reached the back door to find Emma Miller and her daughters rushing around with coffeepots and trays. Not that any Amish woman would confess to being caught unprepared by visitors, but Emma looked distinctly rattled.

She caught sight of them and waved with a coffeepot at the door to the front of the house. "Go through, go through. We're setting up more chairs now."

The Miller house was built along the lines popular in Lancaster County homes, with two large front rooms that could be either separated or opened into one by a partition. That turned it into an ideal space for worship.

The partition was open now, and several people were setting up folding chairs facing the middle, where the three members of the board could be seen in a huddle.

"Not expecting such a turnout," Daad muttered. "Seems like everyone knew about it except the ones who should have. Lizzie and Zeb have stirred up a hornet's nest, for sure."

Stirred it up, yes. But would that fact work in Cathy's favor or not? Michael wasn't sure. With his eye on an unobtrusive seat in the far corner, he worked his way toward it, only to find himself being greeted by first one person and then another—some of the men from work, others from the group who'd helped after the vandalism at the greenhouse.

Funny, he thought, settling into the corner at last. He hadn't thought he'd run into that many people since he'd returned. Seemed as though he'd been drawn into the web of community without realizing it.

The school board members were seating themselves at a folding table, looking self-conscious. He didn't see Cathy—had she decided not to subject herself to an open meeting? The Stoltzfus family had arrived, of course. Lizzie's color was high, while Zeb preserved a stoic face, and Mary Alice looked as if she wanted nothing so much as to crawl into a hole and pull it in afterward. She squirmed in her chair, seeming miserable.

Before he could consider what that might mean, there was a little stir and Cathy came in, her parents close behind her. Expressionless, she nodded at gestures from those two friends of hers and started toward them.

He'd never seen her look so…remote. That was the only word that seemed to fit. This was hurting her so much, her only defense was to retreat into herself. Like Allie, he realized, only Allie didn't do that anymore, thanks to Cathy.

Michael hadn't realized he'd moved until he felt Daad's hand on his arm, warning. The overpowering need to protect her had nearly made him do the worst possible thing. He had to stay away—to make their relationship nothing beyond teacher and parent. It was what was right, but it went against every instinct he had.

Cathy had reached her friends by now, and she took the chair between them while her parents sat close behind her. They were surrounding her with their love and support, Michael realized…the thing he couldn't do.

James Miller cleared his throat, and the murmur of voices ceased. "You're all most wilkom to join us this evening." He glanced at his colleagues as if enlisting their support. "Seems like a lot of folks know we're making a decision about the teaching position at Creekside School tonight, and I guess you'd like to be heard."

There was a murmur of agreement, and James looked down at what seemed to be a letter under his hand. "I guess it's no secret that some folks have concerns about how things have gone lately. First off, the fact that the police have been called to the school, something that's never happened before."

Lige got to his feet as if propelled by force. "So there was never a reason to do it before—that doesn't mean anything." His tone was so passionate and emphatic that Michael had to blink to be sure this was the Lige he knew.

"Everybody knows about the bad things that have happened at schools in recent years. Teacher Cathy saw a stranger watching the scholars and did just what she should have done. Isn't that what your own guidelines say?" His stare challenged Miller to argue, and Michael could feel the impression Lige had made in the room, maybe because he was normally so slow- and soft-spoken.

Miller cleared his throat again. "Yah, well, yah. That's true enough. We…we have no fault to find with the way Teacher Cathy carried out our own rules."

Lizzie Stoltzfus, who had been growing steadily redder, jumped to her feet. "That time, maybe. But what about the other time the police were there? It's unseemly for an Amish school to have police coming and going like it's a—a tavern."

This was news to some of them… Michael could see it. And they didn't like the comparison to a tavern.

Joanna Kohler rose. "Yah, the police came to the school because they wanted to talk to Michael. But I understand that was a mistake. Chief Jamison has already apologized for that to the bishop and ministers as well as to the school board. How can you hold Teacher Cathy responsible for someone else's mistake?"

Joanna was composed and articulate. Michael was impressed, and he didn't doubt others had been. He saw several people nodding in agreement. She'd defended Cathy in a way he wished he could.

This was going far better than he'd feared. True, Joanna was a close friend of Cathy's and not a parent, but people seemed to admire her as a businesswoman, and that gave added weight to her argument.

If Cathy's supporters had planned to go immediately on the attack, he had to congratulate them. It was far better than waiting until others had presented the negative.

The Stoltzfus family seemed to sense that the tide was going against them. Zeb sent a lowering look at his wife, and Mary Alice seemed on the verge of tears.

But Lizzie wasn't going down without a fight. She turned to glare at Michael, as if pointing him out as the guilty party. "None of this would have happened if Cathy hadn't allowed an Englisch child into our school. We might have known—"

"You are talking about my granddaughter." Daad was on his feet in an instant, and his voice thundered in a way that forcibly reminded Michael of one of his scoldings. "She has a right to be in the school I support, just like her cousin Ruthie. You can't keep her out."

"She was raised Englisch," Lizzie retorted. "You can't deny that."

"I don't need to deny anything. Bishop Eli, what do you say?"

Michael hadn't noticed the bishop in his preoccupation with Cathy, but he found him quickly. Eli Fisher's beard was a little longer and a little whiter, making him look even more like the prophet Michael had once thought him.

The bishop leaned forward, hands on his knees. "This should never be a subject of argument between brothers and sisters in faith." His expression was more sorrowful than angry. "When one of our families takes in foster children, do we not welcome them into our school? Josiah's granddaughter has her proper place in our school."

Not a murmur broke the silence for a long moment. Daad sank back in his seat. Had he been so sure what the bishop would say? Michael couldn't help but wonder if he'd spoken to him before. But at least—

There was a rustle of noise at the kitchen door. Michael turned to see a group of what were surely the older scholars at Cathy's school filing in. James Miller looked as surprised as Cathy did at the sight of them.

Boys and girls both, they stood quietly in a row.

"John?" James Miller's expression actually held more than surprise as he looked at the tallest boy. By his reaction, this was his son.

"We would like to speak to the school board." John seemed to be the spokesperson. A girl next to him nudged him, and with a look at her, he added, "Please."

Miller looked questioningly at his fellow board members and then nodded.

"We wanted to say that we heard you might not bring Teacher Cathy back next year. We think...all of us...that she's the best teacher we ever had. We don't want to lose her." He seemed to falter for an instant. At another nudge from the girl he continued. "It's nothing against Mary Alice," he added quickly. "We just...just..."

"I'm not ready." Mary Alice had suddenly found her voice. She clasped her hands together in front of her as if needing support and carefully didn't look toward her mother. "Not now. If I could spend a year or two helping Teacher Cathy, maybe she could teach me to be like her...at least a little bit." Tears started to spill over, but then she saw Cathy smiling at her. She sniffled a little, smiled and sat down.

So. Michael struggled to hold on to a stoic expression. The children had pointed out the obvious—the reason why the Stoltzfus family brought their complaint in the first place. And Mary Alice was declaring herself at last.

Miller looked as if he'd give anything to have this whole thing over with. There was no doubt now about the mood of the room—or the mood of the other board members.

"Does anyone have anything to add?" he asked, looking around as if daring anyone to speak.

Lizzie Stoltzfus started to rise, but her husband caught her arm and sat her back down with a firm hand. Everyone heard his murmured, "No."

Miller had a brief, whispered consultation with the other board members and then straightened. “The board offers Teacher Cathy a teaching contract for the Creekside School, renewable each year. This meeting is closed.” He sank down and mopped his brow.

The danger was over. Cathy’s job was safe, no thanks to him. She was surrounded by friends and well-wishers. There was nothing he wanted more right now than to join them, but he wouldn’t go anywhere near her. He’d hurt her enough already.

If loving someone meant putting her happiness above his own, then he must surely love her.

BY THE TIME Daad turned into the drive to drop him off, Michael had managed to convince himself that his every glance didn’t give his feelings away to anyone who was watching. He was pleased and relieved about Teacher Cathy for her sake and Allie’s sake, and that was what he would say to anyone who mentioned it.

He suddenly realized that all of the downstairs lights were on, including the gaslight outside the back door.

“Why’s Verna got the house all lit up?” Daad asked, coming to a stop by the porch.

“Something’s wrong.” Michael fairly flew off the buggy seat and took the porch steps in a leap. When he reached the kitchen, Verna came hurrying in, and he realized Daad was right behind him.

“What’s happened? Allie?” He seized Verna’s arm.

"Allie's fine," she said. "Hush, don't you go waking her again."

"What do you mean again? Was she up?"

Verna patted his shoulder. "It's nothing, just a nightmare. She woke up yelling out, but it was only a bad dream. I got her soothed down and gave her some milk, and she settled back to sleep again."

"That doesn't tell us why you've got every light in the place on," Daad observed. "Komm, Verna. Something scared you, and it wasn't a nightmare."

Aunt Verna glared at Daad for a moment, but then she nodded. "All right, then. I'll tell you, even if it makes me look foolish." She turned to Michael. "I was sitting in the front room sewing, and I thought I heard someone walking around the house…bushes moving, brushing against the house even though the wind wasn't blowing. Bunch of nonsense. I've never been afraid to be alone in this house, and I'm not going to start now."

Something cold seemed to grab Michael's heart. "What did you do? Are you sure Allie's okay?" He was torn between hearing what happened and running up to check that she was all right.

"She's fine. Maybe she heard me going around trying to see what it was, and that started her bad dream." Verna shrugged. "Could be, I guess. Truth was, I thought it might be vandals back again for another try."

"You didn't go out to confront them, did you?" His blood ran cold at the thought of a woman in her eighties confronting a bunch of vandals.

"I did have that much sense," Verna said tartly. "I lit all the lamps, thinking to scare them off, and I made sure the doors were locked."

"Didn't you think to call for help?" There'd been trouble, and he hadn't been here to deal with it. Could it be someone who'd guess he'd be out at the school board meeting? Or just chance?

Aunt Verna looked embarrassed. "Didn't think I wanted to go out to the phone shanty in the dark if someone was out there. And I for sure didn't want to leave Allie alone in the house."

Of course. He'd forgotten that. "You did the right thing, staying safe."

He put his arm around her in a quick squeeze. She should have a phone in the house. At her age, it wouldn't be safe, her being alone here, even if it weren't for the trouble with vandals. After all, she could easily have an accident. A business phone in the house was acceptable in the community, he knew, and he'd see to that before she was much older.

"I'm going to check on Allie, and then I'll look around outside." He met Daad's gaze, and his father nodded.

"I'll meet you outside. Verna, why don't you make up some cocoa for us? That'd certain sure taste gut."

Verna seemed to know she was being kept out of harm's way, but she nodded and was rattling pans by the time Michael hastened up the stairs.

She'd left Allie's bedroom door ajar, and he eased it open a little farther. Allie lay on her side, snuggling her favorite dog, and he could hear her even breathing. He stood there for a moment, feeling the weight of tenderness and responsibility that came with being a parent. But at least he was no longer alone.

Flooded with thankfulness, he hurried downstairs and outside to find his father, pausing only long enough to grab the most powerful of the flashlights.

Daad was using his own flashlight to scan the area along the driveway. “Nothing here. Thought there might be tire marks if it was the vandals coming back.”

“She said it sounded like someone or something close to the house.” He started along the side facing the drive, flashing his light over the grass verge and the flower beds. Daad added his light, and they moved along slowly together.

“Nothing,” Daad said. “Maybe the side away from the drive—somebody’d be less likely to be spotted there.”

They checked along the front, and as soon as they rounded the corner, they spotted the marks…an indistinct trail of disturbed shrubs, broken twigs and a trampled flower or two.

“There.”

Michael aimed his flashlight at the soft soil of the flower border. Footprints showed plainly enough. It looked as if he’d paused by the window, maybe peering into the front room, where his aunt had been sewing. The hairs on the back of his neck stood up at the thought.

He glanced up at the window of Allie’s bedroom. Thank Heaven she was on the second floor. Had she heard a disturbance, even in her sleep? It might very well have caused a bad dream.

Should he ask her in the morning what she'd dreamed of? Or would that be the wrong action? So much of parenting seemed to be trial and error. And if he made a mistake, he might not know it for years.

"Let's have a look through the outbuildings," Daad suggested. "Just to be sure."

"You go on home, Daad. I'll do it."

"We'll both do it," he said firmly. "I wouldn't sleep unless I made sure."

Sleep? He suspected he would do very little sleeping tonight. And tomorrow, like it or not, he'd best talk to Chief Jamison.

CHAPTER TWENTY-ONE

DESPITE THE LATE night after the school board meeting, Cathy was on the go Saturday morning, arriving early at the Mud Sale grounds to help with Joanna's stand.

"Here's the person of the week," Joanna said, lifting her foam coffee cup in a mock toast. "Do you have a big head after all the wonderful good things people said about you last night?"

"No, but I feel about ten years younger than I have all week." Cathy accepted the coffee cup Rachel was holding out to her. "Looks as if you two have done all the work without me."

"Ach, no, we saved some for you. We're just taking a break for coffee." Rachel produced a plate of sticky buns from a basket behind the counter. "Eat. Don't worry," she added quickly, apparently seeing a warning forming on Joanna's face. "I have something to clean up with. We won't touch your quilts with sticky fingers."

"In that case..." Joanna helped herself. "Yum, still warm. What did you do, get up in the middle of the night?"

Rachel laughed, shaking her head. "I put the dough to rise in the refrigerator, of course. It's a gut thing you don't have a husband to feed, or he'd be eating out of cans."

"Since that's unlikely, I'll enjoy the fruits of your baking," Joanna retorted.

Marriage was unlikely for all three of them, though Joanna hadn't pointed that out. She didn't seem to look further than her business for satisfaction, and poor Rachel was so tied to that father of hers it seemed she'd never get loose.

As for her...at least she knew now what it meant to be in love. That was something to hold on to. She had her job, loving family and good friends. Plenty of people didn't have that much. She'd learn to be content again.

Joanna launched into an account of the school board meeting for Rachel's benefit, giving it an air of humor that Cathy hadn't felt at the time. Cathy studied their familiar faces, swept with gratitude for them. She could so easily have been the only unmarried woman from their little group. They would still have been friends, of course, but there was an inevitable chasm between married and unmarried women in the community, no matter how deeply they cared for each other.

Their morning break finished, the three of them made short work of setting up the rest of the sale items. Cathy lingered over a child's quilt—one made for a little girl, it seemed, with traditional patterns in delicate shades from rose to palest pink. It would be perfect for Allie, but she didn't have the right to buy a gift for her. Their relationship was teacher and pupil, and that was all.

The fire hall grounds gradually filled with people circulating, stopping at stalls, but looking rather than buying at this early point in the day. Things would really start rolling around eleven, when the auction began.

Rachel leaned against the counter next to her. "Looks like a wonderful gut day. You should get a nice amount for the school from this day's work."

Cathy nodded. "The board is talking about a new roof. That'll take a chunk of it, but I'm hoping to have enough extra for bookshelves and new books."

"If we have anything to say about it, there will definitely be enough for that," Joanna said. "Why don't you take a walk around? We're not going to be very busy until this afternoon." She gestured toward the crowd. "Aren't those some of your nieces and nephews coming?"

"Looks that way." Cathy waved. "I think I remember promising them caramel apples."

"Go on, then," Rachel urged. "Take your time. We'll switch off later."

"Denke." Cathy slipped out of the booth and a moment later was surrounded by nieces and nephews, all talking at once.

That was one thing about being the youngest in the family—her siblings had provided her with plenty of young ones to spoil. Two of her nephews had grasped her hands and were tugging her across the grounds toward the caramel apple stand.

"Wait, wait." Laughing, she freed herself, pausing to be sure the smallest ones were holding hands with an older sibling or cousin. "All right. Now we can go, but don't lose the little ones."

They must, she thought, resemble an amoeba as they moved in a cluster with the crowd. She'd have to remember that for next week's science lesson.

"Hurry, Aunt Cathy." Her sister Mary's daughter, Emma, had a voice just like hers. "They might run out."

"Emma, it is not quite eleven in the morning. There isn't the slightest chance that Ben Miller's stand will run out of caramel apples."

That particular branch of the Miller family had the largest orchard in the area, and no one would think of getting caramel apples elsewhere. That was a comforting thing about the Mud Sale—the same people were here with the same stands every year, and if they weren't, they'd be missed.

When each one of the kinder had been provided with a caramel apple, Cathy accepted a handful of napkins. "We'll need these," she said. "Unless I turn them back over to their parents covered with caramel."

Ben grinned, holding out another apple. "How about one for you, Teacher Cathy? On the house."

"No, thanks. I just finished one of Rachel Hurst's sticky buns."

"Later, then," Ben said. "Don't forget."

Nodding, Cathy moved her herd onward. She'd best let them eat the evidence before returning them just in time for lunch. Though on a day like this, no one worried too much about regular meals. If—

She stopped suddenly as a small figure burrowed its way through the group. "Allie?" Her breath caught as she realized the child was shaking. "What is it? What's wrong?"

Allie buried her face in Cathy's skirt, whispering something Cathy couldn't hear.

"Hush, now, it's all right." She bent over the child, thankful that her nieces and nephews made a screen for what was happening. "Tell me."

"It was him," Allie whispered. "I saw him."

"Who?" She patted the trembling child.

"Mommy's friend. The one I saw. He—he looked at me, and I was scared."

A shiver of fear seemed to pass from the child right through Cathy. How could that be? She'd assumed—Michael had assumed—that the man visiting Diana had been a boyfriend, someone she'd met in Harrisburg. How could he be here?

"We'll find Daadi," she said. "He'll know what to do. Is he here?"

Allie raised a tearstained face to her. "I—I don't know. He left me with Aunt Verna because he had to talk to somebody. He said he'd come soon."

She looked around, hoping for a glimpse of his familiar face. The grounds were crowded with both Englisch and Amish, but she didn't spot him.

"Here's what we're going to do." She gathered all the children around her. "We need to get back to Joanna's stand. Allie's upset, and she needs your company, so we all go close together. All right?"

They nodded, seeming to catch the seriousness in her voice. Young Daniel, the smallest, held out his caramel apple to Allie, offering her a bite, and she managed a smile despite her apprehension.

Cathy moved slowly, scanning the crowd for her brother-in-law Daniel or Lige or any of the adults from her own family. Where were they all?

Wherever they were, no one seemed available at the moment. She'd get the kinder to Joanna's stall. Joanna had her phone with her, so she could call for help. Cathy had a wry thought for how someone like Lizzie Stoltzfus would react to her needing the police again already.

It seemed to take forever, inching their way along so that Allie could be kept in the midst of a small horde of Amish children, hopefully indistinguishable from them. If the man was here, if he'd seen Allie as she'd seen him—what then? What would he do if he'd read the fear in her face and known she could put him on the spot when Diana died?

Finally they reached the stall, where Joanna stood alone. Apparently Rachel was off seeing the displays.

"There you are. What—" Joanna stopped, obviously reading trouble in Cathy's face.

Cathy did a quick survey of her young relatives and picked out Emma as the most responsible. "Emma, I want you to see if you can find your daadi or your uncles or Grossdaadi. Send them here at once if you do. Do you understand?"

Emma, eyes bright, nodded. Without a word, she turned and darted through the crowd.

Cathy gathered the others close to the stand. "Stay where Joanna can see you, all right?" She turned to Joanna, lowering her voice. "Call the police. Tell Chief Jamison that Allie was frightened by seeing a man who used to come and see her mother. That's all. He'll understand."

"Got it." Joanna was already punching her phone.

"I'll take Allie in the back, where she's out of sight until he comes."

With a quick look around, she slipped past the curtain at the back of the display area, drawing Allie with her into the storage space behind. She sank down on a box and pulled Allie close to her, smoothing her hair back from her little pale face. She seemed to be all big eyes—frightened eyes. It wasn't right for a child to be so afraid.

"You're safe now, Allie. You're here with me, and soon Daadi will be here, too. How did you get to be all by yourself?"

She couldn't imagine Verna letting a child Allie's age go off alone at the sale.

Allie seemed calmer, but her lips trembled. "I was with Aunt Verna, but she…she stopped to talk to someone. I let go of her hand because I wanted to see a box of bunnies that a man was carrying. He let me touch one." Her face shone with remembered pleasure. "But then when I started to go back to Aunt Verna, I couldn't see her anymore."

Her face crumpled, and Cathy hurried to reassure

her. "It's all right. It's easy to get separated in a crowd. No one will blame you. Tell me what happened next."

"I…I thought she was by a woman with a dog, but I couldn't see the woman or the dog or Aunt Verna. So I went toward where I thought she was, but I couldn't see anybody that I knew." Tears trickled down her cheeks. "I wanted Daadi or you, and you weren't there."

"No." Cathy patted her back soothingly. "But I'm here now. What happened next?"

"There were a lot of people. I thought maybe I'd see somebody I knew, but then I saw him." Her voice broke, and she buried her face in Cathy's lap.

"There, now, you're safe now. But you need to tell me, so we can do something about him. You're sure it was the man you saw walking into your house to visit Mommy?"

Her eyes still bright with tears, she nodded solemnly. "It was. I know it."

"Okay. I believe you. Do you think he knew you?" How could he? How could this anonymous man pick out Allie in a crowd of similarly dressed Amish children?

Allie nodded, a shiver making her whole body shake. Cathy wrapped her arm around the child. "Are you sure? How could you tell?"

"Because he looked like he…he hated me."

Cathy's heart twisted, and she gave Allie a fierce hug. "No one could hate you. He's afraid, that's what. Afraid you'll tell on him."

And she would, if Cathy had anything to say

about it. Allie could identify the man, which meant the police could start investigating him. And leave Michael and Allie in peace.

"It's going to be all right, dear child. I'll keep you safe."

Even as she said the words, Cathy saw the canvas at the side of the stall twitch. Before she could catch her breath, someone had pushed his way inside.

It was Randy Hunter. He stood a few feet away from her, but she hardly recognized him. The pleasant, ordinary face she knew was twisted with rage and fear.

Allie gave a tiny cry, clinging to Cathy, her hands and legs wrapping around her like a baby animal clutching its mother. Cathy struggled to get her legs free and rise to her feet.

"Randy, what are you doing here? This is Joanna's stall." She kept her voice even with an effort.

If she screamed…someone would come, of course. But Randy was only a few feet away, and if he got his hands on Allie…

She couldn't risk it. *Talk to him, calm him, don't do anything to set him off.*

"Randy!" Sharper, demanding his attention. "Look at me. It's Catherine Brandt. What are you doing here?"

Hear me, Joanna, please. Get help.

Nothing, no response, and he took another step. Loosening Allie's stranglehold, she pushed the child behind her, taking a step backward.

Obviously, it was no good talking to him. He

wasn't hearing anything but his own fear. She had to try to get Allie away from him.

"Allie, when I say go, you run to Joanna. Okay?"

But there was no response. The child was too frightened. She couldn't run. She couldn't even move.

And Randy advanced even as Cathy backed away, pushing Allie along. She groped with her hand for something, anything, that she could use to deter him.

His eyes were blank, expressionless—it was like looking at something less than a person. His hands were reaching toward her, clutching… A shiver of revulsion went through her.

Her groping fingers closed on a roll of quilt batting. She yanked it from the box, threw it toward him and screamed.

People burst into the stall from all directions. She stumbled backward and felt her father's arms close around her. When she managed to look, Randy was swathed in quilt batting as Chief Jamison and a young patrolman grabbed him. Then family surrounded her, blocking her view of what followed.

Michael had his arms around Allie and partially around her as well, but no one seemed to notice that as they were escorted out of the stall.

They were safe. Allie was safe, crying in her father's arms, and suddenly Cathy's legs were shaking so that she sagged against Daad, who had appeared from nowhere, it seemed.

Joanna thrust a chair behind her and pulled her into it. "It's all right, Cathy. I heard you. Everyone came."

Arms wrapped around her—her mother's, Joanna's, Rachel's—until she could scarcely breathe. She looked over their heads and saw Michael holding Allie, similarly surrounded. For just a moment their eyes met, and then someone moved between, and the moment vanished.

IT WASN'T UNTIL evening that Chief Jamison came to the house to see Michael. He looked faintly surprised at the number of people who were there—Lige and Sarah and their children, Daad, Aunt Verna, Michael's two brothers—no one had wanted to go home, as if the only safe thing was to stay together.

"Komm, komm," Aunt Verna said, ushering him into the kitchen. "You'll have coffee. And some pie, ain't so? I brought cherry and apple home from the sale."

"Just coffee, thanks." He pulled out a chair, sinking onto it and propping both arms on the table. "I hope I never go through another day like this one. Seems pretty clear now what happened, so I wanted to bring you up-to-date." He grimaced. "That Harrisburg cop was all for keeping everything quiet, but I told him you folks deserved the peace of mind of knowing the truth."

Michael saw Sarah and Aunt Verna exchange glances, and then they were shepherding the children toward the door. "You boys take the young ones outside to play ball." When his brothers looked loath to miss the explanations, Aunt Verna gave them a look that permitted no argument. "You'll hear it all later. Go."

Obediently, they gathered up Allie, Ruthie and the boys. Little Sally was already asleep on her mother's lap.

When the door had closed behind them, Jamison gave a satisfied nod. "It's not suitable for youngsters to hear, especially not little Allie." He glanced at Michael. "I'm just sorry we didn't figure it out before she had such a scary experience."

"She's safe, thanks to Cathy." A cold hand gripped his heart at the thought of what might have happened. "How he thought he could get away with it in the middle of a crowd…"

"That's just it—he was past thinking, at least by the time we got him down to the station. According to Cathy, he acted like he was in a daze from the minute she saw him."

"You've talked to her, then." He longed to ask how she was, but he feared giving himself away when his emotions and his thoughts were in such a tangled mess.

"Just briefly, to get her account of what happened. She'll come in and make a formal statement on Monday, but that's enough to go on with."

So it wasn't over for Cathy yet. He tried not to let his mind dwell on her.

"Anyway, the case is wrapping up pretty well. I think Randy was so demoralized by the realization of what he'd almost done that it was a relief to him to spill it all. His lawyer kept trying to hush him up, but nobody could stop him from talking."

"You mean he confessed about Diana?" He'd been

picturing Diana's killer as some sort of monster, not the broken remains of a human being he'd seen led away to the police car.

Jamison nodded. "It seems she called him sometime ago, asking him to come and see her. I'd guess the truth is, he'd never gotten over his crush on her, so he went. Turns out she wanted him to be an intermediary with her grandmother, thinking he could sway the old woman's feelings. All she wanted, she said, was to have the life she'd left."

Michael tried to rub away the tension that always built behind his forehead when he thought of Diana. "She seemed to be thinking of that a lot that last year or so—the life she'd have had if we'd never run away together."

As he had, he supposed, except that he wouldn't exchange anything for his daughter.

"I suppose Randy would do whatever she asked. He was always crazy about her, not that she'd ever paid any attention to him." Randy had just been another of her court of admirers, from what he remembered.

"Seems to be the case. The old lady is having memory problems, but he'd spent a lot of time with her, talking about Diana. Apparently he was convinced he'd gotten her to the point of welcoming Diana back with open arms."

"I don't guess Bernard Wilcox would be happy about that," Lige commented.

"If he knew." Jamison shrugged. "He won't admit it, I'm sure. Anyway, when Randy told Diana, he says she was delighted. Then he made the mistake of assuming they had a future together." He hesitated, looking around as if weighing whether to say something or not. "He hedges about her response, but I'd guess she laughed at him. Something that infuriated him anyway."

Michael could imagine. Diana had been good at hitting a man's vulnerable points.

"He says it was an accident—that he pushed her, not meaning to knock her down the stairs. And ran away."

"Do you believe that? That he didn't mean to hurt her?"

"Doesn't matter what I believe," Jamison said. "That's what his lawyer will argue."

"When I came back to River Haven, he must have panicked. The vandalism, the feelings against me… he stirred that up, didn't he?"

"He didn't want to be reminded of what he'd done by your presence. He wouldn't admit to stalking Allie, but I'm more or less certain he was afraid she'd seen him. If you'd settled anywhere else, she wouldn't have had a chance to recognize him. I'd guess he was trying to see which child she was, but he didn't know for sure until the day he followed her and Cathy home from school."

"If he'd gotten to Allie today…" His hands knotted into fists.

"He didn't," Daad reminded him. "God protected her, and it's over now."

Over. Somehow he couldn't quite believe that the cloud that had darkened his life was gone for good.

"Yah," he said at last. "It's over. We can get on with our lives."

Even as he said it, he wondered. What lives? Should he even think of picking up the pieces of that life out in the world? At one time, that had been all he'd wanted, but the past month had made that life seem remote. Now…

Now, he realized, a lot depended on Cathy. He had to see her before he could know what his future held.

AS FAR AS Cathy could tell, what had happened had disrupted the Mud Sale pretty thoroughly. Still, people had rallied and they'd eventually gotten back on track. Joanna, stopping by after it was over, claimed she'd sold more than she ever had, primarily because people wanted to get close to the scene of the action.

Cathy was feeling overwhelmed by the solicitude of family and friends by the end of the day. When two of her sisters were still hanging around after supper, she'd slipped away, letting them think she was going to rest. Actually, she'd evaded them, gotten out of the house and sought refuge in the barn.

Silence, other than the soft whicker of a horse and the occasional thud of a heavy hoof on the wooden floor—that was what she craved. She needed peace to get her thoughts together and process everything that had happened.

Blackie, the oldest of the buggy horses, put his head over the stall bar and rested it heavily on her shoulder. "All right, all right. I love you, too. Give over." She shifted him with an effort, and he switched to nuzzling her hand.

Giving in, she got a carrot from the bin and brought it to him, generating a lot of interest from Belle, Cathy's own buggy mare.

Cathy rested her head against the upright between the stalls. From what Chief Jamison had said when he'd questioned her, it seemed fairly certain that Michael was finally in the clear. The newspapers would trumpet the arrest of Randy Hunter, and everyone would know that Michael was innocent. He'd be able to go back to his Englisch life, if that was what he wanted.

For sure he would, wouldn't he? She rubbed Blackie's forelock and let him nuzzle against her shoulder. Standing there, relaxing at last, she felt the tears come to her eyes. She had been telling herself this would get easier, but not yet, obviously. When? How long would it take before she stopped yearning for Michael?

She heard a step behind her, and a shadow moved across the late-day sunshine streaming through the open doorway.

"I thought I might find you here. Cathy?" He took a step toward her. "Are you crying?"

"No, of course not." She wiped away the trace of tears. What had happened to her control? Today's events seemed to have shattered it.

"There's no need to cry now. It's all over." He sounded tentative, as if unsure what to say to her.

"I know. I'm just trying to get away from my family," she managed.

"Same here." He came to lean on the stall next to her. Not touching, but comforting all the same. "Jamison finally left. He's satisfied they have all the answers now."

"So it was Randy who came to the school that day, scaring us all." He was so close that it seemed she could feel the warmth radiating from him, warming her as well.

He nodded. "He didn't think that through very well, did he? He seems to have felt compelled to see Allie, even though he knew there was little chance she'd recognize him. He should have realized you'd react as soon as you spotted a stranger on school grounds."

A shiver went through her. "It was every teacher's worst nightmare. I'm wonderful thankful we'd been prepared. Even a few years ago, we'd have thought an Amish school the safest place in the world."

Grief slid through her for the innocent children whose deaths had ensured that the Amish no longer assumed their kinder were safe.

"And he was the one who chased you and Allie that day. If I'd been a little faster, I might have spotted him and saved us all this day."

He would blame himself, as any parent would. "And if I had been a little braver, I might have gotten a look at him."

"And paid with your life for slowing down." His hand closed hard over hers. "I'm very glad you didn't."

She had to say something, something to move

them away from disturbing emotions. If she were stronger, she would draw her hand away, but if these fleeting moments were all she'd have, she wouldn't give them up.

"The police in Harrisburg—will they know by now?"

He nodded, the faintest of smiles tugging at his lips. "I think Jamison took pleasure in calling that detective to tell him he'd arrested Diana's killer. Small-town cop bests the big-city detective, I guess."

"Chief Jamison had a head start on the truth. He knew you."

His fingers tightened a little on hers. "That's the thing that I'm just finally getting used to. The fact that so many people here believed in me even when reason told them not to."

"That's the very definition of faith, isn't it? To believe that way? People who know you had faith in you."

"Yah. Even Daad. He never thought I was guilty of anything but running away from the life he'd given me."

"But you're all right now with your family." She took a breath to have strength to say what she must. "Even when you go back to your Englisch life..."

"What makes you think I'm going back?" He shifted, and his face was so near her that she could see every tiny line around his eyes, almost count the lashes. So near she couldn't seem to breathe.

"You—you can now, can't you? I thought that was what you wanted."

"I could, I guess. Maybe I did want that once. But now…what would I be going to? Everything that's important in life is right here—work to do, a place to bring up my daughter, family, good friends, church… and love, if I'm more fortunate than I deserve."

She didn't dare think about what those final words might mean, not until she was sure. "You told me once you'd lost everything that was important to you out there. You could have it back now."

"Ach, Cathy, I didn't value the right things outside. Now I know what kind of life I want—one that balances all the important things, not just success and money." He lifted his hand slowly toward her face, so slowly that it was clear he was giving her a chance to pull away.

But she didn't. He touched her face, moving his fingertips gently over her features as if memorizing how they felt.

"Everything I want is here." He almost breathed the words, and they seemed to touch her skin. "I love you, Teacher Cathy. I won't rush you. Not as long as I know the end means the two of us together, forever."

"Allie…" she began.

"Allie will be delirious, don't you know that? She loves you already."

"And I love her." Her heart winced at the thought of how close they'd come to losing her today. "But I think we should give her some time."

"You'll decide," he said promptly. "I'll wait until you say it's time. Good things are always worth waiting for. Well, Cathy? Will you marry me?"

She was sure now. Happiness didn't come with guarantees, but he was offering her a love that would last, that would only grow. She raised her lips to his in answer.

A long, satisfying time later she drew back just far enough to see his face. "There's a little matter to be put right first, you know."

He chuckled, deep in his chest. "The penitent has to return. What do you suppose Bishop Eli will say to that?"

"He'll be delighted," she said promptly. "It won't take long. And then..."

"And then?" His dark eyes were lit by love.

"I think I'll have to give Mary Alice a crash course on becoming a teacher," she murmured as his lips closed on hers again.

* * * * *

Ready for more love and mystery in River Haven?
Don't miss the next book in the River Haven series
by Marta Perry,

Amish Protector

Available April 2020 from HQN Books.

SPECIAL EXCERPT FROM

An Amish widow and a lawman in disguise team up to take down a crime ring.

Read on for a sneak preview of Amish Covert Operation *by Meghan Carver, available July 2019 from Love Inspired Suspense.*

The steady rhythm of the bicycle did little to calm her nerves. Ominous dark blue clouds propelled Katie Schwartz forward.

A slight breeze ruffled the leaves, sending a few skittering across the road. But then it died, leaving an unnatural stillness in the hush of the oncoming storm. Beads of perspiration dotted her forehead.

Should she call out? Announce herself?

Gingerly, she got off her bicycle and stepped up to a window, clutching her skirt in one hand and the window trim in the other. Through her shoes, her toes gripped the edge of the rickety crate. Desperation to stay upright and not teeter off sent a surge of adrenaline coursing through her as she swiped a hand across the grimy window of the hunter's shack. The crate dipped, and Katie grasped the frame of the window again.

"Timothy?" she whispered to herself. "Where are you?"

LISEXP0719

With the crate stabilized, she swiped over the glass again and squinted inside. But all that stared back at her was more grime. The crate tipped again, and she grabbed at the window trim before she could tumble off.

Movement inside snagged her attention, although she couldn't make out figures. Voices filtered through the window, one louder than the other. What was going on in there? And was Timothy involved?

Her nose touched the glass in her effort to see inside. A face suddenly appeared in the window. It was distorted by the cracks in the glass, but it appeared to be her *bruder*. A moment later, the face disappeared.

She jumped from the crate and headed toward the corner of the cabin. Now that he had seen her, he had to come out and explain himself and return with her, stopping whatever this clandestine meeting was all about.

A man dressed in plain clothing stepped out through the door.

"Timothy!" But the wild look in his eyes stopped her from speaking further.

And then she saw it. A gun was pressed into his back.

"Katie! Run! Go!"

Don't miss
Amish Covert Operation *by Meghan Carver,*
available July 2019 wherever
Love Inspired® Suspense books and ebooks are sold.

www.LoveInspired.com

LISEXP0719